THE TWISTED MARK

SOPHIE WILLIAMSON

Storm
PUBLISHING

Ebook ISBN: 978-1-80508-138-8
Paperback ISBN: 978-1-80508-141-8

Cover design: Eileen Carey
Cover images: Shutterstock, iStock

Published by Storm Publishing.
For further information, visit:
www.stormpublishing.co

ALSO BY SOPHIE WILLIAMSON

The Binding Mark

For Freddie, Georgiana, and Archie.
Everything for the family, always.

PROLOGUE

In the first of my three endlessly recurring Gabriel Thornber dreams, I'm walking along a deserted London street at midnight. I'm perfectly calm. My powers mean the dark and the dangers of the city hold little fear for me, either in reality or in my subconscious. And then I turn a corner, into a narrower street, and he's there.

"Sadie Sadler. It's been a while." Gabriel is smiling as though bumping into me—or more likely, finally tracking me down—is the best thing that's happened to him in a long time. He's wearing tight jeans and a blue and white striped shirt, with his shoulder-length hair pushed back and his customary sunglasses hiding his terrifying eyes. Even through my mounting terror, I can appreciate his beauty. A demon in the body of an angel.

I freeze, barely able to breathe, but quickly summon enough self-preservation to spiral my arms around myself and throw up a strong shield.

He steps closer and lazily waves a hand in my direction, probably more for effect than anything else. His magic requires nothing as crude as hand gestures. My shield drops before I can even think about resisting.

"Come on, Sadie, you're not playing fair. I only want to take what you promised me. You know full well it's breaking all the rules to resist a lien."

I nod shakily. It's very difficult to resist a lien. The power of them sort of compels you, sort of puts practical barriers in your way. And if you push your resistance attempts too far, you'll die.

Hiding out down south is not exactly in the spirit of the thing, but it's not really resisting... just making things a little more difficult for Gabriel. But trying to stand against him now would be completely unacceptable. Besides, as he's amply demonstrated, I'm in no position to do so.

"Come here," he whispers, half command, half lover's entreaty.

I stay where I am, incapable of movement.

He shrugs and closes the distance between us, until he's facing me, close enough that I can hear his steady heartbeat and feel his breath, but deliberately not touching me.

"Sadie. I've waited six years. May I?"

Such a pointless question. As if he'd simply smile and walk away if I said no. But he always has to play the gentleman.

I take a deep breath. When I speak, my heart is racing but my voice is gratifyingly calm.

"I'll honour the Old Ways."

There's nothing more to say or do.

PART 1

ONE

LONDON—PRESENT DAY

I pour black coffee into my favourite mug and Evian into my silver scrying bowl. Once I've taken a swig of the coffee, I breathe rhythmically and wave my hand over the water until it's steaming and swirling.

I've sworn off magic nowadays, but I make an exception for checking up on Tinder dates.

After a few seconds, the water calms and the vision comes into focus. Christopher looks just like his photos, which is a good start. His apartment is clean, decorated, and seemingly only occupied by him: another tick. Judging by his outfit, he's about to go out for a run. No obvious red flags here. He seems as blandly pleasant as the messages we've exchanged suggest.

We're going to view the latest exhibition at the Tate Modern art gallery, then try some new Indonesian restaurant. It'll be lovely. It'll be unbearably dull. I'll have to grit my teeth to avoid letting my emotions or my powers get out of control. If I let my guard down, I'll end up setting the gallery's Turbine Hall on fire with an idle thought.

Later, I imagine we'll come back here. Christopher will no doubt be gentlemanly to a fault, like he's trying to win the prize for Feminist Ally of the Year. We'll probably sleep together, probably instigated by me. I'll probably come, despite it all. I almost certainly won't feel satisfied in the slightest.

I try to make an effort to go on dates, but I ruined myself for other men six years ago, aged eighteen. When I look at Christopher's earnest blue eyes in the scrying bowl, in my mind I see a different face—eyes with diamond-shaped pupils like mine, glowing red like the fires of hell and trying to see into my soul. *You made a bargain.*

The image fades away, and I make a mental note never to spy on my dates again. I'm about as likely to stick to that as my semi-regular hungover vows to give up gin.

More coffee is definitely required. I methodically grind the beans before putting them into the cafetière. They cost ten pounds for a single serving. My mum would kill me if she knew, but then my family's principles are rather skewed. Controlling an entire town with magic, fine. Enforcing magical debts, no problem. Demanding obedience from acolytes and plotting against enemies or rivals, absolutely. Wasting money or seeming too pretentious and intellectual, no way.

Luckily, as my relatives still live three hundred miles north of London, they don't know much about the habits I've picked up or the traits I've abandoned in a desperate attempt to seem normal.

If I'm going to force myself to go on a date, I might as well attempt to look good. I grab my make-up bag, my laptop, and a small mirror, and drag them all to my one table. It functions as an eating place, a storage space, and, when I'm working late into the night, a home office. My home's well-situated and beautifully decorated, but spacious it ain't.

I blow-dry my hair with more enthusiasm than skill. Left to its own devices, it's naturally the deep black of a teenage goth who has gone overboard with the cheap hair dye, in stark contrast to the pallor of my skin. It's also a tangle of curls with a tendency to frizz. Back home, I used to straighten it with spells. Nowadays, I rely on the pseudo-magic of the local salon. Between the Brazilian blow-dries to keep it straight, the spectrum of deep brown highlights, and the shoulder-length cut, I look more like a young urban professional and less like a fairy-tale witch.

Once my hair is fully dry and vaguely sleek, I fire up a YouTube tutorial on sexy but casual make-up styles. I dip my over-priced eyeshadow brush into the palettes, but my hands are shaking too much to be allowed anywhere near my face. One wave of my hand, one carefully concentrated thought, and I could make my hair and make-up perfect or create a Chanel dress out of thin air. And my mind, my body, my soul is pleading with me to do just that. But I resist and brandish the brush like a recovering alcoholic sipping a lemonade.

Eventually, I'm ready. Beautified through entirely natural means. There's one final step. I peer into the mirror and carefully insert my over-sized brown contact lenses to disguise my diamond-shaped pupils and unusually large irises, which tend to change colour under pressure or when I use magic.

Back home in Mannith, most people understand the significance of eyes like that, but it's not as if anyone in London would take a look and damn me for a witch. Even so, they're one more barrier between me and being normal. So, I force the contact lenses in and throw sunglasses on for good measure, despite the overcast day.

I glance at my watch. Train or taxi? The eternal dilemma. *Just use magic,* my mind screams. I cross my arms, blocking out the annoying voice with a new podcast about the link between politics and psychology, and dash to the tube station before I can crack.

.   .   .

The platform is hot, crowded, and full of an unholy mixture of confused tourists, rowdy recent graduates, and a few people who, on the surface at least, look interchangeable with me.

"The Northern Line is experiencing severe delays, due to unplanned engineering works."

I'm going to be late for my date. And not fashionably, nonchalantly late, but late enough that Christopher might give up and go home.

I look at my watch again, then at the screen showing when the next train arrives. It's gone ominously blank. There's a restless crowd on the platform and an endless stream of people filing on to swell its ranks.

My heartrate's increasing, and my chest is tightening. Anger and irritation and frustration and impatience. They're not safe emotions for me. If it weren't for my coloured contacts and dark sunglasses combo, everyone on the platform would see my irises turning red. And if there happened to be any practitioners about, they'd see the cloud of magic that surrounds me—that always surrounds each of us—change from a placid blue lake to a stormy grey sea.

I take a deep breath like my nan always used to teach me. *In for four. Hold for seven. Out for eight. Repeat.* The real trick is to close your eyes and let your mind sink into the earth and become one with it. You can both neutralise and strengthen your power that way. Back home, it's easy. But London's not conducive to magic or to core meditation at the best of times. Too many people. Too many buildings reaching into the sky and tunnels buried deep underground. The Tube is a particularly awful place in which to attempt to ground yourself in the earth. So I settle for breathing.

It's sufficient to steady my power to the extent that I'm in no imminent danger of blowing up the platform. But it's not enough to undo my panic about being late for the date, and resisting the urge to traverse—that is, to travel there instantly using magic—is like torture. As a teenager, I barely travelled any other way, apart from when I wanted to show off in one of my family's fancy cars or travel through the Dome.

For those of us born with a connection in our blood to the magic all around us, making use of it is as natural as breathing. Magic grows stronger within us and sustains the practitioner in turn. It's almost unheard of for a practitioner to resist the pull of their power—particularly a practitioner as strong as I am. Or at least, as strong as I used to be. I can only assume my strength has waned over six years of barely being used. Not using magic —real magic, not just a touch of ill-advised scrying—is a mental struggle and a physical strain, but I stick to my vow.

When I finally make it to the gallery—arriving by tube and only fifteen minutes late—Christopher is waiting by the entrance. He's got the generically bland attractiveness of a professional in their mid-twenties who takes their exercise and grooming about as seriously as they take their career. Mid-brown hair in a neat cut. Clean shaven with clear skin. Developed, but not over-exaggerated muscles.

"Hey, Christopher, it's me. Sorry I'm a little late."

Dates generally have a hard time recognising me in person, as my profile is entirely made up of my eldest brother's drawings of me. They're simultaneously true to life on the detail and flattering in their overall effect. God knows how many people swipe left due to their horror at my pretension or their suspicions about the physical defects I must surely be trying to hide. But those who swipe right tend to really, really like the pictures, which they assume demonstrate my cool, artistic nature, rather than my literal inability to show up in a photograph.

"Sadie! So good to finally meet you." He leans in and kisses me on the cheek. "Ready to go inside? I've heard great things about the new exhibition."

I take his hand and lead the way.

"Where are you from?" Christopher asks, while we gaze dutifully at the bunk beds and steel monsters that make up the display.

I get that question a lot. My accent is about as stable as the voice of a teenage boy. Sometimes, it's generic estuary English with a few odd vowels. Sometimes, thanks to the effects of university and all my well-bred colleagues, it's disconcertingly posh. And then, when I'm excited, scared, or stressed, I sound like I did when I was eighteen: northern as hell.

"Mannith," I say. "You've probably never heard of it. It's in Yorkshire. Your standard post-industrial wasteland."

That's not true in the slightest. There's nothing post-industrial about Mannith. Nothing run-down. For better or for worse, it's like something from the fifties. The steelworks in the town and the mines out in the countryside are thriving; the local pubs are buzzing; people leave their doors unlocked and chat in the street. And my parents and their Dome are the ones to thank for that.

Chris frowns like he's scanning his internal encyclopaedia for some fact about my hometown. "Wasn't their football team in the FA Cup semi-finals a few years ago?"

"Yep. A heart-warming underdog story until Manchester United destroyed them."

Their victories were courtesy of Liam, my youngest brother, who's an obsessive fan.

"Let's go and look at the Magrittes," I say. "They're my favourite."

Christopher nods, and we stroll through a succession of galleries until we reach the right room, stopping now and then en route to gaze at an exhibit that catches one or both of our eyes.

As we idly browse, Christopher continues with his safe

small talk. "You're a lawyer, aren't you? What do you specialise in?"

"Human rights stuff. Immigration appeals. And criminal work—defence mostly. Whatever their faults, I believe everyone deserves a fair trial."

I love my work, and I love talking about it, but sometimes I think I might as well just get a badge that declares 'I'm trying to be a good person'.

"Sounds fantastic. I work for a charity that's focused on increasing the number of girls in education in developing countries."

Glorious. Now we're having a self-righteousness-off. I can almost hear my dad mocking us both.

Christopher gestures at one of the paintings. "Have you seen that new show about the creation of this at the National? It's meant to be fantastic."

"Not yet. But I've read some great reviews." Probably exactly the same reviews as him.

"Perhaps we could go next week?"

I smile in a noncommittal way. Through force of habit, I glance down at my right hand, but the lien mark is hidden safely under one of my large collection of costume jewellery rings. At home, I tend to take the contact lenses out and the sunglasses off, but the rings always stay on. I can't bear to look at it. I can't let it flash red. I can't be found.

The lien will be binding. I may have chosen not to collect last night. But I reserve the right to do so.

"Have you seen everything you want to see?" Christopher asks, after another half hour of wandering. "I was up for looking at the Flavin exhibition, but the dinner reservation's for eight. Have you tried Indonesian food before, by the way?"

"The restaurant sounds amazing. But I'm not really feeling it tonight. It's been a long week."

Chris looks like a kicked puppy.

"Why don't we go back to mine?" I suggest. "Order some-thing in? Chill out."

He smiles at that. This time, I order a taxi. I can't face the Tube again, and traversing in front of someone on a first date is not a great look.

I lead Chris into my open-plan, grey and teal-toned kitchen/dining room/sitting room, peruse my extensive collec-tion of fancy bottles, and fix us both a Graveney gin and Fever-Tree tonic, with tons of ice.

When I look up, he's staring at the family drawings.

"Did you do these?"

"They're my brother's handiwork."

"He's an amazing artist."

It's true. With or without the aid of magic.

"That's him, there," I say. "Brendan. And the woman with white-blonde hair down to her waist is his fiancée, Leah. The guy in the boxing ring is my other brother, Liam, and that's his best friend, Shane. He's practically a third brother to me. The one who looks sort of like me but about ten times hotter is my older sister, Chrissie—"

"I don't think that," he interrupts.

"That's an objective fact, not self-esteem issues," I reply, handing him his drink. "Anyway, the man who's about twice her height and four times her weight in muscle is her husband, Ray. They met when she was on holiday in Jamaica. It was love at first sight to the extent he came home with her. The two baby girls are theirs. Ceridwen and Chioma."

I ought to stop talking, but while he struck me as the sort of person who'd politely feign enthusiasm, he's staring at the draw-ings in genuine fascination. There's something about my family that captures people's attention, even from a distance of three hundred miles.

I don't mention that I've never met Leah, Ray, or the gorgeous little twins in person. They all came on the scene after my self-imposed exile started.

"What about the photographs?" Chris asks, gesturing towards the opposite wall, which boasts several larger prints.

"Mannith in all its glory. Something to stave off the home-sickness."

According to Chrissie, Ray loves photography about as much as Bren loves drawing, and he imbues his art with the same carefully honed skill and magical touch. It's an odd hobby for someone who can't show up in a photograph themselves or capture images of most of his friends and family, but he focuses on haunting landscapes. The Witches' Church. Summer Hill. The idiosyncratic design of the Sadler family home.

As soon as Christopher finishes his drink, I pounce. I want to do this, but I want it over with. I pin him against the wall and kiss him frantically, releasing him just long enough to wriggle out of my dress and unbutton his shirt.

I relish the look of stunned arousal on his face. I'm far more turned on by my own self-confidence than his admittedly well-honed chest.

"Sadie, I'm not sure this is quite what I was expecting when you invited me back. You're absolutely gorgeous, and you're so funny over text, but you seemed a bit distant today..."

I grin, stepping back to give him a better view of my lingerie-clad body. "I'm full of surprises."

I grab his hand and half drag him to the bedroom, then sprawl out on my hygge-chic cinnamon and slate patchwork quilt. His jeans come off in seconds, then he lays down beside me. Before he has a chance to collect his senses or take control of the situation, I straddle him, lean over, and kiss him with renewed passion.

He slides a hand between my legs, and I return the favour. I don't mess about waiting for him to bring me off with his surprisingly skilful fingers. I grab some protection from the bedside drawer and jump on top.

My arousal is building, but then I look down at him. There's something in his ordinary, friendly face that suddenly bores me almost to the point of disgust. I'm seeing those flame-red eyes again. Dirty-blond waves in place of Chris' short brown hair. Dangerously sharp cheekbones in place of his soft facial features. And that evil, alluring smirk in place of Chris' wholesome smile.

Don't do this, brain. For once, stay in the moment. Appreciate the perfectly pleasant, perfectly attractive man in front of you.

But it's too late. I close my eyes, and my unconscious mind is running my favourite fantasy again. I come with my sweetly bland date's hands all over my body, but my utmost enemy's face and voice all over my brain.

Once we wake from a brief, post-coital nap, Christopher smiles and attempts to pull me into an embrace. "That was amazing. Do you want to curl up together, or shall we get dressed, order that food we skipped, and then do it all again?"

I prop myself up and look down at him. He's cute naked, and while he's no doubt influenced by the sex, he's gazing at me as if he really likes me. He seems like a nice guy. I could try to be nice back.

I give an exaggerated yawn. "It was lovely to meet you. But I'm super tired, and I've got to do some prep on a case for tomorrow. Let me fix you another gin and tonic, then I'll order you a taxi."

He stands up on autopilot. "Really? Are you sure you don't want me to stay the night? I can head off early?"

My smile is becoming stiffer by the minute. "Maybe next time."

I head across the landing to the open-plan kitchen before he can debate the matter further, and pour us both a strong drink. Despite the awkwardness of the situation, I take the time to add ice and a slice of lime. Neglecting that step is practically heresy. I drain mine before he manages to throw on his clothes and join me.

He takes a tentative sip of his drink then perches on my breakfast-bar stool. "There's something I need to say before I go."

I tense. I've never had a date refuse to leave before. I do my due diligence, I pay attention to my intuition, and it all works out. Maybe he's just a little overenthusiastic and not great at social cues. But maybe he's someone who doesn't deal well with rejection and can't take no for an answer.

A little twinge of that primordial panic that all women know far too well hits me, despite the fact that, if push really came to shove, I could incinerate him with a thought. But I really do try so hard not to do that sort of thing.

"I'd like you to leave now, please." For the moment, I cling to politeness and pray he'll respond in kind.

He holds out his hands. "Sadie, I'm not some creep, I swear. I need to deliver a message, then I'll leave you in peace."

"You've got five minutes. Then creep or otherwise, I need to get on with my case prep."

"I'm an associate of the London Coven. They were tasked with tracking you down, and I was selected to be the one who made contact."

I take a hurried step back, then raise my arms and throw up my shields before he can say anything more. A simple touch of defensive magic shouldn't be enough to trigger the lien mark, and even if it were, it feels like the lesser of two evils for once.

I've never had the pleasure of meeting any members of the London Coven face to face. But my dad had dealings with them when he was younger, and he's told me enough stories. I'm powerful enough and have a strong enough pedigree that they'd probably welcome me with open arms if I still performed magic. But I don't, so despite the fact I've lived in their city for six years, I've stayed out of their way and they've stayed out of mine. Chris didn't seem to be a practitioner. How the hell could I have missed the signs?

Chris doesn't respond to the appearance of my shield—a translucent, red-tinged bubble visible to all those with the power to see it. Nor does he raise a shield of his own or prepare any kind of attack. I glance at his eyes. Still blue. Pupils still circular, irises still normally sized.

"You're not a practitioner, are you?" I stutter out after a moment. My body's rigid, poised to take more dramatic steps if I need to.

"No." There's awe in his voice at the very idea. "But they've promised to teach me their magic if I spend a few years working for them on the side."

I laugh incredulously, even as I keep my shield firm. "Lavinia and her cronies would never teach a human. Besides, it's barely possible, even if they were willing to put their prejudices aside. They could show you a few cheap party tricks at best."

He shrugs as though he doesn't care, though the question of whether he's being used must haunt him.

"Lavinia trusted me enough to carry out this mission on behalf of one of her closest allies. A bit of research suggested I'm broadly your type. Or, at least, what you try to convince yourself is your type, nowadays."

I barely hear the end of his self-congratulatory little speech. I make it as far as "closest allies" before my heartbeat starts to drown out all other sounds.

"I need to take you back to Mannith," he continues.

I close the distance between us and take a firm grip of his arms with my suddenly clammy hands. "If you try, I'll kill you. And failing that, I'll kill myself. You won't take me to him." My voice is so high-pitched it could be heard by bats. I sound hysterical. I couldn't care less.

Burn him, my mind screams. *Mesmerise him. Break his will or break his body or bend his mind. Do something. Anything.*

Using magic is a risk. But right now, it seems safer than the alternative. Better to give Gabriel Thornber some clue as to my location than to be dragged to him.

I tighten my hold on Chris' arm, close my eyes, and let my power flow. Even through my fear, it gives me a wonderful sense of release. When I let go a few seconds later, he's frozen in place. I stroke a finger over his lips so he can at least speak.

"Let me go, please. It's not the Thornbers who asked Lavinia for a favour. Your family want to bring you home."

"They wouldn't. They know why I can't go back to Mannith."

"They need you. However much they miss you, they wouldn't normally ask. But they're desperate."

He's not got any body language to play with and can barely move his eyes, but something in his tone manages to convince me. I stretch out a trembling arm and make a scooping movement as though dragging my magic back out of him and towards me. He crumples to the floor as his muscles come back online.

My lien mark flashes red, bright enough to be visible even under the rings. *No. No no no no no.* Is it enough to allow Gabriel to track me? It's a one-off and he's hundreds of miles away, but I don't like those odds.

Having risked everything on breaking my magic ban—seemingly needlessly—it's tempting to carry on and melt the skin off Chris' bones for having dared to put me in this position. The London Coven probably wouldn't be overjoyed with me, but they generally put a practitioner's right to safety over a human's right to life.

I take a deep breath. I'm not that person. "Get out."

He grabs onto the bar stool and pulls himself back to his feet. "I swore I'd do this."

"You've delivered your message. Go and get your little pat on the head from Lavinia. I'll take this up with my mother."

He heads into the hallway and towards the door without further objection, his movements jerky like someone who's pushed themselves far too hard in the gym.

"I wasn't acting under sufferance tonight, you know," he says, opening the door. "And other than hiding my allegiance to the Coven, I wasn't pretending to be someone I'm not. Until that last ten minutes, I'd been having the best evening I've had in months. I don't suppose you'd like to meet up again when your business up north is finished with?"

"Seriously, get the hell out of here before I do something I regret more than I already regret this entire evening."

Once he's finally gone, I collapse onto the sofa. The red glow has already faded from my finger, thank God, and Gabriel Thornber does not appear to be bursting through the door. I ought to call Mum right now and find out what the hell's going on. Instead, after five self-indulgent minutes of moping around, I stand up, strengthen the wards around the house, then bury myself in case prep, using work to drive everything else out of my head.

When I allow myself to sleep, it's inevitable I have yet another of my recurrent Gabriel Thornber dreams. There are three broad types. Sometimes, it's a straightforward, vivid re-enactment of the night he imposed the lien. Sometimes, it's one I'm basically too embarrassed to admit to. Tonight, it's once again the version where he tracks me down and takes my power, as he's perfectly entitled to do under the terms of our bargain.

Once again, I'm walking along a deserted street at midnight. Once again, I turn a corner, into a narrower street, and he's there.

"I only want to take what you promised me. You know full well it's breaking all the rules to resist a lien."

If you use magic to try to escape your deal, the universe will turn your own power against you and kill you on the spot. The same thing happens to any friends or family who try to help you. If you don't use magic, then fate will kill you anyway over weeks or months. Strike you down or waste you away. And, while they're waiting for that moment, the one who imposed the lien is perfectly entitled to kill you for breaking a fairly struck bargain.

"I'll honour the Old Ways."

"Thank you." He wraps his left arm around my upper back to keep me in place, presses his right hand against my sternum, taps his fingers three times to open a channel, then closes his eyes. Mine slam shut in response.

There's a gentle pressure at first, along with a sense of my muscles contracting. I breathe steadily and attempt to zone out and pretend this isn't happening. There's a voice at the back of my head screaming that I ought to resist. Punch him. Try a magical attack. Run for it. Or just beg him not to do this. But that's human thinking. He can stop whatever spells I attempt. He'll show no mercy. And ultimately, if I tried to prevent this, by all our rules and customs, I'd be the one in the wrong.

There's a chill building at my chest. At first, it's like running my hand under cold water. Then it's more like pressing an ice cube against my skin. It'll grow and grow until I feel like I'm running through the Arctic in a bikini.

He's taking my magic.

Of course he is. That's the whole point of the bargain. But

the sudden thought makes me panic. Against my better judgement, I snap out of my semi-trance and attempt to push his hand away. I succeed only in turning the unpleasant but bearable coldness of a semi-voluntary magical transfer into the shocking pain of one in which I'm not cooperating.

I scream, like Bren screamed the night I made the bargain to save him. Some of it's from the pain, some from the horror of what's happening to me. The fact that I'm losing my magic and the fact that I've lost. Only his firm hold on my back is keeping me standing.

"Sadie, try to relax. This has to happen. But it doesn't need to hurt you."

"Stop, please."

"I'm merely taking what I'm owed. You could have let me have your brother's magic instead, all those years ago."

After that, I'm incapable of any more conversation, even the simplest of pleas. Somehow, I stay conscious, though that may be more a curse than a blessing.

I may never use my magic these days, but there's something comforting about its presence. It's a part of who I am. Losing it will be like losing a sense. Already, the colours of the night seem less sharp. I'm less connected to everything and everyone around me. Apart from Gabriel, who I'm utterly aware of, almost as though he's a part of me.

I don't know how long it goes on. The pain and the unreality blur time. But eventually, he taps his fingers again and removes his hand, while keeping me supported.

"Done. That half of the debt is repaid. Can you stand?"

I nod, a tiny, weak movement that's all I can manage. He releases me, and I slump to the floor, showing my claim to be a lie.

He reaches out an arm. "Let me help get you home."

I huddle into myself on the ground. "You got what you came for. Now leave me alone." I hesitate as an awful thought strikes me. "Unless you're planning to claim the other half of the bargain tonight, too."

"Not tonight. But that part of the lien holds."

I don't reply. The pain's fading rapidly, but the deeper, psychological agony of being cut off from the magic in the air is hurting more by the minute.

He disappears into thin air, leaving me a broken wreck on the ground.

As always, I wake up sweating, with my pulse racing like the dream was real.

I turn on the bedside light and take some slow, deep breaths. Gabriel has made no attempt to claim on the lien in six years. To the best of my knowledge, he never visits London. I'm careful not to use my magic, but the odd slip-up never seems to result in disaster. Though maybe he's just biding his time. Hiding away down here is one thing. Returning home to Mannith would be quite another.

TWO

LONDON—PRESENT DAY

The next morning's depressingly overcast for late June, which doesn't help my state of mind. Everyone always claims that English summers were warmer when they were a child, but in my case, thanks to the effect the Dome had on Mannith, it's objectively true.

As I walk to work, the questions keep coming. What the hell do my parents want? Why would they send the London Coven after me, rather than getting in touch themselves? And how dare those stuck-up southern witches trick me into going on a date and letting my guard down?

Nonetheless, after a few minutes, the exercise, the river views, and some Lana Del Rey on my iPhone start to push my worry and anger into the background. At least there don't seem to have been any obvious repercussions from panicking, using magic, and triggering the lien mark. I just need to be careful not to do it again any time soon.

I stop at my favourite little coffee shop en route and get a flat white to take away. Caffeine's probably not a great idea when I'm this on edge, but I need a treat, and decaf is a sin.

By the time I'm crossing Waterloo Bridge, I'm feeling

almost cheerful, at least on the surface, until a phone call cuts off my music. A glance at the screen shows it's my mother.

I walk to the side of the bridge, both to get out of people's way and so I can ground myself—physically by holding onto the side, emotionally by watching the river ebb and flow.

"Hi, Mum." I make my voice as cheery as humanly possible.

"Hopefully Lavinia's man told you that we need you to come and stay for a few weeks," she announces, with no preamble or any hint that I might refuse.

My hand tightens on the bridge. "You know I can't. And I can't believe you sent someone to track me down."

Mum's voice is firm. "I thought it might be harder for you to ignore a stranger in person than one of us on the phone. But that's not important. Brendan needs you."

I glance down at my Fitbit. It tells me my heartrate is in the cardio zone, despite the fact I'm standing utterly still.

"Brendan? What's he done now? And what's so bad that he can't sort it out himself with the usual magic and charm?"

My oldest brother is brilliant. He's also a bloody liability.

"He's been charged with the murder of Niall Thornber."

My vision blurs. Niall is Gabriel's father. The head of the Thornber family. My family's only rivals. "You have got to be kidding me. Did he do it?"

"Your father says that if we want you to help with his defence, we shouldn't talk casually about the details."

"For goodness' sake, Mum! Am I a part of this family or not?"

"You tell me."

I really walked into that one. I take the deepest breath I can and start to cross the bridge. There are two contradictory ways to keep unconscious magic at bay. One is to still your body and mind, and basically go into a trance. The other is physical exertion. I can't hold a conversation with my mum while I'm running or while I'm meditating, so a brisk stroll will have to suffice.

"Of course I'm still a Sadler. I want to help Bren. But there are lots of good lawyers. Why do you need me?"

"We need absolute loyalty, total dedication, and someone who understands what's really going on here."

It's a fair point. If you didn't know about the magic, the family feuds didn't make that much sense. Chances were that the circumstances of the murder didn't either.

"Couldn't you just—you know..." I wave my hand vaguely in the air to demonstrate my point. Couldn't the family *just* mesmerise the entire prison staff into letting him go and forgetting this ever happened? Or *just* blow a hole in the prison walls with the power of their minds and bust him out. *Just* solve the problem with magic, essentially.

Mum understands my meaning all too well. "If we'd acted more quickly, then yes. We'd have dealt with this in the normal manner."

Very few crimes are committed in Mannith to begin with—there's little need when everything's peaceful and plentiful and when a significant percentage of the population can achieve what they want with magic. When an incident does occur, my family and the other senior practitioner families tend to punish the perpetrator themselves if they're an outsider; cover it up if they're a member of the inner circle. And the few police who live in the town are firm Sadler loyalists.

"But?"

"But it was out of town police who came for Brendan, supported by a few Thornber scum. They struck while he was weak. And once they had him in the prison, it was too late."

I frown. I'd forgotten about the fact that all major prisons and their staff are warded against practitioner attack, psychic or physical, internal or external. Some sort of covenant with the

Crown, centuries ago, to ensure our kind couldn't be entirely above the law.

In Mannith, and a few similar places controlled by other families, practitioners are a known fact. In most of the country—and indeed, the world—our existence, like that of vampires and all the rest, is much more secretive. But there have always been people at the top of society who are aware of us and have worked to put both polite agreements and protective measures in place. Ironically, it was the Sadler ancestors who agreed to arrange the wards in most of the local jails.

All that said, I've never represented a fellow practitioner, so I'm hazy on the details. "Do those weird old protections apply in the courts, too?"

"There's some of the same sort of power in the air. But nowhere near as strong. We couldn't just traverse him out of there or strike the case from the records. But in theory, we should be able to influence the judge and the jury or put ideas in the witnesses' heads. Unfortunately, so can the other side—and Niall's darling son has promised to block any magic we attempt and mesmerise the entire court into locking Brendan up for life."

I shiver at the mention of the Thornber heir. Actually, physically shiver. It's pathetic, but I do. I glance at the Fitbit again. It thinks I'm doing CrossFit.

"We need a lawyer who can't be mesmerised themselves, and who can prevent that bastard from mesmerising the judge and the jury. Perhaps turn his magic back on him, too. Even Dad couldn't manage that. Not against Gabriel-fucking-Thornber."

The whole family call him that whenever they have cause to refer to him. Gabriel-fucking-Thornber, like it's a double-barrelled name.

"Mum, you make it sound like I can block his magic where others can't because I'm some amazing practitioner. You know full well the only reason I can stand up to him is because we made a deal. If I come back, he's going to collect."

I pull out the mirror I keep in my pocket for just this purpose and check my irises. Despite my contact lenses, they're a glowing orange. I lean against the balustrade, slam my eyes shut, and try to breathe. My temper is one of the less welcome inheritances from my father. If I don't calm down, I risk channelling the physical manifestation of my rage into the earth and cracking the bridge in two. Already, waves are rising on the usually placid river.

"Brendan needs you, Sadie. And family always come first. Change your name, keep your new accent, Chrissie will sort out your face. You can just be our lawyer. No one needs to know you're also our long-lost daughter. Just get up here tomorrow."

"Tomorrow? When did this happen? The case won't start for months. I've got a big trial down here."

"Niall died on the fifteenth of June. Your brother was charged yesterday. The case starts in a fortnight. Things move fast in Mannith, as you well know. Someone else can take your other trial. We'll sort the logistics."

Bren's my brother, he's in trouble, and I'm the only one who can help him. Conversely, Bren got *himself* into trouble, and I've helped him enough for one lifetime.

It'll be nice to see my family again. But there are good reasons I never go home.

Technically, Gabriel could call in the lien at any point, no matter where I am in the world. But outside of the Dome, I'm harder to find, especially if I don't work magic, and his powers hold less sway.

I don't know why I'm even pretending to have this debate with myself. I might be able to resist mesmerism, but I'm a sucker for a bit of emotional blackmail.

THREE

By five PM the next day, I'm on a train heading north. I haven't agreed I'll take the case. But I've committed to visit Mannith, talk to Bren, and then make my decision.

The intervening thirty-six hours have consisted of a toxic mixture of internal debate and hurried logistics. I should have been in the Old Bailey today. But when my parents want something to happen, they make it happen. And I've never known them want something this much.

My clerk was mesmerised from a distance by my mother. My chambers know not to expect me back for a month or two. The other trial was delayed by a few days. Another lawyer was found. Maybe they'll win and get the credit that should have been mine. Maybe they'll lose, and my poor client will be screwed over. But Brendan's the only thing that matters now.

It usually takes months from a defendant being charged to the start of a murder trial, but Bren's will be starting in around two weeks—neither the Sadlers nor the Thornbers want this to drag on longer than it needs to. Goodness knows what cases have been pulled to make space for it.

I'm not sure my parents have quite appreciated the subtlety

of my position. As far as they're concerned, I'm now Bren's lawyer. But as I've repeatedly tried to explain, I reserve the right to head straight back to London if the case seems unwinnable or I feel in danger.

Chrissie's worked a spell on me from a distance to make me look just different enough that no one should recognise me. Disguise spells are surprisingly difficult, considering that the natural magic in the air and the earth tends to simply respond to our commands. You can play around with hairstyle or a few degrees of skin tone, but attempts to change people's facial structure or body shape rarely last more than an hour or two.

In our teens, Chrissie and I occasionally attempted body-switching for the purposes of practical jokes, despite or perhaps because it's famously meant to be impossible, almost up there with reviving the dead. Unsurprisingly, we never managed it.

Chrissie's settled for shifting the way the light reflects off me and the overall impression I leave in people's minds. It wouldn't be enough to hide me from those who see me regularly, but I'm already fairly unrecognisable after six years away, a spot of natural ageing, and a total change of hairstyle and dress sense. The magic should tip the balance.

I've got a first-class seat on the train. Mum would be furious if she knew. I usually travel in standard, but if there was ever a day I deserved a little treat, it's today.

I drink three awful train coffees before we reach Sheffield, after which I change from the intercity train to a slower, smaller, local line that links the surrounding towns and villages.

Thirty minutes out, the train reaches the edge of the Dome. I see it before me as an iridescent curved red wall rising from the earth to the sky—invisible to everyone except those born with the power needed to see it.

It catches me by surprise. I remember its boundaries as starting a mile or two farther north, just before the train station, but my memory must be playing tricks on me. The Dome is a constant. It's been in place for generations, and despite Bren's efforts years ago—the efforts I paid for so dearly—no one's ever succeeded in moving or expanding it.

The train passes through with ease, though a few of my fellow passengers shiver or stiffen for a moment without knowing why.

For me, the effect is more pronounced, like I've charged headfirst into an electric fence. I dig my nails into the seat of the train and wait for the burning sensation in my nerves to subside. It only lasts a second or two, though those seconds are endless. Then we're through, and into the outskirts of Mannith.

I shrug off my suit jacket. It's summer, therefore the weather's sunny and warm here. Things happen according to expectations in my hometown.

A glance in my trusty mirror shows that my irises have turned a light pink. I throw on my sunglasses. Merely being within the boundaries of the Dome is enough to set my magic surging towards the surface.

Contrary to what many people in town believe, the Dome isn't the source of my family's power. Our ancestors and a few other practitioner families have lived in Mannith for centuries, working our personal magic. The so-called Witches' Church was built in medieval times, and there are family records of sixteenth-century spells, whereas the Dome is only about a century old. It allows magic to take place on an industrial, automated scale. It keeps the whole town permanently blessed, without us having to contribute anything towards this on a day-to-day basis. Were it ever to fall, we could still work love spells, curses, and all the rest of it, but Mannith would no longer be protected from everything from inclement weather to economic recessions. Those are the upsides. The downsides, as I understand them, are more complicated.

According to my watch, there are five minutes before the

train reaches the station. I use the time to sink into a core meditation deeper than anything I've managed in years.

*"We are now on the approach to Mannith. Mannith is our
next station stop."*

I shake myself back to full consciousness, grab my suitcase
and head for the doors. No one else follows. Mannith isn't
exactly the sort of place that encourages casual visitors. It's
astonishing it still has a regular train service. My parents' doing,
presumably.

The Victorian station is small, but pretty and perfectly
preserved, as though it's a microcosm of the town. There's a
little stone waiting room, painted dark blue and cream. A
flower display of pink fuchsias and purple pansies that lightly
scent the air. A rickety wooden bridge crossing the track. It's
all made more pleasant by the evening sun and the gentle
breeze.

I stand there for a moment, gently reacclimatising to the
town, until a man in his early-twenties strides towards me.

"Miss Elner?"

For a moment, I almost don't respond to the assumed name
we've agreed I'll use for my stay in Mannith. Then my brain
catches up with events. If someone were to look through the
records of Gray's Inn, they'd find evidence of a lawyer called
Kate Elner having been called to the Bar. If they were to look on
my chambers' website, she'd be listed there, and all my
colleagues would nod in recognition of the name. Kate Elner
apparently has an impressive track record. It's just one more
example of the myriad complex strands of magic my family has
spun over the last day or two.

"My name's Connor Colson. The Sadler family sent me to
pick you up and take you to your hotel."

I stare at Connor, trying to place him. There'd always been
a few Colsons in my father's employ, but this one can't be more
than about twenty-one. I've probably met him at some long-ago

family gathering, but if he's a couple of years younger than me, he'd never have factored on my radar as a teenager.

The Colsons are another practitioner family, and if my parents have entrusted him with escorting me, his powers are presumably first rate. With his tight jeans, sleeveless T-shirt to show off his muscled and tattooed arms, and closely cropped brown hair, he looks nothing like the popular perception of a wizard—ruggedly handsome would be the polite way to describe him. "A nice bit of rough" would be the alternative.

I glance at his eyes. Diamond-shaped pupils, unsurprisingly. The sure sign of a Born Practitioner. Hopefully, the contact lenses and sunglasses are effectively hiding mine.

"Pleased to meet you, Connor," I say, as he leads me towards his car. My local accent has naturally faded in the years I've been away, but now I play up the southern accent and the middle-class manners.

The way he slings my over-packed suitcase into the car suggests the muscles aren't just for show. Probably one of my father's enforcers—the brawn rather than the brains of the operation. But a well remunerated enforcer, judging by the shiny new Merc. Presumably, he's perfectly capable of traveling by magic should he wish to do so, but nice cars are a status symbol for practitioners, the same as for anyone else. And though magic is always quicker than more mundane forms of transport, it has a really draining effect on the body over longer distances.

My brother Liam had wanted to pick me up from the station himself, but we'd agreed it was a bad idea. At best, an actual Sadler family member taking the time out to collect me would look distinctly odd. At worst, we'd start hugging and screaming, and he'd forget to call me Kate Elner. Not a great start to my cover if there were Thornber spies around.

"You'll be staying at The Windmill Hotel." Connor opens the passenger seat of the car and helps me in like a fancy chauffeur.

Mum had wanted me safely tucked up in my old bedroom, but however much they attempted to sell it as a sensible way of protecting their prize lawyer, it'd be utterly unbelievable. As I know all too well, the family home is sacrosanct. Hence my room in The Windmill, the closest hotel.

"The Windmill's nice enough," Connor continues, starting to drive. "I'll be staying there, too, in the room next door. It'll be like being on holiday."

"Why are you staying? Don't you live nearby?"

I know the answer, but I ask the question to keep up appearances. I'm on the London circuit, but I've done a few provincial trials and stayed in the local hotels. I've never been assigned a bodyguard-cum-chauffeur by my clients, still less had them check into my hotel.

"I don't want to worry you, but your client has some dangerous enemies. There's always a chance they'd try to get to you."

"Nothing worries me. Besides, he's not officially my client yet. And it's sweet that everyone's so concerned, but I can take care of myself."

He shrugs, and it's obvious what he's thinking: *If only she knew the sorts of enemies she's up against.*

If only he knew just how well I can look after myself, I think by way of silent reply.

"Brendan's family will explain when we get to the hotel. They'll give you twenty minutes to get settled, then they want to meet you and plot."

I frown, half keeping up the act, half nervous about seeing them all so soon. "This is all very unorthodox. I'll have a conference. Tomorrow. With my potential client. And there'll be no 'plotting'. We'll go over his statement and talk about possible defences."

Connor crosses his arms in frustration. The car keeps

steering perfectly. He's driving it with his mind, as he's presumably been doing all along.

"I was told you were prepared to show total loyalty and commitment. That's why you were chosen. I thought all that was made clear before you accepted?"

"I'm a lawyer, Connor. Not a gun for hire. And once again, I've not accepted the job yet." The irritation in my voice isn't faked in the slightest. Damn my parents for putting me in this position.

"Let me make one thing clear then, Miss Elner. People round here don't say no to the Sadlers."

"I say no to whomever I please," I reply. "And with you here to protect me, I have nothing to worry about."

"I need to protect you from yourself as well as our enemies, with an attitude like that."

I just about manage not to laugh.

The Windmill is situated in the old, quaint bit of town that my family's powers have long protected from both modernisation and decay. I know the bar on the ground floor all too well from endless drunken teenage birthday parties featuring enthusiastic dancing and furtive kisses away from Bren's ever-watchful eye.

It hasn't changed a bit in the six years I've been away. But then again, it probably hasn't changed all that much in the hundreds of years it's been in existence. Few things do, in this town. Mannith was in the Domesday book, and though most of the buildings in town are from the early 1800s, the pub's been there almost from the beginning. It's got the flagstone floor, oak-beamed ceiling, and rustic wooden furniture you'd expect in the sort of place middle-aged couples would visit for a genteel pint after a long country walk with their dog. But it tends to be full of disreputable young people drinking heavily and even less reputable old people drinking even more.

Glancing around is like stepping back in time to my teenage years. The same smell of beer and smoke in the air, the same constant swell of laughter and cheerfully shouted remarks. Some of the clientele are practitioners, some humans in my family's employ, others just ordinary, loyal townsfolk.

I vaguely recognise a few people from school and from family gatherings. I was never exactly Miss Popularity as a teenager—I was far too quiet and studious for that—but my family name and the efforts of my more sociable siblings meant I was always included in most social circles. And I did have a few closer, like-minded friends. But keeping in touch with them after I fled was too much of a risk, and by the time I'd been away for a few years, it seemed increasingly unlikely I'd have much in common with people who were still living the life of a practitioner. I'd love to catch up with some old acquaintances, but it's more of a risk than ever.

Thanks to Chrissie's prowess and my natural changes, even the magical ones show no sign of penetrating my disguise. Indeed, no one pays me much attention at all, until they realise I'm with Connor. That piques their interest.

"Who's the new lass, Connor?" someone calls. "How've you found the time for a dirty weekend in the middle of all that's going on?"

I can't help but reflecting that it would be nice if that was actually what was happening here. Almost anything would be better than the reality of the situation. Besides, even if he's not my usual type, Connor's objectively good-looking and seems like a decent guy.

"He's nothing but trouble, love," one of the others says to me. "Come here. I'll buy you a drink."

I'm on the verge of saying something back. Perhaps a jokingly flirtatious line, perhaps a withering putdown. But that doesn't seem a very Kate Elner thing to do, so I stay silent and mimic the nervous smile I've seen time after time on the face of outsiders who find themselves in our town.

For a second, Connor smiles, too, and the same desire to make a witty remark lights up his face. There's a pleasant energy running through the room, a real sense of people who know, trust, and like each other, who are equally happy to sit in companionable silence with their pints or lovingly tease and mock each other all night.

He opens his mouth to speak, and I pinpoint the precise moment he remembers he's there on business and meant to be protecting the outsider.

"This is Miss Elner, the Sadlers' new lawyer. It's her job to get Brendan out. It's my job to keep her safe until she does."

I relish the pride in his voice and don't attempt to point out for the hundredth time that I've not committed to being their lawyer yet.

Everyone turns weirdly respectful when they hear that, like some diluted version of the reception I'd get if they knew who I really was. The Windmill is a solidly Sadler establishment. Most bars, clubs and restaurants in town are owned by or under the protection of the Sadlers, the Thornbers, or one of their associates. And even those that aren't tend to have an informal loyalty one way or the other. There are few people in Mannith who don't know both families and owe at least a vague sense of allegiance to one of them.

My family's commercial interests are a swirling web of magic and business. Firstly, there are the companies they own, which magic helps to protect from competition or recession. Secondly, endless numbers of people within the Dome owe them fealty and pay for the privilege. It's sort of like a protection racket, but a very civilised and consensual one, based around respect and love, rather than fear and violence. And thirdly, in what was the foundation of the family business a few centuries back, they sell spells at an eye-watering but ultimately fair price.

"I'm taking her up to see the family now," Connor continues, despite the fact I'd argued this would be a terrible breach of protocol.

"Good luck, love," someone says. "I hope you've got what it takes. Brendan needs a bloody miracle."

I grin back at him and allow a tiny hint of my personality to shine through. "He's got me."

They all raise their pints then down them in support. It's a little off-message, but it's worth it for their reaction.

Connor whispers a few words to the barman, who doesn't need asking twice.

He hands him a key, then gestures towards the stairs. "Top floor. Do you need a hand?"

Connor shakes his head, scoops up my suitcase, then leads me up the stairs. I can't help but check him out as I follow behind.

I've never visited the hotel part of The Windmill before, but unsurprisingly, my bedroom is lovely. Everything in this town is lovely. Whitewashed walls with black beams. A big bed with pure white cotton sheets that give off a freshly laundered scent. Views out over the courtyard garden at the back, and a gentle cooling breeze drifting in through the sash window. It's nicely quiet considering it's only two floors up from the noisy bar. Probably some sort of soundproofing spell.

"Step outside for five minutes," I say to Connor. "I need to get ready. If you're insisting I meet my potential client's family tonight, I want to make a good first impression."

It's ridiculous. I spent years slobbing round my parents' house in pyjamas. But my family cares about outward appearance, and I care about what my family thinks of me, especially after being away for so long.

I throw off the smart-casual dress I'd travelled in and pull on a black, sleeveless suit dress, cut just above the knee, along with a matching tightly tailored jacket.

I rummage around in my suitcase until I find my make-up bag, and start to redo my face. It'd looked pristine when I'd left London, but travelling, nerves, and now the heat of Mannith have faded it. My hands are trembling far more than when I was getting ready to meet Christopher. A date is one thing. My mum and sister are quite another.

It's weird looking in the mirror while I'm under Chrissie's glamour. I look like myself, and yet not. Light bends around me in a different way. It makes getting my make-up right even trickier than usual. And in the magic-laden air of Mannith, it's a real challenge to stick to doing it by hand, but it's even more important that I don't give in to temptation.

I manually slick on some bright red lipstick and spritz myself with a citrus perfume. Once I pop my sunglasses back on, I'm done. There'll be no need for them with my family, but I ought to be careful around Connor, at least for the moment.

Connor's nervousness is saturating the air, even through the door. He doesn't want to be held responsible for the meeting with the Sadlers starting late. Neither does he want to hurry me along when he's meant to be taking care of me on their orders.

"Right, done," I say, bursting through the door. "Let's go and meet the family."

"You look great. Now, can you do me a favour? Don't argue with Mr Sadler about whether you're taking the case. If you really decide against, you can always take it up with his wife later."

"Fine." I'll argue with Dad as much as I want, but if Connor's worried, I'll try to have the decency not to do it in front of him.

My dad is a good man. He uses his powers to protect Mannith and make it a wonderful place to live. And on a day-to-day basis, he helps people out with magic in ways both big and small. But as he told me endlessly as a child, being good is not the same as being weak. Sometimes, it's not the same as being nice either.

Dad treats acolytes with respect and kindness, but he asks for absolute obedience and loyalty in return—the risks of betrayal or even just half-hearted service are too high to contemplate. Likewise, he does what needs to be done to keep those who'd want to harm Mannith or the family at bay. And to stop anyone who doesn't treat magic with the necessary seriousness from abusing it.

Keeping Mannith perfect requires both magic and strength. He *is* a good man, definitely. But, if I'm absolutely honest, if you didn't know him well, you'd probably also say that he was something of a scary one.

Connor escorts me back down one flight of stairs, to a familiar room on the middle floor. My dad's used it for both business meetings and family gatherings for a long time. It's got oak-panelled walls, a thick red carpet, no windows, and is almost as well warded as the family home.

Connor knocks. "It's me, sir. I've brought the lawyer."

"Come in."

Once the door swings open, I stare at my father. He appears older than the last time I saw him. Hardly surprising, considering six years have passed, but he looks good for his age. Greying but full hair swept back. His hard face softened by a few lines. A dark suit, cut to show he still has the kind of muscles a twenty-something would be jealous of.

He seems forbidding as hell, but I'm desperate to run over and give him a massive hug. Instead, I keep my body still and my voice professional.

Connor bows his head. "This is Kate Elner, sir."

"Ms Elner. Thank you for joining my son's legal team at such short notice."

I've not agreed yet. I long to snap out the words, but I

honour my promise to Connor and smile sweetly. "My pleasure. I always like to ensure justice prevails."

I'll try once more to make my position clear to Dad after the bodyguard's left us alone.

"Quite. While you're working for us, we expect the highest standards. Your absolute loyalty to the family. Your absolute discretion."

I bow my head in imitation of Connor. "Yes, sir."

"And you, Colson, I'm trusting you to protect her. She's my son and heir's only hope. You'll guard her like you would a member of the family. If the Thornbers or anyone else try anything, you *will* stop them. And if you don't, you'll pay the price."

I surreptitiously glance at Connor's arm. A lien mark rings his bicep. It's not clear whether it relates to a promise to guard me or to a general vow of loyalty to my father and the Sadlers. Either way, like all liens, if he breaks it, then one way or the other, he'll die.

Connor glances at the floor for a moment then rallies and looks my father in the eye. "You can count on me, sir. But what about her? Will she be... marked?"

Dad shrugs. "Ms Elner comes highly recommended. She's a consummate professional, not a hired thug. If push comes to shove then yes, I'll mark her. But there's no need for that now."

I shudder. Hopefully this is purely for Connor's benefit, an exercise in keeping up the charade. Dad would surely never actually brand a lien mark into my skin. My existing one is more than enough.

"Now leave us, Colson. Guard the door. Don't let anyone in. I want to talk to our lawyer alone. This is family business."

Connor bows properly this time, gives my arm a little squeeze, then heads out.

Dad waits until he's closed the door, then bursts out laughing. "Come here, sweetheart."

I laugh in turn, then dash over for that hug. "Great performance."

He hugs me back, and I feel like I'm ten again. "We'll be utterly convincing. No one will know who you are. Especially not that Thornber bastard."

I nod. Too many emotions to speak.

"Dad, you know I've not decided if I'm taking the case, right? I only sounded so certain just then because my poor bodyguard seemed convinced you'd kill us both otherwise."

"That's my stubborn baby girl. No pressure. But I'm sure you'll take the case once you've heard the full story. Once you've seen Brendan."

"Maybe. I want to help him if I can."

Dad takes my right hand. "Have you still got that damned mark?"

"You know better than anyone that those things don't just disappear."

Lien marks can't be removed or hidden by magic. Or indeed, by laser skin treatment. Believe me, I've tried.

He pulls off the ring that covers it. Other than a quick glance the other night to check it'd stopped glowing, it's been months since I've looked at the intricate interlocking spirals that encircle my finger. The ring stays on when I shower, when I work out, and when I sleep. I flinch at the sight, but that's nothing to my father's reaction. His eyes switch from a neutral blue to a glowing red in seconds. The mirror on the back wall shatters.

"We'll break him. We'll get that removed. We called in a favour with the London Coven and then dragged you up here because we had no choice. But perhaps it's a blessing in disguise."

I shrug. I've long given up on escaping the lien forever. Making it through the trial and out the other side is the best I can hope for.

"Let's go and see the others. And we'll try to avoid talking about the trial tonight."

He takes my arm and leads me to the door at the back of the room. There's a larger room beyond, and when he throws the door open, the rest of the family are perched on and around a long, low sofa, like they've posed for a tableau.

I dash inside, a wild grin on my face, then freeze to soak in the scene.

Mum's in a dress that's about ten years too young for her, but she's still got the body for it. Chrissie's wearing a similar dress that's about ten years too old for her, but she's got the style for it. Her husband, Ray, has got one arm around her, and Ceri and Chi are nestled on their laps.

Liam is dressed much the same as Connor was, but with muscles that put even his to shame. He's sat beside Shane, who's been his best friend since they were two, and a permanent fixture at family gatherings ever since.

I've never met the woman perched next to Shane in person, but I recognise her from Brendan's drawings: Bren's fiancée. Leah. She's dressed like Chrissie always used to dress, like the whole world is her personal runway. White-blonde hair is piled up on her head, showing off her delicate shoulders and the ultra-pale skin of her exposed back.

At the sight of me, the whole room erupts with noise and movement and chaos. I've never been hugged by so many people in such a short period of time.

"My baby girl." Mum pulls me into a tight embrace with her toned arms. "I can't believe you're actually here."

"Want a drink, Sadie?" Liam asks.

I nod, and he walks over to the bar in the corner and fixes me a gin and tonic without having to be told.

Chrissie examines me critically. "Sadie, really. When did you let yourself get so pale?" She waves her hand and, in a moment, I'm as gloriously, artificially tanned as she is. It's a different, lighter kind of magic than her attempts to make me go unrecognised. More like make-up than a mask. Mercifully, she doesn't try to magically bleach my hair to match hers and Mum's.

Leah walks nervously over to us. "Hey. We've never met. But I've heard a lot about you."

I give her a big smile. "Likewise. And I trust Bren's judgement. If he loves you, consider me your sister."

"I'm just so worried. He's always seemed so strong, so in control. But the Thornbers struck while he was weak. And now they've got his powers in check."

I put a hand on her arm. "None of them can touch him. Barely any practitioners are a match for my brother."

Other than Gabriel, but let's not go there.

"That's true right now, but they'll break him down over time. I can't stand it. I'm not sleeping. We should have been planning the wedding. Instead, we're fighting for his freedom."

I look closely at her face. I'd thought her eyes were red from her magic, but they're actually swollen from tears and exhaustion.

"It'll be okay, I promise. You'll be shopping for cakes and flowers in no time."

Though that's only true if I agree to take on the case. And even then, the outcome's far from certain. Somehow, I manage to sound a lot more confident than I feel.

Chrissie calls over to Shane. "Get Leah a drink. Then sit down and chat with her for a bit."

Shane's mum is one of the family's most loyal acolytes, and we've all known him so long we treat him like an additional annoying baby brother. He even looks a little bit like Liam, as if they've started to meet in the middle after all their years of friendship. The same shaggy black hair. The same pale skin. The same impressive muscles, though Liam's are that bit more pronounced. The facial features that hover somewhere on the boundary between hitman and model.

Shane gives a mock bow, then drags Leah away.

"That girl. Highly strung's not in it," Chrissie says, once our future sister-in-law is out of listening distance.

"But what did she mean about the Thornbers striking when he was weak? And about his powers being kept in check?"

I'd been wondering how the police had managed to arrest him despite all his power, and Leah's emotional ramblings raise more questions than answers. And now I come to think of it, Mum had said something similar in that initial phone call.

"You better talk to Bren about it. Hear it all first-hand."

Then she beckons to her husband, who comes over with their twin girls.

"Ray, meet my baby sister, Sadie. And Sadie, these are our little demon princesses."

I stand on tiptoes to give Ray a kiss on the cheek, then scoop my two-year-old nieces up in my arms. The fact I've never seen them, let alone held them, sends a shiver down my spine. It feels so right to be here with my family.

"Drinks are ready," Liam calls.

We all decamp to the various sofas. I take my place next to my sister and sip my gin. There's a Bren-shaped hole in the room and a nagging fear at the back of my mind, but other than that, it feels like I've never been away.

There are only two things I want at that moment: for that feeling of belonging to last and for the hole to be filled. I stand up and lead Mum and Dad into a quiet corner.

"I'll take the case, but I have a few conditions."

My mum crosses her arms. "Conditions? We're talking about your brother's life."

"And I'm the only one who has a chance in hell of getting him released, so we do it my way."

"Go on," Dad says.

"The first point's pretty simple. No magic and no intimidation of witnesses. Inside or outside of court. By you or by me. I'll neutralise Gabriel-fucking-Thornber's magic, but I won't use any of my own. For my own protection and for my conscience."

Mum frowns like she's about to protest, but Dad simply nods. "Fine. We can stick to that for now. If your legal skills don't seem to be working, we'll review as a family."

"Sure. Next, it's against all my professional ethics, but I'll lie for Bren if I have to. In return, I need the whole truth from all of you."

"You're our daughter, his sister," Mum replies. "No one's going to lie to you."

It's striking that, so far, no one's explicitly said Bren didn't do it. I'm assuming he didn't, but I wouldn't one hundred per cent put it past him. He certainly hates the Thornbers, even more than the rest of the family. With the possible exception of me.

I don't ask my parents the question again. I'll discuss it with my brother. With my client.

"Glad to hear it. But for the moment, I'm your lawyer and that's it. Which means we definitely can't socialise as a family, and I'm going to keep my distance from the rest of the town, too. I need to focus and keep my cover intact. We'll have the party to end all parties once Bren's out."

"We have a deal," Dad says, with a smile.

For a moment, I almost think he's going to formalise it with a lien mark, but I'm being ridiculous. Besides, he knows as well as I do that when it comes down to it, those sorts of theatrics aren't necessary. A deal's a deal and a debt's a debt, whether it's branded on your skin or simply spoken out loud.

FOUR

Walking into a prison is hardly an unfamiliar experience for me, even if HMP Wakefield—originally built in the Tudor era, rebuilt in Victorian times, and looking halfway between a haunted asylum from a horror film and a Soviet hellhole—is particularly grim. It's been home to murderers and rapists for four hundred years and you can feel it in the air.

Brendan's not my first client, and he won't be my last, but I usually keep my composure in these situations by drawing a cloak of professionalism tightly around me. I've always got a little thrill out of the way that hulking great men who treat women like crap shrink into themselves at the sight of tiny little me. My tailored suit, stern expression, and big words are a magic all of their own. It's amazing how much respect you can force out of someone who'd never normally show politeness to anyone, let alone a young woman, when you're the one thing standing between them and a long sentence.

Some of my clients are unfairly accused or acted out of desperation. Some, I have to admit, can be pretty unpleasant. But perhaps partially as a reaction to the way my family has always run Mannith like a medieval fiefdom where their will is law, I believe in the rule of law. Never in lying for my clients, but always in putting their story forward, ensuring a fair trial and, one way or the other, seeing justice prevail.

But all of that's when I'm dealing with faceless criminals and anonymous victims of the system. Knowing it's my brother I'm here to see makes it a thousand times harder to summon the detachment I need. I've seen family visitors far too many times. Those who cry, those who scream abuse at the staff, and every-thing in between. I look like my usual polished, educated self. But inside, I feel like one of them.

I also feel vaguely hungover. I'd forgotten how much my family can put away when we all get together. The drinks were on the house at The Windmill, and Liam kept those gin and tonics flowing.

Even through my self-inflicted headache, it's evident from the moment I step into the visiting area that Brendan's not the only practitioner inside. I can feel their presence. Gabriel's men, no doubt, there to keep an eye on Bren, if not try some-thing worse. It's rare anyone from Mannith ends up in jail, despite their crimes. They must have been planted. They wouldn't be able to do overt magic given the protections build into the prison walls, but practitioners who can't defend themselves are as susceptible to a physical attack as anyone else.

I've been reading through the case files this morning, and things don't look great. Niall Thornber was shot in the chest at point-blank range, in his own home. There's no hope of spin-ning this as an accident.

The murder weapon was a Victorian silver revolver, left at the scene, which I recognise as an old Sadler family heirloom. There are several similar guns in town—an ancestor of ours had them made and distributed to his closest acolytes—but this one was covered in Bren's prints. Which is odd, because if Bren wanted to kill someone, I'd expect him to use magic. It's cleaner, and much easier to present as a natural cause and keep out of a human court.

Then there are the witnesses. The star attraction is Gabriel himself, who supposedly saw the murder. But the prosecution—or more likely, Gabriel—have mustered any number of further witnesses who claim to have seen Bren on the night of Niall's death. Some of them supposedly saw him out and about in town at the start of the evening, in contradiction of his alibi. Others claim to have caught sight of him later on, close to Thornber Manor around the time of the murder.

"Your client's in here, Ms Elner," the prison guard says, pointing towards a private meeting room. "I'll wait outside."

I nod. He lets me in, then locks the door behind me. I immediately throw a bubble of silence around the room. The prison is meant to respect client-counsel privilege, but you can never be too careful, and I can get away with tiny bits of protective magic like that without triggering the lien.

There's a hint of resistance in the air. Presumably, it's from the wards that would stop me from simply breaking Bren out of there, but they let that token spell go.

The room is chilly and smells faintly of drains. I swallow hard at the sight of Brendan, sitting on a plastic chair across a worn table under a sickly florescent light. He's always had delicate features, a slender build and wide, faraway eyes. *Too much time practising magic, too little time down the gym*, as Liam is fond of telling him. In stark contrast to Liam and Shane, of whom the exact opposite is true, he looks a lot sweeter than he is.

On one level, he's his usual beautiful self today, but his almost feminine charms are stretched to breaking point. He's just a little too pale, a little too thin. Some of the hyper-masculine swagger that balances out his looks and makes the overall effect work has dimmed. And more worryingly, so has most of the all-encompassing clouds of magic that always used to surround him. I've not seen him in years, so it could be the passage of time, but I'd put money on the fact that he looked as glowing as I remember him being, right up until the point he was incarcerated.

I toss prison rules and professional appropriateness to one side, dash around to his side of the table and throw my arms around him. There's probably CCTV, but my bubble should block it. "It's so good to see you."

"And you, at long last. Are you here as my sister or my lawyer?"

I straighten up and take a step back. "Lawyer. And you're right. We shouldn't blur the boundaries."

"Right you are then, Miss Elner."

"You can call me Kate," I say, allowing myself one little grin before I force my expression back to its most serious.

I'm about to launch into my usual spiel about the need for him to be as open and honest with me as he can—without actually incriminating himself—when I notice his handcuffs.

They'd vaguely caught my eye when I'd first entered the room. It's a little unorthodox to keep someone cuffed for a conference with their lawyer, but not out of the realms of possibility in a high security place like this. What I hadn't previously noticed is that they're gold and engraved with swirling symbols.

I reach out and touch the left cuff and flinch at the coldness of the metal and the sense, even in that split second before I pull my arm back, of something being pulled from me.

"They've got you in blockers? What the hell? How did this happen? Are you in those all the time? This is a breach of your human rights."

Or it surely would be, if those who'd come up with the concept and the legislation knew about practitioners. The point of blockers is to stop the person wearing them from doing magic. But they don't just stop the magic from flying out of you as spells and influence. It's more like they stop it from flowing into you in the first place, stop you even sensing it in the air and the earth. It's less like putting someone in handcuffs, more like putting them in a portable sensory deprivation chamber.

I've seen my father—and Brendan himself, to be fair—use them in extremis, when an ally needs to calm themselves before they do something stupid, or an enemy refuses to stay down. But just until the situation is under control, not for extended periods of time.

"Apparently, it's standard practice for imprisoned practitioners. They don't catch one of us very often, but when they do, there's ancient procedure in place about what to do. Only a handful of seniors in the prison system know about magic and how to deal with it, but the practicalities get filtered down to the guards on the ground—who just believe I'm a particularly dangerous human prisoner.

"I tried to fight back when they arrested me, but I was weakened. I didn't manage to gain a foothold before they got these on, and then I was essentially helpless."

"That's what the family told me. But what on earth weakened *you* enough that some human police officers could overpower you before you could just wipe their memories or influence them or something?"

"I'll explain in a minute. It all ties in with my alibi."

I frown. That sounds like some story. But if there's one thing I know, it's that though you might need to push and probe a client, you ultimately need to go at their pace.

I lean over and place a hand lightly on his chest. "If your magic's blocked, take some of mine. There's enough to go round, and it's not like I use it much."

"Thanks, Sadie. I mean, Kate. It's like water for a dying man."

Normally, when you share magic with a fellow practitioner, they sort of suck it in through their skin. At least, based on things I've seen and the one time I experienced it myself from the other side. But with Brendan's own magic blocked, I basically have to pump it into him. I don't share too much, as he can't do anything with it while he's wearing the cuffs. It's like a blood donation when you need a heart transplant.

Sharing magic with someone creates a special kind of bond. Usually, you'd be a bit more ritualistic and reverent than this, but as brother and sister, we've already got bonds of blood. Sharing magic also reduces the power of the giver and proportionately increases the power of the receiver, but at these low volumes and with our respective powers similar in strength and style, the difference should be negligible.

I give it two minutes, timed precisely by my watch, then step back. I've not given him much, but the exchange is still enough to give me a headache and a desperate desire for a coffee. I really do need to snap into lawyer mode sooner rather than later. I sit down on the hard, uncomfortable chair on the opposite side of the table.

"Okay, back to the trial. First things first, the more honest you are with me, the more likely it is I can help you. I can't operate at my best if I get surprises flung in my face."

Brendan nods. "I know, I know. Ask the question."

"Did you kill Niall Thornber?"

"No." His eyes are open and honest.

"Did you hurt him?"

"No." His breathing and his voice are perfectly steady.

I breathe a little sigh of relief. It's bad not to have had faith in my brother, but he's never been the calmest of people. It's not beyond the realms of possibility that he could have killed Niall, whether in a flash of anger, in self-defence, as a show of power, or just as part of a plan that went wrong.

Of course, despite his convincing tone and body language, he could be lying. With Brendan's power blocked and mine buzzing in excitement at the thought of being home, I could check. But we never probe each other's minds. It's one of the first rules of the family. Something you just don't do, regardless of the provocation. And call me naïve, but I trust him.

For the last six years, though I've missed Bren, I've also—fairly or unfairly—resented him for the way his actions ended up with Gabriel marking me. Now though, face to face with him for the first time in far too long, a wild montage of scenes from our childhood and teens cascade through my brain. He'd always taken care of me, always let me tag along with his games and his friends, never just dismissing me as an annoying little sister. He'd helped me practise my magic, never pushing or patronising, but striking just the right balance. He'd let me sit and watch him draw and paint. Sometimes, he'd sketch me—pretty portraits, funny little cartoons and caricatures and everything in between. He'd tried to teach me to draw, though had given up once it became clear I had zero ability for art, with or without magic. After which, he'd settled for letting me talk to him about books and history, and told me stories about the Old Ways and about Mannith in centuries gone by.

Of course I trust him. Of course I'll do anything I can to get him out.

"So, who did kill him then?" I say.

"No one on our side, I'm ninety-nine per cent certain of that. Any Sadler acolyte would brag about it rather than cover it up, and I really don't think any of them would let me go down for a crime they committed.

"It could be someone from out of town. But I think it was probably one of the Thornber acolytes. Some sort of attempted coup."

I flick through the case file. "The murder happened out at Thornber Manor. So the main evidence against you is an eyewitness account of the murder from—from the victim's son." I can't bring myself to utter Gabriel's name. "Wouldn't he want the person who actually did it to be punished?"

"You'd think so. He always seemed to revere his father, and

it went both ways—he was his spoilt little golden child. My best guess is that Gabriel killed the actual murderer himself—probably horrifically—then covered it up to hide the existence of dissent in the ranks. And then, added bonus, he decides to frame me as a perfect cover-up, one big screw you to the Sadlers, and a chance to claim the town. He always says he has at least two reasons for everything."

I nod, though I have no idea of the Thornber family dynamics. I'm so disconnected these days from the thread of rumour and history that swirls around the town.

"Anyway, never mind the Thornbers. Where were you the night he died? Really."

There's an answer in the case file, but it doesn't make much sense.

"At home with Leah. She cooked some food. I watched the football. The usual. Then around ten, I travelled out to Summer Hill."

I lean over the table. "Summer Hill? By yourself? Why?"

There's only one reason any of us would make the trip to one of the furthest flung and most difficult to reach areas of the Dome, and that's to perform the annual Ritual that keeps Mannith protected. I shiver inwardly at the thought. The Ritual isn't for the faint-hearted, and it's only a few weeks away. Mum had better not have deluded herself into thinking I'm going to take part this year.

Bren's supercilious expression fades for a moment. "I wasn't actually by myself. The missus was there, too."

"So, on a random evening, you and your fiancée travelled out to our Ritual spot. And while you were there, someone else happened to kill Dad's only rival. What aren't you telling me?"

Bren slams his palms down on the table, making the blocker handcuffs shake. "I can't think properly through these damned things. It's hard to explain."

"Just do your best."

"We're trying for a baby."

I give a very unprofessional squeal. "That's lovely! So, I get it, you took advantage of a warm summer's night to get frisky in the great outdoors."

Bren laughs, and for a second, the strain in his face disappears. "Something like that. Leah's surprisingly traditional sometimes."

Under the Old Ways, practitioners are meant to conceive outdoors. Find somewhere beautiful. Connect with the forest or the river or the trees. Genuinely feel the earth move.

"*Something like that?*"

"You know what they say about Gabriel-fucking-Thornber, right?"

My back tingles at the sound of the name. "People say lots of things. I try not to listen."

"Sorry to bring him up again. But you know the rumour I mean."

"That his mother was half-demon?"

All Born Practitioners have some demon blood, by definition. That's where the power comes from. We're essentially what happens when a human and a demon love each other very much. It's just that in most cases, the demon genes were introduced into the bloodline centuries, perhaps even millennia ago, and then passed down through generations of practitioner marriages. It's rather more disturbing when the unholy union is meant to have happened in the twentieth century. And it has a rather more impressive effect on power levels.

"It's not fair for the Thornbers to have that advantage. We wanted to attempt something similar."

My whole body goes as cold as when I touched the handcuffs. "What? What... would that even involve?"

Nowadays, demon blood is something that tends to be more associated with vampires than with practitioners. Vampires are born human, of course, and then turned by other vampires, not directly by demons. But the same creatures that created the earliest practitioners through sex and reproduction also created the earliest vampires through blood and death. You don't get many vampires in the north of England full stop, and you certainly don't get them in Mannith, because the Dome keeps them out unless they're explicitly invited in. But I've come across the odd one over the years and they are deeply disturbing. Just for their political views, before you even start on their bloodthirsty way of life. We like to at least pretend that we're a bit more human than that. Or at least, most of us do. Maybe Bren begs to differ.

Bren shrugs. "It didn't work. All those teenage warnings about how a baby is practically inevitable when two practitioners don't use protection were a load of bollocks. But the summoning attempts left me too drained to put up a magical or physical fight when they arrested me later that night. Or to come up with a good cover story. That's what I mean when I said I'd been weakened."

"I still don't get it. I hate to feed your ego, but you're a ridiculously strong practitioner. I can see this weird sex magic might be quite intense and wear you down a bit. But surely not to the extent that you're left helpless to protect yourself."

He shrugs. "It *was* intense. And maybe I'm losing my touch."

I reach out and touch his arm. Unthinkable with a normal client. "Oh, Bren. Why do you always have to make life difficult for yourself?"

He doesn't answer. Like mine, his mind's surely on that night six years ago, the last time I paid the price for his ambition.

I straighten up, tuck a loose strand of hair behind my ears, and frantically channel Kate Elner instead of Sadie Sadler.

"We can work with this. Leah's an alibi. Not the best one—people are often willing to lie for their partners—but it's a start.

And as long as you don't mention the demon aspect, going out into the woods for a romantic, sexy night makes a degree of sense."

I glance at my watch. I'm thirty minutes into day one of being Bren's lawyer, and I've already lost count of the lines I've crossed and rules I've broken. Still, everything for the family.

That night, I dream about the day it all went wrong. That's hardly an unusual occurrence. It haunts my sleep just as it ensnares my fantasies. But this time, back home in Mannith for the first time in years, it's not merely vivid, it's almost like I'm reliving it all.

FIVE

The night that everything changed started with me dressed in leopard print pyjamas and working on my history homework. The wildest of Saturday nights.

Chrissie and I nominally shared a room, more out of habit than necessity—though she also had a separate room for bringing back conquests or sleeping off hangovers. We had a four-poster bed each and had filled the remaining space with an eclectic selection of cushions, candles, blankets, books, clothes and posters. It smelt of cheap perfume, and complex herbal potions and was the single place in the world where I felt calmest and most content.

Chrissie was blasting out Beyoncé numbers while cycling through a variety of form-fitting dresses, using only her mind. "Come out with us," she demanded. "Have a bit of fun. You're totally gorgeous when you get dressed up."

"I'm alright, honestly. Besides, you know what happens. Some bloke catches my eye, we have a little dance, next thing, Bren's throwing Greenfire at them. It's alright for you. You're the big sister."

Chrissie planted her hands on her hips. "If Brendan starts

any of that over-protective big brother crap while I'm out with you, I'll blast him. Put him right back in his place."

I laughed, knowing she meant it. Technically, she was also younger than Bren, but only by two years, instead of my six, and he'd long ago given up on treating her like a kid.

"You look great," I said. "I might come out next week. I need to get this essay sorted tonight."

"Girls, come downstairs!" Mum called. "Your father's called a family meeting."

Chrissie pouted. "This had better not take long. I've really not got the energy for it tonight."

"Any idea how many people we've got to get through?"

"Nope. But for goodness' sake, put some proper clothes on."

I laughed. "If Dad insists on parading us like we're prize ponies, he can put up with me wearing pyjamas."

"Chrissabelle. Sadie. Hurry up."

We held hands and traversed ourselves downstairs together. It would have taken about two minutes to walk, but there was something to be said for making an entrance.

The main room downstairs had a black leather sofa that curled around three sides of the room, a huge TV on the front wall, and speakers in every corner. It was generally the place where we gathered as a family to watch the football or cycle through the music channels. But that evening, the TV was off, the curtains were closed, and the lights were dimmed.

Mum, Dad, and Liam sat comfortably on the sofa, like they were about to watch a cheesy film, but there was one of the family's acolytes in each corner and another by the door. The hard-faced men and women greeted me and Chrissie with a smile.

Mum patted the sofa, and we sat down beside her.

Dad smiled. "My gorgeous girls. Now, has anyone seen Brendan?"

"We should make a start," Liam said. "Bren's pissed off

somewhere for the night. And I want to get out and meet Shane and the other guys."

Mum glanced over at the forty-something woman on the door. Connor's mother, in her prime. "Colson, bring the first one in."

These evenings had been an occasional part of my life for as long as I could remember. Every few weeks, my father held court as though he was a medieval king meeting his subjects. He needed his enemies, allies, and customers to see the power of his perfect offspring. His hyper-magical elder son. His lethal younger son. His beautiful elder daughter. His clever younger daughter. We all had our parts to play in proving that Dad didn't just have his own power, he had a dynasty.

A scrawny man in his late twenties slunk into the room, while one of my father's acolytes kept a close hold of his arm. The man glanced around, clearly unsure what to do, until the guard pushed him down to his knees.

My father stared at him from his position on the raised sofa. "What's your name, young man? And what can we do for you?"

He kept his eyes on the floor. "I'm Paul. And there's this woman at work…"

"Love potion or curse?" There was no judgement or emotion in Dad's voice. He was just a businessman doing a deal.

"I want her to love me. I don't really believe in magic and stuff. But I'm desperate. And I met a guy in the pub who insisted you're the real deal."

"Have you thought about going to the gym and getting a better haircut?" Liam asked.

Mum glared at him, and I tried not to laugh. Poor Paul didn't reply.

"It'll cost you," Dad said, as though Liam hadn't spoken.

Paul's head slumped down. "I don't have much money…"

Dad shrugged. "Who could ever put a price on finding love?

Our magic works. If you live on bread and water for the next year and don't buy yourself anything new, won't it be worth it when she's yours?"

Paul nodded frantically.

"I'll need a payment upfront. Then a further one every month until the debt's paid. And believe me, it will be paid."

Paul reached into his pocket and took out a wad of notes. The acolyte guarding the left corner crossed the room to take them from him, then reverently handed the money to Mum. She counted it, nodded, then slipped the money into a secure box on her knee.

Some of this was for show. One of my parents' acolytes would have explained the exact costs and payment schedule outside the room, so my father didn't have to get too far into the grubby detail. Five thousand pounds or so tended to be the going rate for this sort of thing.

"Bring him forward," Dad ordered.

The man twisted his head back and forth, seeming suddenly uncertain, but everything was moving too fast for him to back out. Colson propelled him to the front of the room.

"Chrissie, darling, will you do the honours?" Dad asked.

My sister reached into her bag and pulled out a vial of love potion. "Drink half of this now. Then dab a little on your wrist and neck every time you see her. It won't take long for her to succumb."

None of the family needed potions, for love or for anything else. Magic was everywhere in the air and the earth around us, and we'd been born with a connection to it. All we had to do to get the things we wanted was to use our minds and our will to channel it. The more complex the desire, the more mental control was required. Potions, charms, and invocations were a shortcut to achieving the same ends with less concentration and allowed us to give humans a little taste of magic.

"Give me your arm," Dad demanded, once Paul had taken the vial. "We need to make sure you pay up, after all."

Paul complied, though his arm was shaking. Dad closed his meaty fist around the man's underdeveloped bicep and squeezed. I saw the swirling black lines of magical energy that Dad dragged from the air and channelled into Paul's arm, but lacking the sight, the customer would have seen nothing, only been aware of a mild burning sensation.

When Dad took his hand away, a perfect black line encircled Paul's upper arm. He rubbed it gingerly.

"The lien mark will remain until the debt is paid." Dad was all smiles. "And if it's not paid, there will be consequences. But I'm sure that won't be a problem. So, in the meantime, I hope you have a wonderful time with your new girlfriend."

Colson led him out.

The next two were straightforward. A man and a woman, both already bearing lien marks, arrived to pay the next instalment of their debt. She'd wanted to advance at work. He'd longed for a baby. They both seemed satisfied with the outcome and paid up with no issues.

The next participant was dragged into the room by two acolytes, trying to lash out but immobilised and silenced by their magic.

His lien mark was visible even through his long-sleeved shirt. It glowed red, in the tell-tale sign of someone who'd tried to renege on a deal.

"You're two months overdue with your payments, Mr Gibbins," Dad said. "And we can tell when someone who has a debt to us tries to exit the Dome."

One of the men holding Gibbins snapped his fingers, and the debtor managed to speak. "It's not like that. I was just having a weekend away. I was going to pay on Monday."

Dad waved his arm towards Gibbins in an almost dismissive

gesture, and, immediately, Greenfire surrounded the unfortu-
nate man. He screamed as my father's magic burnt through
him.

Greenfire attacks the mind, not the body. The pain is an
illusion, and as long as the person inflicting it stops before your
heart gives out from shock or your mind cracks, it does no
lasting harm.

For most practitioners, imposing Greenfire on someone
would require complex hand gestures and perhaps some incan-
tations. It would certainly require a hell of a lot of concentration. For my father, it was all but effortless, magic flowing from
the earth into his body and out again with no resistance. Bren
could do that sort of magic, too, but the scary thing was that
increasingly, so could I. My connection to the earth and my
control of my powers were growing by the day.

My father kept up the assault for five minutes, then waved
his hand just as casually, and drew the fire back into himself.
"You have seven days to pay the debt in full. Next time, it'll
count as breaking our lien."

And we all knew what happened to people who broke liens.
Dad wouldn't even have to lift a finger.

Gibbins lay on the floor, gasping for air. An acolyte lifted
him to his feet and led him out.

As I've said, Dad is—and was—a good man, but he couldn't
afford to appear weak. If magic were granted to everyone who
asked, with no tests and no payment, demand would far outstrip
supply. The result would be utter chaos.

He used the payments as a form of rationing—and ensured
the debts were paid for much the same reason. He couldn't
stand it when people tried to avoid their obligations. Left
unchecked, that sort of lack of respect for him and his family
could start to undermine the order of things in Mannith. But it
also demonstrated a lack of respect for the magic itself and for

the solemnity of the magical deal. Treating things like that lightly was dangerous for all concerned.

All that said, as a family, we did pretty well out of those deals. We could achieve most things with magic if we really needed to, but sometimes, it was simpler or raised fewer questions to do things the human way, and all the cash certainly helped that along.

"We're done for tonight, ladies and gentlemen," Dad announced.

Some of the practitioners in the room traversed themselves away, some used the door. I excused myself and surreptitiously followed Gibbins and his guard out to the driveway. He flinched at the sight of me, as though an eighteen-year-old girl in pyjamas was more terrifying than the scarred, muscled, forty-five-year-old guarding him.

"Can you afford to pay the next instalment?" I tried to mimic my father's authoritative but dispassionate tone.

"I'll pay. I swear I'll pay. Don't hurt me."

My family's reputation protected me from a lot of things, but it made it hard to have a civil conversation.

"If you don't pay, you'll die. I don't think you have the money. And I don't think you have any way to get it in seven days."

I reached into my handbag and withdrew a pile of notes. "Here. It's a gift, not a loan. Enough to pay up next week. That'll give you a month to find the following payment. Don't expect me to help you again."

The acolyte gave me an exasperated look. "Miss Sadler, please. We've talked about this before."

I understood all the arguments about only giving magic to those who were willing to make a sacrifice; about the need to treat liens with the seriousness they required; and about the importance of maintaining authority and control for the good of the town. And on an abstract level, I agreed with them. But that didn't make it any easier to see an individual suffering just because they'd been foolish enough to play with magic they didn't understand.

"I wouldn't give family money to debtors, but this is my tutoring cash."

Gibbins took the money. "Thank you. You're an angel."

"Hardly. Now get out."

I went back inside, hoping the rest of the family would assume I'd simply taken an extended bathroom break.

I'd just settled back down on the sofa with one of my history books when the screaming started.

Chrissie jumped to her feet. "That's Bren."

Chrissie was a much stronger empath than I'd ever be. If she thought that was our brother screaming, she was almost certainly right. But this was our house. Our sanctuary. Protected by magic and strength. Nothing could go wrong here. Besides, Bren was the strongest practitioner out of all of us, and more than capable of looking after himself... right?

We all glanced at each other, then dashed outside.

There was an unfamiliar convertible car on the driveway, and by the back porch, Brendan sprawled, contorted in agony.

I stared at the man standing over him. I'd never actually met Gabriel Thornber in person before, but I knew the son of my father's only rival by reputation. By all accounts, he was the most powerful practitioner of magic in town. Perhaps in the entire country. Though he was a few years older than me— around Bren's age—he was a subject of fascination amongst the practitioners in my year at school. Some had insane crushes on him thanks to his cheekbones, wavy blond hair, power, and general air of mystery. Others repeated dark rumours about his background, his magic, and his family.

"I heard he can mesmerise most practitioners as easily as we can mesmerise humans."

"*I heard he can change his appearance at will. Like really change it. Body-switching, that sort of thing.*"

"*He drains people's magic while he screws them.*"

"*He killed his mother with Hellfire.*"

God knows what was and wasn't true. The Thornber faithful probably told similar stories about Bren. And considering that the most popular rumour of all was that Gabriel's mother was some sort of literal demon, the idea that he'd killed her seemed both far-fetched and not necessarily a bad thing.

"What the hell are you doing?" Chrissie yelled out the question. The rest of us were unable to speak.

"Your brother was playing with things he shouldn't have been," Gabriel replied. "Trying to extend the Dome. I'm evening the score."

Trying to extend the Dome? Through my panic, I could barely make sense of the extraordinary claim. It was something the family had talked about attempting for generations, but no one had known where to start. Bren was undoubtedly an impressive practitioner, but surely he couldn't have had any chance of doing something like that alone?

"Stop. You're draining him." Now that she'd had a few seconds to compose herself, Chrissie's voice took on the mature edge of the trained empath who saw and felt all things, making her sound decades older than her twenty-two years.

"He can't be trusted with this much power," Gabriel said.

I couldn't stop staring. It was dark out on the driveway, but his magic lit him up from the inside. He really was as gorgeous as people at school claimed.

I shook my head to drive the thought away. *He's torturing your brother. This is no time to admire his narrow hips and broad shoulders. Or those strikingly delicate facial features.* It was like I'd been bewitched myself. Which was basically impossible. Whatever those rumours claimed.

Chrissie glanced at me, and I snapped out of it. I closed my eyes and focused on the sense of my sister by my side, Liam beyond her, and Bren writhing on the floor, his screams as agonised as ever but growing less frequent. Invisible strings flowed from Gabriel to Bren. Energy pulsed in both directions: Gabriel's will going one way, Bren's power going the other. It made no sense that Bren couldn't break free. He was incredibly powerful himself.

My father screamed out a torrent of words, half incantation, half obscenities, threw both arms into the air and poured out two parallel streams of power, one directed at the bond, one at Gabriel. I sensed the intensity. Dad was giving it everything he had—and that was a lot. Surely the draining spell ought to break? And surely, Gabriel ought to collapse, or at least have to focus all his energy on putting up shields and firing back, which would force him to leave Bren alone. But somehow, the only effect was that Bren's screams intensified.

I reached my hand out, too. It was unlikely I could achieve something that was out of my dad's reach, but I'd been getting stronger, and I had to try. I'd have liked to just throw my hands in the air, will Bren to be free, and have it be so. But panic was making my magic unstable, so I went back to basics. I made a slicing gesture with one hand while I visualised the dual bond falling away. And I held the other hand flat and pushed air in the direction of Gabriel, imagining him being shoved away. My head ached and my hands burned, but nothing else changed.

"He's burnt himself out working that spell on the Dome," Gabriel said, as though he'd read my mind and understood my puzzlement. "And I've linked my magic with his. It's like he's draining himself. You won't be able to break the connection or harm me without killing him."

I let my hands drop to my sides, trying to understand how that would work. I'd never heard of a spell done that way before.

Liam took a few steps forward, fists raised.

"The protection of the bond applies to physical attacks as well as magical ones," Gabriel said, staring at him. "So don't even think about trying to put those famous boxing skills to use."

"Stop, please," my mum cried. She was a powerful practitioner herself, albeit not quite on the level of Dad and Bren, and she rarely showed weakness. But at that moment, she sounded like any frail human mother terrified for her child. She lifted her hands as though about to attempt a spell, then let them drop as Gabriel's warning sank in.

"What he did is utterly unacceptable. The Dome can't be expanded. He needs to pay the price."

Gabriel sounded completely calm. How could he hold a conversation while working such complex and deadly magic on someone so powerful in their own right? Not only were there none of the hand signals or chanting you might expect, there seemed to be no conscious effort at all, as though the magic in the air couldn't wait to do his bidding.

I couldn't understand his strength of feeling on the matter of the Dome. In the unlikely event that Bren had pulled it off, surely that was cause for celebration, not fury? Inside the Dome, all was peaceful and prosperous, while outside, people suffered. If it *could* be extended, wasn't that the only moral thing to do? Sure, the process of maintaining the Dome was rumoured to be messy, but it was worth it for the greater good.

Bren screamed again. He wasn't truly conscious anymore. What I could sense of his mind was nothing but pain and panic with an underlying fury and frustration at his inability to break free. I was going to be sick.

"Or else, someone needs to pay the price on his behalf." Gabriel's voice was almost hypnotic. If it weren't for our own powers protecting us, it probably would have been *literally* hypnotic. "There are less painful ways to siphon off magic."

He released his mental grip on Bren, just a little. My brother was still utterly in his grasp and beyond our reach, but at least the flow of magic out of his body had stopped for the moment.

My father was the sort of man who could be provoked to anger by someone cutting in front of him at the bar—not that there were many people stupid enough to do such a thing in this town. The sight of his beloved eldest son in pain and at someone else's mercy must have required every inch of his small level of self-control to stop him lashing out, whether with his magic or with his fists. But he was smart enough to know he couldn't risk attacking Gabriel while he was connected to Brendan. Hurt one and they'd both go down.

"You mean sex?" Chrissie demanded. "You're not really my type, but I can handle that. Put Bren down, I'll come back to yours, and you can take some of my power in the heat of the moment. Job done."

Sex had never seemed to be a big deal for Chrissie. She got a real kick out of seduction. Sometimes it was about ego. Sometimes about fun. Sometimes, she liked to take a hint of their life force if they were human, a hint of their magic if they were practitioners. Never enough that either party thought it an unfair deal. Even so, I shivered at the thought of her giving herself to an enemy of the family, to someone capable of this sort of cruelty.

"Or me," Liam added desperately.

As our nan never tired of telling us, as part of her wider lectures on practitioner lore, our kind had traditionally only cared about people's souls and auras, not, in her inimitable words, "their naughty bits". By which she meant there had tended to be little to no gender preference amongst practitioners. In this, as in most things, Gabriel Thornber followed the Old Ways.

"Good to see a bit of good old-fashioned family loyalty from you both," he said, smiling at Chrissie and Liam in turn, without letting his onslaught on Bren drop. "But no. If we're doing this, I want her." He pointed at me and locked his eyes on mine. "Strongest magic, prettiest face, most likely to make the whole damned Sadler family feel like Brendan's been well and truly punished."

All the blood in my body rushed to my head. Surely he couldn't mean it?

"No." My mum's voice was firm, but her hands were clutched to her chest. "Not Sadie. She's not like that. She's not like one of us, not really. She's going to university next year. She's getting out."

"Well, she won't need all of her magic then, will she?" Gabriel replied.

My father didn't speak. Probably because if he stopped focusing all his attention on keeping his fury—and thus his magic—in check, he'd blow the whole house up around us.

"Please," Chrissie pleaded. "Take me."

Gabriel tightened his mental grasp on Brendan. The power started to flow out of my brother again, and the screams that had almost fallen silent intensified.

Each scream physically pained me. I had to make this stop. My siblings had volunteered themselves, I needed to be strong enough to do the same. But my heart was beating so fast it had to be audible to everyone else. Gabriel was utterly terrifying. How could I possibly do what he was asking?

I closed my eyes. "I'll go," I shouted, hysteria in my voice. "Anything for the family. Always." It was the closest thing to a moral code we had.

Brendan rallied at my words. His reaction when sweet guys from school hit on me with my utmost consent was not pretty. It wasn't beyond the realms of possibility that the concept of his sister being ravished by a psychopath for his sake would be enough to break the spell. I felt him fight, but it wasn't enough.

"Stop draining him." I dashed towards him on shaking legs. "I said I'll go with you."

Gabriel smiled. My brother collapsed, truly unconscious now, but he was no longer in pain and no more magic was being leeched out of him. The connection narrowed to a thread just strong enough to prevent my father from trying anything stupid.

"Marvellous. Though... you could at least dress for the occasion."

He clicked the fingers of his right hand, and my comfy pyjamas turned into a rose-gold 1950s-style tea dress, while my hair sprang into a complicated up-do.

"I don't think so." I was on the verge of tears, but I had to maintain some semblance of control. I clicked my own right fingers. Panic made the gesture clumsy, but the magic in the air still did my bidding, and the clothes were replaced with tight jeans and a clingy white T-shirt with embroidered black swirls. The sort of thing I'd wear for a night out if left to my own devices.

"Fair enough. Now, Jag or shall we traverse?"

This didn't feel real. My breathing was too rapid. If I didn't calm down, I was either going to pass out or let my magic get completely out of control. Gabriel was staring at me intently, waiting for an answer, and it was almost impossible to block him out—or stop my mind from throwing up lurid and horrifying images of what might happen to me once he got me alone.

I forced myself to breathe in deeply, and let my mind join with the earth. *Inhale, exhale.* With each breath, I went deeper into myself and into the ground. At its simplest level, the exercise was merely calming. Go deeper, and it started to get dangerous. Push through that, and you could literally move mountains.

"Your eyes are turning black, Sadie. No damned core meditation on my watch. Jag or traversing?"

I didn't want to come back to reality. I longed to linger in this passive state. But mess around too much and Bren would be screaming again within seconds. So, I breathed faster, and drifted up to the surface, into my body and into the room. As soon as I did, all the panic retuned like a tidal wave.

"Do you even need to ask the question?" I choked out the words. "Do I look like some impressionable human girl you've worked your charms on? I'll traverse there myself."

"For the record, it's a really nice car," Gabriel said. "But hell, let's do this the easy way. You're coming with me, though. Not a hope I'm letting you travel by yourself."

I wrapped my arms around myself. "Fine. Expend your energy on posturing, see if I care."

I was aiming for confident and nonchalant, but my voice cracked on the last few words, showing just how much I actually did care.

None of my family had spoken for at least five minutes— pretty much a world record for them. No one wanted to break the fragile equilibrium.

I looked at each of them in turn, trying to read their expressions, trying to understand what they wanted me to do. My dad had clenched fists and a set jaw, but was somehow holding himself in check. Tears were running down Mum's face. Chrissie and Liam were wide-eyed with shock.

They had different ways of expressing it, but the same conflict played out on all their faces. They couldn't quite believe I'd volunteered. I was the baby of the family. Everyone had always tried to protect me. They wouldn't accept this in a million years, if they had the choice.

But Brendan was the family's hope—its heir. His magic was strong, and he had the ruthlessness to go with it. He could make us a true force to be reckoned with. We could strengthen our hold on Mannith, defeat our rivals, and expand our reach into other towns. Apparently, we might even be able to expand the Dome. But not if Gabriel leeched all the power out of him while he was in this unusually vulnerable state. So, for Bren's sake, they needed me to go through with it.

Or perhaps I was just projecting my own swirling thoughts onto their tortured expressions. Unlike Chrissie, my empath skills were half-hearted at best.

"Take my hand," Gabriel whispered. "The second you do, I'll release your brother, and we'll disappear."

Anything for the family. Always. But for all my attempts to be brave, this felt like more than I could bear.

Gabriel's eyes had never left my face, but now, I finally made myself return eye contact. He had diamond-shaped irises, not just the usual diamond-shaped pupils. And his pupils were currently red, too. *Don't look him in the eye,* practitioner class-mates had whispered.

Technically, there was little he could do to me against my will that I wasn't already offering freely. My body and my magic, served up on a plate in return for Bren being left alone.

It was the right thing to do for the family. But that didn't make it any less awful for me. How much magic was he going to take? And as far as the other side of things went, what exactly was he planning to do to me?

It wasn't like I was entirely naïve about sex or had never been touched—I'd had a few fumbles with schoolmates who'd got past Bren's over-protective radar—but I'd never gone all the way. I wasn't saving myself for marriage or anything, but I was fairly emphatically saving myself for something a little more romantic than this nightmare.

I swallowed hard. It was too late to back out now. I couldn't let Bren down, let the family down, be that weak. But Gabriel's eyes were burning into mine and magic was radiating off him with an intensity I'd never felt before. My vision started to blur.

Before my thoughts could send me cowering to the floor, I put my trembling hand in his. Everything happened within an infinitesimal fraction of a second. Our skin touched. The connection with Brendan broke. And we left my family's sitting room and reconvened in what I could only assume was Gabriel's bedroom in Thornber Manor.

SIX

The Thornbers were different to us. We lived in town and were a part of it. Our house had belonged to my great-grandparents originally, and they'd managed to gradually buy up an entire row of terraced houses and knock them together.

The Thornbers—the actual family and those who swore loyalty to them—had properties in town, too. But the core family's central home was on the outskirts of Mannith, where the city gave way to the moors. They'd lived there for centuries. At some point in the distant past, they must have taken it from a local gentry family, whether by force, by mesmerism, or in payment for a debt. The bedroom's canopied bed, heavy window drapes and wall hangings, combined with an open fireplace, made it look like it hadn't been redecorated in the intervening period.

Once, long ago, the Thornbers had worked for my family as their most trusted and powerful lieutenants. But a couple of generations ago, the head of the Thornber family had rebelled, taking various acolytes, both human and practitioner, with him.

They operated on a smaller scale than us—we controlled the Dome, after all—and though they were powerful enough that my family didn't simply crush them for their intransigence, it had always been accepted that they were the weaker family. Gabriel's father, Niall, could never stand against my father in a magical duel, but there'd been whispers for a while that his son and heir was in a different league. The performance we'd just seen seemed to back that up.

I still felt dizzy from both the rapid journey and from the shock of it all. But I'd die before I'd let Gabriel see that. Or let him know how scared I was. Or indeed, how inexperienced I was.

He settled down on the four-poster bed. I deposited myself in an armchair by the fire before my legs gave out. I'd presumably have to move to the bed before too long, but one step at a time.

"Let's get this over with," I said, like I sold myself for my family every day. Like I sacrificed my magic on a regular basis. I tried to make eye contact again, but couldn't quite do it. I settled for looking somewhere in the vicinity of his chest.

Gabriel's gaze locked on me. I raised my bowed head for a moment, needing to see his expression. I expected him either to be undressing me with his eyes or else simply looking unbearably smug about his victory over my family. Instead, he looked oddly reverent, like he was admiring a prized treasure he'd been hunting all his life. I was hardly unattractive or lacking in self-esteem, but it wasn't the sort of look I was accustomed to.

I swallowed hard, closed my eyes, then pulled my T-shirt over my head. When I dared to open my eyes again, I saw I was wearing an insanely lacy pink bra. His doing rather than mine. At least the heat of the fire kept me from shivering.

Still perched on the four-poster bed, Gabriel looked at my face rather than my exposed body and laughed. "Put that back on."

I crossed my arms over my chest. "Sorry, what?"

"What sort of a monster do you think I am?"

I jumped to my feet, all dizziness and nerves extinguished in a wave of fury and confusion. "The sort of monster who just tortured my brother and kidnapped me."

Gabriel patted the bed next to him. I drifted over there, then sat as close as I could manage without actually touching him.

"Brendan deserves everything he gets. But I'm not in the mood for dealing with you right now."

My heart pounded as I dragged my T-shirt back on. I'd steeled myself to go through with it. At the suggestion I might not have to, the adrenaline drained away.

"What the hell? Why am I here then? Is this some sort of joke?"

Gabriel sprawled back on the bed. "We'll see where the night takes us. But for now, I mostly just want to mentally torture your father and brother. I'm that much of a monster at least."

My breathing ought to have been stabilising, but it became more frantic by the moment. "What am I supposed to do with myself all night?"

Gabriel stretched out on the fur throw. "Anyone would think you *want* to be ravished to save your family. I don't blame you. I am every girl's dream man."

"Before you so rudely intruded, I was doing my reading. Any chance I could find a computer and get it finished?"

Which was literally the most "me" answer I could have come up with. The most beautiful, most powerful, most deadly man I'd ever met was holding me captive, his to give whatever pleasure or pain he desired, and I demanded to finish my homework.

He smiled as though the same thoughts had crossed his mind. "What's your essay on?"

"The Visconti and the Sforza. They were the rulers of Milan in Renaissance times."

He sat back up. "I'm sure you're used to the majority of this town having no clue about anything outside their own bubble. But I *have* just graduated in history from Cambridge. I know about the Dukes of Milan."

I frowned. "Really? That doesn't quite fit with my mental image of you. And if it's true, why did you come back?"

"Good to know you have a mental image of me to call on. And I came back because the town's in my blood and my blood's in the town. Surely you of all people can understand that."

When I didn't reply, he stood up and held out an arm. I took it gingerly and let him help me down from the bed, though my hands were still shaking.

"I'm not leading you into a trap," he said. "Just taking you to the library."

The room was everything you'd hope and expect from a library in a centuries-old house owned by a family of witches. High shelves. Lead-paned windows recessed into the deep walls. Leather-bound books everywhere, some neatly shelved, others sprawled over tables, all giving off a distinctive, comforting scent. Unlike the bedroom, hot from the fire, this room had a chill despite the evening's warmth, but that only added to the general ambience.

Gabriel led me to a somewhat out-of-place computer desk and pulled out the seat so I could sit down.

"I've got some books here you'll probably find useful," he announced, then strode over to one of the further shelves.

He could have stayed where he was and made the books come to him, but we traditionally considered it more personal to perform favours we could carry out magically by hand.

He returned a moment later, with a little pile that he deposited on the desk. "*Plenitude of Power* gives a great over-view. *Art and Authority* is good on the cultural side of things.

And *The Duke and the Stars* is a fun read. Come to think of it, I've probably got some old essays on that topic, too."

I couldn't stop myself from picking one of them up, but I maintained enough self-control to keep my expression stern. "Just leave me to it. I'll stay here tonight to honour this debt, but it doesn't mean I have to talk to you. It certainly doesn't mean you need to help me with my homework."

Gabriel laughed. "The deal is still in effect, you know. For now, I'll be over here, reading. But I might still take you up on your offer once you've got your work done."

I stared at the computer screen as hard as I could, trying to pretend I was in my own room and to block out the sense that his burning eyes with their weirdly shaped irises and coloured pupils were fixed on the back of my head.

Gabriel was toying with me, that much was clear. Not yet claiming my solemnly promised sex and magic, but never quite letting me forget that he could do so whenever he chose. Making me welcome, but not entirely allowing me to relax.

But what did he actually intend? Was this all a bluff and he'd return me unharmed in the morning? Or did he think it'd be all the sweeter to finally make me submit once he'd lulled me into a false sense of security?

Somewhat against the odds, I made good progress with the essay. The books Gabriel had recommended were as useful as he'd claimed.

"I'm going to bed," Gabriel said eventually. "I'd normally be causing a scene in town at this time on a Friday night, but I can't let anyone see me when I'm supposed to be taking advantage of you."

How many of the rumours that swirled around him had been carefully curated for his own purposes?

"And where am I going to sleep?" The words came out in a whisper, the question concerning more than simple logistics. If he were going to make good on our twisted deal, now would be the time to do it.

He hesitated for a moment or two before replying. "With me," he replied, eventually. "But I'll take the sofa."

I bowed my head. "Just stop this, please. You need to keep me here overnight to prove a point, fine. But if you're going to claim what you're owed, then get it over with. If you're not, then put me out of my misery. I'd like my own room, for a start."

I sounded reasonably calm, but for all my brave words, I once again felt ready to pass out with nerves.

He crossed his arms. "I want to keep an eye on you. And I want to keep my options open. As your family love to tell people, don't make magical bargains if you're not prepared for the consequences."

I followed him back to his room in silence. I tensed when we crossed the threshold. Was this the moment he was going to act?

A gentle surge of magic flowed out of him, and I jumped, but all he'd done was make up the sofa bed.

"There's an en suite bathroom if you want to get yourself ready for bed," he said, as though I were a normal house guest.

I did as he'd suggested—dashed to the bathroom, sorted my face and teeth with a simple spell, then conjured up something resembling the cosy pyjamas I'd been wearing when the evening began.

When I got back to the room, Gabriel was laid out on the sofa bed, shirt off, striped cotton pyjama bottoms on, apparently asleep—though I found that hard to believe.

For a long moment, I just stood and stared at him. With his eyes closed and his body still, he was like a beautiful statue. Some of his swagger had fallen away, and he seemed less wild, less dangerous.

I shook my head and turned away. That was probably what he wanted me to think. One more attempt to make me let my guard down before he finally pounced. I shouldn't let myself relax around him, however tranquil he looked in the moonlight that drifted in through the window. And I certainly shouldn't admire his body—whatever he did or didn't intend to do with me, he was still a monster.

The only thing I could do that would be even more stupid would be to attempt to run. Even if he were actually asleep, rather than trying to catch me out, it was dangerous to try to escape a bargain. Even weaving some sort of spell of protection around myself would be cheating and it could be instantly swept away.

I needed to stay put, stay on my guard, and hopefully, by the morning, this would all be over. Surely if Gabriel were going to do something about our deal, he'd have done so by now?

I climbed into the four-poster bed, propped up the pillows, and just sat there, trying to stay alert. However much I tried to empty my mind, the sheets smelt faintly of Gabriel. I could hear his steady breathing, and his aura filled the room from floor to ceiling.

I was bone-tired, but between all the adrenaline of the evening and the knowledge that Gabriel was there with me in the room, the risk of falling asleep seemed low.

And yet, at some point during the night, my exhausted body must have overruled my watchful mind, because I suddenly found myself waking up, with sunlight streaming through the windows.

There was no sign of Gabriel in the bedroom. He'd seemingly let me sleep in. I wandered downstairs. Gabriel was already up and about, dressed for the day and cooking sausages on the old-fashioned stove. His father was still nowhere to be seen.

"I'll take you back shortly," he said. "Breakfast first. I don't want to face your family's vengeance on an empty stomach."

At his words, some of the tension that had lingered since I'd arrived fell away. I'd made it through the night. He was taking me home. I was almost off the hook.

"Nothing for me." The sausages smelt delicious, but one of the first lessons we learnt was never to accept food from enemies. At worst, it could be drugged. At best, it put you in their debt. Things were looking up, but I still needed to maintain a little caution until I was actually away from enemy territory.

Gabriel studied me intently, with a frown on his face, as though surprised I was being so cautious, surprised I was still afraid of him.

"All things considered, I took a little too much magic from poor dear Brendan last night," he said, in an oddly placating tone. "Let me give you some back. As long as it equals out, he can't object. *Everything for the family*. That's your motto, isn't it?"

I frowned in turn, caught off guard by such a strange and surprising offer. The idea seemed to have come from nowhere, and was the complete opposite of what we'd supposedly agreed. "Will it be Brendan's magic, or will it be yours?" It was a stupid question, the sort of thing someone newly come into their powers would say. Magic doesn't work like that. But even so, there was some essence of Gabriel in his magic that I simultaneously longed for and yet didn't want anywhere near me.

"My magic, mostly," he replied, as though my question made perfect sense.

I shuddered. Magic exchange occurred in two opposing circumstances. It was a sacred, magical, quasi-romantic occurrence, perhaps between actual lovers, perhaps just between best friends, family members, or the closest of business associates. Or it was the sort of thing that had happened on the previous night, when Gabriel had torn some of Brendan's power from him through force and pain. It wasn't something you calmly and logically did with an enemy you barely knew.

But stronger magic was stronger magic after all.

"Go on then." I was proud of how confident I sounded.

He walked over to an old sofa in the corner of the room and beckoned for me to follow.

I sat down beside him. "Will it hurt?" I wasn't sure if I meant me or him. All I could see was Brendan screaming on the floor.

"Why don't you find out for yourself?"

He turned to face me, placed his right hand on my sternum and his left hand on my waist, then touched his forehead to mine. I shivered. This felt far more intimate than the experience I'd escaped last night.

After a few seconds, heat arose in the three places where his body was connected to mine. I closed my eyes to avoid looking at Gabriel or thinking overly logically, and simply focused on the sensation.

The heat spread round my body, as though something physical were being injected into me, and the points of contact grew hotter and hotter. At first, it felt like lying in the sun. Then, like standing right by a radiator. After a few moments, as if I'd stepped into a bath that was far too hot. What did it feel like for him? Could he feel the heat, too, or was he growing colder and colder as the warmth of the magic left him? Perhaps he was on the opposite trajectory, from pleasant summer breeze to falling into an icy pond.

At the precise second when the heat-feeling changed from discomfort to pain, Gabriel moved his head and left arm away and the feeling disappeared. All that remained was a half-jittery, half-energised feeling, like I'd downed four coffees in a row.

"How much did you give me?" I whispered.

"Enough that you'll notice. Not so much that it'll make any appreciable difference to my powers. I need you to be strong."

He tapped each of the fingers of his right hand against my

chest, one at a time, three times each, to close the connection. Then he leaned back and stared at me in silence, with the same admiring expression he'd worn last night. I returned his gaze, allowing myself to look into his strange eyes and really study him. With some of the fear evaporating, I could appreciate just how gorgeous he actually was. And how oddly right it felt to sit by his side: calming and exhilarating in equal measure.

It was a huge relief, obviously, that he hadn't actually forced the issue the night before. Sex in those circumstances would have been a violation and probably left me traumatised as hell. But there was a guilty part of me that couldn't help wishing that I could have enjoyed a more conventional night of passion with the hottest and most intriguing guy I'd ever spent time alone with.

He raised one eyebrow, as though he could tell what I was thinking. It was probably only my imagination, but that didn't stop a deep blush from spreading all over my cheeks and chest.

He leaned back towards me, as though he were going to commence the magic transfer again, but this time, he touched his lips to mine. I gasped slightly, then kissed him back, wrapping my arms around his waist to draw him closer. It was the gentlest, sweetest kiss, our lips only just open, our tongues only just touching. But my heart raced, and my stomach fluttered with a thousand times more intensity than I'd ever experienced before. I wanted to rip off his clothes. I wanted to curl up in his arms. It was almost impossible to keep in mind the way he'd hurt my brother, dragged me here, or made my family sick with worry.

All too soon, he broke the kiss with a little sigh. "We should get you home before your family come and burn this place to the ground."

My shoulders loosened and my jaw unclenched as the last residual bits of fear fell away. It made no sense, but if that was how he wanted to play things, then fine by me. I could go home, reassure my family and catch my breath. And maybe I'd even choose to come back later in the day... if he'd have me.

"So that's it? Instead of taking anything from me, you give me some of your power and a little kiss and send me on my way?"

Gabriel frowned. "For now. But I'd be foolish to turn my back on a bargain that's been willingly struck. Are you familiar with the concept of a lien?"

I pushed his hand away from where it still rested almost tenderly on my shoulder. I'd thought my heart was beating fast during the kiss, but that was nothing compared to the way it pounded at his words. "I'm a Sadler. I've been brought up with magic since I was born. I know what a lien is."

I took refuge in righteous indignation, because I knew full well what a lien was, and I saw the shape of the rest of my life. How could I have walked into his trap?

"You made a bargain," he whispered, as though I were about to deny it.

I nodded. I was starting to sweat, but somehow, I kept my voice more or less calm. "I understand the old laws. I was stupid to forget them, just because you seemed reasonable for a moment."

"The magic is a gift. And the kiss was wonderful. But the lien will be binding. You promised me your body and your magic in exchange for leaving your brother's power alone. I chose not to collect last night. But I reserve the right to do so."

I nodded again. What else could I do? Some people might claim I should have argued with him, sought to reason with him, or run for my life. But I understood how magical debts worked. It didn't stop me feeling like the room was spinning around me.

"Give me your hand," Gabriel murmured.

I slipped my trembling right hand into his left without having to be told.

If we were making the deal from scratch, I'd have to promise whatever it was I was committing to. But I'd said those words last night. Deep down, it was already binding. This was just the formality.

He pressed my hand against his chest, then with his other hand, squeezed the base of my ring finger between his thumb and finger, employing a massaging motion. A few moments before, I'd no doubt have found the sensation romantic or erotic. Now, it filled me with terror. After a few seconds, he let go.

I was all too familiar with the marks my father burnt into the flesh of his allies and customers. Large, ugly bands around the upper arm. This was different. A tiny, elegant circle of twisted, interwoven lines around the base of my finger. It almost looked like a wedding ring.

I flexed my finger a few times. Technically, it meant only one thing. At some point, he was entitled to have sex with me, during which he could take some of my magic. Nothing more, nothing less. But perhaps it was the design. Perhaps it was his magic circulating in my veins or the lingering aftereffects of the kiss. Either way, I felt like I'd made a much deeper, much more binding commitment.

"The magic I gave you will make you immune to my mind control," he said, matter-of-factly. "You should be anyway, with your natural power, but I'm strong enough to mesmerise some pretty serious practitioners, and I need you to be sure. A vow is a vow. I don't want or need to control your will to make sure you pay up."

I pushed him away and stood up, despite not being entirely sure my legs would be able to support me. The magic in the air combined with Gabriel's intensity had made the whole thing seem unreal, like something from a fairy story. But now, the implications were catching up with me.

"Any time you feel like it, you can ask for sex and magic, and I have to comply," I snapped. "Mesmerise me or don't.

Imprison me or don't. There's no such thing as consent with this branded into my skin."

He shrugged, as if the situation was out of his hands.

"Can I leave now?"

"I'm not holding you prisoner."

"Keep telling yourself that, Gabriel." I practically shrieked the words. "Tell yourself whatever it takes to convince yourself you're not a total psychopath."

I raced out of the door and traversed straight from his gravel driveway into my family's back garden without a second's hesitation. As I landed, the mark on my finger flashed red, as though to remind me that my magic was only my own as long as Gabriel allowed me to keep it.

I walked into the family home, and the entire family, minus Brendan, were there in seconds.

My mum won the race to reach me and pulled me into the tightest embrace I could ever remember. "Are you all right, darling?"

"I'll murder him," my dad snapped, throwing his arms around my mum and me and squashing us all together.

"You can't," Liam, always the voice of reason, muttered. "Dad, be sensible. You can't kill someone for something they've done as part of a legitimate bargain. It's like turning your powers on yourself."

My dad knew that better than anyone. But when he was in a blind fury, he sometimes needed reminding of the basics.

"He took your sister!" Dad yelled, as though I wasn't there. They'd probably been having variations on this argument all night.

"I'm fine, I promise," I said. "He didn't do anything. And I got him away from Bren before he could do him any real harm.

Even if I'd had to go through with it, it would have been worth it. Now, where is he?"

Chrissie shook her head. "Bren's upstairs, sleeping it off. He'll be weak for a few days, but then he should be fine. He'll have a little less power, but he had enough to spare."

I planned to tell them about the lien eventually, but just then, it seemed like pouring fuel on an unpredictable fire.

Dad stormed outside. I watched through the window as he smashed Gabriel's 1950s Jaguar into a million pieces, using a hammer at first, before moving on to fire and lightning, then a spell that seemed to be practically tearing what was left apart at the molecular level.

When we reached Bren's room, I saw Chrissie's description wasn't quite accurate. He wasn't so much sleeping as forcibly tucked into his bed under the power of my mum's magic. At the sight of me, he broke through the invisible barrier just enough to sit up. I dashed over and threw my arms around him.

"Oh God, Bren, how are you feeling? You look awful. Like you've lost a load of blood or something."

"I'm fine, thanks to you. But I would never, ever have let you go if I'd been able to stop you. I can't believe the others agreed to it. Once I came round, Mum had to telepathically pin me to the bed to stop me storming over to Thornber Manor."

"You know how bargains work, Bren," I snapped, trying not to look at my finger. "Besides, I made my own choice. I knew what I was getting into."

Still, it had been his fault I'd had to make the choice to begin with. He'd taken a risk by trying to enlarge the Dome, and I was the one paying for it. Unlike with my parents and innocent siblings, where I couldn't reassure them fast enough, I was in no hurry to put Brendan out of his misery as to what had actually happened last night.

"I'll kill him, Sadie, I swear. It won't be linked to your

bargain, but I'll find an excuse, I'll find an opportunity, and I'll make the bastard pay."

I took a deep breath. "He didn't sleep with me. He didn't take my magic. It was all just a game to him."

Once again, I didn't mention the lien. I'd tell my family once everyone started to calm down. I'd buy the biggest ring I could find to hide its physical manifestation. I'd go to The Windmill and get wasted to hide the mental manifestation. And then I'd leave town and escape his clutches. Move into my university accommodation a few months early. Magic was weaker outside Mannith. It'd be harder for him to track me down, especially if I didn't use magic myself. The thought of going away for good and restricting my powers hurt in equal measure, but I tried to put a brave face on it and change the subject.

"Anyway, is it true what he said? Did you really try to extend the Dome? Did you manage it?"

Bren smiled as though he'd already forgotten about what I put myself through for him. "That bastard stopped me before I could complete the spell. But now I've got the basic idea, I reckon I can make it work at some point in future. I'll have to build my strength back up first though—the attempt really took it out of me. That's why Thornber was able to overpower me."

I hugged him. "Bren, that's amazing. You're absolutely brilliant."

It was too bad I wouldn't see my family finally achieve the one thing we'd aspired to for generations. But I couldn't stay here.

All he's entitled to is one night of sex and some of your magic, I told myself again. *It's not that bad. It's not worth running away. You were willing to do it last night.*

But last night had been an emergency. You'd run into a burning building to save a loved one; you wouldn't casually stroll into the flames when you didn't have to.

If he claimed his "right" to sex, the fact that I'd have no real choice in the matter meant that would be a terrible violation of my body.

As for the magic, it was possible he'd only take a token amount, but there was no guarantee he wouldn't all but drain me. For a practitioner, losing your power—and by extension, losing your extra senses and your connection to the earth—is akin to losing your soul and your eyesight at the same time.

Just those two considerations would be enough to make getting out of town the only sane answer. And everything about him and his overwhelming power and unpredictable ways terrified me beyond all reason.

But apart from all that, I'd felt something I couldn't quite describe, first when he'd shared his magic with me—why the hell had I been stupid enough to accept?—again when he'd kissed me, and once more when he'd imposed the lien. Some sort of connection greater than anything I'd promised out loud.

I needed to get away.

I wake up in a cold panic. *It's okay. You're in London. He doesn't know where you are. He can't touch you.*

It's the little mantra I use every time I have a dream like this. Then I remember where I actually am and how that reassuring statement isn't entirely true anymore.

I lay there for an interminable amount of time. It's so much darker and quieter than my room in London, where the streetlights penetrate my curtains, and sirens and shouting drunks can be heard all night long.

In an attempt to shake off the strains of the day and the terror of my dreams, to my shame, my mind goes to its darkest place and my fingers between my legs.

Let me be clear here. It's not the masturbation I'm ashamed

of. I'm a fully paid-up subscriber to the modern view that it's healthy, natural, maybe even empowering. It's the things I think about to bring myself off that scare me. Fantasies are meant to be healthy, too, however filthy, however twisted. But surely not like this.

In my horniest moments, it's always a variation on the same theme that screams through my mind. It's that night, six years ago at Thornber Manor, but Gabriel Thornber's intent on collecting.

There are a hundred and one little subtleties and differences each time, but two key different versions.

In the first, after all the fury and spectacle at my parents' house, he turns utterly sweet the moment he has me alone.

"You made a sacred deal," he whispers, as he unzips my dress. In these fantasies, I'm wearing the pink dress he put me in. "You need to go through with it, but I'm not the monster you believe. Let me make it good for you."

I look at him, and all the fear and the anger drains away. All I can see is the beauty of his face, and, as he unbuttons his shirt, the muscles of his chest. In my imagination and in my bed, I'm melting inside.

He scoops me up, lays me down on the four-poster bed, and kisses me from my neck to my hip bones, taking his time, while I sigh and whisper his name.

Eventually, his kisses lead him to my thighs. He settles down between them and gets to work with his tongue. I'm gasping within seconds, screaming in pleasure within minutes.

"I told you I'm not a monster," he whispers, as I come from his ministrations.

Then he slips inside me and slides in and out, agonisingly gently, as I arch my back and push up against him. We come in unison, and strands of my magic slip into him as his slip into me.

I imagine we kiss and cuddle afterwards, but I always finish myself off before the film in my head gets that far.

. . .

The second version couldn't be more different.

"We have a deal," he growls, picking me up and throwing me face down on the bed.

"Please," I gasp, and it's not clear to me or to him whether I'm pleading for mercy or demanding satisfaction.

He tears the dress off me with some combination of force and magic.

With one hand, he holds my wrists together, pinning me to the bed. The other slides between my legs.

"Surprisingly wet for someone who's doing this under sufferance," he says with a laugh, rubbing me harshly.

I cry out with a mixture of pleasure and pain, then without further preamble, he enters me from behind. I'm pinioned under the weight of his muscle, but I still push back and meet his thrusts as far as I can. I still feel the pleasure build.

It ends the same as the other version. In the dream, we come in unison, our magic flowing from one to the other, and in my bed, in real life, my fingers move faster, and I come with a muffled cry.

I'm never sure which of the two versions makes me feel the guiltiest. And I don't understand where they come from. A way of processing the trauma of that night? A side effect of the lien he put on me? Or just proof that my mind is a twisted place? Either way, it's ruined me for other men. No flesh and blood date can make me feel like he does in my fantasies.

PART 2

SEVEN

On the first day of the trial, I slide into my tailored black skirt suit like I'm putting on chainmail. I plait my hair, as I always do for court. I'm so practised at that style that the desire to use magic barely even surfaces.

I read the brief one more time, trying to focus on my proposed lines of questioning, and not the fact that my brother's freedom is at stake or that I might need to face the man of both my nightmares and fantasies.

The prosecution have lots of consistent, reliable witnesses who claim to have seen Brendan at various key points on the evening of the murder. It's not yet clear whether they are Thornber acolytes or some combination of bribed, blackmailed, and bewitched. I won't be able to tell until I see them in court. Anyone who's in the Thornbers' inner circle will sport a distinctive heart and star tattoo behind the ear. The bribed and blackmailed will look scared. The mesmerised will sound utterly confident, but wear a glazed expression.

Or they could all be ordinary people who are telling the truth and Bren's lying to you, my subconscious chimes in.

At nine, there's a knock on my door. "Are you ready, Kate?"

I smile at Connor's voice. I've spent the days since my arrival hiding away in The Windmill, working on the case, pausing only for solitary meals in the bar, walks round town to focus my mind, and online workouts in my room. He's been lurking in the pub all week, a comforting but unobtrusive presence.

The rest of the family have been constantly trying to get me to come round to the house or meet them at a restaurant or a club, but I've kept telling them I need to concentrate and keep emotions out of this.

"Coming." I slick on my favourite bright red lipstick again, then head out to the corridor.

Connor takes the wheelie suitcase containing my files with one hand and my arm with the other, and leads me to his car. Even if he knew I was a practitioner, we'd still have to take a car today. You can't magically travel through the Dome in either direction.

"Good luck, love," several patrons shout as we leave. "Show those Thornbers what the Sadlers are made of."

I appreciate the sentiment. I've been friendly to the other patrons, but I've tried to keep myself to myself as much as possible. So it's nice to see they've got some faith, rather than just seeing me as a stuck-up, standoffish lawyer.

In the car, while Connor is absorbed with the traffic, I allow myself a quick, light core meditation. The process is intended to stop your magic getting out of control, but it's surprisingly good for calming you down and helping you focus in more prosaic situations.

I shiver as we drive through the Dome, first from the almost physical sensation as the barrier presses against my skin and my mind, and then from the colder air on the far side.

The slight chill isn't the only thing that's different on this side of the Dome, in Rivley, as the neighbouring town is called. Even with most of my attention focused on preparing for the case, it's hard not to notice the graffiti, the homeless people, the boarded-up shops and run-down houses. And beyond what's immediately visible, I know the local hospital will be over-stretched and there'll be unemployment and crime and people struggling in ways both big and small. It's not like it's some hell-hole either. It's just a normal town, suffering from the recent effects of recession and austerity, several decades of underin-vestment and industrial decline, and the general vagaries of human nature. Mannith suffers from none of that. Never has, never will.

That said, though Mannith has many amenities, it's too small for its own Crown Court, particularly as the official crime rate is so low—Sadlers and Thornbers deal harshly with those breaking the law without their blessing and protect those doing it on their behalf. The trial will be held in the rather less magical surroundings of Sheffield Crown Court, a concrete, glass, and red-brick edifice built a few decades ago.

Sheffield's had some regeneration since I last lived nearby and is in a far better state than Rivley and its ilk, but compared to Mannith, there's still a slightly depressing air. But then, the same is true for most of London.

Connor manages to drop me off right outside the court, which is a relief, as I've worn the highest heels I own as a confi-dence booster. Walking halfway across town in them would have been agony, and traversing would have got things off on entirely the wrong footing, even if I'd dared to risk it.

Think lawyer. Think professional. Think coolly detached stranger.

Against the odds, I keep my breathing steady and my head held high. Other lawyers, heading to their own cases, give me friendly nods. It's exactly the reaction I've always had in London, but somehow, I'm both surprised and grateful that they're not either crossing themselves at my approach or laughing in my face.

In a normal case, I'd try to find the prosecution lawyer and establish some rapport before we seek to tear each other's arguments apart. Show it's nothing personal. But today, it *is* personal, and I can't face the conversation.

Before my arrival, Bren's case had been handled by the family lawyer. The usual thing would have been for them to carry on with the backroom side of things while I stood up in court, but I'm now working on a "directly appointed" basis, responsible for all aspects of my brother's defence.

We're supposed to put on our wigs and gowns in the robing room. Instead, I change in the ladies' bathroom, then drop the rest of my belongings in the approved place as quickly as I can and head to the courtroom for one last look at the files.

Everywhere I go, Connor trails at a discreet distance, but there's been no sense of danger so far. Once I'm in place at the front of the court, he leaves me to it and heads for the visitors' gallery, where most of my family are already gathered. I give them a brief smile, then try to blank them out. They've positioned themselves in a way that would allow them to block any physical or magical attack aimed in my direction.

The courtroom is much the same as the exterior of the building: the sort of blandness that passed for modern twenty years or so ago: pine wood, cream paint, and polyester chairs, overheated with a tinge of chemical cleaning products in the air. I thrive on the old and on the beautiful. On those rare occasions I appear at the Old Bailey, my skills flare to life as though I'm possessed by the centuries of lawyers who've spoken there before. This room gives me nothing to work with.

I almost expect the judge to announce that there's no such person as Kate Elner, but of course, my parents' magical preparations work perfectly.

I shudder at the sight of Bren when he's led out into the dock. He's standing tall and looking straight ahead, a noble smile on his face. But the damn blockers are still clamped to his wrists, his power is dimming around the edges, and a mental, physical, and spiritual exhaustion has him in its grip.

It makes me want to run up there and hug him or else find the person who put him here and strike them down. Instead, I give him a small nod of recognition, lawyer to client.

The rest of the family aren't so restrained. Despite my best attempts to ignore them, I hear Chrissie's strangled cry and Leah's rather more full-blooded sob. My father remains outwardly silent and stoic, but there's a shift in his energy and a wave of fury.

And then, from the other side of the public gallery, the Thornbers enter. I force myself to stare straight ahead rather than look at them, but I can see enough through my peripheral vision. The men, young and old, are wearing tight-fitting black jeans and tighter white T-shirts, cut to show their biceps, like it's some sort of uniform. The women are evenly split between those dressed in similar jeans paired with low-cut tops, and those in skimpy dresses. They're all wearing sunglasses indoors, half as a fashion statement, half to hide their practitioner eyes. The Thornber heart and star crest is visible just below the ears of the men who've cropped their hair and the women with updos. The brands mark them as trusted members of the family or senior associates. This is the real inner circle.

There are two exceptions to the dress code. Jim Thornber, the dearly departed Niall's brother and right-hand man, and my father's usual interlocutor when he needs to do business with the Thornbers, is in a sensible suit. And Gabriel sports an expensive pinstripe three-piece suit cut close to his body. I'm no longer using peripheral vision, I'm outright staring, and I'm in imminent danger of having a panic attack in the middle of court. I wrap my arms around myself and try to breathe.

The judge says something, but I don't quite catch it, so fully is my conscious and unconscious attention focused on Gabriel.

Despite all the talk of him over the past few weeks and the

way he's lived rent free in my mind for years, I've almost ceased to think of him as a real person, as opposed to an abstract symbol of all our problems. He's more beautiful than I remembered. More terrifying, too. I can't see his famously eerie eyes through his sunglasses, but there's something in his composure and in his aura that chills me.

He's also more or less invisible. As a witness for the prosecution, he shouldn't be watching the case lest his testimony be corrupted by listening to the other witnesses. So he's put a spell on himself to hide him from the eyes of those without the power to see through it. I'm not sure whether all practitioners can see him or just those with enough magical strength.

Today, my job is relatively straightforward. The prosecution will put their case first, so there'll be no need for me to speak or use my knowledge of the law. That will come later. For now, I'm purely focused on keeping Gabriel's magic at bay. He shouldn't be able to influence Brendan, even with my brother's magic tamped down, but the judge, jury and witnesses are a different matter.

My legal opponent gets to his feet. In London, I know most of the lawyers I find myself up against, but I've never had much to do with the Northern Circuit. And thanks to my nerves, isolation, and stubborn avoidance of the usual protocol of a pre-trial chat, this is the first time I've set eyes on him. He's a tall Pakistani guy around my age with an unusually cheery and honest-looking face for a lawyer. The slightly clouded look in his eyes and something barely perceptible in his aura tell me he's already deeply in Gabriel's power. It's a stronger connection than I can break without getting him alone and working some serious magic, but I'm not too worried. I'd expect the counsel for the prosecution to be working against us, mesmerism or no mesmerism. It's everyone else I need to protect, and they're seemingly not yet touched.

Even as I think that, Gabriel pushes his sunglasses away

from his eyes and up onto his head, and power emanates from him and fills the room. I flinch. It's a cross between the pressure in the air you feel just before a long overdue storm and the sense of water rising up over your head in a sealed room.

It takes little effort to keep my own mind out of Gabriel's clutches—he made sure of that when he gave me a hint of his magic—but I'm still acutely, almost painfully aware of his power and far from certain I can protect the whole room.

I normally make my psyche sink down into the earth when I'm under pressure and needing to concentrate or perform difficult magic. But now, I do the opposite, and let my awareness drift upwards, free of the constraint of my body and looking out over the court. Oddly, I feel a little calmer now the pressure's on and I have to do something about it.

Gabriel smirks at Brendan as his magic gets its claws into the room. Brendan simply smiles back, glances at me (or rather, at my corporeal body), and nods. He could have been a touch more subtle, but at least he's got faith in me.

I focus on Gabriel's power until my mind gives it a semi-physical form. Then I slightly raise my hands and physically shove it away, while my mind exerts a similar force on a mental level. It's like trying to push a truck uphill, and all the while, I have to look calm and professional and keep my gestures as discreet as possible.

My magic's naturally strong, but I'm out of practice and have done everything I can to repress my power. So it's no surprise that, at first, my best efforts make no difference. But after a minute or two, the intensity of the force radiating from Gabriel drops by several degrees. I'm not arrogant enough to think I've achieved this directly. His concentration and will have wavered, presumably from surprise that someone's fighting back and confusion about who's doing it.

I seize my moment and push back harder still while the power's weaker and his guard's down. Somewhere in the background, the prosecution lawyer is opening his case. It would be useful if I were able to listen, but all of my energy and senses are focused on driving back Gabriel's mesmerism. Despite the danger, I feel eerily calm, removed from the real world and purely concentrating on the task at hand.

Against anyone else, my family could help, but Gabriel's too strong. In his heyday, my dad might have had a shot, but his powers are waning with age. And if Bren were free, he'd have a fighting chance, but wearing the blockers, he's less attuned to magic than the average human. But I'm both powerful in my own right and supported by whatever protection Gabriel gave me against himself.

I ball my hands into tight fists, dig my nails into my palms hard enough to leave a mark, and push back with renewed force. The power recedes further, and this time, it's definitely my doing. I almost want to do a little celebratory dance, but courtroom decorum issues aside, I can't lose concentration now.

Something in the magic shifts. The tendrils of mesmerism still infuse the entire room, but Gabriel has seemingly realised the source of the resistance. Though I'm looking straight ahead, I can tell his mental and physical gazes are focused directly on me. It's like he's trying to read my mind, gaze into my soul, and undress me with his eyes all at once.

And then his direct attention recedes, but power explodes out from him, tripled in intensity.

If fighting back was like pushing a truck uphill before, now it's like the brakes have come off and the vehicle is going to mow me down. He's seemingly less interested in bending the court-room to his will and more interested in seeing how much the inexplicably magical defence lawyer can take.

I strongly suspect the answer is *not much more.*

"This was a cold-blooded, pre-planned attack by a young, fit man on a vulnerable older person. The defendant broke into the victim's house, found him in bed, and shot him at point-blank range, for no better reason than an old family rivalry that had got out of hand."

The prosecution's words drift into my mind for a moment, then fade as the power intensifies once again.

My calm, professional veneer is slipping away by the moment. My head feels ready to explode from the pressure and a wave of nausea rises and falls in my stomach. I close my eyes and press my hands to my head.

The prosecution's speech stalls. "Your Honour, my learned friend does not look well."

I ignore both him and the sudden wave of concerned faces turned in my direction. I take a deep breath, stand up straight, and turn to look at Gabriel. He does not look like someone working powerful magic or pitting his strength against an opponent. His hands are clasped in front of him, and his handsome face wears a faintly bored expression. His uncle, Jim Thornber, tries to take his arm, presumably to funnel more magic through him, but Gabriel shakes his head slightly and shrugs him off.

The only thing to indicate that his efforts are costing him anything are his eyes. Where they'd been pale gold, they are a deep red, like all the fires of hell are burning behind them. I probably shouldn't be able to tell at this distance, but somehow, they're practically the only thing in the room I can see.

Hopefully, my oversized, coloured contact lenses are ensuring that my eyes appear to be a placid blue, but underneath, in the face of all this exertion, they're probably a similar shade to his. That, or sliding beyond into a dark, dead grey.

As kids, we always used to say you shouldn't look into Gabriel Thornber's eyes. I guess it was just some sort of anti-Thornber propaganda, but between the shape and the way the colour change doesn't restrict itself to his irises, they *are* eerie, even by practitioner standards. The famous demon blood, presumably. Now, I indulge myself and make proper eye contact from across the room. It's kill or cure—with our gazes locked, I might be able to find a way into his power. Equally, he could knock me out.

His glowing eyes narrow, and his studiously neutral expression slides into a slight frown, though the flow of power doesn't abate. It hurts my head more than ever.

The rest of the Thornbers and their hangers-on are staring at me, too, but I keep my focus firmly on Gabriel.

Despite all my mental exertion, I'm only resisting magic, not performing it myself, so it hasn't triggered the lien mark and explicitly given me away. Hopefully, Gabriel will assume my parents scoured the country and found someone who's both a qualified lawyer and an exceptional practitioner. I've no reason to believe he knows Sadie Sadler was ever called to the Bar—or anything about my life over the last six years—so he won't necessarily jump to conclusions. But I'm playing a dangerous game.

"Ms Elner, are you quite all right?" The judge stares at me in concern. I must look really terrible if he's being this informal.

It's imperative that I face him, reply to his question, and show proper respect. But I'm locked in Gabriel's eyes like a bat trying to fly to the moon.

Without warning, his eyes widen, their fire dims, and they turn a sort of rose-gold. At the same time, his lips curve into what almost looks like a genuine smile. And the flow of power stops like he's flipped a switch.

He carries on looking at me like he could stare all day, but with the crushing weight of his will removed, I'm able to break eye contact and turn back to the front. My head still aches from the exertion, but it's down to the sort of level a few painkillers will easily resolve.

"Apologies, Your Honour. I felt a little faint for a moment. I suspect it's the heat." I take an exaggeratedly slow swig of water. "I'm fine now. My learned friend should continue."

With one last worried glance at me, the other lawyer does

just that. This time, I'm able to listen as intently as I usually do and scribble down some notes.

"The defendant was heard talking about his plans earlier in the evening and was seen by numerous witnesses both when he entered the house brandishing a weapon and when he left, covered in blood."

When I dare to glance at the balcony, Gabriel is gone. The rest of the Thornbers remain, and they make an effort to take over the mesmerisation process, but I wave their power away with ease. I'd forgotten how strong I am.

Though I manage to keep my attention on the speech, I'm dimly aware of the old brand on my finger tingling. Perhaps it's psychosomatic, but even with my disguise and without having triggered the lien mark, I can't shake the feeling that Gabriel now knows exactly who I am and is planning... something.

EIGHT

Once the day's proceedings are over, my family surround me.

"What happened in there?" Mum, hands on her hip.

"I thought he was going to break you, but then you made him leave." Liam, slightly awed.

"What do you make of that other lawyer?" Chrissie, frowning.

I cross my arms. "That was okay for day one. Now I need to make plans for tomorrow."

Even if Gabriel's left, there are other Thornbers around, and there's no way I can keep up a sustained conversation with my family in public without risking my cover. My body language, my emotion, all of it will just be wrong.

Connor glances at my father. When Dad nods, the enforcer leads me back out to his car.

"Well done," he says, once we're inside. "How are you feeling? You look tired."

"I'm fine. The first day's always the hardest." Sadly, that's not strictly true, but I need to keep up morale.

"Have you still got a headache?"

"It's fading."

"Then how about grabbing some food? It can't be healthy, always eating by yourself, never leaving The Windmill."

He's leaning forward like he's about to launch into a stream of arguments in favour of this idea, but I surprise him with a nod. "Where did you have in mind?"

"There's this great new Indian restaurant if you're up for heading into town."

"Perfect. It'll be fun to explore the centre."

We tend to refer to the whole area within the Dome as Mannith, but it encompasses a variety of elements. The bit where my parents live and where The Windmill is situated is the original medieval town, but by modern standards, it's basically suburban. Farther out, there are some completely rural places with isolated farms and houses—Thornber Manor, for a start—and some slightly more developed small country villages. In between, there's the late Victorian town centre, half of which is still given over to industry, while the other is busy with shoppers during the day and those seeking a good time in the evening. My family owns many of the bars directly and a large proportion of the others are run by those involved with or at least loyal to the family, but even as a teenager, unless Chrissie near-forced me, I never visited much.

We head straight to the new restaurant, the Cardamom. It's nothing special, but the food is decent and the atmosphere cheery. Connor doesn't say much, but he's a relaxing, comfortable presence, as well as easy on the eye. I don't speak much either. I'm worn out from the day I've had, and it would be tiring to spin a cover story about Kate Elner's life. He looks at me protectively and doesn't seem to mind. I try to study his body language. Is he still just doing his duty, or does he see this as something resembling a date?

"Fancy a quick drink before we head back to The Windmill?" he asks, once the last plates have been cleared away. No bills have appeared. The restaurant must also be under Sadler control.

"I ought to get some prep for tomorrow done. But one drink won't hurt."

"Are you okay to walk? There's a great bar five minutes away."

My shoes are killing me. I wish we could travel with magic. But I nod, and he takes my arm.

It's a beautiful evening—it's always a beautiful evening in Mannith. The air is warm but fresh, and the stars are visible despite the bright lights of the city. Different food smells mingle in the air, complementing rather than clashing with each other, and music and chatter drifts out from bars. Everywhere, locals are out, dressed up and enjoying themselves. People make more effort here for a casual trip to the pub than they do for a big party back in London.

We turn the corner into a deserted courtyard that separates two side streets. At almost the same moment, Gabriel and his entourage enter from the other side.

It's unclear whether it's an ambush or the universe toying with me again. Either way, they stride towards us like they already own the town.

They've obviously been enjoying a night out, too. Most of the women are heavily made up, with the plump lips and sculpted contours that only magical enhancement can achieve. They've presumably got the long eyelashes that Chrissie and Leah sport as well, though their dark sunglasses make it impossible to tell. There's a sameness about them, as though overuse of beautification spells over several years has gradually erased their natural differences. The prettiest one—wavy blonde hair down to her tiny waist and glorious bone structure—is hanging onto Gabriel's arm possessively.

There's one notable exception. The woman on Gabriel's other side—not touching him, but standing extremely close—has dark hair cropped to her chin and no make-up bar a slash of scarlet lipstick. She's wearing jeans and a black T-shirt in place of a tiny dress, though her heels are still several inches high. Her brown skin is a depressingly rare sight in Mannith.

The men are in the ubiquitous black jeans they all wore to court, but now accompanied by a variety of smart shirts. They've all got aggressively gelled-back hair, aftershave I can smell from several metres away, and of course, massive, mirrored sunglasses.

I'm studying the gang so intently in an attempt to avoid actually looking at Gabriel. It's one thing seeing him across a crowded courtroom, quite another to be face to face with him. But my eyes have a mind of their own, and against my conscious will, I find myself staring. He's in suit trousers and a fitted blue and white striped shirt. His hair is slicked back like his friends and minions, but he hasn't bothered with sunglasses. It's like he wants people to see his haunting eyes. Right now, though, apart from their shape, there's nothing much to see. The over-large, diamond irises are a deep brown. Pretty but unremarkable.

He shrugs off his date's arm and walks right across to me, while the rest of the group stands in place. My blood rushes to my head. I wish there were somewhere to sit down. I settle for huddling closer to Connor.

"Good evening, Ms Elner," he says, imbuing my assumed name with a deep touch of scepticism.

I'd forgotten about his accent. In my mind, he sounds like a stereotypical villain from a Hollywood film. In reality, his voice is pure northern, to an even more pronounced degree than my family, like Sean Bean in every role he's ever played.

"I'm sorry, have we met?" It's anyone's guess how I get the words out through my rapidly constricting throat.

Connor takes a firm hold of my arm and steps in front of me. "Leave it, Thornber. Kate's just doing her job. She's not from round here. She doesn't deserve to get dragged into this."

"What's going on?" I stage whisper to Connor. "Who is this?"

Even as I fight to keep up the act, I know how naïve we've been. Of course he'll see through me. He has spies everywhere. He can scry. And if all of that wasn't enough to allow him to penetrate anyone else's disguise, in my case, there's also the connection he forged through the lien mark and perhaps through the magic exchange, too.

"This is Niall Thornber's son," Connor whispers back, leaning towards me but never taking his eyes off Gabriel. "Head of the family, since whatever Brendan did or didn't do to the old man."

Gabriel glances behind him. "Everyone except Nikki, get out of here. I'll see you back at the manor."

His date pouts. "But babe, I thought we were going on to the casino."

One of the men takes her arm and hustles her away before Gabriel can respond. They walk as a group back towards the side street, then convey out en masse, leaving only the woman who'd stood out for her darker skin and heavier clothes. Nikki, presumably. She stands by the entrance to the courtyard with her arms crossed, like she's preparing to defend a strategic pass in a medieval battle.

Gabriel steps closer. Connor's grip tightens. To the best of his knowledge, he's protecting a valuable but vulnerable lawyer. Easy to do if human thugs or a Thornber minion starts something. Not so easy if Gabriel abandons all reason and decides to fight his own battles.

"My dearest Connor," Gabriel says. "It's you who doesn't deserve to get dragged into this. She's already front and centre. I'd hate to see you lay down your life for a woman you know nothing about, so let me reduce that risk."

Connor is strong, both physically and psychically. In the case of pretty much anyone else—bar perhaps my father or

Brendan—he'd have been able to laugh off their threats. But Gabriel's eyes narrow, Connor's grip on my arm slackens, and I'm genuinely scared.

I spare Connor a split-second glance. He's not unconscious, just frozen in place. Knocking him out would have been kinder than making him watch whatever's coming while he's powerless to do anything about it, but who's naïve enough to expect mercy from Gabriel-fucking-Thornber?

"Now your bodyguard's out of commission, how about we play a little game, *Kate*?"

I look him straight in his now-glowing golden eyes, trying to pretend I'm not feeling physically sick with fear. "What on earth's going on? I'm not here to *play games*. I'm here to represent my client. And intimidating the defence lawyer in the trial of your father's supposed murderer is not going to help matters."

I'm pleased I manage to sound so professional, because inside, I'm shaking.

"Really, Sadie? You're actually going to keep the act up? You're honestly going to make me do this?"

I glance at Connor, expecting to see shock on his face at the sound of my real name, but his expression doesn't change. Maybe Gabriel's blocked his hearing as well as his movement, or—horrifyingly—perhaps he's speaking directly into my mind.

"I have no idea what you're talking about," I reply.

I'd expected a few more minutes of heated back and forth. Instead, he hits me with a wave of Greenfire.

The second it touches me, I scream like I'm being burnt at the stake.

I fight to regain a semblance of reason. The magic of Greenfire is that it's utter agony in the moment. You genuinely feel like your flesh is about to melt off your bones, like you're moments from death. But the second your assailant stops, the awful sensations falls away completely, as if someone's flicked a switch. And there's absolutely no physical injury done.

In our early teens, it'd been a bit of a challenge for me and my siblings to inflict the spell on each other. See who cracked first or who could put up the most resistance. My parents always hit the roof whenever they discovered we'd been playing that game. It was brutal, but that's kids for you. Or perhaps that's just my family.

I scream again. It's been a long time since I've experienced the spell, and it really does hurt. But deep down, I know it's basically an illusion, and that stops me completely losing control. When Greenfire is used on non-practitioners, it's not uncommon for their heart to give out before the assault stops.

I close my eyes. I may not practice magic much anymore, but I'm still a practitioner by blood. That sort of mind trick won't be happening to me. Even so, it's agony. A few more minutes, and I'll be begging him for mercy. The idea of that tortures me more than the pain.

"I don't like hurting you," Gabriel says, and through the onslaught, I can't tell if he's screaming it out loud or whispering it in my mind. "You can stop this with a thought, you know you can."

He's entirely correct. The magic is gentle, a tenth of the power Gabriel could surely produce if he really wanted to hurt me. Summon the slightest hint of my own power, and I could stop the pain. But fighting Greenfire isn't just a case of resisting mesmerism. It's more like putting out a fire with your mind, and that takes real magic, which would blow apart the last remnants of my cover. And at that point, he'd do a hell of a lot more than toy with me.

Despite my attempts to keep up the act, my performance in court surely made clear that I was a practitioner of some strength. But as long as I don't trigger the lien, he has no proof I'm Sadie Sadler. So, I grit my teeth and let his magic burn me.

"I know who you are. Stop being ridiculous. Fight back."

If there were any passers-by—which there aren't, because

the courtyard is deserted and no one is getting past Gabriel's bodyguard—they wouldn't see anything but Gabriel's psychotic calmness and my agony. But I see the glowing ball of unreal flame that surrounds me. And Connor is surely able to as well.

"Stop it!" Connor shouts, snapping sufficiently out of the trance Gabriel had thrust on him to speak but not yet to move. "Stop hurting her."

"She can stop it herself, with ease," Gabriel replies.

"Gabriel, please. I know you're angry at Brendan and upset about your dad, but don't do this. Fight me if you want to fight. Or hell, burn me where I stand while I can't fight back. Just leave her alone."

"Interesting," Gabriel says to me. "Is he terrified about what Philip Sadler is going to do to him if he doesn't bring you home in one piece, or have you found yourself a little admirer?"

I don't reply. I can't formulate an answer in my head, let alone speak one out loud. The pain is driving everything else out. And perhaps even more terrifying, I can feel my dormant magic starting to rise in response to the trauma, with no intervention from my conscious brain. It's the practitioner equivalent of a flight or fight reflex.

For a second, the intensity lessens, as the power inside me forms a shield around my skin and pushes back the waves of flame. With a little more force, I could put them out entirely. Really make an effort, and I could turn them back on my assailant. Every nerve in my body is screaming at me to do just that, and the thought is almost unbearably tempting. Nothing seems to matter more than stopping the pain. And inflicting it on Gabriel would be satisfying as hell.

"That's it," Gabriel whispers. "Protect yourself. Hurt me. I want to feel your power."

There seems increasingly little point in keeping up the charade of being "Kate the human lawyer from London", but I have to try. I grind my lips together and squash my magic down into a tiny ball. The second I do, the pain hits me afresh, stronger than ever, drawing another scream from my burning mouth. The burn of the fire is almost matched by the pressure of fighting my own magic. Not using it in a situation like this is like forcing yourself to hold your breath until you pass out.

"Stop it. Give in. Fight me. You know I'll let you win. If the Greenfire doesn't break you, suppressing your magic like that will."

Is that a hint of panic in Gabriel's voice? Perhaps he expected me to defend myself immediately and blow my cover before any harm was done. Cruel but efficient. But I'm holding out, and he can't back down.

I close my eyes again and try to breathe more deeply. Doing a core mediation is going to be incredibly difficult in the midst of this agony, but if my mind is in the earth, I won't be able to feel the pain, and my magic won't get out of control.

I plant my feet more firmly against the pavement, try to count backwards from a thousand (the numbers make no sense in my head), and let my mind slip.

"I can see what you're doing!" Gabriel shouts. "I don't know why you think this will give you away any less than just blasting me."

His words are far away, as is the pain.

"Gabriel, I'm begging you," Connor pleads. "Leave her alone."

"So, which is it?" he says to Connor. "Is this purely professional, or have you got a little crush?"

"You're going to kill her," Connor screams.

"I really hope for your sake that you're trying to get into the Sadlers' good books, not get into her pants," Gabriel says. "Because firstly, trusted acolyte or not, I suspect Philip Sadler would kill you if you so much as kissed her. And secondly, she belongs to me."

I'm beyond all feeling now, safe in the earth, too far away to really understand his words. But however distant my mind is, my body is still reacting to the danger, and at long last it has the decency to plunge me into unconsciousness.

"Wake up, Kate."

I open my eyes. Connor is shaking me. All of the pain has gone, and so has Gabriel.

"What happened?" I ask.

"You passed out, and I think that bastard realised he'd gone too far. He stopped attacking you, released his grip on me, and disappeared with Nikki, his bodyguard."

I almost smile at the way he's trying to explain the situation without explicitly referencing magic. Without that in your frame of reference, none of it would make any sense. Gabriel revealed a lot about me—not just my name, but his fervent belief in my ability to use magic. Connor clearly didn't hear a word of it. His hearing wasn't blocked, as he responded to the comments Gabriel addressed to him, so my initial suspicion must have been correct—Gabriel was speaking directly into my mind.

If I were really trying to keep my persona intact, I ought to ask a few wide-eyed, leading questions. But there seems little point now. I can take some moral satisfaction in the way I didn't give in to Gabriel, but it's clear he knows who I am. And even more worryingly, that he still puts some credence in the idea of the lien.

On the other hand, I can't face the drama of explaining to Connor who I really am. I'll do it soon, but that conversation needs careful handling, at the right time.

"When I took this case, I was told to expect some things I couldn't quite understand or believe. I guess I know what they meant now."

"I'd explain it if I could. But I wouldn't know where to start."

"Don't worry. Just get me back to the hotel."

Connor puts a hand on my shoulder. "Any chance you could avoid telling Mr Sadler about this? It might make him attack the Thornbers, and that's not going to help Brendan. And I'd be punished for failing to protect you. God knows I deserve it, but I don't want anyone else trusted with the role."

I shiver. He thinks he's at risk of being punished for not protecting a valuable family lawyer. The punishment for not protecting a beloved daughter would be far worse. And yes, there's no way Dad could be relied upon not to lash out at Gabriel if he knew what he'd done to me. Not just the Green-fire, but the way he'd claimed I belonged to him.

"Of course. I'd hate to see you get into trouble, and there's no one I'd rather have guarding me."

After all, unless I stick with my actual family 24/7, it's unlikely anyone else would be able to resist Gabriel's powers any more effectively.

Connor grins. "Thank you. I'm so glad you're okay. I'll never let something like this happen again."

I'm sure he knows as well as I do that there wouldn't be a lot he could do to stand against Gabriel, but for both our sakes, I let him reassure me.

In stark contrast to his usual professional attachment, he pulls me into a bone-crushing hug. For a second, I freeze, then I hug him back. It's comforting to rest against his solid chest.

Gabriel had claimed that Connor had more than just a professional interest in me. The thought had crossed my mind over dinner, too. I'm still not sure whether it's my imagination, but after a day like this, I could do with a bit of fun. It seems worth testing.

"Let's head to The Windmill," I say. "Now I know the sorts

of dangers lurking in this town, I don't want to be alone tonight."

For a moment, he frowns, as though trying to establish whether it's a come-on. Then I wink, and he takes my arm and leads me to the car.

Screw you, Gabriel. I don't belong to anyone, and I'll have whoever I choose.

Against all the odds, we make it back to The Windmill and up the winding stairs to my room without any of the regulars or any of the acquaintances I'm still carefully avoiding attempting to engage us in conversation.

"Do you want a drink?" Connor asks, hovering on the threshold. "Recover from the shock and steady your nerves?"

I shake my head. I've already managed to push the shock deep down into my body where it can't bother me, and my nerves are surprisingly steady. Life might be a confusing mess, but I know what I want right this moment.

"Come here," I demand.

Connor steps away from the door and closes the space between us like he's walking on a rickety bridge over a lake of lava. The second he's within touching distance, I pull him the rest of the way towards me, clamp one arm around his waist, and use the other to wrench off his shirt. I have to stand on tiptoes to pull it over his head.

His eyes widen. Clearly he didn't expect his London lawyer to be quite so forward.

I smile at the sight before me. His tight T-shirts leave little to the imagination, but I'm pleased to confirm his physique is everything I thought it would be.

"You're not going to get in trouble for this, are you? I mean, your boss didn't issue any strict prohibitions regarding his lawyer?"

Connor laughs. "He'd probably like the idea. The more I care, the more I'll try to keep you safe."

Maybe he's right. In any case, my family used to be over-protective as hell, but that was when I was a teenager. They can't object to my love life at this point.

Besides, however over-protective they used to be, when push came to shove, they were still willing to pimp me out to save Brendan.

I push the unwelcome thought away. I've never thought of it in such stark terms, and now isn't the time for lingering on the past or worrying about the future. I've got a gorgeous, half-naked guy in front of me who's eating me up with his eyes. I need to live in the moment.

I bestow my sultriest smile on him and slip off my dress. The main purpose of all the exercise I do is to keep my endor-phin levels up and distract myself from magic, but there's no getting away from the fact that my body looks good as a result. It's one of those things you're not meant to say. It's supposed to be a little unseemly for women to like their bodies. But screw it. There are lots of things I don't like about myself. My defined abs and narrow waist and rounded bottom do not make the shortlist.

He gives a little whimper of excitement at my mostly naked form. I hadn't bothered with a bra, but I had worn hold-ups and sweetly lacy underwear, even though I'd had every intention of returning home alone. It's a point of pride.

"Get those trousers off," I order, half stern, half giggling. He obeys with a dazed look in his eyes. His thighs and bum are as appealing as his chest. And after a night like this, it's good to feel in control.

I pull him in for a kiss. He bows his head and succumbs. My

arms are around his shoulders and his arms are around my waist, and it's impossible to say who's holding on the tightest.

He scoops me up, kisses me once more, then lays me down on the bed.

"You definitely want to do this?" he asks. "It's not some weird reaction to everything that's happened tonight? I wouldn't have thought I was your type."

"I don't have a type. And yes, Connor, of course I damn well want to do this."

He's handsome. He's available. He's into me. This probably isn't going to be a love affair for the ages, but why the hell wouldn't I?

He slips off his boxers, and he's hard as anything.

"Sit down," I tell him, guiding him to the edge of the bed. I throw a pillow on the floor, kneel on it, and put my mouth around him.

He gasps, in what I can only assume is a mixture of surprise and desire. I always like to embrace my assertive side. It gets such a reaction.

I work away for a few minutes, pushing myself to go deeper in much the same way I push myself to manage a few extra reps during my workouts. His hands are on my head, and he seems faintly stunned, though it doesn't stop him from moaning with pleasure.

At what seems to be an opportune moment, I swirl my tongue around one more time, then get to my feet.

I reach into my handbag and pass him a condom. I'm always careful—I never want to catch anything, after all—but the pregnancy risks are much higher with a fellow practitioner. According to some, it's practically impossible for us to get pregnant by a normal person without making a full-blown ritual out of it, practically impossible to avoid it with our own kind without either medical or magical protection. And we generally avoid the pill and the like—messing with our hormones seems to do something to our powers.

"My turn," I say, with a grin.

Connor doesn't seem quite capable of speech.

I'd intended to have him go down on me, but in absolute contravention of all my feminist principles, I'm sufficiently aroused from the naughtiness of seducing my bodyguard, so instead, I get on my hands and knees.

I scream in pleasure when he enters me.

This is different, I tell myself, as he thrusts deeply into me, stroking me with one hand and holding onto my hip with the other. *All those pretentious, right-on professionals couldn't satisfy you. But the fault's not with you, it's with them. Connor's different, and your body knows it. You're not broken after all.*

And then slowly, as he moves faster, grows louder, and holds me tighter, my mind starts to disengage, and it feels like any other polite encounter with a nice man after a pleasant enough date.

I push back against him frantically, trying to regain the magic. *He's hot as hell,* I think. *He's your bodyguard, sworn to protect you. That's pretty much every woman's fantasy. He's a tough guy, but you seduced him, not the other way around. That's sexy and cool. And doesn't the fact that he doesn't know who you really are add a certain frisson?*

"God, Kate, you're so gorgeous. You feel so good," Connor sighs.

He's evidently holding on, resisting his pleasure until I get mine.

It's weird to hear him use my fake name in such an intimate scenario. Hardly sexy at all.

I pride myself on my ability to come, even with a halfway competent date. It's a big part of my self-image. And as well as being sexy as anything, Connor is doing everything right. I close my eyes and try to lose myself in the sensations.

Protect yourself. Hurt me. I want to feel your power.

Unprompted and unwanted, the fresh memories slip into my mind. Suddenly, Connor's touch feels heightened, and I can hardly breathe.

Give in. Fight me.

This is insane. The Greenfire incident was horrific, and the last thing my psyche needs is some new twisted Gabriel-fucking-Thornber fantasy.

Connor. Think about Connor. He's tough and sweet in equal measure. His six pack is jaw-dropping. He's moaning behind me like he can't hold on any longer but is somehow managing to do so through sheer force of will for my sake.

She belongs to me.

I come with a full-body shudder, and full-throated scream, and a crushing feeling of guilt and confusion that cuts through most of the pleasure.

The second I let myself go, Connor stops trying to fight. He comes in turn, before I've stopped shaking.

For a few seconds, we remain frozen in place, then we both collapse back onto the bed.

"God, that was amazing," Connor says.

I nod. "Though... if you can bear to put some clothes on, that drink to recover from the shock and steady my nerves you offered sounds good right about now."

Despite my cheesy chat up line about not wanting to be alone, I gently send Connor back to his own bed after we've had a few more drinks and another round of sex, then spend a couple of hours working on the case. Eventually, I snatch a few hours of sleep. Inevitably, with Gabriel's magic still infusing my skin, I dream the same old dream again, more vividly than ever.

NINE

The next morning, I shower and pull my professional clothes and my professional attitude back on.

When Connor collects me for court, he's professional too, in his own way. He doesn't mention last night, and there's no kissing or over-familiarity. But there's an unfamiliar smile on his face, and he can't keep his eyes off me.

I say nothing either, but I smile back. He may not have been able to achieve the impossible and keep my twisted fantasies at bay, but it was good spending time with him. Both out and about, and in bed. It's an experience I'd like to repeat, and hopefully, he feels the same way. But I'll cross that bridge once I've today's court session out of the way.

"Are you going to be okay today?" he asks once we're in the car and heading out of town. "If Thornber's in court, I mean?"

"I'll have to be. If he tries something like that again, can you stop him?"

Connor turns towards me, ignoring the road for the moment. "Honestly? I don't know. Maybe not."

"That's okay."

"But I'll do my best. And Brendan's family will protect you.

They're not going to let their prize lawyer get hurt."

This time, I go to the robing room like a proper lawyer instead of hiding away. I even manage to exchange a few pleasantries with Imran Usmani, as I've established the prosecution lawyer is called. He frowns when he sees me and insists I have a glass of water. His concern's presumably due to yesterday's performance in court, which I'd almost forgotten about in light of the later drama.

Bren is pacing around the sickly-green interview room waiting for me. "What the hell happened last night?"

He snaps the question out without giving me chance to sit down and without the slightest hint of pretence that I'm merely his lawyer.

"What do you mean?"

"What do you think?"

I honestly don't know. He could mean Gabriel's attack. Equally, he could mean Connor's seduction. It's hard to say which would infuriate my brother more.

"The story's all over—it's like those petty Thornber acolyte inmates got a telepathic memo or something. What did he do to you?"

"What are they saying?"

"The details differ from person to person, but they've loved rubbing it in my face."

I lean over. "Are you checking I'm okay or worrying about your own reputation?"

He shakes his head. "A bit of both. Sorry. I just wish I wasn't stuck wearing these blocker cuffs. That I wasn't under constant surveillance. That I didn't have to be on my best behaviour. I wish things were back to normal—that we were sitting on that old garden bench at Mum and Dad's, and I could sketch a new portrait for you."

"It won't be long now. We've got this." I make myself sound confident for his sake.

"So, are you okay?"

"It was just Greenfire. And I could have turned it back on him if I'd tried. He definitely knows who I am though."

"Dammit. I knew this was a bad idea. I wish you *had* turned it back on him. I'd have loved to see that. Even if you'd blown your cover and ruined my trial, it'd still have been worth it."

I laugh. "Greenfire would be too good for him. I'll save my moment until I've got a clear shot and Hellfire in my palms."

"That's my sister! Now, ready to be my lawyer again?"

Today, Imran will continue the case for the prosecution by starting to work his way through the hordes of witnesses who'd supposedly seen every moment of Bren's murderous rampage. Hopefully, I'll be able to pay more attention today. Scribble down notes furiously so I can use every detail the witnesses give against them when it's time for my cross-examination. And if needs be, perform another round of deflecting Gabriel Thornber's power.

Despite his earlier outburst, Bren is smiling serenely in the dock. Even with shadows under his eyes and a touch of stubble creeping in, he appears too delicately handsome to be a murderer. More victim than villain.

Up in the viewing gallery, my family are watching in rapt attention, quieter than they were yesterday. Mum and Chrissie have just completed a light core meditation. Dad's gripping the barrier hard enough to leave a dent.

On the other side, the Thornbers are back. Gabriel's *in situ*, still invisible and wearing yet another fancy suit, but the sunglasses are on today, and he's making no obvious attempt to unleash his power on the court.

He notices my eyes on him and gives a wide smile of greeting. I look away before he can drag me further into his net.

The first witness is a barmaid from The Angel, which is apparently a bar in the town centre, though it wasn't there in my day. Weird to think of the town changing, even in small ways. In my mind, it's fixed in time.

Her eyes are a clear, cheerful blue, with no sign of mesmerism. Her long, highlighted hair sways as she walks into the witness box, giving me enough of a glimpse of the side of her neck to convince me there's no Thornber tattoo there. Which doesn't prove she's not affiliated with the Thornbers, merely that she's not a full member, not in the inner circle.

She's looking down at the floor, and her hands are trembling slightly, but it appears to be merely the normal nerves of someone giving evidence in a major trial. There's none of the wide-eyed terror I'd expect if the Thornbers were forcing her to lie under oath.

Imran gives her a gentle smile and starts his questioning. "Where were you on the evening of the 15th June?"

Her reply is clear and certain. "At work. At The Angel, on York Road. Started at five, finished just before midnight."

I scribble down a note. For whatever reason, Gabriel's not attempting to project his power on the court today, which makes focusing on my legal duties a damn sight easier.

"Did you see the defendant that night?"

She nods. "He came in around seven, by himself. Sat down at the bar. Ordered a beer."

"Was the defendant known to you? Had you spoken to him before?"

"He comes in every so often. We've had the odd bit of banter over the bar. I wouldn't say I know him personally. But everyone in Mannith knows about Brendan Sadler."

The judge gives the witness and the prosecution lawyer a

pointed look. "Stick to the facts, please. What you think you know about the defendant is not relevant here."

"Thank you, Your Honour," Imran says. "Now, you say he ordered a beer. Did he say anything else to you?"

"That or just thinking aloud. He said something like, *I'm going to make those Thornber bastards pay.*"

I almost laugh out loud. Really? Everything else she's said was in her witness statement, but this detail is new. She's obviously in the pay of the Thornbers rather than merely mistaken, if she's spouting such obviously made up "evidence". She could have tried to come up with something vaguely subtle.

"And how did you respond?"

"Customers talk a load of crap when they're drunk, even if you'd normally take a threat from Brendan Sadler a bit more seriously than one from a random guy. Still, half the point of my job is to be a sympathetic ear. So I was all like, 'Why? What have they done to you, love'?"

"Did he reply?"

"Yes. He stood up and downed his drink. *'I'll make them pay for what they did to my sister. It's been six years. Long enough for the prohibition on taking revenge to have faded. But not long enough for me to have forgotten'.*"

My head swivels in Bren's direction. He's shaking his head. That line wasn't in the witness statement either. But it sounds a lot like something my brother would say, and not much like something someone would make up.

I do the calculation in my head. It hadn't clicked, but the night of Niall's murder would have been exactly six years since the night of the lien.

Imran asks a few more questions to establish the details, then the witness's account ends with Bren slamming down his glass, storming out, and driving off in his open-topped Mercedes, way over both the speed limit and the drink drive limit.

When it's finally my turn to speak, I stand up, bracing myself for another onslaught of power from Gabriel, but still nothing comes. I can't help turning around to check he's still there. He is. Watching silent and expressionless, sunglasses on.

Not that I need magic to distract me. The witness's words rushing through my head are quite enough. Still, I've been trained to do this. I've practiced hundreds of times. I may be emotionally invested in the result and worried my brother's lying to me, but it's surprisingly easy to slip into the role of smooth defence lawyer.

"How many people did you serve that night?"

The witness frowns. "Quite a few."

"Did you have conversations with all of them?"

"A couple of words while I poured their drinks."

"So why were you talking to the man at the bar? Why do you remember what he said so clearly?"

"You don't ignore Brendan Sadler if he wants to talk to you, and he tends to leave an impression."

"You've already admitted that the defendant is an occasional customer and a town legend, not someone you know well. He's a white male in his early thirties, with short dark hair and a slim build. There are endless numbers of people in this town matching that description. How can you be so sure it was him you were talking to?"

"You're not from around here, are you? Anyone in Mannith would recognise any of the Sadlers."

I cross my arms over my chest. "Where I'm from is irrelevant to these proceedings." It's hard to keep the irritation—or the accent—out of my voice. And it's disturbing to hear my family talked of in this way.

I attempt to steer the questioning back onto safer ground. "How's the sound quality in The Angel?"

"It's a bar. There's music and chatter. But I'm used to holding conversations over it. And it's not like he was speaking quietly. To be honest, I was getting a little thrill from talking to him."

God save me from my brother's endless appeal to the opposite sex.

"Can you remind me of exactly what he said?"

She nods and reels it off without looking at her notes. "*'I'll make them pay for what they did to my sister. It's been six years. Long enough for the prohibition on taking revenge to have started to fade. But not long enough for me to have forgotten.'*"

"And what did you think he meant by that?"

For the first time, she hesitates. "I knew he might do something violent. But I was imagining a fight, not a murder. And an attack on someone his own age, not an old bloke. It sounded all gangster and cool. Now it makes me cry to think I didn't do anything to stop it."

"*I'll make them pay for what they did to my sister.*" Somehow, I manage to repeat the hateful words. "Does that mean anything to you?"

"Who knows? I assumed it was Gabriel Thornber he was angry with, rather than the old man. God knows what he did to Brendan's sister. Dumped her, raped her, or got her pregnant, at a guess?"

"There's no need to speculate if you don't know," I snap.

I ask a few more probing questions. She's sure about the time Bren arrived, because he made an entrance. She's sure about the time he left. She followed him outside, and she recognised his distinctive car. I've hopefully managed to create some room for doubt, but it's a depressingly perfect testimony.

"If the next witness has got a story like that, I'm mesmerising them myself," Mum says, after court ends for the day. "I don't know if she was bewitched or out for easy money, but I'm not going to sit there and listen to people lie about my baby boy."

I shake my head. "No. No mesmerism. No blackmail,

bribery, or intimidation. You promised. Just trust me to do my job."

Over the next few days, Imran and I work our way through several more witnesses. A customer in the bar, who didn't hear the conversation but whose description of the basic facts matches the barmaid's perfectly. A man at the petrol station, where Bren apparently parked his recognisable car and showed his infamous face while paying. Someone in the village near Thornber Manor, who'd seen him come screeching in. The manor's gardener, who'd watched him spin to a halt on the gravel driveway and storm inside, holding the extremely noticeable Victorian silver revolver which police evidence suggests was the murder weapon and which was found covered in Bren's prints—hardly surprising, considering that it's a family heirloom.

No one seems obviously bewitched or acting under duress. The neighbour and the gardener are probably Thornber loyalists to some degree or another, but the timings and detail in their stories correspond with the seemingly more neutral and trustworthy witnesses.

My parents honour my request to avoid any attempts at perverting the course of justice, but none of the testimony bodes well for the case. And worse, while I'd never admit it to him or to the rest of the family, I'm starting to doubt my own brother. Next time I meet with him, there are going to have to be some hard questions.

Could he really have done this to take revenge on my behalf and be too ashamed or worried about my reaction to tell me the truth?

TEN

When Friday night of the second week hits, I cannot wait to do some exercise, have a long hot bath, then go to bed.

The bath's a luxury. Growing up, my mum was a big believer in long soaks, for purposes of both ritual and relaxation, and she entirely passed the habit to me. But my London flat only has a shower.

While I'm luxuriating in the water, drink in hand, there's a knock on the door. "Hello?"

"It's me, Connor. Can I come in?"

I smile to myself. Maybe sleep can wait. "Any time."

The door's locked, but his magic makes short work of that issue.

I stretch out in the bubbles, trying to look as languorous as possible and hoping my face isn't too red from the heat.

Connor's grin when he sees me suggests I'm doing something right.

"Care to join me?"

"I guess there's time for a quick splash. But I'm going into town with the Sadler siblings. Or the ones that aren't in jail, at any rate. They insisted I invite you."

He sheds his jeans and T-shirt and slips into the bath before I can answer. For a moment, I don't speak, just revel in the heat of the water and the touch of his body as his hands glide over me.

I probably ought to decline. Tell Connor I'm tired or talk him into a night in, tell Chrissie to lay off the match-making that she's blatantly attempting, and tell Liam—for the hundredth time—that I can't be seen to be socialising with the family.

But the combination of a glamourous night out, a date with Connor, and some family time is too tempting to resist. We all need something to distract us from what's happening to Bren.

Connor and I play around in the bath then finish off laid out on towels on the bed. As soon as we've both had our fun, I jump to my feet.

"Best start getting ready. Got to look good for the clients."

I rummage in my suitcase—at some point, I'm really going to have to unpack properly—and pull out a little black dress.

"What do you think?"

Connor looks away. "I've actually brought you something to wear. Or rather, Chrissie Sadler gave me something and told me I simply had to make you wear it."

I cross my arms. "Truly, this family's respect for professional boundaries knows no bounds. How does she even know my size?"

While I whinge—half keeping up the act, half genuinely irritated at Chrissie's desire to treat me like a little doll—I can't help but smile inside at the certain knowledge that the dress is going to be a perfect fit, absolutely beautiful, and far more revealing than anything I'd buy for myself.

It doesn't disappoint. I tend to prefer floaty, billowy cuts, but this is silk, tailored close to my body, and sitting high on my thigh and low on my chest. In any normal dress like this, I'd be worried about my lumps and bumps, and about showing too much skin. But this flatters me, striking the right balance between sexy and sophisticated. I'm never sure whether it's magic or unerring taste and a unique understanding of the female body that allows Chrissie to pick and create such perfect outfits.

I sit and do my hair and make-up, while Connor changes into a suit he'd also packed into the dress bag. With him watching me appreciatively, I couldn't use magic to help the process along even if I wanted to risk it.

There's a cursory knock at the door, and then Liam and Chrissie fling it open and stroll inside.

I try to imagine how I'd react if they were really just my latest client's siblings, but I'm too excited at seeing them all dressed up to put on much of a performance.

"Why, Miss Elner, don't you scrub up well?" Chrissie says, grinning and perching herself on my dressing table. She's wearing a dress nearly identical to mine, but her hair is in an elaborate style, half twisted up do, half cascading waves.

"Colson, what are you up to with our lawyer?" Liam laughs and slaps him on the back. "Anyway, best get downstairs. Shane and Ray are waiting."

"No Leah tonight?" I ask the question cautiously. I don't want to sound like I know the family too well, but even in my Kate guise, I've met them all before. Hell, I've worked with Leah to prepare her for cross-examination. She's an odd omission.

"She's too upset about Brendan for nights out," Chrissie explains, from her perch.

"The bloody girl needs to pull herself together," Liam adds. "It's not like the rest of us aren't worried sick. But we put on a brave face and have some fun. She'll never make it as a Sadler."

"Are you sure she's not pregnant?" I ask. "Brendan said they were trying. It's in his witness statement."

Chrissie shakes her head. "Trust me, I can tell. Anyway, let's get a move on."

"Where are we actually going?" I ask.

"The Prohibition Casino," Chrissie replies, bounding off the dressing table and onto her feet, and spraying herself with my perfume.

Connor takes my arm and helps me stand. "Is that wise?"

It's a solidly Thornber establishment.

Liam grins as he opens the door and leads the way out. "It's important we get our faces seen."

The bouncer has been waving everyone in front of us through. Some with a cheery greeting, others with a quick pat down or ID check.

"No way," he says, when we reach the front. "No Sadler associates. And absolutely no Sadler family members."

Chrissie crosses her arms over her chest in a gesture of pacification. "It's been a long week. We just want to party, same as everyone else."

The bouncer shakes his head. "I'm going to have to call the manager."

My body tenses enough for Chrissie to notice, but then again, she's always been an exceptional empath. "The manager, not the owner," she whispers to me. "Don't panic. Nikki can be a bit full-on, but she's reasonable."

The bouncer mouths something into his radio. I harbour a sudden fantasy of blasting him aside with magic and storming in there. I sigh to myself. I've been back for a month. Where are these thoughts coming from?

The woman whom Gabriel had left to guard the square on the night of the Greenfire incident strides over to meet us. Tonight, her short dark hair is slicked back, and she's wearing a sharp suit and extremely dark glasses, presumably to hide all traces of the glowing eyes behind them.

She holds her hands out towards us and smiles. "Ms Sadler and her husband. Master Sadler and his sidekick. The Sadlers' favourite young enforcer. And joy of joys, the Sadlers'... lawyer. What a charming delegation."

"We just want a drink, Nikki," Liam says. "We're not looking for trouble."

"People who aren't looking for trouble don't usually travel with their legal representative in tow."

"Are you going to let us in?" Ray asks. His frame practically fills the doorway.

Nikki shrugs. "You can have a few drinks. If you want to use the gaming tables, you'll need to wear blockers. That includes her. The slightest hint of trouble—be that trying to kill someone or just mesmerising the bar staff into giving you freebies—and you're out."

"And who'll arrange that?" Shane puts his hands on his hips.

Nikki frowns. "Me, up to a point. Ably assisted by our bouncers. Though rest assured that the boss is around, too. He's having a nice, relaxing evening with a handsome young practitioner. But if things kick off, I'm sure he'll happily lay him aside and put an end to proceedings."

I glance at the others. "If Gabriel's here, I don't think we should be."

Nikki laughs. "I wouldn't worry. If you'd brought Brendan along, Gabe would probably have tried to kill him in retribution for his father, but as long as you're well behaved, he'll have zero interest in you." She looks pointedly at our little group and then her gaze settles on me. "Or in most of you, anyway."

"Are you done?" Chrissie strides forward. "I think you're overcompensating. And if *"Gabe"* wants to talk to our lawyer, he can come through us. In the meantime, we intend to have a nice evening."

Nikki steps aside with a flourish. "Then welcome to Casa

Thornber. Enjoy your evening. And do try to keep her away from the boss. He's a sweetheart really, but he can be a nightmare when he gets an idea in his head."

I've never been to The Prohibition before. Unlike The Angel, it's been around for decades, but unsurprisingly, my family never really made a habit of visiting Thornber-owned establishments.

It's lavish inside. Provincial clubs, bars, and casinos are often depressing places, trying to emulate the glamour and debauchery of a different place and time. But Mannith's magic has worked its way into the fabric of the venue. The floors are black marble. The walls are red tiles with full-length mirrors. There are no electric lights, only candles. Expensive perfume and crisp champagne scent the air. And though the clientele are mostly just local people, they are all dressed to the nines and looking the part.

"Can we have a go on the roulette wheel?" I'm excitable, like a child at a funfair. There's no trace of Kate Elner's stern demeanour as I skip through the room in my too-high heels.

"Maybe later," Chrissie replies. "You heard Nikki. If we're gambling, we'll have to wear blockers. I'm not in the mood for that. I'm in the mood for finding a table, getting some drinks, and showing we don't give a damn about the Thornbers."

She walks ahead, parting the crowd, her heels clicking on the tiles. There's a circular bar in the middle of the room, with gaming tables positioned around it.

At a pointed look from Chrissie, four people occupying prime position bar stools jump to their feet and dash away.

"Well done, Chris," Liam says, throwing himself down onto one of the stools and dragging Shane over to perch beside him.

Ray sits down, too, and Chrissie scoots up onto her husband's knee. "Connor, Kate, take a seat," he says.

I clamber on to one of the stools. All at once, my excitement at a fun night out with my family and my new lover, and my delight at the extravagance of the venue falls away, to be replaced by a sense of foreboding. I lean against Connor as subtly as I can manage. My siblings are clearly interested in a public show of strength, but I'm feeling anything but strong tonight.

"Can we get a bottle of vodka here?" Ray asks the barmaid. "And in case your manager is listening, we're perfectly happy to pay upfront."

She gives us a nervous nod and brings out an ice bucket, the bottle and some mixers, and six chilled glasses.

Ray takes a couple of photos of the room. It'll be interesting to see how many of the clientele show up in them once they're developed.

"Not a fan of people staring at you?" Chrissie asks, after we've each had a drink.

I thought I had my body language under control, but there's little point trying to hide your emotions from Chrissie, and she's right—I feel like everyone's eyes are on us, and most of them don't feel friendly.

I shake my head. "Can't we get one of those alcove tables?"

Chrissie takes a sip of vodka. "You and Connor could head over there. We'll join you once the management have got the message we're not in hiding."

Connor helps me down from the barstool and leads me past the gambling tables and over to the far corner. There's a space built into a semi-circular alcove with a table in the middle, a sofa around the outside, and some space for dancing or mingling in between. Higher up, there's a balcony recessed into the back wall, though no obvious way of reaching it. Connor waves his hand, and the party that are occupying the space all get up and leave. It's not quite within the rules Nikki set out for us, but I gratefully sink into the sofa. It feels more private here, safer.

"Do you think they left us alone deliberately?" I ask, with an attempt at a mischievous grin.

Connor smiles back. "Who knows? We're both just the staff, after all."

I don't reply. It's long past time I told the truth. This is starting to feel like more than just a fling. Thanks to his body-guard duties, we've spent a huge amount of time together since I arrived in Mannith. And whether he's driving me to court, we're enjoying a meal, or we're alone in my room, he's so sweet and easy to talk to. The sex is great, but so is his reassuring pres-ence. If this relationship—or whatever it is—is going to continue, then he needs to know who I really am. But with every day that passes, revealing that the woman he's dating—and maybe starting to develop real feelings for—doesn't actually exist seems more and more impossible. *I'll do it soon. I have to.* But I can't face doing it tonight. Connor was meant to be a bit of fun, but if he was angry—or if he walked away—it'd really hurt.

"Mind you, the Sadlers are all oddly perceptive," Connor adds, shaking me out of my guilty thoughts. "They might realise there's something going on. In which case, I guess this is one way of showing their approval."

When he says "perceptive" he means Liam's a telepath and Chrissie is an empath, on top of their general magic. I love the way he tries to tell me what's going on without mentioning anything magical. But either way, it's pretty clear my siblings do approve. Which is one more point in Connor's favour.

I'm about to say something. I'm not sure what, exactly. Not the truth about who I am—I still can't make myself. And not anything quite as dramatic as "I love you". That'd be a bit fast, and, for now at least, over-stating things. But something about how much he already means to me. About how I'd like to try to make this work—maybe not forever, but perhaps for more than just the duration of the trial. I just need to find the right words.

Before I can say anything, the sense of foreboding I've been trying to shake off since we arrived reaches a peak that leaves me gasping. I have nowhere near my sister's skill in reading the room nor my brother's skill in reading minds. But though they've honed those abilities into something special, the basics is just the usual application of magic. And however much I try to breathe deeply and tell myself I'm being paranoid, all my senses are screaming that there's something wrong.

Before I can warn Connor there's a problem, a few tough-looking men casually detach themselves from the crowd then pointedly stride towards the alcove.

Connor instantly jumps to his feet and into a fighting stance.

Within the space of a minute, we're surrounded by suited, heavily built practitioners with fire in their eyes, and those distinctive Thornber markings under their ears.

I'm already calculating three things. Can Connor hold his own? Can Liam and Chrissie see or sense what's going on? And if push comes to shove, do I dare use my magic to take them down? I've no idea if I'm strong enough, considering how out of practice I am, and attempting it would show my hand once and for all whether I succeed or fail.

Before I can reach a conclusion about any of that, one of the men blasts a ray of pure power in Connor's direction, which he smoothly deflects. At the same time, an invisibility bubble descends. I scream at the top of my lungs, but whatever else the rest of the casino are up to, they're not going to bear witness to this ambush.

The attacks come thick and fast. The Thornber stooges are throwing fists and spells at Connor in equal measure.

I'm going to be sick. I can't bear to watch this, but I can't look away. I need to help him, but the thought of using my magic to break this up makes my vision blur. I'm still in my seat, panic and horror keeping me from moving.

Connor's fighting back physically and psychically—a punch to the jaw here, a fireball there. It's all so different from the day Gabriel attacked me and put him out of action with one glance. It's terrifying to think how powerful Gabriel really is, if Connor can face down ten strong men but is vulnerable to him standing alone.

"Kate, get out of here!" Connor shouts. "Find the Sadlers."

Even more so than on the night of the Greenfire attack, it wrenches my heart to hear him use my fake name in such a genuine tone. He's clearly more worried about me than about himself, even in the face of all that violence. And in turn, I'm so worried about him that my vision's blurring.

I drag myself to a standing position and attempt to snap out of the haze that's descended. No one's attack has come anywhere near me. I ought to fight, even if that means blowing my cover and putting my neglected powers to an unwelcome test. Connor may be a Sadler acolyte in a Thornber establishment, but it's hard not to jump to the conclusion that his proximity to me is the reason for this level of violence.

"Let's watch the show from a safer vantage point." Gabriel appears out of nowhere. I flinch at the sensation of his hand on my wrist and his voice close by my ear.

Before I can reply or shrug him off, he traverses us to the balcony overlooking the alcove. It's as firmly concealed by the invisibility bubble as the alcove below.

"Get the hell off me!" I shout.

Slightly to my surprise, he lets go of me.

"What do you think? Can your protector take down ten men? Place your bet now. This is a casino, after all."

I swallow hard. "Connor has done nothing wrong."

"Connor is one of your family's top enforcers, as is his

mother. I don't need any excuses to attack him. Though I never do anything without at least two good reasons."

I step away from him to the very edge of the balcony and grip the rail as I stare at the scene below. Two of Gabriel's men have gone down, and Connor's still holding his own, but his movements are getting slower. A few of his opponents' physical blows are connecting, and some of their magical attacks are only being diverted at the last minute. He's good, but he can't be expected to pull this off alone. Where the hell are Liam and Chrissie and the rest of the group?

Gabriel strides over to join me and stands by my side, closer than politeness would allow, but carefully not touching. "The rest of your family and associates can't see through the bubble."

It's not clear whether he's answering the question because he's taken it from my head or because my thoughts are obvious from the way I'm glancing around.

"Don't be ridiculous. They're all powerful practitioners."

It's a tacit admission of who I am, but I'm past caring. Little point attempting to keep up the charade when the main person it was intended to fool clearly knows my real identity.

Gabriel shrugs. "I've put the bubble up myself. No one can penetrate it unless I let them."

Now I look closely at him, I can sense he's doing magic. Something to keep up the more powerful than usual bubble, and something else, too. Perhaps he's giving strength to his men, perhaps he's slowing Connor down. Normally, powerful magic requires a degree of concentration, and it surges out of people, impossible to miss if you know what you're looking for. But it's flowing out of Gabriel like the air he breathes, barely causing a ripple. And the entirety of his attention seems to be focused on me, while he leaves his spell to get on with whatever it's doing.

"It's anyone's guess who's going to win," Gabriel says. "But it'll go on for a while yet. Leave them to it. Sit down. Have a drink. Let's talk."

I have nothing to say to you! I want to yell it out like a heroine in a gothic novel and then run screaming from the balcony and go to Connor's aid. Not that there's an obvious exit —it's seemingly only accessible by magic. But I'm not a hysterical damsel in distress. I'm a professional, and I need answers. Besides, if it comes to it, I can probably fight Gabriel off with my magic. Unless he calls in the lien, of course. Then I'm screwed. Literally and metaphorically.

"I'll talk." It feels like abandoning Connor, which is the last thing I want to do, but there's only so much I could realistically do in a pitched battle—I win my wars with words. "No drinks, though," I add. "We both know the score on that one."

You should never accept drinks in another practitioner's house unless you trust them absolutely. It's an easy way for someone to draw you into their power. Buying drinks in the casino is safe enough, but taking a drink from the owner feels borderline at best.

"Suit yourself. Now, are you ready to drop all this 'Kate' nonsense? I've known exactly who you were from the moment you pushed back my magic in court. You don't spend six years thinking about someone every day, then fail to recognise them when they're right in front of you."

"Sorry, what?" I'd thought about him nonstop, sure. But I'd been the victim of his magic and his wiles.

"The thing about a bargain is that it cuts both ways." With one hand, he pushes my sunglasses onto the crown of my head. With the other, he removes the oversized ring that hides the twisted mark of his lien.

He nods in satisfaction at my practitioner eyes and his brand. "Like I said, I never do anything unless I have at least two good reasons. But that doesn't mean I always go about things the right way."

"Are you calling in the debt?" My legal training kicks in and allows me to make my voice as dispassionate as when I'm cross-examining someone about the details of a child's murder. "I guess it'd explain getting my bodyguard out of the way. And this impenetrable bubble and sealed off balcony."

He takes my hand and strokes the mark. "There's truly nothing I'd like more than to lay you down on that sofa and screw you till you're screaming. Then take you home to Thornber Manor, have dinner, talk, and then do it again, softly and gently this time."

Every muscle in my body tenses, and my hand burns where he touches it, like he's unleashed the Greenfire again, though he's done no such thing.

"But that's not what I'm here for tonight. Unless you particularly happen to be in the mood. And I've told you before, I'm not a monster."

"There are plenty of people who'd disagree. Everything else aside, the way you blasted me with Greenfire the other day's not exactly working in your favour. And if you're too much of a *gentleman* to use the lien, why inflict the thing on me in the first place?"

"I never said I won't use it. But, to answer your question: I put you under the lien to hurt your family, and to strengthen the connection that was already there. It wasn't a spur of the moment decision to take you back with me that night. It was half the point of the evening."

I frown and snatch my hand back. "What are you talking about? We'd never even spoken to each other before that night."

A loud cry cuts through my confusion, and I dash back to the edge of the balcony. Connor's movements are increasingly heavy. The conversation with Gabriel had almost driven away all thoughts of the danger my sort-of-boyfriend is in, which leaves me furious and guilty in equal measure.

Two more Thornber men are on the floor, but that still leaves six, and one of them has made it through Connor's defences. A blast hits his right arm, rendering it useless. It essentially means he can no longer attack and defend at the same time.

"Stop them, please," I whisper to Gabriel, who's back beside me, watching the heart-wrenching scene with mild interest like it's something in a film.

He shakes his head. "No. You stop it."

Two reasons. He clearly wanted to have this conversation in order to say his piece and make me confirm my identity. But just like with the Greenfire, he also wants to see what I can do.

During the Greenfire incident, I refused to give him the satisfaction. But that was virtual pain—Connor's sustaining very real injuries. And that was my body on the line, meaning resisting was stubborn and brave. This time, it's the body of my lover—who's also a decent man that I've lied to and put in danger. Letting him take the hit out of some mixture of self-preservation and principle is selfish and cruel.

"Be careful what you wish for, Gabriel. I've spent years trying to suppress my powers. Force me to start using them again, and one day, I might just turn them on you."

"Repression's bad for the soul," he replies.

I try to ignore him. He may be able to pour out magic with his attention on something else, but I'm out of practice, and I need to focus on the spell and nothing but the spell. But he's difficult to disregard, so close I can feel his body heat and hear his heartbeat.

Furious as I am at the way these Thornber bastards are ganging up on poor Connor, I don't want to kill anyone. Besides, if I tried anything lethal, I could just as easily hit the person I'm trying to save. But there's something I saw Dad do once, to break up a fight between two of his acolytes. The inter-section of physics and magic defies meaningful description, but in effect, you enclose a space and pull all the oxygen out of it, until everyone slumps down unconscious. Let the air back in a few seconds later, and after a minute or two, they all wake up, groggy but unharmed. At least, that's the theory.

I turn my left hand palm up, spread my fingers, and curl them in towards one another. I turn my right hand palm down and keep the fingers straight and stretched. It's a clunky way of doing things. Once, I'd have been able to throw my hand out and make my will reality. Now, I'm going through the motions like someone who's just learning.

I'm dimly aware of the fight going on down below. Connor's still standing, but he's taking more and more hits. And I'm painfully aware of Gabriel right next to me, saying nothing but watching me with a little smile.

What if I can't do it? The idea is terrifying on two levels. Firstly, because Gabriel seems so confident in my powers, there seems a good chance he'll let the fight run until it's too late. Secondly, because it's one thing to voluntarily turn your back on being special, it's quite another to have no choice but to be normal. Magic's a part of me, whether I'm using it or keeping it in check.

"Do you want a hand?" Gabriel asks. "There's no shame in being a little out of practice."

I'll show him—even if that's exactly what he wants. I visualise what I need to happen, rotate both hands a few times, throw them out and down, draw an arch to enclose the space, then pull them back towards me, drawing the oxygen with me. It's a painfully literal way of casting the spell.

Down below, the fight stops and everyone freezes in defensive stances, staring up at the balcony. Magic is flowing from me to create the airlock and towards me to pull the oxygen away. It's swirling around me, visible to anyone with any capacity to see it. This started as a carefully controlled paint by numbers spell, but it's rapidly turning into something wilder and more primal, emanating from my subconscious rather than my rational brain. It's the sort of magic Gabriel and Brendan do, the sort I used to love. My finger is glowing red from the activated brand, but it's too late to worry about that.

The men don't know quite what's hit them yet, only that they're in the grip of some sort of spell. Unlike something more lethal, oxygen deprivation takes a few minutes to kick in fully. Only the people within the bubble can see me, but they're all staring at me with universally stunned expressions. I can't hear anything they're saying through my airlock, but it seems clear the Thornber henchmen are shouting to Gabriel for help. I don't care about them though. Connor is wide-eyed with betrayal.

His expression makes my heart contract. It's too late to do the right thing and be honest with him now. If we make it out of here, all he'll see is someone whose cover was blown. He'll never believe I was going to tell him the truth. And right now, the whole situation is so chaotic that he might even believe I'm working with Gabriel—who I'm seemingly standing side by side with—and trying to hurt him. After all, my spell isn't discriminating between him and his attackers.

Somehow, though, through all the horrible emotions, I keep the magic going, wave after wave of it, out from me and back towards me. God, I've missed the high of this. Slowly, slowly, all the fighters, Connor included, sink to the floor.

I keep drawing out the oxygen. None of it seems real. I'm supposed to break the lock and let the air back in now, but the magic is beyond my control.

"That was worth waiting for," Gabriel says. "You're out of practice, but I can feel the power radiating off you. Now please don't kill ten of my men and your father's enforcer."

I snap out of my almost trancelike state. "I can't stop." I gasp out the words as though the spell's stealing away my oxygen, too.

Think rationally. Go back to basics and the painfully literal spellcasting. One hand needs to push the oxygen away from me and channel it back into the room. Some sort of pushing motion. The other needs to tear apart the airlock. A clawing gesture perhaps. But pushing seems to force more magic towards the unconscious men, and clawing seems to tighten the grip of the airlock. I can't think this through logically, and my subconscious magic is all over the place.

I clench both hands into fists and draw them towards me, gasping.

"Just breathe. It's like you've tried to run a marathon when it's years since you've done more than a fun run." Gabriel steps behind me, closes his arms around my waist, and takes a tight hold of both hands. "Your magic knows what it needs to do. Let it do it." He eases my fingers open, moves my hands away from my chest, and wraps them in his. He holds our entwined hands out in front of the two of us.

"If it comes to it, I can cut your magic off and let them breathe. I'll do it before there's any serious harm done to any of them, so don't panic. But I know you can do it yourself."

His heartbeat is slow and steady behind my back, and his breathing is deep. My heart and lungs copy his pace. And his own magic is wrapped around mine like a comfort blanket.

I visualise air in the room, the men below breathing as easily as I now am, and the barrier gone. I raise my hands a little, lifting Gabriel's at the same time, and let a fresh surge of magic rush out of me. The barrier shatters and the oxygen flies back in. Instead of stopping, my power surges again. This time, it tears the impenetrable bubble around us into shreds, and the noise of the rest of the casino surrounds us.

Gabriel guides our hands back towards my chest. He grips them a little harder, and it's like turning off a tap. He lets go of me as soon as the magic stops, but when I fall back against him, he wraps an arm around my waist. It's both an attempt at comfort and the only way to keep me standing. Never mind a marathon, I feel like I've done an Ironman Triathlon.

Down below, Connor and the others stumble to their feet, all thoughts of fighting extinguished. And attracted by the surge of magic now the protective shield is gone, Liam, Chrissie, Ray and Shane all suddenly appear on the balcony, hands raised ready for attack.

"Get your hands off my baby sister!" Chrissie screams, panic evidently making her forget I'm supposed to be undercover.

Gabriel doesn't move. I don't want him to. This is all his fault, but right now, the touch of his body and the sense of his magic are both equally comforting. I'll feel guilty about this later no doubt, but right now, there's no arguing with my lizard brain and my frenzied powers.

Liam clenches his hands into fists. "Let go of her now, Thornber, or God help me, I'll take you down. I'm not Brendan. You'd beat me in a magical duel any day. But I'd like to see you take a punch to those pretty cheekbones."

Gabriel only tightens his grip. When I asked him to let go of me earlier, he complied in seconds. He'll listen to me. But he lives for defying the rest of my family. And right now, he doesn't seem quite in control of himself. I'm certainly not. I should tell him to let go or I should tell my family I'm fine. But I can't speak any more than I can stand unaided.

The marathon metaphor was an apt one. Like exercise, using magic as a practitioner is good for you. Never do it, and you'll get weak. Do it regularly, and you'll get stronger and stronger. But work out for the first time in years, and you'll be sore afterwards. Go in too hard when you're out of shape, and you risk giving yourself a heart attack. I think I've just done the magical equivalent.

"You know the rules, Liam," Gabriel replies. "Your sister and I have a deal. And you can't attack someone for something they've done as part of a legitimate bargain."

Liam takes a step closer. He's quite evidently going to hit

Gabriel, and to hell with the consequences. And being punched by Liam with intent never ends well.

Shane closes his hand around my brother's right fist.

"Whatever you've done to her tonight has nothing to do with your twisted bargain," Shane snaps. "I'm happy to fight, and I bet the universe won't tear me in two for it."

"Same," Ray thunders. "Maybe I'm not attacking you over her. Maybe I'm upset about the fact your men jumped Connor?"

I'm upset about that, too, obviously I am. But somehow, thoughts of the attack have drifted to the back of my mind, like it happened a long time ago.

"I'll take you all," Gabriel states calmly. "Fists, knives, or magic. Bring it. There are four people who could ever match me in a fight. But Philip Sadler's past it, my mother's dead, Brendan's incarcerated, and she's passing out in my arms. Which, I hasten to add, was not my intention."

There's a flicker at the back of the balcony as Nikki transports herself into place. Her earlier supercilious composure has all but deserted her. She steps towards us.

"Gabe, let go of her, for goodness' sake." She closes the gap and puts a hand on his clenched arm.

"Nikki, get the hell out of here. They can't hurt me, but they can tear you apart."

"Bullshit. I can look after myself, just like they can. Now give her to her family, and let's go and get a drink."

Pressed up against Gabriel and encircled in his magic, I don't need the skills of an empath to sense his mood. At Nikki's words, some of the tension and determination drifts away.

I'm trying to pay attention to all the drama going on around me, but my body and mind don't want to play ball. I really have utterly drained myself through too much magic too soon. My vision blurs, and my shaky legs crumble.

"Sadie!" Gabriel drops his almost bored tone, and practically screams my name. Far from putting me down, he scoops me up into his arms. "Just keep breathing," he whispers. "Let your magic flow through you. Let it heal you. Let it grow again."

"What have you done to her?" Chrissie and Nikki ask the question in perfect sync. My sister sounds equal parts furious and terrified, while Nikki seems more shocked and curious.

"I just need a lie down," I manage to say. "And no one needs to hurt anyone."

"Here's the deal. I'm not putting her down, because she'll collapse," Gabriel states. "But I'll pass her to one of you. She burnt through too much magic too quickly. Her power outpaced her body's capacity to deal with it. One of you needs to give her some of your magic, the other needs to work some healing spells. I'd happily do both of those things, but if I started pouring dark Thornber magic into her, I suspect you really would try to kill me."

"Give her to me," Ray says.

Gabriel nods and passes me to Chrissie's husband. It probably feels like less of a capitulation than handing me over to an actual Sadler.

Liam takes hold of Ray's arm with one hand and Chrissie's hand with the other. Shane closes the circle.

It's a struggle to keep my eyes open, but I manage to glance back at Gabriel. He's staring like he might stop me from leaving after all. Nikki's got a firm hold of his arm and is frantically talking him down in a way few people would dare.

Then my family pull me out of there with magic and drop me in my childhood bedroom, where I finally give in and let myself collapse.

ELEVEN

When you wake up following a traumatic experience, you're supposed to not know where you are. But the second my eyes flicker open, it's clear that I'm truly home. Safe in the ostentatious four-poster bed that dominates my childhood bedroom, which has barely changed since the day I left, except that Chrissie's things have been moved out, though what was once her side of the room is still pink. School textbooks mixed in with hundreds of teen novels. Posters from magazines. Lots of pretty little trinkets, some of which have a magical usage, others that simply look like they do. I'm sure I can smell some shadow of my teenage perfume in the air, though that's probably just my mind playing tricks.

I'm surrounded by my family, who've dropped any pretence that I'm nothing more than their lawyer.

Chrissie has her palm flat on my forehead, trying to revive me, seeking to heal the cells my magic tore apart.

Liam has a tight grip on my wrist, and he's funnelling his own magic into my skin to replace that which I burnt through. Like when I topped up Bren, this familial magic exchange lacks most of the ritualistic nature of sharing with someone who doesn't already have bonds of blood.

Mum and Dad are at the back of the room, observing in a trancelike state.

I gently shrug off my brother and sister's hands and wriggle myself into a seated position. My muscles can barely support my weight, but the fact I can move at all is a good sign. Magical burnout is no joke. It's not something you see very often—few people exert themselves that much nowadays, particularly not from a standing start—but I was brought up on stories of people who tore themselves apart.

"I'm awake," I murmur. "Or I will be, once I've had some coffee. Strong coffee."

"Sit still, darling." Mum almost snaps the words out. "Liam, give her a little more strength, for heaven's sake."

I shake my head vigorously, which leaves me feeling dizzy. "I'm fine."

Liam freezes with his hand hovering above my arm, glancing from me to Mum and back again. Eventually, Chrissie takes his hand and lowers it, then passes me a glass of water.

I down the drink in one gulp, then give everyone a little smile.

"What the hell happened?" Dad asks, finding his voice at last.

"Exactly what I said would happen if I came back here. Gabriel-fucking-Thornber tried to call in his debt."

It's not strictly true, but I've earned a bit of melodrama.

My father punches the aqua-striped wall. "That bastard. We should have killed him years ago. And where was Colson while all this was going on? I don't know what I pay him for."

I sit up straighter still, trying against all the odds to give the impression of health and wellbeing. "It's not his fault. He was ambushed. Ten against one. And he did a pretty good job of holding his own."

My father just frowns.

"Is he okay?" I force the words out when the silence drags on too long.

I should have asked the second I woke up. All the worry and horror comes flooding back, until I think I'm going to pass out again. Ten against one, indeed. Ten vicious practitioners who were out for blood. And one utter bastard who was controlling them.

"He's in better shape than you," my mum replies. "He needed a fair bit of healing, but it was only physical. None of the burnout that's hit you."

"Can I see him?"

Mum shrugs. "Why not? I guess if Gabriel-fucking-Thornber knows who you are, along with half the Thornber casino, there's not much point trying to keep up that London lawyer performance. You might as well start acting as one of the family."

"So, should I bow?" Connor's expression is blank. He's attempting to frame the words as a light-hearted joke, but there's anger behind them.

He ought to be a wreck, but there are no obvious signs of broken bones and black eyes—his condition is testament to the power of magical healing. But there's a potent mixture of exhaustion and fury in his body language, which the restorative spells used on him haven't quite managed to tackle. He's all slumped shoulders, tensed muscles and bloodshot eyes. And his aura is churning through the colour spectrum.

"Sit down. It's still me. There's no need to treat me any differently."

He sits on the electric-blue inflatable chair by the bed (*ah, teen décor*), but his entire body is visibly stiff. "How could I possibly not treat you differently? You're a Sadler. You're my boss's daughter. You're a powerful practitioner."

"None of that makes any difference."

"Then why didn't you tell me?"

"I didn't tell anyone. Only the immediate family knew. It seemed safer that way. And then when things got that bit more serious, I wanted to tell you, but I could never find the right moment."

"Then how did *he* know?"

"Spies? Scrying? Those demonic powers he's supposed to possess? It's not like I cosied up to him and told him who I was while keeping it from you."

Connor drops his head into his hands. "Look, Kate... Sadie, I mean. It's pretty depressing that neither you nor Mr Sadler trusted me enough to tell me the truth, but I can live with that. It was a family decision for your own safety."

"Then what's left you looking angry enough to punch another hole in the wall beside the one Dad made?"

"Firstly, how the hell was I meant to know how to protect you properly if I didn't know? Gabriel Thornber's focus on you makes sense now. But at the time, it was a load of random events I couldn't predict."

I think of Connor frozen in place while I was blasted with Greenfire, then attacked and surrounded in the casino so Gabriel could prove some sort of point to me. None of it was fair on him. But would knowing who I was have made any difference? Perhaps he'd simply never have allowed me outside the house.

"I should have guessed something was up. Intimidating your rival's lawyer makes some sense, but there was something so all-consuming about it. The way he toyed with me when I was with you. *She belongs to me.* I thought it was part of his usual crazy posturing. But I understand now."

I shake my head. "There's nothing to understand. It *is* just his crazy posturing."

"There were rumours when you left. I was too young to be entrusted with any details, but I still heard the stories. The Sadlers' youngest daughter and Gabriel Thornber."

There's real anger in his voice now, and a scorn in his expression that I can't bear to see from someone who was looking at me so sweetly a few hours ago.

"You sold your soul, Sadie. And he's not forgotten."

Though I'm still shaky, I force myself to my feet. "I didn't sell my soul, Connor, I sold my body and my magic. I've never paid up, and I only made the promise to save Bren. Just like I'm putting everything on the line for my brother now. So don't you dare look at me like I'm some sort of traitor, some sort of whore. Everything I've ever done has been for my family."

Connor stands, too. "And what about screwing me? Was that for the family? How could you possibly put me in that position?"

"What position is it you find so distasteful? On your hands and knees behind me, or on your back with me astride you?"

I'm not helping the situation. But there's something in his expression that makes me want to be anything but rational and constructive.

"You let me sleep with you, let me care about you, without telling me who you were. At best, you were messing with my heart and my head. At worst, you could have got me fired. Tortured. Killed. Whether at the hands of your over-protective father—who happens to be both my boss and the king of this town—or at the hands of Gabriel Thornber, who's an utter psychopath, unspeakably powerful, and seemingly convinced that you're his property."

"You're completely over-reacting. Dad would never hurt someone for caring about me. And I've no idea what Gabriel would or wouldn't do, but I'm not responsible for him."

Connor laughs, and it's one of the worst sounds I've ever heard. "You know *your daddy*, but you know nothing about *Philip Sadler*. Sleeping with his lawyer on duty was pushing the boundaries, but something he could let go. Neither sleeping with his daughter nor letting the enemy get to her are remotely forgivable."

I reach out to touch his arm, but he jerks out of my reach. "I'm sorry not to have told you. And to have started something while I was forced to lie. But don't worry. Dad will listen to me. You'll be fine."

He shakes his head. "I'm sure you've got the boss as thoroughly wrapped around your little finger as I was. I probably *will* be fine. It doesn't make up for lying to me, for using me, for walking me into danger."

"I'm sorry." What else can I say?

"You can find another bodyguard. If you even need one—your magic's probably stronger than anyone's. And you can damn well find another toy to play with. But you're deluded if you think you can manipulate Thornber like you've manipulated me and live to tell the tale."

With that, he storms out of the room, seemingly too angry to even use magic.

I spend the rest of the day in bed. It's hard to tell whether my exhaustion is due to the physical after-effect of magical burnout, unhappiness about Connor—I can't believe I've blown things with him—or worry about Gabriel. Maybe it's all three.

As though they can sense my mood—which, thanks to Chrissie, they probably can—the family leave me well alone, other than popping in with occasional coffees and biscuits.

The next morning, I force myself to get up and put a brave face on things. A quick glance in the full-length mirror that dominates the hallway outside my room shows that I'm paler than ever and my hair's regaining some of its natural frizz. I can't summon the energy to tackle either issue. Or to do anything about the fact that my irises are still tinged with red.

Mum's the only one around, and she's busy in the kitchen, starting the preparation for the immutable tradition of Sunday lunch. As soon as I walk in to join her, there's a knock at the door. I glance at Mum, and when she nods, I go to open it.

I smile when I see who's waiting outside. "John! Good to see you. It's been years." It's nice not to have to pretend to be someone I'm not.

"Lovely to see you, too, miss. Just dropping off the weekly offering."

He hands me a wicker basket, which I take with thanks. "Do you want to come in? Get a cup of tea? Or something stronger?"

"I'll be on my way, miss. Give your mother my regards."

He dashes away as though he's scared one of us will turn him into a frog if he lingers too long. I'd almost forgotten about the weekly offerings. It's strange, the things you do and don't remember after a long time away.

Every Sunday morning, John Rose, a local chicken farmer, brings us a bird for a Sunday roast. Likewise, every Friday, Peter Mound, a local pig farmer, brings us sausages and bacon for a Saturday morning fry-up. In return, once each season, the family blesses their farms and their animals. There are no lien marks here, and no money changes hands. It's a much more old-fashioned approach, and the tradition goes back through goodness knows how many generations of Mounds, Roses, and Sadlers. All of the farms beneath the Dome get a good harvest, aside from those rare instances where my family has seen fit to curse one of them. But those that are given our special attention produce meat that tastes like nothing else on earth. Especially when it's then cooked by my mum.

"I've got a chicken for you," I call through.

"Bring it in, then help me chop some vegetables. I'm making the batter for the puddings."

Mum makes Sunday lunch by hand, rather than with the aid of spells. It's a point of pride. But something of her natural magic always seems to infuse proceedings. Her Yorkshire puddings rise so high they seem to defy the laws of physics. Her chickens are tender inside with perfectly crisp skin.

I busy myself chopping carrots and peeling potatoes. It's surprisingly restful. I've grown far too reliant on ready meals and takeaways in London. Mum says nothing about the events of last night or the trial.

At some point, Liam, Shane, and Dad return from the football. Mannith won, thank goodness, which means they're all in a cheerful mood.

Chrissie, Ray, and the little twins appear soon afterwards, and my sister helps with the final preparations. My family's generally pretty equal opportunities, but there's something about Sunday lunch that really brings out the gender roles.

After what feels like hours of cooking, we all gather around the huge table where two former front rooms have been knocked into one oversized dining room. I've been known to eat at award-winning fancy restaurants in London on occasion, but between the enchanted meat, Mum's skills, and the sense of family, it's the most delicious meal I've had in a long time.

Once the washing up's done, I attempt to head back up to my bedroom, but Chrissie takes my arm.

"Now your cover's blown, we don't have to mess around pretending you're not one of the family. And that means we can have a proper night out. Mum's on babysitting duty, and I've got just the thing in mind to cheer you up."

I frown at her. "We tried the whole night out thing on Friday. Look where that ended up."

Chrissie laughs. "That was us taking our lawyer out. Not us taking our sister out."

"But Gabriel—"

She places one of the toddlers carefully on the floor, sits down on a stool and crosses her arms. "Firstly, you are not living your life in fear of that dickhead. Secondly, I know for a fact he won't be where we're going, because the only person in the world he'll listen to will have told him to stay away."

"And where is that?"

Liam walks in wearing a tracksuit, grinning. "My fight, of course."

I shiver. "I'm not sure watching my brother get punched in the face repeatedly will help my nerves."

Liam shakes his head. "Have some faith. I'll win, I promise."

Chrissie shoos Liam out, then descends on me. "Shower. Now. Then I'm getting you ready."

"Manually or magically?" I drag myself to the door with exaggerated slowness, putting on a show.

"Whichever makes you look the most stunning. Now move it."

There are a lot of bathrooms in the house. The fact that it had originated as an entire row of terraced houses makes for a huge array of rooms, a massive garden out back, and a charmingly disjointed vibe.

I head for the largest bathroom, created in what had once been a master bedroom in one of the houses towards the left-hand side of the row. There's a bath I can lay out full length in, and I suspect even Liam could do the same. It's always been used for both long luxurious soaks and purification rituals. There's also a walk-in shower with a dinner plate showerhead and jets on the walls, which I choose in the interests of time. There are many things my parents don't believe in spending money on. But when it comes to things they think are worthwhile, like their cars and their clothes—or in this case, their bathrooms—they go all out.

One of the things Mum definitely *doesn't* believe in

spending money on is expensive toiletries. I use some home-made concoction which, to be fair, probably smells better than anything sold in a little boutique.

I linger under the hot water for ten minutes, then wrap myself in a towel and wander back to my bedroom, feeling slightly more alive.

Chrissie is in there waiting for me. "Right, sit. First things first, I'm removing any lingering traces of your disguise. I want you looking exactly like my sister again."

She waves her hand in a spiral over my head, and judging by her satisfied smile, I'm back to my old self.

Chrissie hands me a copy of *Vogue*. "Flick through. Pick a dress and some shoes. It's tempting to choose for you, but I'm trying not to be too much of a control freak."

I grin as I open the magazine. I'm not that interested in high fashion, but I always enjoyed this game as a teenager.

"That one," I say eventually.

It's longer and looser than anything Chrissie would have picked out for me if left to her own devices, but the emerald lace is still pretty sexy, and my sister nods approvingly.

"Stand up. Towel off."

I do as she orders. I've never really felt naked in front of Chrissie, and though it's been years, there's still no awkwardness. She scrutinises my body like a sculptor inspecting a block of marble, then looks away and stares at the picture in the magazine as though she's trying to see through it. She puts one hand on the picture and one hand on my collarbone, then closes her eyes, clearly concentrating hard.

I shut my eyes, too. When I open them, I'm wearing a perfect replica of the dress, cut to fit my body, and Chrissie is smirking in triumph.

"Okay, that's pretty impressive," I say.

"I know. Now sit down and let me sort your hair and make-up."

She drags her fingers through my hair in a complex pattern. Each time she reaches the bottom, it grows by about an inch. She continues until my shoulder length locks are almost down to my waist.

"That's enough of the magic for now," Chrissie says, plugging in some tongs. "I prefer to do this bit by hand."

I relax as she methodically waves my hair.

"Should I invite Connor tonight?" Chrissie asks, as she twists yet another strand around the heated barrel.

I attempt to shake my head, but she holds it firm. "It's definitely over now. He's right—I never should have lied about who I was while I was sleeping with him."

A pang of sadness goes through me when I think about Connor's anger and pain. Hopefully we can try again in a few weeks' time, when he's had time to calm down. I think he could forgive me and might like to make another go of it. But if I attempt to contact him too soon, he'll probably never speak to me again.

Chrissie raises her eyebrows. "So you did get together? I wasn't sure. I still think of you as my sweet, innocent baby sister."

"And I still think of you as a wild thing, when you're a happily married mum of two. It's scary how things change."

"I still like to flirt, but it doesn't mean anything. From the moment I met Ray, deep down, I wasn't interested in anyone else."

"The whirlwind Jamaican holiday romance."

She smiles. "Something like that. Ray's family have a similar set-up to us. A domed village in the Blue Mountains, with loads of factories in Falmouth and hotels in Montego Bay. They're all very strong practitioners, and they were seeking an alliance. Then his sister had a vision of me."

"Are you saying it was a fated marriage?"

Traditionally, practitioners tended to believe there was one person in the world who was right for every other person. If you were lucky, someone would have a premonition and discover who was meant for you. Sometimes, they'd be next door neighbours. Other times, they'd live on the opposite side of the world. Either way, you pretty much had to track them down and make them yours.

Chrissie laughs. "Kind of. Mum persuaded me to go and meet him. She wouldn't have forced the issue if we hadn't hit it off and neither would his mother. But his sister was sure we were right for each other. And from the moment we set eyes on each other, it was obvious it was true."

I smile outwardly at the romantic story, but the fact it's the first time I'm hearing the details makes me sad. I was right to stay away from Mannith all these years, but I could have made a better attempt to stay in touch.

"I guess I need to find my Ray," I say, as Chrissie finishes with my hair and steps around me to make me up in a far more elaborate way than I could ever manage. "Maybe tonight's the night?"

I say it to drive the serious look off my sister's face. Deep down, I know I'll never have a vision of some fated, perfect partner and neither will anyone ever dream of me. Even if Connor does forgive me, it'll never last. I was ruined for love the moment that mark appeared on my finger.

"Today, there's no skulking around. There's no apologising for our presence. There's no pretending Sadie is our lawyer. Tonight, the Sadlers are on the town, and we are making a spectacle of ourselves."

It's a rather dramatic statement for Liam. More the sort of thing Bren would say, were he here. In his absence, Liam has seemingly appointed himself family spokesperson.

Chrissie could not have done a better job with me. The green dress is as perfect as my hair and make-up. She's fashioned something similar for herself, only in black, which is striking against her ultra-pale hair. Shane and Ray, in tuxedos, look just as glam as the pair of us. Liam, on the other hand, is channelling a rather different, but no less impressive, aesthetic, in athleticwear and a T-shirt that shows off his biceps, ready for his fight.

"I wish Bren was here," Shane says. "If only to draw a picture of us all dressed up."

I agree. I also can't help but wish I'd swallowed my pride, tried again to apologise to Connor, and let Chrissie invite him along.

"Is anyone else tempted to traverse straight into the middle of the arena?" Ray asks, grinning.

"How about we compromise by landing in the reception area?" Shane suggests. "There's something to be said for a bit of subtlety."

Everyone nods. Outside the Dome, no practitioner would use their powers so publicly. But in Mannith, everyone knows about magic, and if anything, we like to remind people of our powers. Remind them who they have to thank for their blessings.

"You okay to do this?" Chrissie asks.

"Have a bit of faith."

We land in perfect sync in the entrance to Mannith Hall, a Victorian building built in the gothic revival style and used for everything from wedding receptions to political gatherings. A few people stare. It's not clear whether they've noticed our unnatural mode of entrance or know us by reputation.

Liam gives me an appraising glance. "Sadie. Straight back.

Long and confident stride. Arrogant smile. You're a Sadler again, and we have a reputation to uphold."

I nod and attempt to mimic Chrissie's posture and expression. We all link arms and stride into the main room, pretending not to notice everyone's eyes on us.

The room has stone walls, a high ceiling, and large, paned windows. Today, the space is dominated by a boxing ring in the centre, with about fifty round tables, each seating ten people, arranged around it in concentric circles.

Liam leads us to one close to the ring. "Sit down. I need to go and prepare. I'll come over and say hi before the fight."

"I'll go and order some drinks," I say, gesturing to the bar along the back wall.

I try to swagger to the bar in my best imitation of my siblings' style, but I'm conscious of their worried eyes on my back.

There's a wait at the bar, but people can't get out of my way quickly enough. It's unclear whether they know who I am or just who my associates are. Within seconds, I'm at the front, waiting only for a female couple ahead to be served.

The woman on the right is distinctive even from the back—taller than most men, near-black hair cropped close to her face, powerfully built shoulders showing through her cocktail dress—but it's not until she turns round that I recognise her.

"Are you okay to take the drinks back to the table, babe?" Nikki says, speaking to her companion but staring at me.

The other woman nods. I can't tell whether I've met her before or not. She's one of those generic blondes that always swarm around Gabriel, with a little bit of power and a lot of hair. Nikki gives her a peck on the lips, then the woman scoops up an ice bucket full of champagne and several glasses and disappears from sight.

I glance around as subtly as I can and ready my internal defences.

"He's not here," Nikki says. "Though I'll tell him you were looking for him. It'll make his night."

What are the odds of her attacking me on Gabriel's behalf? Should I fire first? I glance up at her face to check her uncovered eyes aren't going any particularly deadly colours. They emphatically are not. Her irises are brown and a regular size. And her pupils are round.

"Hang on. Your eyes. So you're not..."

Nikki narrows those unremarkable eyes. "And here I heard you were a nice person underneath it all. I'd have thought a little London lawyer would understand about respecting people's identities? Besides, the last person who claimed I wasn't a practitioner because I don't have mood-ring eyes got a fireball to the chest for their pains."

I can't help but smile at 'mood-ring eyes'. I'm more relieved than ever that mine are hidden away behind sunglasses.

To underline her point, she methodically draws fire into her palms. Her lips whisper the words, and her hands make the shapes. It's very slow compared to the way I'd do it, but impressive, nonetheless.

"You're a Learnt Practitioner."

It isn't a term that gets used very often. Most people tend to prefer the more offensive alternatives. But Nikki's right. I've always done my best to avoid all of the more human prejudices and to be a good ally on a variety of fronts. The least I can do is check my magical privilege and put my family's outdated views on witchcraft to one side.

I strongly believe in the principle that magic isn't some rarefied thing that lives in chosen people's blood, but a science like any other, capable of being learnt. But accepting the theory is different to talking to the sort of person my father constantly sneers about, and attempting to be polite.

"If we have to draw a distinction at all, I prefer the term *Taught* Practitioner," she adds. "It's more accurate in any case."

I frown. It's not quite clear why we're having this conversation or exactly where it's going, but Nikki doesn't seem like she's planning to attack me, and deep down, I'm just bigoted enough to believe I can stop her if she tries. Besides, this is oddly fascinating.

"Really? Who taught you?"

Learnt Practitioners are a relatively common phenomenon. They find the right books or dig deeply enough on the internet, and come to understand that magic's real. And then they dedicate their lives to learning individual spells, one at a time, step by step. It's rare they find one of us though. And when they do, they tend to be overawed, and we tend to be underwhelmed.

The idea of a Taught Practitioner is altogether older. Basically medieval. Masters and apprentices and all that. Seven years of study. But even then, it tended to be those who were at least vaguely of the blood. A practitioner grandmother who'd fled from her family, that sort of thing.

It was presumably what Chris, my ill-fated date back in London, had convinced himself the London Coven would do for him, but he was deluded. Nikki, on the other hand, has got the firepower to back up her proclaimed identity.

"Who taught you?" I ask again, when she stays silent.

"Who do you think?"

"Are you joking?" There's only one person she can mean, and it hardly seems likely.

"After my parents moved here, I grew up in one of the cottages adjacent to Thornber Manor. I befriended Gabe when we were about five and both lonely, only children. It didn't take long for me to realise there was something different about him, and it didn't take long for him to start to show me how to be different, too."

"Forgive me if I find this a little hard to get my head around. Gabriel Thornber does not strike me as the sort to take a human girl under his wing and teach her magic."

"Believe it. Though to be fair, he didn't do much of the actual instructing himself. He's an awful teacher. It was more a case of strong-arming all his wide-eyed acolytes into helping out."

I smile. That sounded marginally more like it. "Awful teacher how?"

"Not the way you're smugly imagining. Let's try a little experiment. That night Gabe unleashed the Greenfire on you, he seemed sure you could have fought back, and he's rarely wrong about that sort of thing. You only didn't break his hold on you because you wanted to prove a point. But say you had wanted to turn it back on him. How would you have done it?"

I wave my arms about indiscriminately, trying to put something that's utterly instinctive into words. "You know. Sort of squash the fire down. Throw it away from you. Direct it towards your opponent."

Nikki smiles. "If you asked a Learnt Practitioner, they'd say something like '*You have to form your hands into the shape of protection. Chant words of reversal in your head. Wear an ice crystal.*' And then they'd spend hours teaching you the shapes and the words or showing you their charms.

"If you asked your average Born Practitioner, they'd tell it differently. They'd say you had to imagine a bubble around yourself. You'd have to breathe steadily and convince yourself that neither the fire nor the pain was real and then will the fire away. Perhaps using the words or signs or charms at the margins to help your focus.

"The night it happened, I asked Gabe the opposite question: how can I create Greenfire? He looked bemused by the question. '*Just summon it and throw it at your opponent.*' And that's basically the same answer you've just given, in reverse. I saw it at the casino, too. You started with hand signs and things. By the end, you were dragging magic out of the air.

"Magic's barely a conscious thing for people like you and

him. It flows through you, and you direct it where you want. And that's why he was hopeless at teaching me himself. It wasn't something he'd had to learn or something he could really explain."

I shake my head. "Magic's overrated. Most of the time, I try not to use it."

"Then you're a fool who doesn't know what she has and how lucky she is. And that's true of a lot of things with you."

"What's that supposed to mean?"

"Never mind. The point is, I don't care what you or anyone else thinks. The only person whose opinion I give a damn about is my best friend's. And he's happy enough to regard me as a practitioner, without any caveats."

She sweeps back her hair where it falls just past her ears in order to show me the mark below her right lobe. It's the star and heart symbol that Gabriel brands on all his most trusted lieutenants, but the extra little stars all around it presumably mean she holds some rarefied position in his organisation. Whatever else she is, she must be seriously reliable and entirely capable of looking after herself while spells are flying.

All that aside, I'm not sure whether it's the mark itself or her smug reaction to it, but it's all hitting a little too close to home.

So I do something I never voluntarily do. I hold out my right hand and slip off my oversized ring. "Don't act like it's a badge of honour. Anyone can get themselves branded."

Nikki lets her fire fade away, then takes my hand for a closer look and runs her middle finger over the swirls that encircle my ring finger.

I close my eyes. "If you're such a good friend of his, I presume you know about the lien he imposed on me. So don't try to tell me with a straight face that he's some perfect gentleman."

By the time I open my eyes again, Nikki looks a little like she's about to cry, which I can't imagine happens very often.

"He told me all about it at the time. Though, seeing the actual mark is a bit different from hearing about it all in the abstract. Not exactly his finest moment, I'll admit."

I'm saved from responding to that under-statement of the year by the arrival of Liam, who's changed for the fight into shorts and a silky dressing gown. He throws an arm over my shoulder, clearly delighted at no longer having to pretend I'm just a professional contact.

"Nikki."

"Liam."

I slam my ring back on before my brother can see the mark and work himself up into a righteous fury.

"My money's on you, Nik."

"Likewise."

"Not brought your boss along for moral support tonight then?"

"I've banned him from watching my fights, as you well know. He gets far too emotionally involved. And he's not exactly the most calming presence. What about you? Not brought your delightful big brother along for back-up? Oh wait, I guess that's not an option anymore."

Despite the verbal sparring, there's an odd friendliness to the exchange, two people who obviously respect and like each other.

"Who needs Brendan when I've got my sister? Sadie would give him a run for his money any day, if she'd only let herself off the leash."

Nikki looks me up and down. "I don't doubt it for a second. You people barely notice magic, it's so commonplace for you. But I can sense it. And it pours off her. Just like him."

I'm not sure which 'him' she means. Gabriel or Brendan.

"Can we get a drink, Liam?" I can't bear another minute of this conversation.

"Sure. Just water for me till my rounds are over. But you look like you could use a gin or two."

Nikki waves a hand over herself until she's standing there in shorts and a sports bra. I'd never burn through magic for something that would take two minutes to accomplish by more conventional means, but I guess it's a point of pride for her, particularly in front of us. "And I'd better get ready for my fight. But once I get home, I'll be sure to mention to Gabe that you were asking about him."

I steer Liam away before he can ask any difficult questions. The server gives him his drinks gratis. Heavens knows whether it's competitor perks or the family name. Either way, I down the gin in one.

There are a few matches to get through before it's time for Liam's fight. I watch the first two with detached interest, focusing most of my attention on sipping my drinks, chatting to the family, and watching the crowd. Though I can't help flinching at particularly vicious punches. Ray takes pictures that would put a professional sports photographer to shame. If only he could capture us on camera.

When it's time for Nikki's fight—the only female match of the night—my interest peaks. I stop short of cheering her on, on the grounds that would basically be treason, but I can't help a smile when she wins on points, with no magic involved. Raucous cheering emanates from the table of her girlfriend and other Thornber associates.

Then it's Liam's turn, and suddenly, the whole thing seems more real. Less a fun sporting event to provide a backdrop to a night of glamour, more a battle in which my brother could get hurt. I put down my gin and sip some water to quash the rising fear-induced nausea.

For the first few seconds, I close my eyes. When I force them open, Liam seems to be holding his own. Without my mind's conscious intervention, I'm on my feet, cheering and screaming along with the rest of my family. It's like something more primal has taken over my usually reasonable brain.

The rounds go by in an absolute blur as I shout myself hoarse. At some point, the referee gives Liam the victory by technical knockout, and I sink back into my chair, as exhausted but exhilarated as if I'd fought myself.

Liam comes over and we all hug him tightly, despite him being a sweaty and slightly bloody mess. For the first time since my return—for the first time in years, really—I feel like a part of the family again.

TWELVE

The next morning, the weekend's over and it's time for court. It's fair to say my preparation has been somewhat limited.

At nine AM, there's the usual knock at my door. In the ten seconds it takes me to slick on a last coating of lipstick and grab my bag, my mind races through all the different things I want to say to Connor. Apologise. Demand *he* apologises. Be staunchly professional, like there'd never been any relationship or any argument. Be flirtatious as hell.

But when I push the door open, there's a stocky middle-aged guy standing there. I fight to hide my mingled relief and disappointment, while I focus on trying to retrieve his name from the reaches of memory. He'd always been around in the background when I was a kid, albeit he'd looked rather younger then.

"Hi, Jack," I manage eventually.

He nods solemnly. "Miss Sadler. Your father says I'm to keep an eye on you from now on."

I nod. I daren't ask about Connor.

We head straight downstairs, but before we can leave, a

woman who's drinking coffee in a corner of the bar beckons me over. "Miss Sadler, could I speak privately?"

She's about my age and I vaguely recall her from teen years. We were never particularly close, but we were in some of the same classes at school, ended up at some of the same parties, that sort of thing. Nice girl, from what I remember.

I've seen her around in The Windmill a few times over the last few weeks, too, but I've kept myself to myself, and Chrissie's disguise was enough to keep old acquaintances at bay. I wrack my brain for a name. *Becca*, I establish eventually.

I walk over to her. "Call me Sadie, please. What's up?"

She glances nervously at Jack.

I turn to him. "Could you give us a moment?"

"I'm not meant to let you out of my sight. But Ms Wellburn is a well-regarded acolyte, so I suppose there's no harm in it. She works directly for your older brother."

He waves everyone but the two of us outside, then goes to stand by the door, far enough away that he shouldn't be able to overhear the conversation, close enough to launch into the defensive mode the second anything untoward occurs.

Once we have some privacy, I sit down opposite her on a wooden chair. "Go on then, Becca." Close to, I can feel her magic. It's not as spectacular as Bren's—or indeed, Gabriel's—but it's strong and steady.

She smiles at the fact I've remembered her name, then starts to twist her hands together.

"It feels disloyal to tell you this. There was no way in hell I was going to mention it to a random lawyer. But once I heard about who you really were—I can't believe I didn't recognise you, by the way—I thought you ought to know. I came here this morning specifically to catch you at a quiet moment."

"If this is something relevant to the case, you need to tell me. The more I know, the more I can help."

"The night Niall Thornber was killed, Bren was in here.

Late on. Well past the time he claims he was out at Summer Hill with Leah. And it's just like those witnesses said. He was in a weird mood. Barely talking to anyone, then making random threats when he did."

I go cold and have to grip the little round bar table for support. I'm still convinced the witnesses are some combination of bewitched, blackmailed, or mistaken. But Becca is self-evidently too strong a practitioner to be mesmerised, and from what Jack said—not to mention the fact she's sitting cheerily in this Sadler stronghold—she's too loyal a supporter of the family to give in to Thornber threats, and too close to Bren to be confused about his identity or to lie about this.

"How many people saw him?"

Becca gestures around the bar room. "Everyone. But don't worry, no one will say a word. We all love your brother in here. Love your whole family. I don't know if Bren killed him—he certainly didn't inform me of any plans to do so, and he's usually pretty open—but if he did, I'm glad. I just wish he'd killed his son, too."

I shiver at her tone. Could Bren have killed Niall Thornber? On some level, I don't care that much if he did, which amply demonstrates the way that being back home is skewing my judgement. But I damn well care if he's lying to me about it.

I take a few calming breaths then touch Becca's shoulder as reassuringly as I can manage. "Thanks, Becca. It might just be confusion about timings, but I can only present a good case if I have the whole picture."

"Please don't tell him I told you."

"Of course not."

"By the way... maybe we could get a drink some time, catch up?"

I nod. "That'd be nice. I need to stay focused on the case for now, but once it's done, I'd love to."

It's coming back to me now. Becca was more than a random

acquaintance. We hung out loads, in small groups or even one to one. It's like I've blocked out half my teen years for self-preservation. She was that bit quieter and more thoughtful than a lot of people in Mannith. Less obsessed with making herself look like a cut-price version of Chrissie or chasing after Bren—indeed, even now, though she's wearing a nice summer dress, she looks a bit dowdy by Mannith standards, with her mid-brown hair and her un-made-up face.

Even in the unlikely event she would be willing to lie to the Sadlers in general, I really don't think she'd lie to me. But what does that mean as far as Bren's concerned?

"See you soon," I say, dashing for the door.

Jack and I drive to the court in silence.

My quiet is partly because Jack and I have nothing much to say to each other. I miss Connor, and I still can't quite believe I've blown it. Partly, it's because Becca's claims are churning through my mind, difficult to explain away convincingly. But it's predominantly because I'm all too aware of what's coming today.

On arrival, just like on the first day, I barricade myself in the bathroom to get changed. It seems to take forever to change into my court uniform. I fiddle endlessly with my wig and retie my ribbon three times. When I'm finally more or less satisfied, I stay there and perform a core meditation. It's not the greatest place in the world to sink my mind into the earth, but we're close enough to Mannith that I do it with ease. Then I stride into the courtroom, head held high.

I zone out while I wait for proceedings to start, deliberately avoiding eye contact with anyone, be they friend, foe or casual observer.

After what feels like an age, Imran stands up and calls the

final witness for the prosecution. I clench every muscle in my body as Gabriel takes the stand.

He's dressed rather more conservatively than usual today, wearing a plain black two-piece suit with a dark blue tie rather than his usual waistcoats, pinstripes, and flashes of colour. His sometimes wild hair is ruthlessly slicked back and—somewhat recklessly in the circumstances—he's neither wearing sunglasses nor has a pair perched on his head. He's clearly decided that looking smart, respectable, and conventional is more important than avoiding people seeing his eyes.

Gabriel's testimony will be absolutely key. All the other witnesses' evidence has been mostly circumstantial and there's no CCTV or DNA to work with. But he claims to be an eyewitness.

Imran clears his throat. "What were you doing on the night of 15th June?"

Gabriel leans forward in the stand, head bowed. The perfect image of a mourning son forced to relive horrific memories. A terrified, traumatised witness, not a cocky liar driven by revenge.

"I was at home. Dad and I had dinner. Steak and ale pie. Then he went to bed, and I started getting ready for a night out."

His voice is shaking, his words hesitant. I've never heard the slightest hint of nerves from him before. It's presumably an act, but I'm not entirely sure.

"And then?"

"I was in my room. I heard the front door open, and someone come in and go up the stairs. Not making a scene, but not really making any attempt to disguise their presence either."

I'm holding my breath and it feels like the whole court is doing the same. I'm staring at him, but for once, he's paying me no attention. He's looking from Imran to the judge to the jury, sucking them into his words.

"How did you react?"

"We weren't expecting anyone, so I grabbed a knife. Stepped into the corridor. I saw the defendant heading for my father's room. I called out. He made a run for it. I chased him, but he wasted no time. No drama, no hesitation, no panic. Straight into my father's room. Shot him through the chest as I came through the door."

His voice cracks on the last few words. The public gallery gasp in horror like they're at a theatre production.

"And then?"

Imran has to keep asking gently prompting questions in order to justify his fee, but there doesn't seem much need. Gabriel's on a roll. He'd quite clearly perform an hour-long monologue if left to his own devices.

"I've always thought of myself as someone who'll stand and fight, but I simply froze. Nothing made any sense. Blood was cascading out of my father's body. Brendan stood there, still holding his old revolver, just as still as me, as though he was in shock at what he'd just done."

Witnesses are supposed to stick to a cold recital of the facts, not this sort of melodrama. The lawyer is supposed to ensure they do so, and if they don't, the judge should step in. He's not actually mesmerising them, but they both seem too enchanted to intervene.

I force my eyes away from Gabriel's magnetic face and check in on my brother. I'm still not one hundred per cent sure whether or not Bren murdered Niall Thornber, but from his clenched jaw to his equally clenched fist, he looks more than capable of murdering the victim's son given half the chance.

"I thought he was going to shoot me, too. I'm the one he hates. I braced myself to run or to tackle him. He pointed the gun at me, looked me straight in the eye, whispered a single sentence, and then jumped out of the window before I could react."

"Did you give chase?"

He cries a single, strategic tear. "I let him go. All I cared about was trying to revive my dad. I called an ambulance, balled the sheets up and tried to stop the bleeding, gave some amateur mouth to mouth. None of it did any good. At that point, I just collapsed down on the bed next to him and cried. The next thing I knew, the police and the ambulance arrived."

"Do you need a moment, Mr Thornber?"

He shakes his head and stands up a little straighter. "I'm fine. It's just hard to talk about."

"Then can we take a step back? You said the defendant 'whispered a single sentence'. Do you recall what it was?"

The moment in which he considers the question stretches out for an eternity. He's the comedian preparing to deliver the punchline, the musician waiting for the beat to drop. *"This is for my sister."*

I glance at Bren again. He shakes his head just a fraction.

"Do you know what was meant by that?"

"Yes, but it was all a long time ago. We were in a relationship for a while. He didn't approve."

"Did you break up with her?"

"No. She left me. Moved to London. I guess she's always been the one that got away."

He doesn't look at me as he says all this nonsense, but he might as well be whispering the words into my ear.

I'm consumed by an urge to make him stop talking. My power is prickling under my skin, demanding to be let free. It's worse than the time he inflicted Greenfire on me. I force my eyes closed and try to breathe, but I can barely get standard breaths out, never mind the deep ones necessary for a core meditation. I try the opposite tack. Instead of zoning out of the room, I focus on the physical. Feel the heat of the room. Smell the sweat and the bleach. Stare at the royal crest on the back wall. That doesn't help, either.

My magic's pooling around me, visible to anyone with the eyes to see—which would include the defendant, the witness for the prosecution, and most of the people in the public gallery.

Gabriel's doing an admirable job of keeping his eyes a neutral brown, justifying his decision not to wear sunglasses. I can only assume mine are some hellish shade.

What would actually happen if I inadvertently struck him dead where he stood?

High up in the courtroom, a windowpane shatters, causing a few gasps and shrieks. My magic's filling the room, rage driving it out of control. It'll either kill Gabriel, knock me out, or destroy the building.

Gabriel finally bothers to look at me. He just raises an eyebrow, then turns away again.

A second window shatters. Even the judge, usually a model of composure, flinches this time.

I sense my father's eyes boring into my back and turn to face him. He makes determined eye contact, takes the deep breaths I can't manage, and draws the excess magic into himself. It's like he's dragging me out of a raging river. He nods in the direction of my mother, beside him and holding his hand. I turn my eyes towards her. She raises and slowly lowers her free hand like a priest offering a blessing. The remaining magic softens and stabilises.

I give them both a smile of thanks, then focus back on Gabriel. He's on marginally less triggering topics now. How high the windowsill was. How he recognised Bren. That sort of thing. It's a damn compelling performance. I'm beyond relieved when it's over.

I throw up a silence bubble the moment I get Bren alone.

"I'm going to ask you one more time. Not as your lawyer, but as your sister. Did you kill Niall Thornber?"

Bren smashes his bound hands down on the interview room's plastic table. "What, you're taking that bastard's word over mine now?"

"That bastard and his hordes of very consistent, very compelling witnesses. I wouldn't judge you. I just need to know."

And as well as all those random witnesses, someone who's a loyal acolyte of Bren himself and an old friend of mine. Who's told me in confidence and has nothing to gain by lying. But I promised Becca I wouldn't mention her name.

"Sadie! I did not kill Niall Thornber. If I was going to be stupid enough to provoke a war between the two families, I wouldn't have wasted time on the old man. I'd have killed Gabriel himself. Slowly."

I stare at the table like it contains the secrets of the universe. If my brother says he didn't do it, I should take that as gospel. But various witnesses' testimony keeps ringing in my ears.

"Both the barmaid and Gabriel claimed you were taking revenge for me. And you did once swear to do exactly that."

"I know I did. And honestly, I'm sorry I never made that vow come true. If I had, I wouldn't be hiding it from you or from anyone else. I'd be bragging about it."

"I don't care either way. I just want to know the truth. For my own satisfaction, and so I can run the case to the best of my ability."

Bren just shrugs. If he wasn't my brother, I think I could hate him at times.

"If the Thornbers are trying to frame you, those words make no sense," I continue. "Without the background about the lien, it doesn't add up. It won't sway the jury. If it's all a lie, why didn't he invent something more straightforward?"

"How slow on the uptake are you, Sadie? That little line

wasn't for the benefit of judge, jury, or anyone else. That was squarely aimed at you. Partly to make you doubt me. Partly to get under your skin. This is all a game to him. We're just pawns. You're the queen."

"Bren, I... I'm going to need more than that."

"What's that supposed to mean?"

I take an audible breath. "I want to trust you, really I do. But there's just so much evidence stacking up. I need to know for sure."

In a normal case, the last thing you want is to dig too deeply. If a client confesses to you, you can't outright lie for them. And I generally take those sorts of principles very seriously.

In this instance though, if I need to lie for Bren, I'll do it. If he killed Niall Thorner, I'll still do everything I can to get him out. But I need to know where I stand.

"You really do think I killed him. You think I'm lying to my own sister."

"I want you to let me read the truth from your thoughts."

Bren flinches like I've hit him. "Sadie! We don't do that within the family. I appreciate you've been away for a while, but you must know that's wrong."

I swallow hard. It's an effective form of magic, and it's one I'm personally particularly good at—I suspect I sometimes do a low-level version on autopilot when I'm dealing with normal clients. I certainly have a higher-than-average ability to get the truth out of people, which is handy for a lawyer. But Bren's absolutely right. My family are pretty gung-ho when it comes to principles around magic, but reading each other's minds is firmly forbidden. It's not quite as bad as using a compulsion spell or something designed to kill or maim, but everyone regards it as in the same sort of ballpark. Just asking makes me feel nauseous, never mind going through with it.

"If you want me to continue with the case, I need this."

"Fine." I expected Bren to shout, but he's quiet and

resigned. "If that's what it takes to convince you. If my word isn't good enough. If you can't trust me. Go ahead and do it."

"Bren, it isn't that I don't trust you..." The words sound hollow even to me. If I trusted him, I wouldn't do this.

I'd assumed I'd need to put all my powers of persuasion to use and spend ages explaining my reasoning. His rapid, but grudging, agreement has left me feeling like I'm in the wrong.

"Just get it over with," he replies.

I take a few deep breaths, then close the gap between us. "Thank you. In that case, let me ask you formally: may I look into your mind and seek the truth of whether or not you killed Niall Thornber and what you were doing the night he died?"

Rather like magic transfer, reading minds is something that can be done either forcefully or voluntarily. And both the magic required and the moral issues are very different depending on which you're attempting. If you're going for the consensual approach, you need to be absolutely sure you genuinely have agreement.

Bren closes his eyes and keeps his voice neutral and equally formal, though even dimmed by the force of the blocking hand-cuffs, his aura pulses with rage. "You may."

My heart pounds. I don't want to do this. Bren's been difficult to deal with, but do this and from my family's moral stand-point, I'm tipping the dynamic towards a scenario where I'm the one in the wrong.

Before I can change my mind, I place my right hand on his forehead and my left hand on the back of his neck. I close my eyes and let the magic flow.

At first, there's a pressure that almost pushes me back across the room. Some protective mechanism within Bren fighting back. I grit my teeth and steady myself and it falls away.

Though I could manage it with most people, it'd be basically impossible to do this to Bren if he were at full strength and actively resisting. But the handcuffs have dampened down his defences, and he's trying to cooperate. That little flash of defiance seems to have been mostly a reflex action.

And now I'm in his mind.

Reading minds isn't like scanning through an encyclopaedia or roaming a bookshop, reading whatever you choose. It's not even like an internet search. It's more like standing in a formal reference library and asking the efficient but grumpy librarian to find you the information you need. A librarian who'll refuse to help if you ask for too much or don't give enough precise detail and who might throw you out if you push your luck too far.

"Did you kill Niall Thornber?"

It's a question I've asked Bren several times since I've arrived, both directly and through more implicit questioning. It's a question I've asked the rest of the family on multiple occasions. And it's something I've asked myself endlessly. But now, I imbue my voice with a tone of command, safe in the knowledge that the answer I get will be the truthful one.

"No."

Bren doesn't hesitate. He doesn't caveat his answer or try to come up with something clever. He speaks the word out loud, he speaks it inside my head, and I can sort of see it in my mind's eyes, like I'm reading a binding document.

Oh. That's a relief, surely. My brother hasn't been lying to me. He didn't commit the awful crime he's been accused of. I can defend him with a clear conscience. Yet, I feel a bit empty, like I'd psyched myself up for a race then been granted the victory by default. I'd been expecting to have to be clever and careful and get the answer from him by cunning.

And deep, deep down, I was expecting the final answer to be a yes.

"Were you involved in his death in any way?"

"No."

"Who did kill him?"

"I don't know."

I bite my lip so hard it bleeds. I'm good at spotting loopholes and half-truths, but that's all pretty clear and conclusive. I ought to stop. This is a massive betrayal of trust and family bonds. But the damage is essentially done. I might as well make sure I have all the information I need.

"What were you doing the night Niall Thornber was killed?"

"I was with Leah, at Summer Hill, trying to make a baby."

I can see it all like I'm watching CCTV. The footage cuts out before I see anything too explicit, thank goodness—my self-preservation instincts kicking in, rather than Bren trying to hide things—but it's enough to show that his alibi is real.

Bren looks slightly weak and ill in my mental images. It seems like some of the pallor and dark circles I'd blamed on his imprisonment actually pre-dated his arrest, but I can't tell why. Leah looks slightly wrong, too—glancing over her shoulder and almost trembling at times. It's an odd reaction to heading out into the countryside for some al fresco fun with your fiancée, but she's a bit highly strung and the idea of trying to conceive a demon baby must be nerve-wracking.

"Why do so many witnesses think they saw you in town or out by Thornber Manor?"

"I don't know."

Normally, he'd speculate. Like me, he no doubt has theories around blackmail, bribery, and intimidation—even if none of that really explains Becca's private evidence. But this sort of magic forces you to stick to the facts.

"One final question then. How were the human police able to arrest *you*? I can understand keeping you imprisoned, once they had you in blocking handcuffs and in a cell, but not how they got you in the first place."

I've asked both him and Leah a variation on the same question, but never quite been happy with the answer.

This time, the pause is longer. And there's something wrong about it, as though he's doing what I expected him to attempt in the first place—trying to come up with a clever answer that tells the truth but not the whole truth.

"They had some practitioner officers with them, who were allied to the Thornbers. Usually, I'd obviously be a match for anyone. But I was weak."

I nod. That tallies with what I was seeing on the video.

"Weak, why?"

What little magic remains in his control through the confines of the blockers flares. Consciously or unconsciously, he's pushing back.

"I've told you before. That whole 'trying to create a demon baby' thing had taken a lot out of me."

I push harder. I forget he's my brother, forget we're meant to be on the same side. It's like he's a key opposition witness and I'm going for the jugular. I need to stop this. I've got the answers I came for. But I can't bear the idea that family members don't think I'm worthy of their confidence.

"That's not the whole story, is it? That might have been the last straw, but something else had already left you drained."

"No, it's not the whole story. But once again, I did not kill Niall Thorner or have any involvement, direct or indirect, with his death. The reason I was weak had nothing to do with any of that and it's none of your business. Are we done now?"

"I release you," I say, all scripted solemnity again now. "I thank you for your answers and sever the connection to your mind."

I wrench my hands away from Bren's face like they're about to be burnt off.

We open our eyes at the same time.

"So, are you satisfied?" Bren asks, his head and shoulders slumping down.

I press my hands to my own face. "I'm sorry, Bren."

He takes a long, deep inhale and then exhales even more slowly. It's a perfect mirror image of the way I breathe when I'm determined to calm myself down. Something Nan taught us both. "It's okay. I can understand why you did it. Just promise me you'll believe me now? That you'll stop asking me if I did it? And that you'll never do that again?"

I nod rapidly. "I promise. Anyway, forget all that. I know the truth for sure now, and I need to defend you. Gabriel can't merely be mistaken, and you clearly didn't do it. So the next step is to cross-examine the hell out of that bastard. Prove he's setting you up."

It's only when I leave Bren that I think to wonder what on earth Becca's claims were all about. I push the thought away. I need to concentrate on Gabriel, and I can afford no distractions.

When the lunchbreak ends, I drag myself back into the courtroom. I honestly can't remember ever being more nervous about anything. I never normally bite my nails, but I've chewed them down to stubs and torn my lips to shreds, too.

I've cross-examined literally hundreds of people over the course of my career. I've had witnesses who were vicious and threatening, and I've not been scared. I've had others who were vulnerable and terrified, and though I've never been deliberately cruel, I've not gone easy on them. I've never taken those with a weak story for granted or been fazed by those whose credible and carefully rehearsed testimony didn't suit my client's case. I'm passionate about what I do, but at the end of the day, it's always just been a job.

I've worried all along that this case would be too personal, that I wouldn't be able to stay professional in the face of my worries about my brother. Against the odds, I've held it together. But I don't know the meaning of the word 'personal' until I'm face to face with Gabriel Thornber in court.

He gazes straight at me, his eyes locked on mine. I expect a facetious or flirtatious remark, but he's still playing the role of the perfect witness.

I glance down at my notes and think about my various possible lines of questioning. His relationship with his father. His bad character. How Bren supposedly got in—and then out again—so easily. How he knew Brendan and was so sure he was the intruder.

Gabriel is a polished speaker with a compelling story that tallies with other people's accounts of the evening. But there are no other eyewitnesses or anyone who can even confirm he was at the scene. I've picked holes in equally believable evidence before.

The thing about a bargain is that it cuts both ways.

I can't seem to find my voice. This must be what stage fright feels like.

It wasn't a spur of the moment decision to take you back with me that night. It was half the point of the evening.

He's staring at me expectantly. For all I know, the rest of the court could have got up and left.

Just stay awake. Let your magic flow through you. Let it heal you. Let it grow again.

We can pretend to be an anonymous witness and a detached lawyer all we want. That strange, surging connection is as present as it was when he unleashed the Greenfire or provoked me into burning through my magic at the casino. I can't do this.

"Ms Elner." The judge gives me a stern look. "Do you have any questions for the witness?"

I grind my heels down into the floor and gather every ounce of self-control I possess into a tight little ball. "How do you know the defendant, Mr Thornber?"

He smiles. He looks terribly amused. He's probably going to look amused for the entirety of the cross-examination.

"We're the same age. Grew up in the same small town. Moved in the same overlapping circles. Our fathers had similar business interests—sometimes complementary, sometimes competitive. And as I mentioned—a few years ago, I had a thing with his sister."

I ought to pursue that blatant untruth, but if I'm going to manage to speak at all, I need to stay on safer topics.

"How was your relationship with your father?" My voice trembles a little, even with the relatively innocuous question.

"Very good. I'm an only child, and my mother died when I was fourteen. Since then, we'd been a little family unit. Two men together against the world."

I should probably ask a follow-up question, but my brain won't cooperate. It's time to bring out the big guns.

You were the only eyewitness to the actual murder. I put it to you that you're lying about who committed it, and you've paid or threatened the other witnesses to support your story.

At least, that's what I try to say. I open my mouth, I think the words, but no sounds come out.

I've seen people have silencing spells put on them, but it's hard for one practitioner to enact a spell on another at the best of times, and I'm strong. I'm also supposed to be resistant to any of Gabriel's mesmerism, though come to think of it, I only have his word for that.

He can do spells without any outward signs of strain, but he really doesn't look as though he's doing magic right now. He might be able to keep his hands still and maintain a neutral expression, but I'd still see the change in his aura, and feel the pressure in the air. Besides, his frown suggests he's as surprised as me. A glance around the room gives no sign of anyone else attempting to bewitch me.

I shake my head. I'm not under a spell, I'm just nervous and triggered as hell. My chest's tight and my stomach's loose.

I squash down the internalised anger my mind tries to throw at me. This isn't my fault. Gabriel basically made me sell my soul to him. He's haunted my dreams for years and my reality for the last few weeks. I'd quite reasonably be trembling if I merely had to hold a casual conversation with him. It's no wonder my body won't cooperate when I'm supposed to be interrogating him in such a formal and high-stakes situation.

Then I catch Bren's eye. He's slumping down in the dock, his confident veneer cracking with every second I stay silent. This isn't about me. This court case isn't some extended therapy session. I promised I'd get my brother acquitted, and trauma or no trauma, I'm going to do it. I give Bren my most reassuring smile, then let it turn into something more akin to a smirk as my gaze shifts back to Gabriel.

"I put it to you..."

This time, it's not just that my mouth won't cooperate, I can barely remember what I wanted to say.

As I struggle to get the words out and maintain my composure, a burning sensation strikes my finger. It's as if my ring had been heated in a fire, but it's not actually coming from the metal, but from the mark underneath. As I grimace, a similar expression passes over Gabriel's face. Not only is he seemingly not doing this to me, it appears to be hitting him, too.

Stopping my cross-examination would be a betrayal of my family, a dereliction of my professional duty, and completely contrary to my core value of never backing down. But I can't do this. I just can't.

If it were merely the pain in my finger, then however excruciating, I'd try to push through. But I can't speak. I can't think. My throat's constricting, my head's spinning, and I've no idea what's physical, what's mental, and what's magical. I need to sit down. I need to shut up. I need to get away.

"No further questions, Your Honour." The words are barely audible, but I get them out.

I glance at Gabriel one more time before he leaves the witness stand and I collapse into my chair. I expect him to be smirking and triumphant, but he's still frowning. He almost looks concerned.

———

"What the hell was that?" Dad snaps the words at me in the lobby.

I can't remember the last time he shouted at me. Even as a child, I was both well-behaved and adored. But now, I'm putting darling Brendan at risk with my weakness.

"That was exactly what I said would happen if you forced me into this," I shout back.

"The whole point was that he can't mesmerise you," Mum says.

"It wasn't him doing it. Not directly, anyway. It's some side effect of the lien."

I push past Liam and Chrissie, throw myself into the family car my new driver was using, and get the hell out of there. In the last three days, I've had an emotional break-up, a physical breakdown, and a professional meltdown, and they all have the same cause. It's time to do something about it.

THIRTEEN

I drive the family car straight to The Windmill, exercise furiously, shower—no time for a bath tonight—then perch at my dressing table. I stare into the mirror, think about all the times I've fought the almost overwhelming urge to prettify myself with magic, and let the resistance fall away.

I don't even have to make a conscious effort. One moment, my face is scrubbed clear and my hair is limp and damp. The next, I look like I'm ready for a photoshoot. Probably one themed around angelic shepherdesses frolicking in some bucolic Victorian landscape.

If I'd been attempting to drive the magic by force, I'd probably have gone for something sleeker and sultrier. But my subconscious seems to have decided that tiny curls and subtle pastel pinks is the order of the day. It's a long way from my default look, but there's no doubt it works.

I've tried to keep my magic at bay. But when the person I've been hiding from knows who I am and understands the extent of my powers, what's the point in trying to do things by hand? Unlike in the casino, where I'd cast a huge spell and felt hideously drained, this small-scale, voluntary blast of power leaves me invigorated and psyched for what I'm about to do.

Once I'm ready, I jump back into the "borrowed" Porsche. I drive on autopilot, with the gas pedal slammed down, the convertible roof open, and my mind elsewhere. It's fifty-fifty whether I'm taking a brave step to secure my freedom or walking into a trap of my own making.

The built-up part of Mannith is hardly on a par with central London, but it's still good to get out of town on such a hot evening. I could have traversed, since I've entirely abandoned my magic ban for the evening, but speeding along with the wind in my hair and music blasting helps to clear my mind. The vaguely village feel quickly becomes very rural indeed, and I relish driving through a tunnel of overhanging trees. Once the woods recede, a centuries-old stone bridge leads into the little hamlet of Brinkerton. Typing its name into my satnav had yielded no results—a magic block or just too rural to register?— but a bit of water-scrying had burned a mental map into my brain. I could have done with Chrissie's help for that part, but I hadn't dared even to hint at my plans.

An ancient church, an equally old pub, and a few quaint cottages combine to create the sort of scene an American tourist would have spent their lifesavings to glimpse upon. I ignore both the view and the "go slow" signs, and floor the car to the end of the narrow, winding road, where Thornber Manor stands in splendid isolation. I screech to a halt in the long, pebbled driveway, kicking up a spray of rubble. It's not that I want to make a scene, exactly. I just don't have enough spare mental energy for attempting to be subtle.

I turn off the engine, cutting the music, and swing myself out of the vehicle. I walk up to the arched front door, with my open-toed sandals crunching satisfactorily on the stones.

There's a suitably gothic-looking skull in place of a doorknocker. I stand there for a moment, hand raised a few inches from the unsubtle piece of decoration.

Eventually, I summon up the courage to knock. The sound reverberates down the hall and echoes back to me, lingering far longer than it should. Impossible to tell whether the effect is caused by centuries-old magic, modern technology, or something in between.

One of the Thornber acolytes opens the door. After that display, I'd almost expected a hunched-over butler, but he's one of the gang I've seen in court and around town. He's around my age, dressed in tight black jeans, an even tighter white sleeveless tank top, and Havaianas sandals. He's holding a bottle of beer and staring at me in confusion through his aviators.

"Are you here for the BBQ? Aren't you that lawyer?"

Great. I've walked into a Thornber summer party. An audience is exactly what I don't need.

"I'm here to talk to your boss." My words sound stilted and awkward, but I can't bring myself to say his name.

"I don't think that's a good idea," the door-opener replies.

"Please just tell him I want to speak to him."

I consider trying to exert some mental influence. This guy doesn't look wildly powerful. But the last thing I want is to try, fail, and really get things off on the wrong foot.

"What's your name again?"

I took a deep breath. "Tell him it's Sadie Sadler."

His fists clench. "Okay, there's no way in hell I'm leaving you unaccompanied."

"Well, there's no way *I'm* leaving without seeing the person I came here to see. And that certainly isn't you."

He glances away just long enough to call over to a companion. "Mike, get Mr Thornber. It's that bloody lawyer. Or the Sadler girl. Apparently, they're one and the same now."

"Come on, Jamie," Mike replies, leaning out from the house's dark interior. He's dressed identically. "Mr Thornber's not exactly in the habit of standing on his doorstep chatting to people. They come to him."

"I'm not being held responsible for inviting her in if she brings the house down around her, or for sending her away if the boss feels like speaking to her."

"Fine." Mike's footsteps recede towards the back of the house, leaving Jamie and me to stare at each other in silence.

Two minutes later, Gabriel appears out of thin air. In stark contrast to Jamie and Mike, he's wearing a white linen suit.

"Far be it for you to have to walk the five minutes from your back garden to your front door," I say.

It's stupid to provoke him when I need to get on his good side, insofar as he has one, but it's a point of principle.

"Sadie Sadler. On my own doorstep, dressed up in a pretty summer dress, and using her real name. To what do we owe this honour?"

"I want to talk to you. Alone," I reply.

"I'm in the middle of hosting a party for fifty of my closest friends. Mostly to celebrate your brother's impending conviction. But an opportunity to 'talk to you alone' sounds far too good to refuse."

"Can we go inside? Find somewhere quiet?" I ask. "I wasn't expecting all these people."

"Nikki, search her for weapons," he replies, ignoring me for a moment and speaking into the ether.

There's no sign of Nikki, but presumably they have some sort of telepathic connection set up in order for her to best perform her role as lieutenant.

I stiffen at the indignity, but it's not unreasonable. I'd considered bringing a knife, just as a precaution, but I'm not exactly a great fighter. And it risked giving quite the wrong impression.

Nikki appears in place and proceeds to frisk me. She's thorough, but professional, and doesn't say a word. I stare Gabriel down while he watches in silence.

"She's clean," Nikki announces, in a tone of voice that suggests this is a crushing disappointment. If she'd found a weapon, she'd probably have used it on me.

Gabriel nods. "Excellent. Not that a weapon was my biggest concern in this situation. Slip these on, and we'll go inside." He holds out two delicate golden bracelets.

"I don't understand."

"These are much the same as the handcuffs your brother has to wear. But handcuffs are so uncomfortable and inelegant for a friendly conversation on a hot summer's day."

"You mean they'll block my magic?" I can't take my eyes off the jewellery, and I can't quite control my breathing. "I'm not letting that happen."

"Then leave. You're the one who wanted to speak to me. Unlike far too many people in this town, I'm not stupid enough to underestimate you. Take it as a compliment."

"If I go in there, weaponless and with my magic blocked, I'll be at your mercy, like any stupid human girl who wants a bit of excitement and danger."

"And if I let you in there *without* your magic blocked, you could murder me and my guests. You turn up unannounced, you demand a private conversation, you give no explanation. You can see the dilemma I'm in."

Breathe in for four. Hold for four. Out for four. Hold for four. My mind sinks into the earth, just slightly, and my body starts to calm. I've been at his mercy for six years, when you look at it one way. Up the ante a little today, and that'll never be a problem again.

"Sadie, your eyes are burning so brightly I can see the fire through your glasses. It's such a turn on when you do your core meditation thing. I've never seen anyone go so deeply into it as you."

I don't reply, and I don't come out of the trance I've fallen into. I just hold out my arms. The bracelets are unnaturally cold as he slides them over my hands, his fingers brushing against mine. The second they settle against my wrists, I'm jolted back into the moment with a little cry. They've cut my connection to the earth and to everything else around me. It's like I'm looking through a pane of glass, listening with earphones in, smelling through a slightly blocked nose. Presumably, this is what it's like for normal people all the time. And what poor Bren has had to put up with for weeks.

Goodness knows what Gabriel sees in my expression, but even he softens. "I take zero pleasure in taking your magic away, Sadie, even temporarily. This is simply self-preservation. Now, do you still want that conversation?"

I nod gently, not trusting myself to speak.

"Go back to the party," he tells Nikki and Jamie. "I'm taking her to the study. Don't let anyone disturb us."

Nikki frowns like she's about to protest, but simply shakes her head at him, glares at me, and disappears back out to the garden.

Gabriel holds out his arm. He probably expects me to shrug it off, but I take it. It'll be practice for later.

He leads me into the hallway and up a sweeping staircase. "Not using magic to take us there?" I ask.

He smiles. "It'd rip you apart in that condition."

Wow. I can't quite get my mind around how deeply embedded magic is in my day-to-day life, even when I think I've turned my back on it.

Once we reach the study, he closes and locks the door, then sits down on an old green leather sofa that looks like two armchairs have been melded together. The exposed stone floor keeps the room cool even on this hot evening.

"Drink?" he asks.

"You're not stupid enough to let me in here unblocked. I'm not stupid enough to accept your offerings," I reply.

I'm sure I said something similar to that last time I was here. I certainly sat beside him like this. The whole situation seems all too familiar.

"So, what is it you're so desperate to ask or tell me? What made you come all this way, when you'll usually go out of your way to avoid me?"

I close my eyes. *Breathe in, breathe out,* slipping into my usual meditation on autopilot. The simple flows of oxygen help my nerves a little, but it's impossible to reach the earth, and that terrifies me.

I force my eyes open again, hold out a braceleted arm, and place my right hand at the centre of his chest, mimicking his years-old gesture.

"I want to cash in the lien," I whisper. "I want to give myself to you, just once, and then be free of it."

He doesn't do anything as crude as gasp, and if I were a little less close to him, I'd think my words had barely registered. But with my hand pressed against him, I can feel his heart race.

"And what if I don't want you to cash it in?" he replies. "Perhaps I value this connection more than I'd value a one-night stand or a little extra magic."

Again, the rise and fall of his chest tells its own story, but I still spin out all my carefully rehearsed arguments.

"The choice isn't yours. I've done my research into the Old Ways. It doesn't matter who a debt is owed to and who imposes a lien. Either party can put an end to it, as long as the debt is settled."

He likes people to fight back, to challenge him. I understood it the day he unleashed the Greenfire on me. Retaliate, and he'll up the ante. Surrender, and he doesn't know what to do. Vulnerability terrifies him, and I'm giving it to him in spades.

"Why?"

"I can't fight against you with this hanging over my head. I couldn't get a word out in court. My relationships collapse. I don't think my family can fully trust me. You tell people I'm yours and on one level, I can't deny it, and the thought horrifies me."

I think about you when I'm in bed with other people. I think about you when I'm in bed by myself. I think about you nonstop. I need this to end.

"If it really bothers you that much, consider the debt written off. I've told you before: I'm not a nice person, but I'm not a monster. I was never really going to cash it in."

My head starts to spin. What the hell? Surely tackling the issue that's defined my life for years on end can't be that easy.

"Then why did you impose it in the first place?"

"I told you. I imposed the lien to dig the knife in deeper with your family and to give me some leverage in case I ever needed it."

I study his face. His eyes look sincere, but some sixth sense tells me this is half the truth at best.

"And why me? The others offered."

"Like I said back then, prettiest face, strongest magic, most effective way to hurt the Sadlers."

He still sounds believable, but this time, I'm sure he's not telling the whole story. For a start, while I've got a reasonably high opinion of myself, no one in their right mind would think I was better looking than Chrissie or more powerful than Bren. Beyond that, he's already told me that he'd thought about me before that night. But why? How?

He leans towards me, takes my branded hand, and slips off the ring. He stares disdainfully at the offending piece of jewellery. "If you were that desperate to hide the lien mark, I could have given you something much prettier."

His hand closes around mine. He presses our entwined hands against my sternum, then leans forward even further, so that his chest touches our hands and his forehead makes contact with mine. I stare deeply into his eyes. I long to close mine, but even with the bracelets blocking my connection to my powers, I can sense the eye contact is part of the magic. It's so like that night that haunts my dreams that I could almost have stepped back in time.

To distract myself from the memories, I start to count. At ninety-nine, I feel a jolt at my chest and a burning in my finger. There's pain and relief all at once, like stretching out an aching muscle.

"It's done," he says, but he makes no move to separate us. "The lien's gone."

I snatch my hand free from his grasp. The mark has disappeared. My hand looks odd without it.

"You've removed it. No tricks and no deals and no debts. You've lost your leverage and your way to hurt my family more. Why would *you* possibly do that?"

"Because I'm beyond delighted that you rocked up at my house on a gorgeous summer's evening, demanding sex, and making clear that you weren't willing to take no for an answer."

I straightened up. "You're utterly crazy. I didn't come here because I wanted to sleep with you. I came here to break the lien, whatever it took. And now it's gone, I'm going to leave."

"It's gone, and you're free to go. But all those things you blamed on the lien. All the facets of our connection. The way you physically couldn't speak against me in court. Do you think a simple deal took away your free will and invaded your mind to that extent? Can you look at me now, free of that old debt, and honestly tell me you feel nothing?"

I look at him, trying to be logical and methodical about it. Trying to size him up like an opponent in court or a casual date. It's impossible. He's already far too deep in my mind.

He's removed the lien; I believe him on that score. But he's not removed my fascination or the questions that lurk at the back of my mind. If I don't act on this in the here and now, I'll continue to play it out in the darkest reaches of my mind, again and again and again.

It's just sex. It's not like I'm a naïve little innocent. I've had casual flings with intriguing strangers, and short-term relationships with people I've liked and respected. But Gabriel doesn't really fall into either of those categories.

"If we're going to do this, let's do it," I say, standing up and taking his hand. "I want to screw you out of my mind."

Gabriel's eyes are wide. Whatever he expected my response to be, it clearly wasn't quite this. But even in his own home, even with my magic blocked, I'm the one in control.

He opens the study door and leads me out into a hallway. A little group of party guests—two men and one woman—are lingering. One of them opens their mouth as though they can barely resist the urge to ask a question, but at one glance from Gabriel, all three of them hold their silence and look away.

We arrive at his bedroom with no further disturbances. It's the one room I really recognise from my last visit. The accuracy with which I've replicated its early Victorian opulence in my regular fantasies is quite impressive.

Finding myself in a bedroom with a strange man and only one thing on our minds is a familiar experience. I pride myself on my poise, my nonchalance. I'm confident about my body. I'm comfortable with my sexual prowess. I'm utterly sex positive. Just recently, with Connor in Mannith and with Christopher in London, all of that's been true. I've shrugged off my clothes and draped myself over the bed or around my wannabe lover. But confronted with the prospect of sex with Gabriel, I'm frozen like a self-conscious teenager.

"Could you step outside for a minute while I get undressed?" I'm barely able to believe I'm saying the words aloud.

"Whatever you say, Sadie," he replies. He uses magic to

disappear, inevitably. The sight disconcerts me more than it should.

I kick off my sandals, shivering as my feet touch the cold stone floor and dashing for the soft warmth of one of the many rugs, then lift my dress over my head. I hadn't bothered with a bra, and for now, I leave my skimpy knickers on. I test the bracelets, but they're too tight to remove. I crawl into the bed, pulling the covers around me. *What the hell am I doing? I should leave, or I should embrace this.* But there's no reasoning with my mind.

"You can come in now," I call.

Goodness knows where he is. There's no way he should be able to hear me, even if he's just in the corridor, but we've both always played fast and loose with the laws of physics.

Sure enough, he appears by the bed in seconds. Wherever he's been, he's stripped down to his boxer shorts and a ring on a chain around his neck. I suck in my breath at the sight. I've seen plenty of half-naked men before, and they've never had quite this effect on me.

Against my will, my brain starts to play a greatest hits montage of every masturbatory fantasy starring Gabriel-fuck-ing-Thornber I've ever experienced. The gentle and the vicious. Which am I going to get? Which do I want? I told myself I was in control, but neither my brain nor my body wants to play ball. I'd never admit it to him, but I'm utterly in his thrall.

"Are you sure you want to do this?" he asks, surprising me. "I've lifted the lien. I want this more than almost anything, but you're free."

I have no idea what I truly want. It's crazy to sleep with him. But I long for it with a force I can't understand.

"I want to do this," I reply, oddly formal, like I'm swearing an oath.

He slips into the four-poster bed beside me without further

preamble. I gasp again, even though he's not touching me. I'm an absolute wreck.

"Turn onto your front then," he whispers.

I don't know what he intends, quite where we are on the spectrum of my fantasies, but I tell myself I'm all in. If I'm doing this, I need to disengage my conscious brain. I need to forget it's Gabriel. I need to live in the moment and go with what he says. I get my mind to obey me to the extent that I'm able to roll over.

Gabriel strokes my back. "Your muscles are so tense," he whispers, right by my ear.

The next moment, there's sandalwood and eucalyptus scented oil everywhere. Magic is good for the little details as well as the big picture. Lying on his side while I lay on my back, he rests his head on my shoulder and digs into my muscles. He has a point. Between all the exercise I do and all the stress I've been under, my muscles are wrecked.

Thanks to the bracelets and my utter discompose, it's hard to tell what's magic and what's skill as he works out all the knots in my back. It hovers on the boundary between pleasure and pain, like all of my interactions with him.

"What is this?" I demand. "If you're going to take me, just do it."

"If we're doing this, we're doing this my way," he replies. "And my way involves making this as pleasurable for you as physically possible."

His ministrations move downwards, working through the knots in my thighs. Little sighs escape my lips every time he soothes a sore spot. He's good, I'll grant him that. Good at healing the individual muscles he touches, good at setting my whole body aflame. His hands haven't strayed close to anywhere remotely sensitive, but I'm dripping wet already.

Slowly, his hands work their way back higher, focusing on the top of my thighs. With his right hand, he turns my head towards him and clamps his lips on mine. For a moment, I tense, and then I kiss him back, careless of the consequences, as his hands continue their exploration of my body.

Slowly, slowly, as though it's the natural and inevitable consequence of everything that's happened so far, his right arm closes around me, holding me closer to him, and his left hand slips between my thighs and inside my underwear. I gasp unashamedly as his middle fingers work their way around the outside of my pubic area.

"Please," I whimper. And unlike in my fantasies, my meaning is entirely unambiguous.

"Whatever you say," he replies, his own voice heavy with want. And then his fingers begin to stroke.

I have a last remnant of logical thought. *How is this happening? How have I let him through my defences?*

And then I give in entirely to the moment, to the sensation, to Gabriel.

Heedless of the rights and wrongs and complications of the situation, I'm outright moaning within moments. His fingers stay in place, alternating between fast and slow, straight lines and circles, while his head moves between kissing me on the lips then draping kisses all over my shoulders and back. I'm not sure quite what I anticipated when I resolved to do this. Perhaps something pleasant that I could enjoy and then forget. Perhaps something awful that I could grit my teeth through and then move on from. But nothing this all-consuming. Every time he moves near enough, I kiss him back.

His finger slides inside me, meeting no resistance, just a fresh round of gasps. I need to come, need to get this over with, but he's not going to make this easy for me. I know from our previous interactions that he likes to play things his own way. Seemingly, sex is no different.

"Turn over," he whispers, punctuating his words with another kiss on my forehead.

The moment I comply, he slides down between my legs and starts to lick. It's just like the sweeter end of the scenes in my imagination, except much, much better.

"Gabriel!" I'm screaming out his name before I can help myself. I can almost feel him smiling at the sound.

He carries on and on. Every time I'm on the verge of going over the edge, he pulls back, just for a moment, just long enough for me to regain some vestige of my composure, then he starts up again.

"Gabriel, please." I'm begging, and I don't care. *Finish me or stop*, I want to add, but I can't form a sentence that coherent.

Eventually, he glances up at me. "Tell me you want me," he says.

"I want you, Gabriel," I manage to choke out. He lowers his head, and with a few expert movements, finally deigns to bring me over the edge. He continues until the tremors fade away.

"May I?" he asks, and there's no question about what he means.

"I'm not sure when you got so polite," I reply, sighing out the words with my eyes closed. "But yes. Of course. God help me, but I want you."

He grabs a condom from the bedside drawer, lifts himself up, slides forward, and slips inside me. All those sounds of my pleasure must have been enough foreplay for him. Or perhaps, knowing him, it's the way I offered myself up, implicitly accepted I was his.

I call his name again once he's inside me. At first, he doesn't move, just presses himself against me and kisses me on the lips. Then he begins to rock, grinding himself against me.

"Dammit, Sadie," he cries out, his pleasure seemingly building in parallel with mine.

If I had any connection to the magic in the air, I could tell whether or not he was using his powers to enhance the experience. The bracelets cut me off from that knowledge and from the ability to do anything about it either way, but I don't care.

There's a part of me that would have liked to have lain there, utterly passive, superciliously letting him take his pleasure and acting like he had no effect on me. Instead, I push up against him, and before I know it, I'm coming again.

He gives me a moment to revel in the sensation and another moment for him to absorb it, then he comes in turn.

We call out each other's names in sync then both fall utterly silent.

I've had a lot of technically good sex in my life. I've had a fair amount of close, intimate moments with people I've cared about. Nothing has ever come close to this. Sleeping with my enemy has satisfied me in a way that no sex with anonymous pretty boys or men I've liked and respected has ever managed. I'd think he'd got one over on me, were it not for the fact that his sleepy eyes show the same shock and awe. He has a different date every night; I've seen that with my own eyes. But I can tell none of them have ever got under his skin and inside his head like this.

He rolls onto his back and pulls me to him. I ought to get up and get out. File this under unexpected surprises and get on with my life. Instead, I rest my head on his shoulder as he wraps an arm around me, drawing me into him. I stroke his chest with one hand and play with the rose-gold, emerald-studded ring dangling from the chain on his neck with the other.

I drift into a trance-like state I'm surprised I'm able to reach through the bracelets. The way my mind works after really good sex is much the same way it works after a really deep meditation. Thoughts collide and coalesce. Half-forgotten memories mingle with suppressed hopes and dreams. Today, in particular, it's like my subconscious brain is trying to get a message to me, but it can't quite break through. I try to cling to the sensation, to the swirling thoughts, but before I can form them into something remotely comprehensible, I fall asleep.

I'm not sure how much later it is when I wake up. The room has turned dark and full of shadows, though there's just enough light remaining for me to see Gabriel's perfect, sleeping face. What the hell have I done? I thought I was walking into physical danger, but it turned out Gabriel-fucking-Thornber was far too much of a gentleman for that. Instead, I've thrown myself into the worst emotional danger I could imagine.

My slight movements are enough to wake him up. "Sadie," he whispers, drawing me back towards him.

I sigh, and wriggle against the bed. The temptation to stay put is almost unbearable, but I force myself into a sitting position.

"I need to go," I say.

"For the last time, I'm not attempting to hold you prisoner. But stay. We can sleep. We can have sex again. We can get up and have dinner or re-join the party that's no doubt still going on downstairs. Or we can just sit and talk."

"I came here to get you out of my head. I don't think this helped, but I'm not going to make things any worse. We're on different sides, and you have no claim over me anymore."

"Give me your hands."

I hold them out, unsure of Gabriel's intention. All he does is slip the bracelets off me, then kiss the back of each hand in turn.

I'd almost got accustomed to the magic being out of my reach, but now it rushes back, like someone unmuting a film. I could strike him down, and he must be aware of that. Is this trust or a test?

I stand up, unashamedly naked, and click my fingers to dress myself. Magic makes everything so much easier.

"Shall I drive you home?"

"I'm fine." If I don't get out of there in the next few moments, I never will. Or at least, I'll never leave with my heart intact.

"Let me at least walk you downstairs then. We don't want any of my acolytes getting the wrong idea."

It's not clear quite what "the wrong idea" would encompass in this scenario, but I nod. As far as anyone in the house is concerned, I'm an unknown interloper at best, an active enemy at worst. Free of the bracelets, I can defend myself against any attack, as long as it's not coming from Gabriel himself, but neither sustaining minor injuries nor blowing Gabriel's associates in two is the vibe I'm going for.

We make it through the house and out the door without being disturbed. In the background, the sounds of the party—indie music and drunken chatter—continue unabated, but no one crosses our path. Perhaps they're all absorbed in their own fun. But more likely, Gabriel is radiating telepathic influences to make everyone stay away.

"You're sure you don't want a lift home? You look a little dazed." He gestures to a row of parked cars, one of which is an exact replica of the one my father smashed to pieces six years ago.

"My car's here. I'm a good driver." I walk towards the vehicle in question, doing my best not to look back.

"Sadie. Stop, just for a moment." His voice sounds raw and exposed, like it did in bed, stripped of his usual certainty and ironic amusement. "Acknowledge what happened in there."

I allow myself the lightest of core meditations before I dare to reply. "What happened is that I paid back a debt. And yes, it was a much pleasanter experience than I was necessarily expecting. But it's over and done with now."

"You screamed out my name."

I turn back to him. "Kiss me goodbye, if you must," I say. "But then I'm going back to my family."

His eyes are on fire. "One kiss goodbye then. And afterwards, if you want to forget this ever happened, be my guest."

I nod and close the gap between us. His hands are in my hair and his lips are rough against mine. We're tipping rapidly into version two of the fantasy, but that doesn't make it any less joyous. I revel in the sensation for a few seconds, then break away while I still have enough composure to do so.

"Goodbye, Gabriel," I whisper, then snap on my sunglasses, turn my back, and throw myself into the Porsche. I screech off the gravel driveway and onto the country roads before I can change my mind.

The whole way back I keep the roof down and drive as fast as I can, with music blasting out. It doesn't help in the slightest.

FOURTEEN

My parents are probably expecting me to stay at the family home now my identity is known, but there's no way I can look them in the eye tonight, so I drive back to The Windmill. The news that Brendan's lawyer is actually the youngest Sadler daughter has spread quickly round town, as all interesting gossip tends to in Mannith. Everyone wants to make conversation. It would be nice to catch up with people I used to know, but tonight is emphatically not the night. I smile while keeping my gaze on the floor, plead tiredness, and make it to my room.

I have a long, overly hot bath, attempting to drive away the scent of sex, of Gabriel, and of that distinctive massage oil. It's easy to get myself physically clean, but in my head, I can sense his presence on my body. The worst thing is that it's not entirely unpleasant.

I remain soaking until the water's cold and my fingers are a mass of wrinkles. Once I'm dry, I climb into bed, despite the fact it's obviously going to be impossible to sleep. The events of the last few hours run through my head on an endless loop. Every few minutes, I glance at my finger. Even in the near darkness of the room, I can see all too clearly that the lien mark is gone.

The next day, I'm back in court, yet again, ready for more prosecution witnesses.

I do my best to avoid bumping into my family, but Dad catches me in the lobby.

"Police, today," he says. "Most of the coppers in Mannith are loyal. But Thornber made sure he got the city force involved. I know you don't want us to use magic on civilians and locals. But surely it couldn't hurt to mesmerise these guys, just a little? They're probably pretty dodgy, if that helps at all."

I put my hands on my hips. "Dad, seriously. What did we discuss? No magic, no intimidation. That definitely includes no attempts to influence the police."

Dad sighs. "If you were anyone but my daughter, I'd either ignore you or take you off the case. I hope for Bren's sake you know what you're doing."

I nod, then dash inside the courtroom before he can debate things further.

I do my best to avoid looking at or thinking about either my family or Gabriel. Instead, I focus all my attention on the first witness of the day, the policewoman who was first on the scene at Thornber Manor.

I do a decent job of casting a hint of doubt on her solid testimony, but it's a challenge to keep my mind on the case.

From time to time, I glance at my finger. I've put my ring back on, to hide the fact the mark's gone, but to my eyes, it still looks and feels different.

As soon as court's over for the day, I drive straight back to The Windmill, lest anyone in the family attempts to start a conversation.

I head for my room on autopilot, but this is no time to be alone with my thoughts. Hiding away made sense when I was trying to disguise my identity and stay in role, but there's no point to that now. Instead, I sit down at the curved oak bar and bestow my brightest and most forced smile on the regulars. "Anyone for a drink?"

It's unclear whether it's the promise of free booze or curiosity about the long-lost Sadler sibling, but I'm soon surrounded, including by several old acquaintances and even vague friends I'd let myself forget about.

Becca's amongst them, but I keep a polite distance despite her attempts to chat. I can't understand why she claimed to have seen Bren, in contravention of his alibi, when I have absolute, psychic proof that he wasn't around. It's not my place to accuse her of anything, still less send her away, but I intend to tread carefully.

The others must long to ask about Bren, about the trial, about my life over the last six years. But instead, we talk about nothing—sports, the weather, celebrity gossip—and every meaningless word takes a bit of my panic away.

Back in my room later, though, the memories of the night before intrude again. I sit at my desk and open my case notes, but they can't hold my attention. I put on the highest intensity interval training video I can find and give it my all, but though it leaves my body exhausted, it's not enough to still my mind. The bath to wash away the sweat and soothe my trembling legs does nothing to calm me down either. What the hell have I done? And what can I do about it now?

The next few days pass in much the same way. I'm holding my own professionally, but on a personal level, I'm about to break in two. The mad desire to speak to Gabriel is almost overwhelming.

On Thursday, Mum corners me in the lobby after court ends for the day. A rush of denials and explanations are on the tip of my tongue, before my conscious mind intervenes to remind me it's very unlikely she knows what happened. Even so, I'm bracing myself for questions around why I've been hiding away.

"Can you pop round and see Leah?" Mum says instead. "See how she's bearing up? Take her red dress and jewels for Saturday. Make sure she's prepared."

"What's happening on Saturday?"

Mum shakes her head. "The Ritual, of course."

I grimace at the thought of the family's annual ceremony to preserve the Dome. It's easy to focus on all the benefits it brings Mannith and forget about the less pleasant aspects. I've never taken part, as it's strictly over eighteens only and I left home before I got the chance, so I'm not one hundred per cent clear on the details, but I know enough to be sure I don't want to be involved. Though if Leah's got one of the starring roles, that at least means I'm off the hook.

Mum hands me a package. She's no doubt already started to think of Leah as a member of the family. Calling on her unexpectedly would be no big deal. She seems to have forgotten my future sister-in-law was basically a stranger to me until a few weeks ago, not to mention that London has leached out what little ability for *ad hoc* socialising I'd ever had. Or maybe she's all too aware of both those issues. Maybe this is all part of the re-education.

"I can't just walk in there," I protest.

"Don't be silly, darling. It's your big brother's house. It's family property."

One of these days, I'll hopefully learn to resist my family's machinations. But today is not that day.

"Fine, I'll go."

"Great. And come over for dinner afterwards. Bring her, too. I've not seen enough of either of you this week."

"Will do," I say, heading to the car park.

"And for goodness' sake, don't knock or ring," Mum insists. "It's rude, really. It's like saying you don't think of her as family."

Brendan's house is only a mile or two away from my parents' home, but unlike their crazy terrace, it's a straightforward 1920s detached property. On arrival, my hand wavers between the bell and the handle as my mother's orders echo in my ears. Dropping in unannounced is so utterly against my usual London way of doing things—social engagements agreed practically in blood weeks in advance—that I almost can't do it. *But when in Rome...*

I grit my teeth and push the door open. Inevitably, it's not locked.

"Hey, Leah. Are you there? It's me. Sadie. I've brought you an outfit."

No reply. No obvious signs of life. But Leah must be around somewhere. Surely even in this town, people don't actually go out and leave their doors unlocked.

I quiet my mental running commentary and let my senses strengthen and do their thing. It's somewhere between listening very intently to what's actually in front of you, and scrying over a distance.

At first, there's nothing. Then as my mind expands, it becomes clear there are two people upstairs. Two practitioners, if I'm not mistaken. Normal people rarely give off such an aura. My physical senses home in on the spot identified by my mental ones. There's noise coming from the same direction. For a horrible moment, it sounds like someone's in agony, then my mind snaps into focus. It's the sound of pleasure, not of pain.

I ought to leave. Spare both myself and Leah the embarrassment. But she's my brother's fiancée. Some practitioners have an open relationship—another potential interpretation of the Old Ways—but I'm pretty sure Brendan and Leah don't. Brendan's never liked to share anything. If she's cheating on him, he deserves to know. And so, with a nosiness and determination my mum would be proud of, I stride into the hallway and up the stairs.

The door to the bedroom is open, meaning there's no need to swing it open dramatically. Leah's got her back to me, but her pinned-up, milky-blonde hair, defined shoulder blades, and almost translucently white back are unmistakeable. And she's emphatically not alone. She's on top, bouncing up and down on whomever she's cheating on my brother with in utter abandon, crying out with each movement.

I ought to sneak away. Either pretend this never happened or confront her afterwards. Anything but interrupt two people in the middle of sex. But my anger on my brother's behalf is growing by the second. He's in prison, for goodness' sake! He doesn't need this.

I cross my arms and stride into the room. "Leah, what the hell are you doing? You're engaged."

She screams, disembarks, and throws a blurring spell around the bed to hide her lover and her nakedness, like a normal person would throw the duvet over them.

"Oh God, Sadie. It's just a stupid mistake. It won't happen again. Don't tell Brendan or the others, please."

I can't see her through the spell (since when was she a good enough practitioner to block me?) but she sounds seconds from tears.

I hesitate, some of the shock and the righteous fury draining away. Haven't we all made mistakes? She loves Brendan, surely. If she's been feeling lonely while he's been away and gave in to some random guy's advances, who am I to judge? I'm supposed to be loyal to the family, but is this really worth ruining an engagement over?

"This puts me in an insanely difficult position," I say. "But get your side guy out of here, and I'm willing to sit and talk."

There are a few rustles before there's any reply. Presumably, she's trying to get dressed before she lets the shield fall.

"Um, you'd better go," she says to her companion after a few seconds. She sounds nervous as hell.

"I don't think so. I'm actually very interested to hear how this conversation is going to go," he replies.

My whole body tenses at the sound of the voice. *It can't be. It just can't be.* But then the shield drops, and I can see the bed clearly. Leah's managed to drag herself into a crumpled dress. Her eyes are wide, and her breathing's far too rapid.

Gabriel, on the other hand, is still utterly naked and seems entirely unconcerned either by that or by being discovered. He's still lounging on the pillows, sprawled out, his characteristic relaxed smirk firmly in place.

My breathing and heart rate accelerate way past Leah's. The rest of the room blurs, until only the bed is real. All the surprise and anger that'd hit me when I'd first walked into the room and just about managed to suppress races back a thousandfold.

"You treacherous whore!" I scream the words, fists clenched and eyes wide.

I've read several articles about how you should never call another woman a whore. About the need to be sex-positive, to be sisterly, to avoid slut-shaming. And I've always agreed with them wholeheartedly. I'd feel bad about my choice of words, were I not so utterly overcome with fury.

"A quick fling would have been one thing. But of all the men in this town, you cheated on my brother with *him*. He's the enemy. It's his fault your fiancé's inside in the first place. What is wrong with you?"

I probably ought to attempt a core meditation, or at least some simple breathing exercises. But I'm way beyond that. I'm wherever my dad goes when people disrespect magic or put the family or the town in danger and he loses it completely. I feel like I could set both of them on fire with the power of my mind. It's terrifying and exhilarating in equal measure.

"I'm sorry," Leah murmurs. She's completely sobbing now.

Gabriel still merely looks wryly amused. "Are you angry on your brother's behalf or on your own?"

I ignore him for the simple reason that if I so much as attempt to engage with Gabriel-fucking-Thornber right at this moment, I'm going to bring the house down around all our heads.

I gasp as a fresh thought hits me. "You've been slipping him information, haven't you? This isn't a one-off thing, and it's not even just sex. You're not just a cheater, you're a spy. You've not only betrayed Brendan, you've betrayed the whole family."

I try to suck in some air. Not to calm myself—there's no hope of that—but to stop myself from actually passing out from the force of my anger. My magic's swirling around me, barely under my conscious control. I dread to think what my eyes look like.

Leah doesn't even attempt to answer, just lays down on the bed and buries her head in the pillow.

"You told him about me, didn't you? You were one of a handful of people my parents trusted, and you told the one person I really needed to keep my identity secret from. You could have got me killed. Or used against my will."

"For the record, she did tell me, straight after that first day in court, but I already knew."

I press my hands to my forehead. "Shut up, Gabriel. You're utterly despicable, but I expect that of you. This is Sadler family business. It's between me and her."

For a second, the smug look fades away, and he closes his eyes. "Are you sure that's what you're thinking right now?"

Leah manages to sit back up. "Sadie, please don't tell Brendan. Please. I've been a total idiot, but I'll do anything."

I fight to keep my hands pressed against my forehead, where they won't do any harm, but I'm crying, I'm trembling, and I'm about to go beyond the point of no return.

My hands fly away from my face, and before my conscious mind catches up with proceedings, they're outstretched towards the bed, and Greenfire's hurtling towards Gabriel and Leah.

Gabriel shields without a second thought, inevitably, but the semi-physical manifestation of my fury surrounds Leah. Within seconds, her emotional sobs have turned to physical screams. I shouldn't be doing this, but it feels so good.

"Sadie, stop," Gabriel says. "You know you don't want to hurt her."

I don't stop. I'm not sure whether that's because I don't want to or I can't. The lines between the conscious and the unconscious and the physical and the mental are all blurred by rage.

Leah is struggling for breath. As a practitioner, the Greenfire shouldn't do her much harm, but she's not a particularly strong or gifted one, and unlike me and my siblings, she probably neither duelled nor messed around with Greenfire much in her youth.

Most of my attention is focused on the trembling, glowing figure of Leah. This must be the first time I've been in Gabriel's presence and not been utterly absorbed with him. But I still notice when he stands up, throws on a dressing gown—my brother's presumably, which seems like adding insult to injury— and crosses the room towards me.

I tense, prepared for an attack, but all he does is come behind me, slip his arms round my waist, and close my hands into fists, just like that night at the casino. As he draws our joined hands towards my chest, the spell falls away and a sobbing Leah drags herself back to a seated position. The pain will have disappeared the moment the magic stopped, leaving no physical harm or discomfort behind, but she looks in shock. I shake a hand free from Gabriel's grasp—he doesn't resist—and perform a simple binding spell on Leah, locking her arms and legs together.

"What are you intending to do?" Gabriel whispers the words. It's unnecessarily intimate.

"Take her back to my parents. Let them deal with this mess. Though it'll ultimately be up to Brendan how far we stick to the Old Ways."

He makes an odd sweeping motion up and down my arm, first the right, then the left.

"Stop that," I snap.

His hands freeze in place. "If you say so. I'm just smoothing down your power. It's a tangled mess right now."

"I'll calm myself down when I get home. My mum and sister can sort out any kinks in my aura."

It takes a lot to say it, because the awful truth is that whatever he just did has levelled me out. Every second he touches me takes away a little more of my anger, a little more of that sense of barely having my magic in check. Which seems unfair, when this is all his fault.

"I know you're angry at me, whatever you claim," he says. "I know you feel betrayed."

I force out a laugh. "Betrayed? By you? For someone to betray you, you have to have some trust in them, some connection with them, some feelings for them."

"What was the other night all about then?"

"That was about sex. It was about breaking a connection, not forging one. I've been with plenty of people. So have you. There was nothing special about them, there was nothing special about us, and there's no such thing as betrayal in this context."

Leah is staring, absolutely open-mouthed. I'd almost forgotten she was there, such is the overwhelming effect Gabriel inevitably has on me at this proximity, but her surprise at what I've admitted seems to be enough to cut through her shock and panic.

"You hypocrite!" Leah shouts out the words between sobs. "So you've slept with him, too? You're not upset for Brendan. You're just jealous."

"I am not jealous! And I've got nothing to be guilty about. I don't have a fiancé to cheat on, and I've not told him any secrets."

Gabriel strokes my hair. I'm not entirely sure whether he's doing the aura smoothing thing again or just aiming for a soothing gesture, but either way, it calms me and excites me in equal measure. I need to get away.

"She's right though, isn't she?" He's whispering again, right in my ear this time. "You're angry on Brendan's behalf, but you're jealous, too. It's really reassuring to see."

"I am not jealous!" I yell the words out at both of them.

"Good. Because there's really no need. I sleep with plenty of people, sure. But if you told me you wanted to be together and wanted me to be faithful, I'd never, ever betray you."

I take a step forward. It's a thousand times easier to think clearly outside of his arms. "Gabriel, get the hell out of here. I'm fairly confident Bren keeps his house warded to high heaven, particularly against you. I can only assume she let you in—one more little betrayal—but I'll fix that."

I walk over to Leah and take her arm. "We are going to my parents' house right this second."

I glare back at Gabriel. He shrugs and disappears, still wearing the dressing gown.

I tighten my grip on Leah, close my eyes, and next thing,

we're in my parents' sitting room, where the whole family, minus Bren, of course, are gathered.

My mum smiles at my furious expression and Leah's ruffled dress, tear-stained face, and bound wrists and ankles. "I knew it. Sorry to put you through that, sweetheart, but I had to be sure about this one. Now, tell me exactly what happened."

FIFTEEN

I spend most of the next day's court proceedings trying to avoid making eye contact with Bren, who looks utterly stricken. The previous evening, Dad had visited him in prison and told him what we'd discovered. A light touch of mind control on my part had ensured Leah couldn't say anything about me and Gabriel to the rest of the family. I'd been unspeakably glad the task of telling Brendan hadn't fallen to me. Under the Old Ways, a betrayal of this magnitude generally means death, but it's for the person who's been betrayed to make the call.

I'd expected Bren to order Leah's execution without a second thought. But according to my slightly bemused father, he'd looked more sad than angry, and merely asked for her to be exiled from Mannith.

Unfortunately, I've also had to drop her as a defence witness. Which isn't particularly helpful, considering she's Bren's only alibi. But given what we now know about her, there's no way I could risk putting her on the witness stand, even if she were willing to go through with it. Who knows what lies she might tell?

The one good thing about this mess is that it's driven all of that twisted desire to call Gabriel right out of my head. I'd thought our sex had been special, but he'd no doubt been giving Leah the exact same lines and experience. And doing it for the exact same reason: to get one over on Bren and our entire family.

At four o'clock, the court rises. It's Friday evening, and Monday is a public holiday, so there's a long weekend ahead of us. I can't spend it all in solitude. I head briefly to The Windmill, pack a small bag, and drive back to my parents' house.

When I walk into the family home, I notice both Mum and Chrissie are wearing red. Somewhere at the back of my mind, it raises alarm bells, but I'm too detached from the rituals of family life to immediately make the connection.

"Hello, darling," Mum purrs. They're a bottle of prosecco down, and in the middle of opening another.

Chrissie looks me up and down, frowning at my pastel blue dress. "You should be in scarlet. Surely you remember what day it is tomorrow?"

Mum passes me a glass of fizz and a little plate of smoked salmon blinis before my brain can catch up with proceedings. "Have a drink while you still can. We need to start the fast in a couple of hours."

Shit, shit, shit, shit, shit. How could I have forgotten? Mum had even mentioned it when I'd gone to visit Leah, but it slipped my mind in all the ensuing chaos. I really have been away too long.

I down the drink in one before replying, "You can't seriously expect me to take part."

My mum shakes her head disapprovingly and refills my glass. "You can't seriously expect *not* to take part. It's a shame you've never had an opportunity to participate in the Ritual, but you're back now."

"And you know we need three," Chrissie adds, putting a calming hand on my shoulder. She's wearing her biggest citrine ring. "Leah would have been taking the third spot. But even if she hadn't betrayed us, her power's not a patch on yours."

The Ritual is our annual ceremony to strengthen and protect the Dome for another year.

It requires three strong female practitioners with some connection to our family, as well as the family patriarch. When I was a kid, it was my nan, my mum, and an aunt, until Chrissie turned eighteen and took one of the spots.

The other adult family members and all our acolytes gather to provide support. As I left Mannith the summer I came of age, I've never attended. And until you do, no one tells you the details.

The rest of what I know is therefore essentially speculation. But based on the rumours I heard over the years—combined with the secrecy around it and the state Chrissie was in when she returned from her first one—it's emphatically not something I want to be a part of.

I stare at Chrissie's ring and try to breathe. "I can't do it. I don't do that sort of magic anymore. And I've got a moral code I'm not willing to break."

"Let's get you bathed," Mum replies, as though she hasn't heard a word of my objections.

I cross my arms.

"Come on. The ground amethysts and the pink salt and the sage oil. You know you love it. A nice relaxing purification bath won't do you any harm, even if you abandon us afterwards."

"Fine. Just a quick soak, if it'll shut you both up."

The second I slip into that bath, I'll have no hope of changing direction. I'll be dressed in red and bedecked with gems. I'll be persuaded to fast and to drink the potion that sharpens our senses and slows down our conscious minds so the subconscious can take control, just like I've watched Mum and

Chrissie do in the past. And before I know it, it'll be tomorrow night. I'll be starving and hallucinating, and looking like an actual witch from a story book. And once I'm standing there under the light of the moon, with everyone watching, it'll be far too late to refuse whatever comes next.

But there's zero point even attempting to argue with Mum and Chrissie when they're in this sort of mood. And maybe the Ritual isn't as bad as I believe? It's probably all quite token and symbolic.

"I'll prepare the bath," my mum announces. "Chrissabelle, make sure your sister doesn't escape."

"How terrible is it, really?" I say to Chrissie. "I know you're not meant to tell kids or outsiders. But if you want me to take part, surely you can talk me through the basics."

She shakes her head. "That's not how it works. It's Old Ways stuff. Telling you explicitly would be dangerous. But the stuff we gossiped about in our teens isn't that wide of the mark."

"Look," I say. "I know you and Mum aren't going to let this drop. I'll have the bath and drink the potion. I'll stand there and make up the numbers if I have to. I guess I'll meditate and whatever. But I'm absolutely not going to do anything I don't agree with."

"See how you feel when you get there. The moment might seize you. It's a little unpleasant, but it's for the good of the town. It's a small sacrifice in the scheme of things."

"Did Leah represent the family before?"

Chrissie narrows her eyes. "Yes. For the last two years."

"I just wondered if this was all part of Gabriel's plan. Seduce her and be found out, so she would be barred from the Ritual and you wouldn't be quorate."

Two reasons for everything.

Chrissie doesn't look like she's in the mood for second-guessing Gabriel's strategies. Maybe deep down, the Ritual weighs heavily on her conscience, too.

"Who knows?" she says. "It still makes me furious even to think about her. We treated her like a real member of the family, and she threw it back in our faces. I don't know how she could bear to let him near her, never mind screw him. I feel a bit sick if I accidentally make eye contact with him."

"He's not that bad," I say.

To the best of my knowledge, Mum hasn't drugged me yet, but it's like I'm already speaking without my conscious mind running a sense check.

"I mean, obviously he's awful," I add quickly. "A soulless, vicious monster. But from a shallow perspective, if all you're looking for is some sex on the side, he's also pretty damn hot."

Chrissie laughs. "Wow. Of all the people I never expected to express that sentiment. You clearly need that ritual purification more than I thought."

"I didn't mean—"

"I know what you mean. If you're a fan of the whole high-cheekboned, floppy-haired, smirking arrogant face thing, then he certainly does that well. Personally, I like a man with a bit more meat on their body and a bit more humility on their face. But either way, Leah should have known better. And if she couldn't keep her legs closed, she could at least have kept her mouth shut about you."

"It doesn't matter. He knew the moment he saw me."

Chrissie stops ranting and pulls me into a tight hug. "Sadie, don't think about him, please. We won't let him hurt you, and we won't let him get inside your head. Remember that night at the casino? He might be stronger than all of us individually, but united as a family, we're unstoppable."

What would she say if she knew I'd done the same thing as Leah? I haven't cheated on anyone or shared any secrets. Does that make it okay, or is sleeping with Gabriel an inherent sin, from my family's point of view? And if so, is being a Sadler by blood a mitigating or aggravating factor?

"Bath's ready," Mum calls. "Pour yourself another glass of Prosecco and bring it up."

Downing alcohol isn't entirely in line with the spirit of purification, but that's the least of my worries right now.

To be fair to Mum, the bath looks and smells amazing. The huge rolltop tub is full almost to the brim—presumably achieved through magic as it's only been running for ten minutes at most —and is a vibrant green, dotted here and there with tiny pink crystals. There's a woody, earthy smell, undercut with something more feminine and aromatic.

I pull off my clothes—body inhibitions have never really been a thing in this house—and slip in. It verges on too hot, but that's half the point, and my body quickly adapts.

Mum sets a thirty-minute timer on her phone, then leaves me to it. Within minutes, my muscles are floppy and my head's clear. By the end, I'm slightly dizzy and struggling to stay awake. When the timer goes, I barely have enough muscle control to pull myself out of the bath and into the warm embrace of the towel Mum left out for me. I want to go and pass out. But in a nice way.

"Drink plenty of water," Mum calls from the hallway. "All the salt and heat will have dehydrated you. You need to be well hydrated by the time the fast starts."

"Mum! I know I've been away for a while, but it's not the first time I've done a purification bath."

"All right, darling. Just making sure you're okay."

I down the first glass of water that Mum's left out for me, then refill it from a large jug. I walk outside, still in a towel, and stretch out on a swinging bench at the far end of the garden, hidden beneath a weeping willow. It'd been a favourite hiding spot for the four of us as children. It's credit to the power of Mum's potions and Chrissie's stone magic that I'm fighting off sleep instead of lying there wide awake with panicky thoughts of what's to come tearing through my brain.

As a general rule, I don't really believe in all this rigmarole. You don't need crystals and scents and fancy clothes to work magic. You simply need concentration, will, and that connection to the earth. But the Ritual is different. I might not know the precise details, but I understand the basic principle: we protect the Dome by pouring something of ourselves into it. It'd be practically impossible without strengthening and focusing our minds, and incredibly dangerous without protecting our spirits.

That's most of the reason for all the song and dance my family put into this one piece of magic. But it's equally as important that we look the part and make a scene, for the benefit of our allies, our enemies, and anyone debating which they ought to be.

I only realise I've fallen asleep—or passed out, it's a fine line in this state—when the buzzing of my phone snaps me back awake again.

> I hear you're doing the Ritual tomorrow night. I can't decide whether to be impressed or disappointed. I just know you've lost what little moral high ground you had. G

Goodness knows how he got my number. Leah, probably. Or else Imran, the mesmerised prosecution lawyer. I shouldn't reply. But with him, I can't help myself.

> I'm loyal to my family. I'm a real Sadler, deep down. I don't know why this is so hard for you to understand.

Somewhere at the back of my mind, scenes flash up. Gabriel kissing me all over. Gabriel under Leah. It's yet more testament to the power of the bath that the first makes me neither disgusted nor horny, and the second makes me neither sad nor angry. They're just two random things that happened recently, no more or less interesting or emotional than anything else.

> It's a fiercely fought competition, but I think the Ritual is the thing I hate most about your family. Still, I'd love to see you in all that high priestess get up. You'll look beautiful. And I'd almost die watching you channel that much energy. You'll be so powerful. My dream woman.

My emotions are clawing their way back to the surface. I'm tempted to reply with something cutting and caustic. Something furious. Something light-hearted and dismissive. I settle for turning my phone off, then I meditate like my life depends on it.

All through the bath and the aftermath, I've been going back and forth on what exactly I might be asked to do and the pros and cons of putting my scruples aside in order to support my family and the town. But that settles it. There's only so far I'm willing to go, but if Gabriel disapproves of me doing the Ritual, I'm at least going to take part.

Thirty hours later, and as I'd feared, I'm standing in the clearing at the centre of a wooded hill, just out of town. I'm semi-delirious from lack of food. The potions I was persuaded to take aren't helping. I've always steered clear of drugs, unless you count alcohol, but as a one-off, there's something wonderful about being this disinhibited and disembodied.

It might be the hunger and hallucinogens talking, but I feel beautiful and powerful in equal measure. Irresistible and unstoppable. The floor-length scarlet dress, cut to the thigh on both sides to reveal a gold wire garter isn't exactly my usual style, any more than the giant crystals are. But it's certainly a strong look. Make-up that your average drag artiste would think was a touch over the top completes the effect.

My father is at the apex of the hill and the centre of the circle. Mum, Chrissie, and I form a rough triangle around him. The other women—distant relatives, those affiliated with the gang, and loyal local practitioners, like my old friend Becca or Connor's mother—create a circle around us, arms linked.

The men make a similar circle a little further out. Liam, Connor, Shane, and Ray will be amongst their numbers, though it's impossible to see them over the tall flaming torches that stand between the three of us and the other women. There are also various crystals between them and the men, plus salt forming an outer circle. It's exactly the kind of over-ritualistic magic I've always vaguely disapproved of, but tonight, it makes me feel safer and more powerful. Detached from the world and what we're about to do.

Without regular maintenance, the Dome could collapse. My family have put so much into the Dome over the years that if it fell, it'd take us with it, certainly if we were in Mannith at the time, perhaps even if we were farther away. And on top of that, decades of change and decay would descend on the town in one fell swoop. For my family and for the local people, I need to do this. At least, that's what I tell myself.

My father always encouraged me to practice my core meditations, but it tended to be a case of do as I say, not as I do. Today though, his mind is deep in the earth, his eyes glowing brighter than the torches encircling us, or the full moon above. Nowadays, Dad tends to rely on his reputation and influence, rather than pure magic. Sometimes I forget where Bren and I got most of our power from.

Not that the genetic contribution was entirely one-sided. Mum's powers aren't as spectacular, but she's a strong practitioner in her own right, and tonight, she looks it, too—dressed every bit as extravagantly and revealingly as her daughters despite her extra decades.

"Mannith is a blessed place," my father intones, like he's on stage. "It's always drawn something from the rivers and mountains that surround it, but for the last hundred and fifty years, it's our power and our sacrifices that have protected it from the decay facing the wider country, the wider world. But that power must always be restored and maintained if we wish our beautiful town to flourish."

The words are simply a statement of intent, something to focus our minds and our magic. I presume they've been the same every year for the century or so this Ritual has taken place. Even so, it's strange to hear such dramatic phrasing emanating from Dad. Odd to hear someone so in love with power and material things talking about rivers and mountains like the old hippies he despises.

I shake my head to clear my brain. The Ritual is no time for rational, cynical thoughts. You need to be led by instinct and the unconscious. The drugs and hunger are meant to help, but my conscious mind's trying to fight back.

My father throws up his arms, pointing them towards the visible moon and the usually invisible apex of the Dome. In this light and this mindset, I can see it flickering in the sky above me.

"Tonight, we rebuild the Dome," he intones, then lets his mind sink still further into the earth below and the Dome above and stands there utterly frozen, barely breathing. It's our cue to move.

Mum, Chrissie, and I walk at a stately pace, marking out a triangle on the ground. Once we arrived at Summer Hill, my relatives gave me a few pointers, but they were barely necessary. Though it's the first time I've done this, the movements feel instinctive, like I'm drawing on some sort of ancestral memory.

In the same way, I know that the women around us will be moving in a clockwise circle and the men beyond them in an anti-clockwise one. I'm barely aware of them in the here and now, though, just of an overwhelming sense of movement. It feels disconcertingly like we're the only still things in existence and the world is spinning around us.

At each corner of the triangle, we pause, kneel on the ground then stand and point our arms to the sky, like I've been instructed. In normal circumstances, it'd feel like the world's most basic yoga class, but right now, every step and every bend and stretch is imbued with significance. We go around three times, then stop in our original spots, arms raised and stretched. All around us, the others continue to move in their opposing concentric circles.

So far, pretty much anyone could have done the steps. The movement and the concentrated desire has stirred up a mass of power within the circle. Now we need to capture and use it. That's the trickier part. A weak practitioner or someone entirely without powers would feel and achieve nothing. Someone stronger but not strong enough would risk blowing themselves apart. Even at our level, the risk of failure or death would be unacceptable without all the preparation and protection.

The power and energy surrounds me like a living thing. Power seeks power, and no one would disagree with the fact I'm the strongest of the inner three. I draw it towards me like I sucked in the air that night at the casino, without anyone having to tell me what to do. Soon, I'll direct it back out. I can tell now that maintaining the Dome's not a million miles away from throwing up a bubble of silence or protection, it's just on a much larger and more permanent scale.

I clasp my left hand to my chest to hold the power there and breathe slowly and steadily. The power wants to burst free or tear me in two, but I keep it in check through sheer force of will.

With what remains of my conscious brain, I glance across the clearing. Mum and Chrissie have their left hands at their chests in an identical gesture, but their right hands are drawing daggers from their garters.

My own hand moves to my dagger, my subconscious entirely in control. As one woman, we swipe our weapons across the back of our left hands—not deep enough to do any permanent damage to the muscles and ligaments, but deep enough that there's immediately a lot of blood. There should be a lot of pain, too, but I'm far too detached from my physical body to feel a hint of it. I hold out my injured hand and let the power flow upwards from the palm as the blood drips down from the back.

I've seen the temporary scars on my relatives' hands after previous Rituals, so I knew something like this was coming even before I was finally briefed. It's unpleasant, but it's not the aspect I'd worried about.

"We give our power to the sky and our blood to the earth," my father intones, coming back from his trance so that he can speak. "We give ourselves to Mannith to secure its protection."

Some whisper of my own power and aura is drifting upwards. Hundreds of metres above our heads, it's mingling with the translucent representation of the edges of the Dome. Sliding into place. Sealing cracks and smoothing rough areas. It's just my mind creating a literal, visual representation of something intangible and beyond human comprehension, but it looks very real. As does the way my blood pools and expands, far more of it on the ground than has really left my body. Soaking into the earth, repairing the fissures.

My father waves his arms and my hand heals instantly, though the unreal blood continues to swirl below my feet.

"Blood and magic are worthy gifts," he says. "But our Dome must be strong, and a greater sacrifice is needed."

It was probably disingenuous of me not to mention that there's a bound and mesmerised man in front of my father and one each in front of me and my two companions.

Apparently, they are all human Sadler loyalists who volunteer themselves and are well-rewarded.

This is the bit of the Ritual I'd heard rumours about and been dreading. We need to cut them, and do it deeply enough that we get a decent quantity of their blood to add to ours.

I know we'll heal them afterwards, but it still goes against everything I believe to hurt someone that badly and in such a coldly pre-meditated manner... even though they've consented, and even though it's for a good cause. I ought to feel utterly sick, but all the preparation keeps most of my emotion at bay.

Even so, my hands are trembling, but I manage to copy the others by kneeling and raising my dagger. And then the magic in the air starts to override both my conscience and my consciousness.

I thought I'd struggle to so much as pierce my volunteer's skin. Instead, everything from the increasingly wild people around me to the moon to the drugs to the burn of power to my father's voice to wanting to be part of something is screaming at me to take my kill.

It's hard. Harder than any time I tried to suppress my powers and resist the lure of magic in London. But I retain enough control over myself that I manage to strike the right balance and make a relatively token cut.

But whether they were overcome or whether it was deliberate, the other three plunge the weapons deep into their volunteers' chests.

I don't scream. On the outside, I barely react at all. I'm far too detached from my body for that. Insofar as I'm having clear emotions at all, the chief one is regret at my own weakness and a sense of not quite belonging.

Power surges from the three lethal wounds, and trickles from the graze I've created. Blood pounds in my head and my trembling hands clench the dagger as if I could snap it clean in two.

Despite my trance-like state, my heart is beating wildly in my chest. I don't think my family lied to me, exactly. They told me I'd have to use my knife on the volunteers—which was essentially the gory rumour I'd always heard as a teenager. It seems I just heard what I wanted to hear. I told myself a small cut would be enough and believed they'd take the same approach.

We stand. We drop the daggers, my hands shaking as I do so. We pace the triangle three times more, my legs barely able to support me. We nod to the sky and the earth, and dizziness blurs my vision.

"Blessed be this town." My voice catches as I chant the words along with the others.

The two other circles finally stop moving. The torches extinguish, then light again. I think I've done it with my mind but who even knows at this point. We each walk away in our own direction, through the ring of flame, the ring of women, of crystals, of men, then scuff the circle of salt with our feet, step beyond it, and crash down on the grass. I'm not convinced I'm capable of ever getting up again.

There's a moment of utter stillness and silence, then the other circles break and people go to find their friends and partners. There's awe on their faces, but they're also chatting amongst themselves. People are throwing down picnic rugs and opening bottles. They're surrounding me, lifting me up to a sitting position, and offering me drinks and praise before I can get away. My mum and dad both hug me, pride in their eyes, even though I didn't actually kill my sacrifice.

I'm torn between screaming at them for their brutality and —insanely—apologising for my weakness, but I can't get a single word out through my rapidly constricting throat.

At the top of the hill, the dead bodies are set alight, and my unconscious victim is carried away. You'll be able to see the pyres for miles, but no one will come near tonight. After all, this town is ours.

And I'm terribly sorry if in mentioning the feud between the Thornbers and the Sadlers, I accidently implied that we're the good guys.

SIXTEEN

There are cheers when I walk into The Windmill the next evening. Actual, goddamn cheers.

"Come and grab a drink," someone calls.

"Whatever you want, it's on the house. I mean, it's always on the house for you. But that goes double tonight."

I was an accessory to murder. I've kept the town cut off from the outside world. I've performed the sort of magic that's not natural. I've lost a bit of soul and given it to the town. While the town's lost a bit of soul and given it to me.

Cheering does not seem like the appropriate reaction. I'd probably throw up if I tried to drink something. I'm quite liable to throw up anyway. We all stayed up until the sun rose, and I've spent most of the intervening time asleep at my parents' house. Hours passed out cold followed by hours more of fitful dreams.

It's not like these men and women don't know what happened. Half of them were there. The others, the ones with brute strength or other useful skills but no magic, weren't so "lucky". Nonetheless, they are all Sadler loyalists through and through. They understand what my family do and what this town is built on, and even if they don't know the precise details of the Ritual, they get the basic idea and wholeheartedly approve. They love the family for it. And now they love me.

"Maybe later." I force my lips into some grim facsimile of a smile. "Right now, I need to sleep."

My audience grins knowingly.

"Of course. Magic like that must take it out of you."

"I don't know how you're still standing."

"I need a nap after I've thrown up a shield half the time."

I nod, as though it's the physical effect that's the problem. The truth is, I don't feel drained in the slightest. I'm brimming with energy. I could run a marathon or work some wild follow-up spell. It's my mind that's about to break.

I make it to my room and the chorus of drunken cheering recedes into the background. My phone feels heavy in my hands as I flick through my contacts list.

Today's revelations put quite a different spin on certain things, and I want to talk that through. Plus, I need to vent. And, given that no one in my family's circle are going to want to hear a word said against them and no one outside of Mannith would believe a word I was saying, there's only one person I can do either of those things with.

This isn't remotely sensible. There was a connection, and I've broken it. I owed a twisted debt, and I've either paid it back or wriggled out of it. The last time I saw him, I quite reasonably told him to get lost. It's mad to reopen this old wound. But to my intense irritation, I need this conversation. *And you're desperate for an excuse*, the least favourite bit of my mind taunts.

He's saved in the phone simply as "X". Part security measure in case anyone flicks through my contacts, part protection against seeing his name every day. It's a kiss, and a warning sign, and the place where treasure is buried.

I press call before my mind can throw up any more nonsense.

Gabriel picks up after two rings. He clearly loves mind games, but seemingly nothing as basic as keeping you holding on the line.

"Sadie."

The way he says my name contains multitudes. It's a question and a declaration and an invitation and a command, all at once. He doesn't sound as surprised as I'd secretly hoped though. He's a hard man to catch off-guard, I'll give him that.

"You know what the Ritual entails, don't you? It's why you hate my family so much." I don't waste any time on pleasantries.

"I mean, there's a generations-old rivalry, a touch of resentment at all their power and control, and some general interpersonal conflict. But yes, all the ritualistic murder definitely plays its part."

"I didn't know. I gathered there were volunteers and sacrifices, but I was imagining controlled blood-letting. A cut, not a kill—which, for the record, is all I personally did. I thought it'd be grim, but just about within the bounds of acceptability."

I sound horribly naïve when I say that out loud, knowing what I now know. And what he's always known.

"Is even that really acceptable, year after year though? And is just maintaining the Dome enough for your family?" Gabriel says.

"You'll grudgingly let them get away with the annual Ritual, but you had to intervene when my brother tried to go one step too far by expanding it," I say, wanting to confirm something I've been suspecting. "We were so proud to hear he'd tried and almost succeeded. So angry at you for stopping him. For hurting him..."

Would it have required a higher number of sacrifices each year, to maintain a larger Dome? Or given that the Dome is preserved by the darkest kind of magic, did Gabriel just disapprove of expansion on principle? I still hate the memory of him draining Bren's magic, and I'm glad I stopped it. But in the light of last night's revelations, I can see his point rather more.

"I should have followed through," Gabriel snaps. "I should have drained his magic while he was caught by surprise and weak from all the power he'd expended."

"Why didn't you?"

"Why do you think?"

"Supposedly you always have at least two reasons for everything."

"Not that night. Where you're concerned, I only ever need one. And that's when things go wrong."

I still don't understand what he means when he hints that we already had a connection before that night. It's hard enough to accept that he's been thinking about me ever since, but you can blame the magic transfer and the bargain. Or hell, maybe I'm that damn irresistible? But prior to that, we'd never even met. At some point, I need to pin him down and demand answers, but that's exactly what I don't feel like doing right now.

"Gabriel, it's been an insane night. I know a lot of that's on me. I should have refused to get involved. But I didn't, and I'm paying for it minute by minute. Please don't be this intense. Just for once."

"Okay. Come over. Or I'll come and get you, though they'll tear me apart at The Windmill, if that's where you are. I'll try to be at my least intense."

It's so unbearably tempting. Get in the car and race out to Thornber Manor. Drink with him. Screw him. Or make love to him. Talk and talk and talk, because for some reason, I'm never at a loss for words with him, and his conversation never bores me. And the more I think about this, the surer I become that my ideas of "goodies and baddies" in this equation are utterly skewed.

"No. I need to vent. But I can't open myself up to you. I absolutely can't."

"Who else could you possibly speak to about this? Anyone in the Sadlers' employ isn't going to want to hear your disloyalty. No non-practitioner will understand what you're talking about. And you don't want to be attempting to chat this through with any of my men."

He's got a point—that's precisely why I called him in the first place. I frown and try to think, then an idea strikes me.

The Jaguar purrs to a halt outside The Windmill, roof down, horn blaring.

I'm perched at the bar, using a skin-tight dress and artistic make-up as armour and camouflage. Though all the bar's inhabitants have sent smiles in my direction, I've made it clear I don't want to talk.

Now, their attention turns away from me to the noise outside. The windows are open to let out the heat, so I hear Nikki calling.

"Come on, babe. Time to party or cry on my shoulder or whatever combination of the two you had in mind."

The barman looks me in the eye. "I don't think this is a good idea, Miss Sadler."

Everyone is so much more concerned about my wellbeing now they know I'm the daughter of their *de facto* lord and master. And they're even more respectful since my contribution to renewing the Dome for another year.

"It's fine. We're just having a girly night."

I stride out of the bar with the confidence that only freshly blow-dried hair and a couple of drinks can give you.

"Jump in," Nikki says, grinning.

"Gabriel actually let you borrow his car?"

"He has quite a few cars. I constantly use the others. But

turns out I only get the keys to the 1950s Jag when it's in the service of showing you a good time."

I laugh and enter the passenger seat by means of propelling myself over the edge.

"Seriously, love, you need to use magic more," she says, then floors the car.

"Where are we even going?" I ask, after a few moments of silence.

"You're the one who's having some sort of revelatory moment slash nervous breakdown. You get to choose. Cosy country pub, flashy cocktail bar, or somewhere in between?"

"I'm a little overdressed for it, but it'd be good to get out of town."

"Perfect. I'll head back out into the countryside. Though not too close to Thornber Manor. I'm not sure Gabe could physically restrain himself from crashing the party if you get within sensing distance. Good call not to attempt to deal with him tonight."

I laugh. "I'm not sure I've ever heard you say anything bad about him before."

"Even if I rarely bear the brunt of them, I know Gabe's faults better than almost anyone."

We drive out of town as the sun sets. Some of my tension and upset fades with the heat.

"So, are we classing this as a date?" Nikki asks.

I glance at her, then look at the floor. "Are you serious?"

"Don't look so embarrassed. 'No' is a perfectly acceptable answer. But I thought all Born Practitioners, were, well... flexible."

"I'm not exactly the biggest proponent of the Old Ways anymore, as you may have noticed. Besides, don't you have a girlfriend?"

She shrugs. "You mean Rachel, from fight night? She's a sweetheart. But I tend to keep things casual. Various women, a handful of men. Taught Practitioners can follow the Old Ways, too."

The pub we pull up outside dates back to 1300, according to the plaque on the wall. It's beautiful in the fading light. We walk through the indoors, where the dark wood and huge fireplace make me long to return in winter, then we exit into a garden on the back, tucked into the shadow of a hill. We sit down at a wooden picnic table, both throwing our legs out along the bench in opposite directions.

"Gin?" Nikki asks.

"Not somewhere like this. Get me the real-est ale you can find."

Nikki returns in record time. Presumably some form of magic and mesmerism was involved. I take an aggressive swig of my beer. It tastes like my late teens. I'm not sure when gin became the default.

"I'm perfectly happy to sit and drink an IPA with you in beautiful surroundings on a hot evening," Nikki says. "But there's obviously something you wanted to say."

I down a quarter of the beer in one go. The benefit of giving in and doing this with Gabriel would have been the way he'd have dragged my thoughts out of me through a mixture of charisma and magic. Nikki has plenty of both, but it's not quite the same.

"My family kill to consolidate their power and to protect the town. I've always known there was blood involved, but I never realised it went this far. I can never decide if the Dome's a good thing or a bad thing. Either way, people pay for it with their lives."

Nikki shrugs and sips her own drink with surprising delicacy. "The original Dome's a good thing, on balance. You only have to spend a few hours outside Mannith to see that."

"I guess that's fair."

"Expanding it, on the other hand, is dangerous. Gabe's

grandfather fought your grandfather over this. You know the basic story, right?"

"Just that my family used to control everything within the Dome, entirely unchallenged, and the Thornbers worked for them. There was clearly a disagreement or a power struggle a few generations back, but it's not something my parents ever really talked about."

Nikki nods. "By some quirk of birth or programme of study, Gabe's grandfather's power matched or exceeded your grandfather's. And so he rebelled. Used his worries about the Dome as an excuse, though maybe he just wanted power. They reached a stalemate. Or so Gabe tells me. Neither I nor my family were around when all that was going on."

"How did your family end up in Mannith? People from other parts of Yorkshire barely ever move here, never mind people from the other side of the world."

She shrugs. "Most of the rest of the family went to Sheffield. My parents wanted something different, and they found this place. File it under fate."

"And you've never had any trouble?"

She draws fire into her palms. "I've been able to do this sort of thing since I was tiny. Plus, I've always been under Gabe's protection. Let's just say that the only person ever to make a racist remark to my face provided a salutary lesson in tolerance to anyone else who might have considered doing so."

I grin. I'd like to have seen that.

Nikki sprawls out full length on the bench. "Anyway, back to the Thornbers' grand origin story. The grandfather had a son. Niall. He could hold his own against your father to the extent that he was able to create an entire separate organisation. But he had one obsession. He'd marry the most powerful female practitioner he could find and sire the most powerful heir. He'd beat the Sadlers in the area they prided themselves on the most."

I down the rest of my drink. It's starting to get dark. The

night is still warm—we're in the Dome, after all—but it's cooling.

"And he managed it," I say. "My family still have the ascendency. But while Brendan's a worthy Sadler heir, Gabriel-fucking-Thornber is the single most powerful practitioner I've ever come across."

"Don't call him that. Anyway, Niall cast his net wide. And eventually, he found Maeve. She fell in love. So did he. I only remember her as a kindly adult when I was a lonely child, but she was beautiful as hell. And dripping with magic, even more than you are. Even more than he is."

"Is it true what people say about her?"

"That she was some sort of demon? Maybe. Or maybe she was just a spectacularly powerful practitioner. Niall wanted that wild, untamed magic for his heir. But as time went on, he was less sure he wanted that for his wife. Her own family crafted the bracelets. He made her wear them every day."

I shivered, remembering the hour or two I'd worn Gabriel's bracelets. I'd not wondered about their provenance.

"How long did she live without magic?" It had been about three hours for me. And that had felt like torture.

"Years on end, until she died when Gabriel was fourteen. She either wasted away through lack of magic or killed herself for the same reason. It's hard to say whether father or son was more distraught.

"Niall wasn't the nicest of people. He disapproved of me and my lack of magical heritage, for a start. He truly loved Maeve though, but that love expressed itself in twisted ways."

I down the rest of my drink with a little shudder. I can't get over the fact Gabriel put those same accursed bracelets on me, even briefly.

Nikki sits back up and looks me in the eye. "You should tread very carefully. Gabe has endless flings, male and female. Though he keeps it casual, he treats them well. And while it's never gone beyond the platonic with me, he's always been a great friend. He understands sex and friendship and cama-raderie very well. But his views on love are skewed by his father's example.

"He loves you, you know. It sounds melodramatic, but it's true. But in his mind, love's all bound up with submission and control and obsession. It's a thin line between putting someone on a pedestal and putting them in a cage. Between longing for their powers and fearing them."

"He doesn't love me. I'll accept obsession, at best. He's met me about five times in total."

"But he's thought about you a lot more than that. In the years since you left town. And in the years before that, too."

I grip the table. "How long has this love or obsession or whatever we're calling it been going on? Why did he choose me for his bargain?"

Nikki tilts her head back and stares at the stars. "Ask him. I've already overstepped the mark. Just keep your guard up."

"I should go."

"No. We should get another round of drinks and move on to lighter topics. Are you aware of the concept of the Bechdel test?"

I laugh, though it's a little forced. "Whether or not a film contains a scene of two named women having a conversation."

"Indeed. But crucially, a conversation that isn't about a man. Now, Gabe's one of my favourite topics, too, but let's draw a line under him for now. Let's get drunk and talk politics, culture, celebrity gossip, anything and everything really."

I grab two more beers. We talk about a book we both happen to have read. A trashy reality show we love to hate. A recent scandal involving a politician. And on and on through various random, entertaining topics until the early hours. Between her company and her warnings, I feel a lot better and a lot worse, all at the same time.

SEVENTEEN

I spend the week at The Windmill, focusing on the case, and avoiding my family and anyone associated with them as much as I can.

On Saturday though, I drag myself over to the family home to finally have the difficult conversation.

Only Mum's there when I arrive. Dad and Liam are presumably out watching football. Maybe I've subconsciously chosen this time for just that reason, so I can do this one to one, rather than being outnumbered.

"It's so good to see you, sweetheart," Mum says, when she opens the door and finds me standing there. "We've all been worried about you. We've barely seen you since the Ritual. I hope it didn't hit you too hard."

I almost laugh. She makes it sound like it was merely a tiring evening.

Still, I go inside, sit down on a stool in the kitchen and accept my mum's offering of a slice of freshly baked apple and cinnamon cake and a mug of milky tea—she doesn't really do coffee.

I don't know where to start. I bicker with my family, but I

never really speak against them. How can I say what I need to say?

"You and the rest of the family kill people. Every year, for years on end. How can you live with that? How can I live with that?"

Mum comes over and puts an arm around me like I'm still a little child. "I didn't realise you'd never worked it out. I'd have taken the time to explain in advance otherwise—and been clearer on the details once I did give you a run-through. It's just how things have always been done around here. It's unpleasant, certainly. None of us enjoy doing the deed. But it needs to happen, and everyone in Mannith understands that—we never have any trouble finding the volunteer sacrifices."

I take a bite of the cake. It ought to turn to ash in my mouth, but it's delicious. Of course it is. "You can't consent to being murdered," I say. "Definitely not legally. I'd argue not morally, either."

"And yet, people do. Every time without fail. Because unlike you, they care about this town as much as us. Those four deaths keep so many more people than that safe for the rest of the year."

"I care about Mannith, Mum. I know that's hard to believe when I've spent so long away, but I had no choice. I love the way our magic keeps it protected. But do you really have to kill to make it that way? My token cut seemed to work just fine."

And even just doing that had made my skin crawl once I'd come back down to earth.

Mum shakes her head. "It worked because you were powerful enough to make that be sufficient and because the rest of us went through with it. If we'd all wimped out, the Dome would have withered and died."

I close my eyes, breathe deeply, and take a large swig of the tea. Hard to believe my mum's trying to act like I'm the one in the wrong here.

"I missed you all so much in the years I was away," I say, keeping my eyes closed. "I was terrified to come back, but it was worth it to see you all. I've loved those nights out with Liam and Chrissie. Getting to know Ray and the babies. Quiet moments with you and Dad."

The less said about conferences with Bren, the better, but it's still been amazing to reconnect with him.

"I love this family and I want to be a part of it," I continue. "But how can I just sit around eating Sunday lunch or going out for drinks with you all, knowing what you do?"

Mum slumps into the chair next to me. When I dare to open my eyes, I can hardly bear to see how crumpled and defeated she looks.

"What are you saying?"

I drop my head into my hands. "I really don't know. Nothing and everything. I'm not disappearing back to London or withdrawing from the case. But I can't just spend time with you all and pretend I don't care about the things you do."

"I know this has been hard for you," Mum says. "I'll tell you what you ought to do. Drive over to the church. Meditate properly. Lay some flowers on your nan's grave. Perhaps have a nice chat with her if she's in the mood. It'll make you feel less on edge. Less conflicted about everything. More connected to the town and our ancestors."

"Actually, that's a great idea. And then... well, I guess we'll see how it goes. I don't want to totally cut contact. But I might need to keep my distance, at least for a while."

I finish my drink and the slice of cake in silence, then head out before anything more can be said.

Non-practitioners call it the Witches' Church. It's a long way out from the centre of town, out past Thornber Manor, almost to the furthest reaches of the Dome on that side. It dates back to the twelfth century, though it's been destroyed and substantially rebuilt at least four times. A fire. A lightning strike. A puritan mob. A WWII bombing raid that aimed for the armament factories and went off course.

I park my car as close as I can manage, which is a good twenty-minute walk away. Halfway up a hill, the road just stops. From there, you have to climb to the top and walk down the other side. The hill is all exposed grassy fields, scorched by the sun. The day is genuinely hot—hotter than Mannith's usual pleasant warmth—and I'm sweating by the time I reach the bottom.

As a kid, I used to complain about the walk. "The walk is half of the point," my nan used to tell me. "It starts to clear the mind."

I'm not sure whether she intended it as deep wisdom or a way to quiet a whining seven-year-old, but today, I understand what she meant. My thoughts move more slowly as I walk and some of my worries subside.

At the bottom of the hill, the landscape abruptly changes. Heavily leafed oak trees form a dark canopy above and a narrow pathway below. Ivy crawls up the trunks and nettles line the way ahead. It must be fifteen degrees cooler in this dense shade than out in the open.

This is by far my least favourite part of the route, and I tread carefully to avoid hitting my head on a branch or stinging my legs, but it's worth it for the moment when I break out into the clearing by the lake and gaze on the church.

Nowadays, the physical building stands in ruins. The west wall is fully intact, barely altered since its medieval origins, but on the other three sides, there are only a few foundation stones to show its original shape. Nevertheless, I've always found it more beautiful than any perfectly preserved cathedral.

There are hundreds of gravestones, many of them accompanied by statues of the grave's occupant. They're all faded and overgrown with ivy, so that those from a few decades ago are indistinguishable from those that are centuries old. Nothing remains untouched for long in the hidden clearing by the lake.

As always, I start by walking the perimeter of the building. Then I take a few moments to look at some of the older gravestones and statues, paying my respects to their inhabitants. There are several families buried in the graveyard, but Sadlers ancient and modern dominate. I've looked at the inscriptions on my ancestors' graves so many times over the years that I feel like I know some of them. There's a sixteenth-century statue that even through the moss and the erosion looks identical to Chrissie, and an eighteenth-century one that could definitely pass as Liam in moonlight. Our family has lived in the same place for too long. We're basically one with the town.

I stride to the shore of the lake and pick a bunch of the white lilies that grow there, breathing in their heady scent. Then I stroll back to the eastern corner on the lake side, to one of the newest statues (not that you can tell, considering the way it's already faded). Many of the people buried here died relatively young. And many of those who survived longer are still depicted in their prime rather than their decline. But my nan's statue shows her aged eighty and looks just like I remember her.

I kneel before the statue, reverently lay the lilies down, and sink into a core meditation. It's ten times easier in Mannith than in London, but it's a hundred times easier again in this spot.

You're supposed to be able to talk to your ancestors in this graveyard. Everything from a flash of insight, to a vision, to an audible voice in your head or a full-blown ghost. But communing with the dead—like clairvoyance or true empathy—is a little different from regular magic, and it's never been a big skill of mine. Liam, on the other hand, not only chats to relatives we've known, loved, and mourned, but to long-ago ancestors and complete strangers.

I stay in place, eyes closed, for the best part of an hour, letting my mind sink into the spirit of the place. Eventually, I stand up, and drop a few purple Quality Street chocolates down next to the lilies. They were Nan's favourite, and if her ghost does make an appearance after I'm finished, I'm sure she'll appreciate them more than the traditional flowers.

A meditation that deep, combined with the general atmosphere of this place and the heat of the day have left me disassociated yet hyper-aware. Suddenly, I'm sure I'm no longer alone in this isolated, lonely place and that my companion is flesh and blood.

I whirl around to look, my heart racing. With crushing inevitability, it's Gabriel. Acting on pure instinct, I throw up my hands and draw a shield around myself.

"Sadie, relax. I'm not here for you." His voice is slower and softer than usual, like the clearing has stolen some of his edge. One hand is gripping a bunch of lilies like the ones I picked. With the other hand, he gestures to a tomb on the woodland side of the graveyard.

I follow his gaze, then step over to the grave in question.

Maeve Thornber.
Devoted mother and wife.
Born 1968, Died 2007.
Power and beauty.

The statue might not do justice to her power, but her beauty is undeniable. And it's in unusually good repair, as though someone has not only been laying flowers, but fighting back the clearing's tendency towards decay with all of their considerable magical strength.

I bow my head. "I didn't realise. Go ahead and pay your respects to your mother. I'm finished here."

It's odd, but in this place, I don't feel any fear, anger or lust towards him. Or indeed, any of the fury I've been feeling towards my family all week.

"Stay, please. I'll only be a moment. I literally swear on my mother's grave that I didn't come here to find you. But as you are here, I want to apologise. Explain. Show you the real me and get to know the real you."

"I... I honestly should go."

"Come on, Sadie. We could head out of town for the evening. Get out of the Dome and breathe the free air. Find a restaurant your London friends would approve of."

The correct answer is obvious. Either firmly tell him to piss off or simply leave and hope he gets the message. It was madness when I visited his house, but there was some degree of reason to it. Since then, there's been the business with Leah, and Nikki's warnings. There'd be no rationale for this date-night thing. It'd be fraternising with the enemy, pure and simple. Betraying my family and messing with my head.

And yet... I'm oddly intrigued by what he's like to sit and talk to. And just thinking the words *date night* in the context of Gabriel has sent the blood rushing to all sorts of inappropriate places.

I stand frozen in place, not wanting to leave, not wanting to reply. Seemingly satisfied that I'm not going anywhere, Gabriel ignores me for once and walks solemnly over to the statue of his mother. Just like I'd done, he places the flowers, kneels, then lets his mind sink down into the earth. Standing behind him and a few metres away, I can't see his eyes, but I can tell he's deep into a core meditation. His body is unnaturally still, and so is the usually frenetic cloud of power that surrounds him.

It's both touching and disconcerting that he's allowing himself to be this vulnerable in my presence. While he's this out of it, it'd be simple to take him down once and for all. But even if I had both the stomach and the desire to harm him, no practitioner would be stupid enough to attack someone in these surroundings, particularly while they were communing with the dead. You'd bring the wrath of a hundred ghosts down on your head, perhaps incur the fury of the very earth.

I shouldn't watch him, either. He asked me to stay, but I ought to give him some privacy. Except I can't take my eyes off him. He looks different like this. Alone, silent, and unguarded.

Eventually, he rises. I'm genuinely unsure how long it's been. In the intensity of my focus on him, I'd slipped into a semi-meditative state myself.

"Will you lay a flower, too?" He stays by the statue but turns his head to ask me the question.

I frown. "I'm not sure that's appropriate. I never met your mother, and I doubt she was a big fan of my family."

"It'd mean a lot to her. And a lot to me."

I walk off in the direction of the plot of lilies by the lake without replying. It's unclear whether he's actually just spoken to his mother—if anyone had the gift, it would be him—or whether he's putting sentiments in her mouth, but it would be disrespectful to the dead to refuse at this point.

When I return to the statue, he's smiling like I've done him the biggest favour as he steps aside to give me access.

I stare at Maeve Thornber's beautiful carved face, thinking of Nikki's story and unsure what's expected of me. Lay the flowers and go? Kneel for a moment? Sink down into another meditation?

I glance back at Gabriel, who's watching me intently but giving no hint as to what he wants.

I kneel, lay the flowers, and close my eyes for a moment. Another core meditation would be over the top, but I can show proper decorum.

Sadie. You've grown up as beautiful as I knew you would. It's so good to see you here with my boy.

The words are in my head, delivered in a strong, rural Irish accent.

I drop my head into my hands. This shouldn't be scary. I've been brought up to believe in spirits, to see them as sources of advice and love. But I've never managed to make contact with my own ancestors. Why the hell is Gabriel's mother, of all people, trying to have a chat?

We were all so sad when you went away. I know I'm biased as a mother, and I know he doesn't always go about things the right way, but you should trust my Gabriel.

I ought to reply, but I'm stunned and unsure what to say. So, I simply bow my head towards the statue, then jump to my feet.

"Okay?" Gabriel asks, taking my arm.

I nod frantically. "Fine. I really should be getting back, though."

"Thank you for doing that. Now seriously, will you join me for dinner tonight?"

I've basically been given orders by a ghost. Besides, against all my better judgement, the idea is still intriguing. And maybe, just maybe, I can get some intel that'll be useful for the case.

"No blockers, no guards, and never mention this to anyone, but other than that... you can pick me up at six."

Gabriel grins like he's won the lottery. "Perfect. I'll sort out reservations."

I dread to think what combination of threats and mind control he intends to employ to get the table he wants, but I'm past caring.

I glance back at the statue of Maeve as a thought strikes me. "Isn't your father buried here? Shouldn't he have a statue by now?"

Gabriel looks away. "It's still too raw. I'll erect one once the case is over. It's probably for the best as far as you're concerned though—I doubt you'd get as positive a reaction from him as from my mother. He was never your biggest fan."

I bow my head. I guess his dad just really, really hated all Sadlers.

"In the meantime, do you want to go inside for a moment?" Gabriel gestures towards the church's one solid door.

"Can you activate it?"

He walks over to the door. "This is the Witches' Church, not the Sadlers' personal family chapel. It's keyed to my blood as surely as to yours."

I run to catch him up, then hold out my hand. He takes it and lifts it up. Together, we grip the massive brass handle and pull. Despite its age, heaviness, and general air of disrepair, it opens smoothly.

With our hands still raised and adjoined—and I'm barely conscious of the fact I'm holding his hand, such is my concentration—we step over the threshold of the ruined church and into its perfectly preserved interior. Where I'd stood on grass moments ago, there's now a stone floor with ornately carved wooden pews at regular intervals. A huge stained-glass window dominates the far wall, with small ones every few feet along the side walls. They show scenes from the Bible, from local history, and from practitioner lore, all artfully depicted by craftsmen who possessed both artistic skill and enough power to bring their innermost visions to glorious life. Everywhere, candles glow, ranging from those several feet high that cast their light on the main window, to tiny ones in holders by each pew. A scent of beeswax and of incense rises around us, and there's a faint, disembodied sound of organ music in the cool air.

Back when I still lived in Mannith, I came to the graveyard every few weeks, but I haven't been inside the church since my nan's funeral when I was fifteen. You need two practitioners with the right strength and lineage to make it snap into life. However many times the physical church has been destroyed, this true heart of it has always survived. It was intended as a sanctuary, impenetrable by those who would do us harm.

"It's so beautiful," I whisper. "I'd forgotten."

"Me too. Mum used to bring me here all the time. She used

to tell me I'd have my wedding here one day. But after she died, Dad had no interest in visiting, and no one else in my circle could trigger the mechanism."

I smile. "It'd be an odd place for a wedding. For a start, you'd have to make sure you had a bride who could see anything except nettles and crumbling walls when she opened the door."

"That wouldn't be an issue. I'd never marry anyone who couldn't."

"Your retinue of flings and admirers will be crushed to hear that," I reply.

I keep my tone jokey, and my eyes averted from his. Because I have an alarming suspicion it's our wedding he's seeing in his mind's eye.

"I'll see you at six," I add, turning to go. "Out by Langley Hill. There's no way I'm having you pick me up outside The Windmill. Or God forbid, my parents' house."

"See you then." He stares up at the stained-glass windows, lost in thought.

EIGHTEEN

By the time I get back to The Windmill, it's three PM. If I'm going to be ridiculous enough to go on an actual date with Gabriel, I could at least have the self-respect to avoid looking like I've made an effort, but I can't resist.

I'd go to Chrissie, normally, but that'd result in a whole load of questions I don't want to get into. I can't even visit any of the salons in town—everyone knows my family and likes to gossip.

Instead, I do the best I can with a mixture of conventional and magical techniques, both of which my sister drilled into me, neither of which I'm quite as good at as her. But I'm happy with the end result. My outfit and hair are simple and pretty: white knee-length cotton dress and light waves around my face, respectively.

The saucy underwear I've conjured into being makes me a little guilty. The love potion I dab on my pulse points makes me feel worse. It's not like it'll have any effect on Gabriel. It's more for my confidence... but it's the principle of the thing.

I keep telling myself this is entirely justifiable as an opportunity to find out what really happened the night Niall Thornber died, but it's not a wildly convincing argument, even to myself.

I've never known three hours go by so quickly. I stuff my heels in my oversized bag and throw on some sparkly flip-flops, then head downstairs, nod at the other patrons, and stride off towards the edge of town.

You should have let him pick you up here, a treacherous part of my mind chides. *If you're doing this, then own it. No need to be ashamed. No need to worry about what other people think.*

Normally, that's exactly the kind of motto I live by. But of course, I should be ashamed of this, and I couldn't possibly let other people know. It'd get back to my family, and they'd quite rightly be worried and horrified in equal measure.

All that aside, it's good to walk in the slowly cooling early evening air. Since I've been back in Mannith, I've started to drive everywhere without thinking about it, while I'll happily walk a couple of miles in London, or at least as far as the train station. Despite all my exercise, my leg muscles must be in danger of atrophying.

Gabriel's distinctive car and even more distinctive profile are right where he promised. No playing games, no running late or making me wait. I take a deep breath and tell myself this is a normal date and I'm playing the role of relaxed, sexy young woman.

"I wasn't sure you'd come," he says, with a huge smile when I stand by the driver-side door.

"Don't tell me that's a hint of self-doubt? That must be a first for you."

"I don't normally have any worries about my charms. But then, I don't usually have such a turbulent prior history with my dates."

He lets himself out of the car then opens the passenger door. I can't help but smile at the sight of him in tight jeans and pale pink tailored shirt, sunglasses pushing back his floppy hair and showing his eyes—a sort of rose-gold right now—in all their glory.

"You look beautiful," he says as I slide onto the low seat. "You always do. But tonight more than ever. Perhaps because you went to all that effort for me."

I laugh as he closes the door and returns to the driver's seat. "Oh, please. I've made an effort for the benefit of the fancy restaurant and of the photographs I intend to post online so my friends back home don't start to wonder if I'm dead."

"Do you really not think of this as your home anymore? That's sad." Then he grins, leans over, and buries his head in my neck. "Sadie Sadler. You are absolutely doused in Vetiver, Ylang Ylang, and all the rest of it. Now don't tell me that's for the benefit of the waiters."

"It's not like it'd work on you anyway," I say defensively, fighting the irrational urge to stroke his hair and press him deeper against me.

"Not on the level of a spell, no. But it still makes you smell sexy as hell. And while I appreciate the gesture, you *really* don't need to attempt to work any love magic on me. That ship's well and truly sailed."

He smells amazing, too. I think it's an expensive aftershave rather than a potion *per se*, but that line is as blurry as the one between magic and technology.

He sits back up and starts to drive. I lean back and feast my eyes on him. If I'm going to do this, I might as well make the most of it.

Please let this be a good night, I silently pray. *Please don't let there be drama. Please don't let there be danger. And for goodness' sake, please let me escape with my heart intact.*

A few minutes later, I feel that disquieting little flicker as the car reaches the outskirts of Mannith and pulls through the Dome. Outside of it, I'm able to think a little more clearly. I steel myself. There's enjoying the moment, and then there's giving in.

"You said you wanted to explain. To apologise. How about we put the flirtation on hold for a moment?"

Gabriel nods, slowly, then turns to look at me. The car continues to speed along, though his eyes are nowhere near the road and his hands barely on the steering wheel. His magic is taking the strain.

"I've told you before that I always have at least two reasons for everything I do. It's true, but it's also a throwaway line. A shield. You deserve more than that."

He alternates between gazing into my eyes and staring at the dashboard like it contains the secrets of the universe. Of course, he could be putting on a show. He's so damn difficult to read.

"It's hard to know where to start with apologies. The lien, I guess. Imposing it on you was a moment of madness. There's no sane way of explaining that one away. At some point, I want to tell you more about what drove me to it, but let's park that for now.

"Then there was the Greenfire. I didn't want to hurt you. I just wanted to know for sure that you were who I thought. And I wanted you to stop repressing your power. I thought you'd fight back within seconds."

"And if I wasn't who you thought? You'd have broken a human with that concentrated an attack. Probably a weaker practitioner, too."

I shouldn't be splitting hairs like this, debating what he knew and why he did it. There is no explaining it away, no justification. He hurt me. That's surely all that matters?

"And then, at the casino, seeing you flipped a switch in my brain. I wanted to be close to you, for you to admit who you were, and for you to stop holding all that glorious power in check."

"You could have got Connor killed." I still feel guilty about that little episode. He sure as hell should.

Gabriel shrugs, as though what happens to Connor is neither of our concerns.

"You nearly burnt me out."

His expression turns more serious. "I miscalculated."

I clench my teeth. I dread to think what my expression looks like, never mind my eyes. "Miscalculated? Gabriel, I'm not your personal experiment. You can't hurt me and hope I'll fight back. You can't force me into using magic and hope I'll thrive instead of nearly breaking."

"I know. And I'm sorry. It just kills me to see you deny your power, deny who you are. It's so antithetical to everything I was brought up to believe."

"I only ever stopped using magic because I was so scared of you and your lien. And it's not the only reason I left this town, but it sure as hell is the reason I didn't visit my family once in six years."

I stare out at the horizon. Am I getting through to him? Is he really sorry? Does he understand why so much of what he's done is so messed up?

"If you're determined to reel off a list of your sins, let's move on to Leah," I say eventually.

He nods. "If you'd asked me not to sleep with anyone else after our night together, I'd have respected your wishes. But you didn't give any sign of wanting to see me again."

"Hang on a minute. This isn't even about me."

"From my perspective, everything's about you, to a greater or lesser degree."

I dig my nails into the leather seats. There's something worrying in his tone. I've always assumed he was toying with me, using me, or slotting me into some wider plan. But the more he tries to apologise and explain, the more obsessed he sounds. Nikki's warnings seemed melodramatic, but I'm starting to believe he truly thinks he's in love with me for whatever twisted reason.

"You used Leah. Either to hurt Brendan yet more or to get a rise out of me. Or both."

"I wouldn't say I used her. She got exactly what she wanted out of the arrangement. And if not me, she'd have given in to someone else's charms sooner rather than later. I basically did Brendan a favour, showing him her true colours before the wedding."

"There's no point even trying to discuss any of this, is there? You just don't accept the normal rules apply to you. You're not apologising. You're attempting to tell your side of an indefensible story."

He closes his glowing eyes for a moment. "Okay then. Let me wholeheartedly apologise for something. Putting the bracelets on you. Blocking your power. Sleeping with you while you were blocked. I was so stunned that you'd appeared on my doorstep that I was scared it was a trap. But that's no excuse. That *was* indefensible, and I'm sorry."

He's a damn good actor, but he sounds so sincere and sad that I reach out on autopilot and touch his arm. "Really? That's what you feel bad about? It's not a sensation I'm eager to repeat, but it didn't do me any harm, and it was a sensible precaution."

He places his hand on top of mine, not even pretending to be physically driving the car anymore. I hate the fact his touch sends shivers down my arm.

"You don't understand. Everything else I've done, it was about trying to get you to embrace your powers and to want me. I shouldn't have curtailed your powers even for a moment. And I should have shown I trusted you."

Presumably, he's thinking about what his father did to his mother, and how putting the blockers on me was like following in his footsteps. But however honest we're supposedly being, there's no way I dare to bring that up.

We drive without exchanging another word for twenty minutes. It's unclear whether it's companionable silence despite everything, or whether we're deliberately not speaking to each other. I should demand he drives me home. Or use magic to get myself out of there. But somehow, I still want to know how the evening is going to go.

Gabriel pulls into an old-fashioned courtyard and kills the engine.

The hotel and restaurant is low and sprawling, built out of the dark local stone but lightened with pristine white paint around each of the mullioned windows and by copious amounts of flowers. It could be any pretty country pub, but I recognise the name from a few newspaper articles that claimed the food can more than compete with any minimalist London restaurant. I try not to think about the bedrooms.

Gabriel helps me out of the car, takes my arm, and leads me inside, where it's a perfect combination of cosy and elegant, rural and sophisticated. We're greeted instantly by beaming waiters. It's unclear whether they are simply well-trained and gregarious, or whether they're responding to Gabriel's charisma and magic. Either way, they show us straight to a linen-covered table tucked away in an alcove by an open fire, which is unlit on this warm summer's evening but still gives an air of comfort.

We sit next to each other on a long, high-backed bench, facing out onto the garden.

"I've ordered the tasting menu," Gabriel explains. "It's focused on local food, seasonal produce, and traditional methods. All of which chimes with the way I see the world—there are few things more important than a sense of time and place."

I smile. "You sound like a restaurant critic. Or else some hipster with a food blog."

He laughs. "Not a word of this to the acolytes. But I truly believe all that. Don't you? I've seen you do your core meditations and sink your mind into the earth. I've felt you draw on the power in Mannith's woods and rivers, and give it something of your own power in turn."

"I guess that's basically the same thing as eating hand-caught scallops and forced rhubarb?" I reply, glancing at the menu in front of us. But despite my flippant tone, I know what he means. It echoes the words that start the Ritual: *Mannith is a blessed place. It's always drawn something from the rivers and mountains that surround it.*

All of the tension of the drive seems to have faded away. We're squarely back in date territory.

The waiter brings me a glass of English sparkling wine—really taking local produce to the extreme—and an *amuse-bouche* that tastes as good as it looks, though despite my attempts at London sophistication, my palate's not quite developed enough to tell what it is. I take a sip of the local equivalent of champagne and relax.

Several delicious courses and a couple of glasses of wine later and I'm feeling more chilled and cheerful than I have in months. I'm snuggling closer to Gabriel by the minute, and in between feeding each other mouthfuls of food, we both seem to be laughing or nodding at every word the other says.

"We could drive back," Gabriel says, once we've finished our after-dinner coffees. "One of the benefits of steering with magic is that it's perfectly safe after a few drinks. But I do have a room upstairs..."

For a moment, I snap out of my flirty, contented mood. Does he really think he's so irresistible that after everything that's happened and everything he is, he could take me for a nice—okay, a very nice—meal, and I'd just fall into bed with him?

But the angry words don't come, because there are two truths I can't avoid. Firstly, as soon as he invited me, I started preparing as though for a date. And secondly, looking at him now, I want him more than I've ever wanted anyone. Perhaps more than I've ever wanted any*thing*.

I mentally scan my body and the surrounding area, looking for any trace of a spell that could be affecting my choices. His powers shouldn't have any effect on me, of course, but who knows with him? All I can sense is my power and his, the forces still, steady and intertwined.

I lean in closer. "It's a beautiful place. And as I presume you kicked out some poor couple who've had it booked for months, it'd be a shame to waste it."

His smile widens, as though, for all his confidence, he'd actually been worried I might say no. Surely not something that's normally high on his worry list.

He takes my arm and leads us out of the restaurant. It's unclear whether the bill for dinner has gone on a tab or he's made the manager forget the meal ever happened.

The room is as lovely as I'd hoped. The furniture is old and heavy, but the bright white walls, curtains, and bed linen make it feel light and spacious. There's a huge, high bed, with a massive carved wooden headboard behind it. I take all this in in a moment, because now we're alone, it's almost impossible to focus on anything but Gabriel. If the room contained the original Mona Lisa or a live alligator, I'd barely notice.

What's glorious and terrifying is that he's staring at me in the same way, as though I'm the only thing capable of capturing his attention, the only thing worth looking at.

"How many people have you brought here?"

I just about manage to make the question sound casual. It's not like it matters. It's hardly as if I'm some sweet little virgin about to be dishonoured. It's not as if I want more from him than sex.

"Here? No one. I'd never deny that I've had plenty of flings and one-night stands. But I want this to be special. I want us to be special."

His words send a cheesy smile to my lips, a blush to my cheeks, and a rush of blood to my erogenous zones. God, he's good. No wonder everyone falls for him.

You can sleep with him if you really must, I tell myself sternly. *But you cannot, must not be taken in by his nonsense. You can't be used or betrayed if all you want is a night with a hot guy and all you get is a night with a hot guy.*

I shake my head. "Less of that. Perhaps you want to stop me freeing my brother? Perhaps you want to score a point against the Sadlers? Or prove no one can escape you or resist your charms? Or hell, maybe I just look hot in this little dress? Dinner was delightful, you're basically more handsome than any guy I've ever seen, and I'm looking forward to ripping off that shirt. Don't try to pretend there's love and romance at the heart of this."

He closes his eyes and takes an audible deep breath, almost as though he's about to start a core meditation. "Okay. If you want to deny you feel anything for me and I feel anything for you, we can pretend this is entirely casual."

I slip out of my dress. Whether he's in love with me, using me for sex, or taking forward some wider plan, I appreciate the little sigh that escapes him at the sight of my body. He stares like he's never had someone naked in front of him before.

I reach up and unbutton his pink shirt, acting like my hands aren't trembling. "Don't you dare be all tender and romantic tonight. I want you to pin me down and take me. I want the version of you that unleashed Greenfire on me. Or the one from the casino. Don't treat me like a lover. Treat me like a captured enemy."

I'm breathing so heavily I can barely get the crazy, dangerous words out.

He looks stunned. It's the same expression I've seen on all sorts of men's faces when I've been rather more sexually confident than they were expecting. But this is about more than me knowing what I want in bed. It's half pushing him away, half opening myself wide.

It's madness to deliberately put myself at his mercy, to demand he brings forth his dark side. But there'll be less room for bullshit this way. And I'm aroused beyond measure. As is he, I quickly discover once I open his jeans.

"Are you sure about this?"

"Once again, I'm not some breakable human girl or half-rate practitioner. If you push me too far, I can fight back."

He pulls me towards him and kisses me softly on the lips. "If you insist."

The next moment, I'm face down on the bed, arms and legs spread, pinned in place by tendrils of his magic.

My breath comes thick and fast. I never normally feel powerless. Even though I barely use my magic, the knowledge that it's simmering away below the surface provides constant reassurance. But despite my reckless words to Gabriel, I'm far from sure I'm strong enough to break out of this if I wanted or needed to. The thought is oddly erotic.

He kneels on the bed between my legs, hands on my back. "You really want to play the Greenfire game again?"

I nod, insofar as I can move my head. Everything about this is insane, but I'm beyond caring.

He doesn't hesitate. The skin-to-skin contact means the spell hits me instantly. I scream. It's every bit as agonising as last time, but I don't feel scared. It's oddly safe, oddly intimate.

With all his prior insistence on making this a nice, romantic evening, I half expect him to lose his nerve and stop at the sound of my screams, but he only intensifies the effect.

He runs his hands up and down my back. Somehow, my

mind is able to sense the soft touch even through the pain everywhere else.

"Beg me to stop," he whispers.

I dig my nails into the pillows and give a miniscule shake of my head.

"Or fight me off, if you prefer. I'm not stopping till you do one or the other."

Just like in the street that night, my magic takes over and fights back without consulting with my brain. This time, I let it. Immediately, the pain lessens. But instead of backing off, Gabriel pushes harder. It's a battle of wills and strength.

"You'll have to fight harder than that to stop me, baby," he whispers.

I try. Unlike last time, when I'd fought my magic every inch of the way, I give it free rein, forcing it out of every pore, pushing back against both the physical manifestation of pain and the incorporeal image of the fire around me. Every time I buy myself a second's respite, he redoubles his efforts.

He trails soft kisses down my back and strokes my thighs, all the time sending wave after wave of pain through me.

I'm shaking, my muscles pulsing and my nerves firing random signals. It's the pain. It's the force of my magic. It's the powerlessness. It's the arousal that's only rising, against all the odds.

"Don't feel bad." He speaks the words right into my ear. "Anyone else would have passed out by now. No one else would have been able to push back at all. And you're still out of practice."

All that's true. Plus, it's hard to be at my best with my hands bound. I'm still far too reliant on those pathetic gestures. Instead of ignoring the pain, I let it build, use it to fuel my magic. One last blast. For a moment, I think I've done it. I win myself five clear seconds free from pain.

Then a new wave of Greenfire hits. That's it. I'm done. "Stop, Gabriel, please."

The second I say the words, the spell breaks and every trace of the pain disappears. His control is as impeccable as his strength.

I lie there trembling from the intensity of it all while he continues to run kisses up and down my body. Then he slips his hands between my legs. I gasp.

"Well, well," he says, alternating between rubbing roughly and slipping two fingers inside me. "Anyone would think you liked Greenfire. It beats spanking, I suppose."

I grind against his hands.

"Stay still," he orders.

I freeze. I'm too strung out to tell whether it's magic or I'm too deep in the moment to defy him.

I'm close to coming within moments.

"Nope. Don't you dare." He takes his hand away, drawing a whimper from my lips. "Not until I say so. *If* I say so."

He leans over me, resting his forehead on the back of my head and holding my wrists. There's a spark of power where his hands touch me, and suddenly, my arousal limits are off the scale. He's doing *something* with magic. Bypassing physical touch and the nerves and going straight for the relevant receptors in the brain.

"I'm also blocking you from actually orgasming," he adds, as though I've said the first part out loud. "The feeling will only build."

For a minute or two, it's frustrating but heavenly. After that, it's almost worse than the Greenfire.

"Please." I don't make a conscious decision to beg this time. "Please let me come. I can't take this."

"You look so beautiful like that. Aroused and at my mercy."

He's still kissing me. It's all too much.

"Gabriel." I whimper his name.

"Is this casual enough for you?"

I can't get out a coherent response, just a succession of little sounds. My body feels like it could fly apart.

Without warning, he sits up and releases my wrists, breaking the immediate connection. The unbearable, heightened sensation falls away, leaving just my very powerful natural arousal. A fresh surge of power, and instead of being pinned in place on my front, I'm on hands and knees.

"You okay?" he asks.

I nod frantically. "No more games. I just want you."

He slips on a condom—I guess all those lessons I was taught about the dangers of unprotected sex with fellow practitioners were drilled into him, too—then thrusts inside me without another word. From the way he grips my hips and pounds, he's not forgotten my warning not to be tender. He slips a hand further around and strokes me with equal force. I come instantly, screaming louder than I did under the force of the Greenfire, spasming against him.

"Oh, Sadie," he sighs.

Then he continues, a little slower now, but still deep and forceful. Whatever magic was holding me still seems to have fallen away with my orgasm, and I move back against him. After a few minutes, I come again, then he pulls me close, holds me firmly against him, redoubles his speed and force, and finally comes himself, showering a fresh batch of kisses on my head as he does.

We're frozen in place for a moment or two, not by magic but by intensity. Then we fall back on the bed, and he pulls me into an embrace.

I wriggle into him as closely as I possibly can, clinging to him.

"I didn't go too far?" he asks. "I've never quite gone down that route with anyone. I think I'd have killed anyone else if I'd tried."

I start to cry, hot tears dripping on his chest.

"Fuck. I did go too far. God, Sadie, don't cry."

I shake my head. "It was perfect. I've just never felt so completely in someone's control. Anyone else, I'd have fought them off. Or if they'd managed, I'd have been terrified. But I was at your mercy, and it felt like a nice place to be."

He doesn't say anything, just pulls me in tighter and strokes my head. I don't know what to make of all this.

"Am I allowed to be sweet again now?" he asks.

"Always."

"Then let me run you a bath and get you some water. You look like you've come back from a war."

I don't want him to move, but there's sense in his words, so I release my death grip. I smile to see him walk over to the bathroom. It's odd to see him walking around naked in my presence. I can compartmentalise sex, but there's a strange intimacy in this.

The sound of running water and the scent of some sort of aromatherapy oil (not a patch on one of my mum's concoctions, but not bad) drifts towards me, then Gabriel reappears with a glass of water. He could have achieved both tasks from the bed with a flick of his finger. Or not even that, in his case. But he's done it by hand, a traditional sign of respect and regard.

He smiles to see me sprawled on the bed, already half asleep. "Drink this. And no sleep until you've had that soak."

I wriggle back up to a seated position and let him hold the water glass to my lips.

Once the bath's run, we slip into it together. I lean back against his chest as the water soothes my muscles and his hands encircle my waist. He's still wearing the ring on a chain I saw last time I saw him naked, and it presses lightly into my back.

Last time we slept together, I couldn't get out of there quickly enough. But now, God help me, I want nothing more than to fall asleep in his arms and wake up beside him.

It's mid-morning when we do wake up. We clearly both needed the sleep. When my eyes flicker open, I'm still cradled against his shoulder. I stroke his chest ultra gently, but it's enough to wake him.

We have sex again. Slow and gentle this time, but every bit as physically and emotionally satisfying. Then it's time for a lazy Sunday morning breakfast downstairs. The staff smile at us, as though we're giving off so much love and joy that it's infectious. My hearty bacon, sausages, and eggs are as delicious and as prettily served as last night's more rarefied selection.

"Ready for the drive home?" Gabriel asks.

"I guess."

I want to put it off as long as possible. Out here, it's just the two of us. Food, sex, and conversation. Back in Mannith, nothing will be that simple. Even so, I get in the car.

For the first few miles, we drive in silence, enjoying the view and each other's company.

"So, what is this?" Gabriel asks eventually, once we're through the Dome and on the outskirts of Mannith. "Do you propose we make a habit of this sort of thing?"

I look away from him, out over the moors. "Do you?"

"I've told you before. You say you want something serious, I'll give it to you. But you don't seem to know what you want. Or if you do, you won't show it."

I want you. It's crazy. Though he's inhabited my mind for years on end, I barely know him. And some of what I do know gives major cause for concern. But while I can attempt to hide the truth from him, there's no hiding it from myself.

"These last fifteen hours with you have been... incredible. But I can't separate what I feel for you from your relationship with my family. Particularly now, while the trial is ongoing."

I'm still angry at my family about the Ritual. But that

doesn't mean throwing my lot in with their old enemy. It doesn't mean letting my brother go down for a crime he didn't commit.

Gabriel swerves the car into a side road and slams on the brakes, jolting us both back in our seats. "Forget about the trial. Brendan does not deserve your help. Not six years ago when you handed yourself over to me to save his magic and not now."

I cross my arms. "Is that what this is all about? You had a fool-proof plan to take down your rival, but Brendan has a secret weapon in me, so you're trying to use sex and romance to neutralise the threat?"

Gabriel cuts the engine. "Let's take a walk. There's something I need to tell you."

I glance out of the window. The road is deserted, and the surrounding area is heavily wooded. Despite the lovely time we've been having, some instinct tells me I don't want to be alone with him out there.

I sit up straighter. "Whatever you need to say, you can say it here."

"Some conversations need to take place in nature." He opens his door, steps out onto the side of the road, and strides into the shelter of the trees without waiting to see if I'm going to follow.

For a minute or two, I hesitate. What the hell is this? Then I sigh and let myself out of the car. Deep down, I'm desperate to hear what he has to tell me.

Gabriel has disappeared from sight, but I can sense his aura pulsing in the distance. It's strong and distinctive—and right now, extremely agitated.

I traverse myself to his location—it's a two-minute walk away at most, but I don't want to waste any time. He's in a little glade, where the intertwined trees above almost block out the sun. He's leaning against the trunk of an old oak, breathing hard and obviously trying and failing to control his emotions.

I stand just in front of him, not quite touching. "Well?"

I expect a smooth, polished reply, but no words come. He closes his eyes and takes another audible breath.

"Come on, Gabriel. You've dragged me out here for some grand revelation. Give it to me."

He opens his eyes, looks at me, and nods. But instead of replying, he starts to pace around the glade.

I stand very still and resist the temptation to demand an answer. He clearly needs time. But my own breathing is getting more rapid by the moment, and I'm unpleasantly hot. What's so awful or so shocking that the cockiest person I know—and there's competition on that front, given my family—can't bring himself to utter the words? It's hardly as if he pretends to be an angel. I've seen plenty of the bad side of him.

Eventually, he stops, facing me head on, but with a good few feet between us. From across the distance, he stares into my eyes.

"I killed my own father to frame your brother."

My hand flies to my mouth and I almost fall to the mossy ground in shock. "You did... what?"

He sounds so matter of fact, his voice stripped of all emotion. It's more terrifying than if he'd screamed the words.

I take a few hurried paces backwards until I'm pressed up against a tree, and with some effort, I raise my shields. I've always known he was far from morally uncomplicated, but someone who'd kill their father could be capable of literally anything.

Besides, though I'd assumed Gabriel had had a hand in Bren being falsely charged with Niall's murder, I'd worked on the principle that it was an opportunistic cover-up to hide dissent in the Thornber ranks or the like. If he could do some-thing so cold and calculated in order to strike at Bren, what might he have planned for me?

I press the palms of my hands over my eyes and try to breathe deeply. This is properly psychotic stuff.

I ought to traverse out of there right now, but I'm too stunned to work the spell. And the curious, thoughtful, almost emotionless part of me that I've honed with years of legal training can't help but want to know more.

"I glamoured Nikki to look like Brendan so she could wander around town giving witnesses something to see," Gabriel adds, after my horrified silence drags on long enough that it's clear I have no coherent reply to give.

"I got Leah to bring me Brendan's gun, take him somewhere he'd have no other alibi and weaken him with sex magic, then get him back home in time to be arrested. I stayed home and did the deed myself."

I swallow hard. There's a lot to unpick there, but one thing leaps out at me. "Body-switching is impossible…"

"Not for me. Everyone talks behind my back about all that demon blood I'm supposed to have. It's always just intended as a veiled insult, but they never seem to wonder what rules it might allow me to break."

"It's true then, about your mother?"

He closes the gap between us. I keep my shields firmly up, but don't try to run. His eyes are wide and he looks so utterly sad.

When he speaks, his voice is little more than a whisper. "She was half-demon, genetically. And an absolute angel, personality-wise. I loved my father in a way, but I watched him kill her with his attempts to constrain her magic. There were other factors at play, too, but if you want my classic two reasons, I wanted to stop Brendan, and I needed to avenge her."

An irrational part of me wants to reach out and put my arms around him, drive away some of the hurt. Then I remember what he's freely admitted he's capable of—the point about his mother makes his actions marginally more explicable, but it hardly makes it okay—and I wrap my arms tightly round myself instead.

It's a minute or two before I can speak. "Why the hell are you telling all this to the defence lawyer?"

"Good luck convincing the jury this was achieved through body-swapping."

It's a fair point. But surely there's something I can do with this information? Assuming I'm willing to see Gabriel go down to save Bren. Which shouldn't even be up for debate, especially after these new revelations, but my heart insists on making things difficult.

"You were so upset a few weeks ago, when you found out the truth about the Sadlers' precious Dome," he adds, running his hands through his hair like he's struggling to find the right words. "Four sacrifices a year, even of willing victims, wasn't a price you were willing to pay. But you're still so blinkered by family loyalty that you never thought to ask the obvious question."

I frown. "What's the Dome got to do with anything?" I shouldn't get drawn into discussion. Or if I must, I need to keep the conversation focused on Gabriel's misdeeds.

"If it usually takes four deaths for basic maintenance, how many do you think it might take to expand the area of protection?"

I slump back against the rough trunk of the tree, as my mind throws up images of that night six years ago. Normally, my psyche focuses on the later bit, at Thornber Manor. But now all I can see is Gabriel pinning Bren to the ground and leaching away his magic.

In the aftermath of my first Ritual, I was able to understand Gabriel's dislike of Bren's attempts to enlarge the Dome rather more than I ever did at the time. But it still hadn't crossed my mind that enlarging it might require deaths on a larger scale.

"Six years ago, Brendan attempted to extend the boundaries of the Dome by a mile," Gabriel says, his arms crossed. "He needed to kill fifteen people. That time, I stopped him before he sacrificed more than five. Earlier this year, though, he tried again—and this time, he pulled it off."

My body goes very still. What he's saying sounds insane. And while my family might have come to think of the annual sacrifices as an acceptable tradition, surely Bren isn't capable of killing fifteen people in cold blood?

He's my brother. I'm not naïve enough to think he doesn't have flaws, but he paints beautiful pictures. He babysits Chrissie's little twins and fawns all over them. As a child, he'd entertain me for hours on end with fun little tricks—making my toy animals dance, that sort of thing.

I'd believed Bren capable of killing Niall Thornber, but even that turned out to be unfair on my part. He's not a mass murderer. He just can't be.

"Even if I *could* believe my brother were capable of that, what would he have to gain by extending the Dome by a mile?" My voice is trembling.

Gabriel steps even closer, his body touching mine, the edges of our auras mingling. "Do you really not know? Are you really that far outside your family's confidence?"

I slam my palm into his chest, pushing him back. "Just tell me, Gabriel."

"It was a trial run. Extending the Dome at all is hugely challenging. But once you've got the hang of enlarging it slightly, expanding it *massively* is simply a case of scaling up the magic—and the sacrifices. He wants the Dome to cover all of the biggest cities in the North."

I dig my nails into my palm and try to ignore my escalating heartrate. "Bren would never do something like that. Or if he did, the rest of the family would never condone it."

I snap the words out without a moment's hesitation, but as soon as I say them, I'm already wondering whether that's true. My family love the Dome. They're fiercely ambitious. And as the Ritual shows, they're flexible when it comes to the sanctity of human life. But surely not something of this magnitude? I'm not clear on the precise numbers, but if it's four deaths for maintenance and fifteen to move it by a mile, the sacrifice required for an expansion of the sort Gabriel is talking about would almost defy comprehension.

But then again, how many people in the cities surrounding Mannith died last year from homelessness, avoidable illnesses, poverty, stress, depression, and all the rest of it? Extending the Dome could save a lot more people than it killed. That wouldn't make it anywhere near okay, but I can just about see how Bren might be able to convince himself he was attempting something heroic rather than evil.

"Mass murder through magic is a hard thing to convince the police and the courts of," Gabriel continues, while I'm still weighing all of this up in my mind. "So, I gave them a simple, believable crime in place of a complex, inexplicable one."

"I don't believe you." I cross my arms and glare at Gabriel. "You killing your father makes perfect sense without the need for any deeper plot. Become head of the family. Avenge your beloved mother. And set Bren up just for the hell of it. You despise him. You slept with his fiancée to drive the knife in deeper, and now you're trying to make his own sister betray him in order to give it a twist."

Part of me wonders if I'm literally being the devil's advocate. Gabriel has always felt like the villain. He's certainly no angel. But I'm not entirely objective where my family are concerned.

"Fine, I hate Brendan. And I do have a tendency to play people. But I wouldn't lie to you."

I sink down to the ground and close my eyes. Despite my strident words, I have no idea what to believe. Gabriel killed his own father. Bren may have already committed multiple murders and be planning a full-scale massacre.

It's too much, too fast. Too much horror surrounding

everyone I care about. Too many lies, and plots, and competing stories. And launching into these terrible revelations and claims straight after the best date I've ever had is emotional whiplash on a nuclear scale.

I dig my nails into the soil to ground myself and press my back against the rough bark of the tree, letting the discomfort keep my mind focused on the physical sensation rather than all this emotion and speculation. I close my eyes and breathe deeply, relishing the scent of sap, pollen, and mulch. Through the effects of nature, I just about manage to get my mind and my magic under control.

Gabriel has the sense not to interrupt. He simply sits down beside me, silent and still.

There's a part of me that wants to run. Return to London; take on a nice, normal case; meet a nice, normal man; put all of this behind me. Let Gabriel and my family sort all this out between themselves. Whatever the precise truths, it's increasingly clear that everyone involved is pretty thoroughly flawed.

There's another part of me that believes Gabriel, and longs to forget about his faults and to fall into his arms.

But back when I was young, and everything seemed simpler, there was a motto I lived by. *Everything for the family.*

I've no idea what the objectively right course of action is right now. All I can do is fall back on that old certainty.

I pull myself up to standing and drive my doubts deep down. I'll interrogate Bren about all this the first chance I get, but in front of the Thornbers, the family needs to show a united front.

Gabriel gets to his feet, too, and once again stands so close that we're almost touching.

I force myself to make eye contact. "I am going to trust my family's word over yours, no matter how good a lay you are. I am going to defend Bren with all the legal prowess and magical force I can muster."

Gabriel leans over me and presses his palms into the tree trunk above my head. His lips are so close to mine that we could almost kiss.

"The second you seem in imminent danger of getting him out, I'm going to collapse the Dome," he whispers. "I'll destroy it before I see him extend it and kill a hundred people in the process."

I duck under his arms and step away, my heart pounding. His words have triggered something that's been drilled into me since I was a toddler.

"The Sadlers are sworn to protect the Dome. Anyone who'd seek to destroy it seeks to harm this town, and we'll do whatever it takes to stop them."

I shout out the words, but I want to cry. *What's happening?*

Gabriel turns and takes a hold of my arm. "Sadie, please. You should be on my side. I'm not always a nice person, but I'm not the villain here. Didn't I manage to show you that last night?"

I place a hand over his. "Last night was wonderful. But that was an enchanted evening. This is real life."

I lean over and kiss him, with tears streaming down my cheeks, then I traverse myself the rest of the way back to The Windmill before my mind can succumb to his charms like my body has.

PART 3

NINETEEN

Monday morning starts with another conference with Brendan. Today, it's meant to be time to start the case for the defence.

I told Gabriel I didn't believe his claims about Bren. But in private, it's not that simple. I've barely slept or eaten since I left. I've just sat in my room at The Windmill, running everything back and forth in my mind.

Bren has his flaws, but he wouldn't commit mass murder, not even for the sake of trying to extend Mannith's blessings to other towns. Would he?

I'd never have believed the rest of my family to be capable of human sacrifices, until I saw it with my own eyes. I've clearly got a bit of a blind spot as far as my relatives are concerned.

On the other hand, I'd all but convinced myself Bren really had killed Niall Thornber, but I was wrong. And I made a fool of myself in going as far as I did to prove that.

I don't want my brother in prison, wasting away without magic. I don't want my family left without a strong heir. And honestly, I don't want Gabriel and the Thornbers to win.

But even though I know for a fact that Bren isn't guilty of the crime he's actually on trial for, if he's really planning some sort of magical massacre, I surely can't have a hand in getting him released. Or at least not without some guarantees that he won't do it.

Either way, I need to know.

I shake my head. I can't believe I've let Gabriel put all these doubts in my mind. He's given me zero proof of his accusations, and he freely admits he hates my family.

I take a few deep breaths and try to still my runaway thoughts. I need facts, not speculation.

I sit down in the small plastic interview chair and cross my arms. For a minute or two, I simply stare at Bren, like something in his expression or his body language might give me the reassurance I need, but it's no good.

"I need to ask you something," I say, eventually.

He gives an exaggerated sigh and leans back in his chair. "If the question is 'did you kill Niall Thornber?' then I think I'm going to scream. You might not trust me, but don't you at least believe in your own truth-reading abilities?"

"Not that. I've found out the truth. Gabriel Thornber's setting you up. He killed his own father. But there's no way I can explain the how and why without talking about magic."

He jolts back upwards. "I knew it was a set-up, but I still can't believe he killed his father himself. And what was the deal with all the witnesses?"

"They all really believed they saw you. It was his bodyguard in disguise. Genuine body-switching."

Which, come to think of it, explains Becca's claims. It's a relief amongst all the rest of this horror to know she wasn't lying or working for Gabriel—I guess that means we can safely meet for a drink at some point. But bloody hell, Nikki had a nerve wandering into The Windmill and pretending to be Bren in front of some of his closest allies.

"What the hell? That's basically impossible, everyone knows that." He uses the sort of tone a regular person would employ to talk about most of the things we practitioners do without a second thought.

"Apparently not for him. Demon blood and all that."

He frowns. This maybe wasn't the best time to remind my brother of the unnatural magical strength of the man who's determined to bring him down.

"So how did you find out? Scrying?"

"Never mind that. Is it true that you managed to expand the Dome a few months ago? That you killed people in order to do it, both then and when you tried years ago? And that you wanted to do it again, on a huge scale?"

His expression changes instantly. With me, though we might have superficial arguments, he always wears an easy smile, big brother to baby sister, even in the most trying situations. But now, he's sporting the cold stare I remember from old family meetings, when a debtor failed to take a binding, magical bargain seriously, or an acolyte showed disrespect or disloyalty.

"Have you been talking to Gabriel-fucking-Thornber again? Taking his word over mine?"

"It's a simple question, Bren. It doesn't matter who put the idea in my head. Is it true, or isn't it?"

Bren gets to his feet. "What would your reaction be if it *was* true? You were so proud when I nearly pulled it off that night you got branded. But you were a proper member of this family back then."

Rage courses through me and the urge to unleash my power is at least as strong as anything I've ever felt when faced with Gabriel, but I take a deep breath. *In. Hold. Release.* My control's getting stronger again.

He strides around to my side of the table and puts his bound hands on my shoulders. "I'm sorry to snap at you, Sadie. I just hate that that bastard is getting inside your head. I'll answer your questions honestly."

I nod. "Thank you. Go on."

Bren stares at the wall in front of us. "Yes, when I tried six years ago, there were people who died. Just like there are every Ritual night. I'm not proud of it, but they were volunteers, and at the time, I thought it was the right thing to do. The aftermath and what happened to you made me realise I'd gone too far, and I've always regretted what I did."

My heart constricts. Some honesty, finally. He sounds contrite, but it's horrible to hear. "And more recently?" I force the words out.

"I've not attempted anything similar since, and I have no plans to do so in the future—it was a naïve teenage dream I grew out of years ago. It'd be nice to extend some of Mannith's blessings to other towns, but not at the cost of what that would require. Besides, it pains me to say it, but I actually don't believe I've got enough power to move it by more than a token amount, even if I did want to try again. Which, once again, I don't."

His eyes are wide open and honest. His touch is calming. His words make sense. And they're what I want to hear. If he'd denied everything, I'd be suspicious. But his honesty about what happened in the past makes me believe he's also being honest about the future.

And the suggestion that he physically wouldn't be able to do it anymore—which can't have been any easy admission for someone so proud of their exceptional powers—is particularly reassuring.

And yet he must know I'd be beyond horrified if he were planning what Gabriel claimed. He must suspect I'd take myself off the case and doom him in the process. He's got every incentive to lie, and he's cunning enough to know the best ways to frame an untruth in order to make it believable.

"Don't you believe me?" he asks, when I don't respond.

"I want to believe you," I reply. We both know that isn't the same thing.

"So, do you want to do the whole mind reading bit again?" Bren asks. "Is that what it's going to take?"

"I swore I wouldn't. And I take promises seriously."

It's tempting. A blast of magic and a few probing questions, and I'll know for sure. But I'd failed to trust him last time, I'd broken all our rules, and I'd turned out to be wrong. If I do it again, then not only will I be going back on my word, I'll destroy any chance—whatever the answer—of a functioning sibling relationship once all this is over.

My mind once again jumps to our childhood. I try to avoid looking at the old memories through rose-tinted glasses. Bren could be as overbearing at twelve as at thirty. Sometimes we argued, or he was just grumpy in general. Sometimes he pulled rank as the eldest. Sometimes he'd demand I left him alone. But even at his worst, it was always obvious that he cared, that he saw himself as the protector of the family in general and me in particular.

Even after everything that happened six years ago and even after the way he's acted since my return, when I think about the need to help my brother, it's not just arbitrary ties of blood I'm concerned about, it's real love and affection. I don't want to destroy that. And it means nothing without trust.

"I'm not going to drag the truth out of you with magic. Swear to me that what you're saying is true, and I won't ask again."

"I swear," he says, without hesitation.

It's not some magic, sacred promise. It's just my brother's word. I either have to accept it or walk away.

I stand up and pace the room. I freeze and drop into a brief, but deep, core meditation. And eventually, I sit down and gesture for Bren to do likewise.

I put my hands on top of his. "I believe you," I say. "I'll get you out."

It's not a binding, magical deal, any more than his promise was. But I imbue it with the same sort of solemnity.

Everything for the family. I can't let him rot in here. All I can do is choose to believe his solemn promise, choose to stand by my family.

"Now, let's get on with preparation," I say, after what feels like an eternity. "The prosecution have got you on the ropes, but today's your chance to tell your side of the story."

We talk tactics, practice a few questions. Nothing's really changed. We're sticking to the same tale.

Sticking to the true story, I tell myself.

"I'm going to give you another dose of magic before you go out there," I announce, once we're done. It's sort of an apology. Sort of a show of trust. And in large part, just a practical measure—he'll make a far better witness once he's borrowed a bit of my strength.

He nods gratefully. The toll the blockers are taking on him is evident from his vacant expression and hunched posture. I can't help thinking once again about Gabriel's mother and the suffering she must have endured.

We both stand up, and I place my hand on his chest and let a little of my magic flow out. It's gratifying to see the shadows under his eyes fade and his skin plump out.

Without warning, his hand closes on my right wrist. "What happened to your finger?"

"What do you mean?" I draw my hand out of his grasp and away from his chest, breaking the connection.

"There's something different in your energy, in your aura." He grabs my hand back, pulls off my ring, and stares at my unmarked finger.

"Where's the lien mark? What the hell did you do?"

"What I had to do. You saw what I was like when I had to

cross-examine him. I refused to let my weakness stand in the way of your freedom."

Bren turns and kicks the door with enough force to knock it off its hinges if it hadn't been specially reinforced. "How could you be so stupid? This is exactly what we've fought to avoid."

I huddle down in the chair, arms around my waist, eyes on the floor. "Sit down. Calm down. It's my body, and now I'm free."

He throws out his arms as though he's about to unleash a furious storm of magic, then slams them back down against his thighs when the blockers stop his spell in its tracks. "It's never *just* anything with him. If you let him in your bed, you let him in your head. Look what happened to Leah. I feel physically sick thinking about his hands all over you. About those creepy eyes looking at your body."

"Bren, please—"

"No wonder you've been asking all those questions. '*Are you sure you didn't kill Niall Thornber?' 'Were you trying to enlarge the Dome?' 'Are you plotting to sacrifice scores of people?*' It's like you're his bloody mouthpiece."

Tears are welling up, and I don't feel much more capable of speech than I did when attempting to cross-examine Gabriel.

"Brendan! What's important is getting you acquitted. I'm going to give you one more dose of magic, we're going to practice the trickiest questions again, then you're going to take the stand and turn this case around—"

He leans his forehead against the wall. "No. I don't want your tainted magic. I'll see you out there."

I get to my feet, grab his arm and turn him to face me. He's twice my height, but fury gives me strength.

"If you're going to speak to me like that, you can get another lawyer. And good luck finding anyone who's my equal in advocacy or magic at short notice, never mind one who cares about this case as much as I do."

Bren freezes in my grasp and says nothing.

"Between your arrest and Leah's betrayal, this couldn't have been a worse few months for you. I get that. And I know being locked in here and kept in those blockers isn't helping either. But you can stop taking it out on me right this second."

All my life—whether watching my family impose binding debts on people or practicing cross-examination in bar school—I've been taught the power of words and the value of using them precisely and sparingly. Right now, I'm squandering them, but I physically can't stop.

"You think this has been easy for me? I'd turned my back on magic, on family, and on this town. It killed me, but I did what I had to do. I made a life for myself in London and in the everyday world. And then, when you needed help, I put that life on hold. I broke all my principles. I faced the man I feared most in the world. And all you can do is throw it back in my face."

He opens his mouth to speak, and from his wide-eyed expression, I can't tell if he's going to apologise or argue back. I get out of there before I can find out. I can't give him the chance to say anything that might leave me with no choice but to abandon the trial.

I take a moment or two to refresh my make-up and do a core meditation in the bathroom. By the time I'm seated in court, I'm almost calm again, though I can't quite bring myself to look at Bren, who's standing in the dock, steadfastly refusing to make eye contact.

Chrissie shoots me a worried look from the public gallery. Her senses are clearly screaming that something's wrong.

Once proceedings start, Bren grudgingly meets my gaze.

There's no hint in his expression of his earlier fury but no obvious sign of an attempted apology either.

I tell myself this is just my job. Brendan's just another client.

"Mr Sadler, where were you on the night of 15th June?" I ask.

Bren's a natural storyteller, charismatic even in captivity. His half-embarrassed, half-saucy explanation of where he was and what he was doing that night (the making love outdoors part, not the summoning a demon aspect) gets either a laugh or a scandalised gasp from most people present.

"Mr Sadler, how do you account for the fact that so many people claim to have seen you at different stages of the night?"

Bren raises his hands as expressively as he can, considering the cuffs. "I don't know what other people think they saw or why. All I know is what I was doing. Though, if I had to place a bet, I'd suggest bribery or blackmail."

The judge glares at him. "The facts please, Mr Sadler."

"Several witnesses have stated that you said something about revenge for your sister. The victim's son claimed they'd had a relationship. What's the story there?" It's hard to get the question out, but I keep my voice steady and professional.

"Gabriel Thornber was obsessed with my youngest sister, back when she still lived in Mannith. Basically, he stalked her. But it's all ancient history. I've not thought about it in years until he brought it up."

I think of his reaction to seeing my lien mark gone and almost laugh. He's certainly good at putting on a show.

We don't land any killer blows, but it's a solid performance, and I can feel the mood of the jury starting to shift.

Then it's Imran's turn. He's trying to get Bren to slip up, break from his version, or admit to some crucial aspect that hints at his guilt.

"You don't like the Thornber family, do you, Mr Sadler?

None of your family do. As I understand it, there's a long running family feud."

Bren laughs. "You make it sound like a medieval court or prohibition New York. They have their businesses. We have ours. They don't tend to conflict."

The lawyer is good, but Bren's better. He's got a terrible hand—his flimsy story against several credible witnesses—but he's playing it well.

I nod at him as the cross-examination draws to a close, more proud sister than relieved lawyer. He smiles back at me, as though he's already forgotten about our earlier argument.

That evening, I leave court without speaking to any of the family—or heaven forbid, Gabriel—and head to The Windmill.

As soon as I get into my room, I whip out my scrying bowl. With no mineral water to hand, I have to resort to filling it from the tap, but the water here is very pure.

Back in London, scrying was the one bit of magic I allowed myself to do on a semi-regular basis, but up here, with more visceral powers at my disposal, I haven't really bothered with it. Today, though, it's exactly what's needed.

I start to breathe deeply and wave my hands, but with all the power in the air, it's barely necessary. The vision I'm seeking appears in seconds. I mentally zoom out to get an outdoor image, cross-reference it with a map on my phone, then jump in the car and head out of town.

There's the familiar sense of pressure as I exit the Dome, the familiar chill on the other side, and the inevitable sense of everything being that little bit more dirty and rundown.

I try to focus as I drive through, try to really think about whether the boundary has moved, but I've been through so many times in the last few weeks that I've lost any certainty about where it was back when I was a teenager.

I drive like a homing pigeon in the direction of the place I'd seen in the water. It has to be the closest pub to Mannith on this side of the Dome. It's quiet, compared to The Windmill, with a slightly stale smell in the air and paintwork that could do with being touched up.

There are two barmaids on shift. One's unknown to me and gives a welcoming smile. The other is Leah. On seeing me, she throws up a weak shield and bursts into tears all at once.

I walk towards the bar, trying to look as smiley and unthreatening as possible, even though we both know I could tear her in two with a wave of my hand.

"It's time for Leah's break," I tell the other woman, imbuing my voice with power.

She nods in confusion.

I step behind the bar, loop my arm through Leah's, and lead us to a free table, covered in empty glasses. She makes no move to resist. She's passive. A rabbit in headlights. I throw up a bubble so we can speak in private.

"How's life in exile working out for you?"

She looks a little faded. Still pretty, still perfectly made up. Just not shining so brightly.

"What do you want?"

"You got Bren out of the way that night on purpose. Took him somewhere where his alibi was entirely reliant on you. And spent the evening doing something that would be impossible to explain properly in court and that would leave him weakened enough that the police and a few half-hearted practitioners could arrest him and block his magic. And you did something with the old revolver, too. Made sure his fingerprints were all over it, then smuggled it to Gabriel.

"And as your next trick, you were going to sabotage your testimony, weren't you? Destroy that all-important alibi. Subtly stumble. Add in some little inconsistencies relative to Bren's account, just like you were ordered to. A witness for the prosecution, disguised as one for the defence."

I can't keep the fury out of my voice. She's just a pawn, really, manipulated by Gabriel. But my brother had loved her, and while I can forgive his enemy most things, I can't forgive his fiancée for her betrayal.

Her silence and sobs are all the confession I need.

"I want you to testify after all. But now, you're going to tell the truth. Or most of the truth, anyway. Nothing about Gabriel's body switching. Nothing about Bren trying to impregnate you with a demon baby. Just the fact that Gabriel was setting my brother up for a fall and you were a willing accomplice."

She collapses back on the sofa, stretched out full length. "I can't. Gabriel will kill me."

I shrug. "Possibly. But the mistake everyone makes is to underestimate me. You know he's powerful and ruthless. I promise you I can match him on both scores."

I lift my hand and drag it lazily through the air. Every glass and bottle in the place shatters. Then I slam my hand down and, across the room, the bar cleaves in two. Leah jumps back.

I made my parents promise they wouldn't try to use intimidation to win the case. But I made no such vow myself.

"We never really got to know each other, did we? You never had a chance to tell me about your family. But I can see a lot in my scrying bowl. You've got a sister, haven't you? She means the world to you."

She sinks down on the floor, heedless of all the broken glass.

"If you don't testify, I will go to 33 Lansbury Street, and I will use my powers to stop your beloved Lola's heart."

There is absolutely no way in hell I would ever dream of doing anything of the sort. Just saying the awful words out loud makes me feel physically sick, but with fire in my hands and my eyes, I sound pretty convincing.

To my intense relief, Leah shows up in court the next morning. She's wearing a smart black dress and jacket, her hair in a neat ponytail instead of the usual wild up-do.

From her vantage point in the witness box, she glares at me like I'm the worst person in the world.

Gabriel's up in the viewing gallery once again. I make the mistake of making eye contact for a split second, and he raises his eyebrow at my choice of witness. I give him my most imperious stare then turn away and do my best not to think about him. It's unclear whether or not Leah can see him. It's possible that his invisibility glamour is light enough that any practitioner can penetrate it. Equally, he may only be visible to those with sufficient power.

"Where were you on the 15th June?"

"With my fiancé. My ex-fiancé... I mean. Or rather, he was my fiancé then. He isn't now. With Brendan."

Her words are a messy jumble.

"Talk me through what you did that night," I demand. "Starting from seven PM."

"We ate dinner. Then I suggested a little drive out into the countryside."

"Are you a fan of nature?"

"I like animals and that. But I thought it would be nice to go out there and... you know."

"Go out there and what?"

Her voice is barely audible. "Go out there and make a baby."

"And did the defendant agree with your plan?"

She nods. "Yes. He could hardly move fast enough. Jumped in the car and we were off."

She stares into the distance as though she's looking back through her memories.

"And was this your own idea?"

She doesn't answer. I stare at her, willing her to speak. *Would a little touch of mesmerism be so bad?*

I shake myself. No. I'll win this case fairly—even if I'm pushing professional ethics to the edge—not through magic. Especially not that sort of magic.

"Miss Stockville?"

"No. I was asked to do it. To get him out of the way so he'd have no real alibi."

I can feel the shock in the court like a physical entity.

"Who asked you to do this?"

"Mr Thornber's son. He wanted to set Bren up. And I was sleeping with him... with Gabriel... so I agreed."

She bursts into such hysterical tears that both my attempts at a follow-up question and the judge's warning to be careful with my line of questioning are all but drowned out.

I glance over at Bren. There's an expression of pure anguish on his face. Leah's helping his case, but he looks like he'd rather go down for life than have her set all this out to the court. She's breaking his heart all over again, and I'm helping her every step of the way.

She says everything I told her to say, pausing between questions to sob her eyes out. If they were still together, no one would believe a word of it. But the truth of the messy breakup is written on every line of her face, and in turn, it gives her fantastical story enough of a hint of verisimilitude.

Eventually, it's Imran's turn to cross-examine her. Still in Gabriel's power as well as his pay, his eyes are wide with shock, and he can barely keep the rage out of his voice.

"Was the defendant ever violent to you in the course of your relationship? Or after your breakup?"

"No. Never. Of course not." She manages to answer that one without crying.

It's clear where he's going with this. He's trying to imply Bren's coerced her into giving this testimony. It could be quite a believable line, but she sounds so aghast at the idea that it's falling flat.

He probes every word of the story she just set out, but she stays entirely consistent. Not surprising when she's telling the truth for once.

Eventually, Imran sits down with an exasperated "no more questions".

Leah turns to look at Bren. Maybe she sees fury in his eyes. Maybe love. Maybe forgiveness. Whatever it is, it's enough to make her pass out in the witness box. Still, it doesn't matter. She's done her job.

TWENTY

Back at The Windmill after court, I fire up my laptop and throw on my workout gear. For the first time in weeks, I'm feeling calm enough for yoga, rather than trying to take out my stress on high-intensity cardio.

Forty minutes of Ashtanga, the inevitable long soak, and a chicken salad from room service later, and though it's only nine PM, I'm basically ready for bed.

With crushing inevitability, my phone rings just as I'm slipping into my favourite nightie. I'm expecting it to be my mum or sister—the idea that I'm trying to keep my distance doesn't seem to be getting through to them—but when I glance at the screen, it shows that ominous X.

I ignore it, even though my subconscious is itching to pick up, and my conscious mind wonders if the message could possibly be important. The phone's innocuous ringtone reverberates through me like a warning bell. It rings until my voice-mail picks up. I allow myself to breathe again as soon as it stops, but a few seconds later, it starts again. Still, I hold my nerve.

The cycle repeats twice more, while I make myself a hot chocolate, wash my face, and try to pretend it's not happening. I could turn the phone off. I could block the number. But I can't quite bring myself to do either of those things.

On the fourth ring, I grab the phone. "What?"

"You were terribly impressive in court today. And outside of it, presumably, if you managed to make Leah talk."

I lean against my desk and resist the urge to throw the phone out of the window in the hope it would take all my problems with it. "I'm hanging up and turning off the phone in thirty seconds. If you've got a point, make it."

"I still think it's basically an unwinnable case. But you put together enough of a defence that I need to take precautions just in case he gets off."

"What sort of precautions?" I hate the fact I'm engaging Gabriel in conversation, but I need to know.

"I'm going to bring the Dome down. Tonight."

I sink onto the floor. He'd threatened as much on the drive back from our... whatever it was, but I hadn't taken him entirely seriously. Now though, there's an air of finality in his tone.

I want to shout questions. I want to beg him not to do it. But I take a deep breath before my racing heart explodes and try to focus.

"Then why are you doing the Bond villain thing? Telling me seems a bit counterproductive?" I aim for my best lawyer voice, but I probably sound about as panicky as I feel.

"The blood of you and your family is in the Dome. A side effect of its collapse will be the death of anyone who contributed to its creation and maintenance, if they're inside its perimeter at the time. You need to get out of town, fast."

I drop the phone. My hands are shaking. Is he really saying he'd condemn my whole family to death? I probably shouldn't be surprised, but I am. All the blood is rushing to my head. I want to lie down and sink into the floor. I want to run out into the street screaming for help. Somehow, after a few shaky breaths, I manage to pick the phone back up and force some words out.

"Why do you care?"

"You know why I care. And get your family to leave for the night, too. This isn't an exercise in punishing the Sadlers. It's an exercise in stopping a massacre."

I close my eyes and wrap my free arm around my body. It's impossible to tell whether Gabriel's convinced himself that Bren is really going to expand the Dome and this is the only way to stop him or is playing me yet again. "And if I stay?"

For the first time in the conversation, he hesitates. "I'd mourn you for the rest of my life, but I'd still do the right thing."

The certainty in his voice makes me shudder. I'm going to be sick. I never should have opened myself up to him, even a little. "My family's safety aside, you'd be condemning Mannith. You love this town. How will you feel when you see it decline?"

"Heartbroken. But it'll still be the lesser of two evils."

"How are you even going to do it?" My words are barely audible through my encroaching tears.

"I'm stupid enough to tell you *when* so you can get to safety. I'm not stupid enough to tell you *how* so you can attempt to stop me. Just get out of Mannith by midnight. I'll come and find you when all this is over."

He rings off, denying me even the small satisfaction of hanging up on the bastard.

There are times for keeping secrets and keeping people at arm's length, and there are times for accepting you're part of a family, part of a team. I change back into proper clothes, dash downstairs, ignoring the patrons' worried looks, jump into the car and drive over to my parents, phoning Chrissie on the way. Inevitably, she already knew I was about to call.

Twenty minutes later, Mum, Dad, Chrissie, Liam, Shane and I are all gathered in my parents' sitting room. No one on the fringes has been allowed near, though we'll no doubt need to rope them in at some point. After Leah's betrayal, it's almost a surprise that Shane's still allowed in the room, but the family's always regarded him in a different light to her.

Ray would have been there, too, but on Chrissie's orders, he's taking the twins on an impromptu visit to see their grandparents in Jamaica. The rest of us will stand and fight, but no one wants to put the babies at risk.

Perhaps things ought to be awkward between me and the others, but in the circumstances, no one is making any snide comments about my disloyal reaction to the truth of the annual Ritual or the way I've been keeping to myself of late. And equally, I'm making no attempt to raise the issue or act aloof.

There's also been surprisingly little debate amongst us. No one's suggesting Gabriel might be bluffing. No one's arguing in favour of leaving town. All anyone wants to know is what he's planning and how to stop him.

A tiny part of me wonders if I ought to get out of Mannith and let Gabriel do his worst. It would at least mean an end to the annual sacrifices. But nothing could persuade my family to leave, and in the case of my parents, who've poured their spirit into it for decades, I'm not convinced they'd survive the Dome's collapse even if they were outside the perimeter. And what about all the other practitioners who've contributed to its upkeep over the years?

Besides, what I've learnt about the sacrifices horrifies me, but I like Mannith's weather, prosperity, and sense of community. I couldn't bear to see it become just another run-down northern town with people out of work and at each other's throats. Perhaps with enough research, we could find a way to keep the Dome without having to kill.

"How the hell could anyone collapse the Dome?" Chrissie asks the question for the hundredth time.

Shane shrugs. "No idea. And I don't think anyone in this room has a clue either. But Liam, I reckon you could find out."

My brother stares at him. "How?"

"Ask the person who created it. No one's as reliable as you at talking to the ancestors. Get over to the church and find an older one to chat with. I'll drive."

Chrissie gets to her feet. "Good idea. In the meantime, I'll go and visit Bren. If there's anyone still alive who'd know, it's him. God knows he's studied the thing enough."

A little wave of unease runs through me at her words. Studied it to what end, if not to enlarge it in the way Gabriel claims?

I shake my head. That's not fair. He's admitted he attempted to enlarge it in the past. He's told me he did enough research to convince himself it was impossible.

Liam, Shane, and Chrissie head off on their respective missions, leaving me alone with my parents. I've spent the last few weeks feeling like the family's saviour and only hope, but now I'm useless.

"Go and bathe," Mum orders. "Then get into your ritual clothes. Whatever he's planning, there's a good chance you'll have to deploy some heavy-duty magic. Either to counteract his own or to take him down."

In stark contrast to the night of the actual Ritual, I don't protest.

"I'm calling Colson," Dad informs Mum as I head upstairs. "When push comes to shove, he knows how to fight."

Not against Gabriel. Still, we're going to need every pair of hands we can get.

I'm still dazed from the heat and herbs of the purification bath and draped in a dressing gown when Chrissie arrives back.

"Bren's got no idea. Full of facts about maintaining and expanding the damn thing, but not creating it from scratch or taking it down. And he's freaking out at the thought of Gabriel even attempting such a thing."

"You tried," Mum says. "Your sister's getting herself ready for a ritual. You ought to do the same."

Chrissie leaves the room to run herself a bath, and I follow.

"What's really going on with Bren and the Dome?" I ask. "Gabriel's entire argument is that he's been trying to enlarge it. Bren denied this, I chose to believe him—but it does seem to track with what you're saying."

Chrissie shakes her head. "He's been obsessed with the Dome since we were kids, you know this. But while he might have tried something stupid when we were younger, his research is all theoretical at this point. He wouldn't actually try to enlarge it. For all his strength, he's accepted he doesn't have the necessary power. And for all his posturing, he wouldn't have the stomach for that number of sacrifices either. We've had long talks about all this while you were away."

I sigh. Though I've told myself I believe Bren, he can be slippery. It's far more comforting to hear this from my straightforward and cheerily honest sister. Especially her confirmation that he probably couldn't do it even if he wanted to, which offers rather more reassurance than, "I trust him not to try."

While Chrissie draws herself a fresh bath, Liam and Shane arrive back, faces serious.

Liam is pale and flops straight onto the sofa.

"Success?" Dad asks.

Shane nods. "He summoned the right spirit. I knew he could do it. The way Jeremiah Sadler explained it was complicated. He liked the sound of his own voice, having not used it in a century and a half. But basically, there's a massive crystal and the mass grave of the original sacrifices buried at the top of the hill. Destroy that with the right intent and you can bring it down."

Dad's phone rings. His normal business one is turned off. Only his most trusted acolytes have this number, and they know only to use it in the direst of need. He picks it up and listens to the voice on the line.

"I see. I'll have sufficient protection deployed." He hangs up and throws the phone across the room.

"Well?" My mum's wearing the same frown she always has whenever Dad loses his temper, whether justified or otherwise.

"Thornber scum attacking both The Windmill and the Cardamom restaurant in town. It's a distraction, obviously. I'll send some of our men over there. But we need to focus the family's attention on the hill."

The doorbell rings.

"It's Connor," Chrissie says confidently. She gets up and returns a moment later with him in tow.

I've not seen him since the day we broke up. Even amidst all the overwhelming emotions surging through my brain, the sight of him still brings back that toxic mix of guilt and sadness I felt at the time. I'd almost forgotten how attractive he is.

Connor gives me a longing glance that catches me off guard, then turns to my parents with a more respectful expression. "What is it, sir?"

Dad's still pacing the room, but he gestures to the sofa, and Connor sinks down into it. "You've always been one of the most promising enforcers amongst the younger generation. I don't tend to waste my time with compliments and praise, but I hope you know that's how I feel."

Connor gives a hesitant nod.

"I know the last few weeks haven't been easy for you. Sadie and all that. But I hope I can still count on your loyalty."

This time, his nod's more insistent. "Of course."

I look at the floor and try to pretend I'm not listening. Memories flood my mind. We hadn't spent that long together, but it had all been so... nice. Just sexy, and fun, and comforting. Such a pleasant contrast to the chaos of the rest of the summer.

I'd never felt a tenth of the emotional intensity I've experienced every time I've so much as spoken to Gabriel, never mind slept with him, but is that really a bad thing?

"I'm more used to issuing orders than making requests," my father continues. "But tonight, I need absolute loyalty and total bravery, and so I need to know you're willing to take part of your own free will."

Connor stands up and looks Dad straight in the eye. "What are you asking me to do?"

"Go to Summer Hill with my family. They'll provide a defence and channel magic to you. Your job is to blast Gabriel-fucking-Thornber clean in two."

"No." I say the word almost without thinking.

The family turn to stare, their universal frowns suggesting they're worried I'm developing some Thornber sympathies.

"Connor's a powerful practitioner. But he can't stand against Gabriel. We saw that in the Casino. I can."

Dad walks over and puts an arm on my shoulder. "No one doubts your powers. But you know what you were like in court when you had to cross-examine him. This'll be a thousand times worse. You can help your brother and sister with protecting Colson."

I tell myself I could kill Gabriel to save my family and the Dome, but if I'm strictly honest, Dad's probably got a point.

"Can't you do it, then?" I ask Dad.

He clenches his hands into fists. "Twenty years ago, I'd have taken that bastard out without a second thought. I'll lead the troops at The Windmill—I've still got enough fight in me to bring down his minions. But not him. I'm putting my ego aside. You need to do the same."

TWENTY-ONE

Less than an hour later, we're on the hill. It's full moon again. Maybe that's part of the magic, maybe it's just a coincidence. I'm back in my red dress and jewels. There simply wasn't time for the elaborate make-up and hairstyle associated with the Ritual and there certainly wasn't time for the fasting and the potions.

No one's entirely sure what form Gabriel's plan is going to take. Our best guess is a few preliminary blasts of magic to take out those foolhardy enough to defend the hill, then one huge spell directed down into the earth. Even he'll probably have to do some sort of ritual to summon the necessary degree of power and channel it so precisely. Using just the power of his will surely won't be enough.

Connor's task is simple: attempt to destroy Gabriel before he can do any of those things. My role and that of my siblings is twofold: protect Connor long enough to allow him to achieve that aim, and block any spells directed at the crystal and the tomb.

On the brow of the hill, Chrissie grips my left shoulder like she grips her hair straighteners when she's styling her hair, and

Liam places his hand more gently on my right shoulder. They'll funnel their power into me. I'll merge it with mine and create enough of a shield to allow Connor to fight. He'll be free to focus all his energy on attacking, while Gabriel has to split his attention in order to protect himself.

Gabriel's a hell of a lot more powerful than any of us individually, but together, this just might work.

"How are things?" I whisper the words to Connor. He's a good few metres away, but sound travels easily on the hill.

"Fine. Sorry I haven't been in touch. You were... anyway, I overreacted."

"I was totally the one to blame," I say. "You merely said some things in the heat of the moment. I kept things from you for weeks. I thought I had good reason not to admit who I was, but it was wrong of me."

"I've missed you, you know," he adds. "Tonight's not a great night for a deep conversation... but once this is all over, maybe we could get a drink?"

I study his face. He could just mean as friends. He might just want to talk things through and give us both some closure. But there's something in his soft smile that suggests he's hoping to try again.

"That'd be really nice," I reply, smiling back.

Meeting him for a drink absolutely *would* be nice. The animal bit of my brain has no doubts on that score. I'd love to see that muscular body again and have some fun together. And on a less lust-fuelled level, it'd be nice to have someone to laugh with, someone to take care of me.

I've lied to Connor once before. This time, I wouldn't be lying with my words or wearing a disguise and a fake name. But wouldn't I be lying with my heart?

Connor's a great guy. I like him. But he deserves someone who could love him, and I don't think I'm capable of love. Or at least, not for anyone but the one person I absolutely can't be with.

I shake my head. I always overcomplicate things. I should meet Connor for a drink. Have a fun evening. Be as truthful as I dare and see where things take us. But first, we need to survive the night.

My siblings have given us some peace and quiet for our Serious Talk, but now, Liam speaks up. "How long do you think we'll have to wait?" He glances at his watch as midnight goes by.

Right on cue, Gabriel appears a few meters in front of Connor. He looks unearthly tonight, dressed all in white, and wearing green jewels that must be the equivalent of our rubies. The usual sunglasses are nowhere in sight, and his eyes are already brightly glowing. He's all alone. I'd have expected his uncle or Nikki at the very least, if not a small army. But perhaps the magic he plans is too dangerous to do in the vicinity of those he cares about.

I breathe in and out, trying to close down my conscious brain and let the power flow through me. I get the shield up in moments. If it were visible, it would be a bulbous T-shape. A thin, vertical line in front of the three of us, expanding out to a sphere around Connor. He needs the protection more than we do.

Gabriel's attention is focused on Connor. He knows a duel when he sees one. Besides, even if he'd happily treat me as collateral damage in the cause of bringing down the Dome, I don't think he'd hurt me directly. Not seriously anyway. Or not permanently. Not fatally, at the very least. You can't look at someone the way he looked at me in bed last week and then blast them apart with dark magic... can you?

I slip into the lightest of trances, enough to steady my nerves and strengthen my magic, without leaving me unable to react to changing circumstances. It's sufficient to let me taste the magic in the air, on both sides. Magic is an art, not a science. It's not easily quantifiable, but it's possible to do a rudimentary sort of equation. The power emanating from Gabriel is insane. There's plenty of power swirling around Connor, too, more than enough for him to win any normal battle single-handed, but it's unlikely to be enough to allow him to strike a definitive blow. Gabriel's in a different league. We need Brendan.

We need me, my mind whispers back. *I'm wasted on defence.*

Perhaps, but thanks to my efforts, the shield isn't going to fall. Connor might not be able to take Gabriel down, but the worst-case scenario is a stalemate. Gabriel might be some mystical practitioner prodigy, but he can blast Connor with all the magic he wants. It's not getting past me and my siblings.

To be on the safe side, I slip deeper into my trance. My conscious brain can deal with the aftermath. Right now, we need raw power. My mind is miles deep in the earth, my eyes are no doubt as flamingly red as Gabriel's, and my shield is inviolate.

Connor lifts his hands to strike the first blow.

And then the mystical practitioner prodigy pulls out an antique silver revolver identical to the Sadler family heirloom used to kill Niall—the Thornbers would have been our acolytes back when they'd been given out. Without a word of warning, he shoots Connor four times at point-blank range.

We'd all been so fixated on the magic that the concept of physical protection had never even crossed our minds.

Chrissie and Liam are screaming. I'm utterly silent, too far into the trance to react, though I sense the horror somewhere at the back of my mind, waiting to assault me when I snap out of it.

There's blood all over Connor's finely honed chest and those arms that used to hold me and make me feel secure are limp at his sides. *Surely no one could survive wounds like that...*

Poor Connor. Poor, poor Connor. Once again, he's been hurt by proximity to me. We'll never have a chance to make another go of it now or even just to have that fun night together. Nor will he have the opportunity to move on and find someone else who can love him like he deserves.

"Give me more power," I whisper to my siblings. I feel like I'm trying to make them hear me from one mountaintop to another.

The second they comply, I sink my mind and spirit danger-ously deep into the earth. Time seems to move more slowly here. It already feels like hours have passed, but Connor's only just hit the floor. Everything is clear and simple at these depths. I have my own power, supported by the earth and honed by my fury. And my siblings are willing to give me whatever more I need.

Give me a near-fatal injury to repair and a powerful enemy to kill, and with a little concentration, right now, I could do both. But this isn't just a *near-fatal* injury. Connor's soul hasn't yet left his body, but his life-force is gone. It wouldn't be heal-ing, it'd be practically resurrection. And this isn't simply a *powerful* enemy. Gabriel is off the charts at the best of times, and today, he's performed goodness knows what ritualistic preparations on himself.

I can do one or the other, and I have seconds to decide, before Connor slips away entirely, and Gabriel blows the whole hill to smithereens. In my mind's eye, I hold out my hands.

"Sadie." Liam's voice drifts down to me from a million miles away and a hundred years ago. "Don't do this."

I don't have time to decide which course of action he's warning me against before I raise my right hand and launch Hellfire at Gabriel. No messing about with Greenfire this time. Hellfire is hot enough to melt flesh from bones.

Even with all the power and rage I'm channelling, and even with the element of surprise, he'd probably have raised his shields in time if it had been anyone else attacking him, even Brendan.

But as I'm wrenched out of my trance by the force of the magic, I see the look of utter shock in his fiery eyes. I can read his expression all too well. He didn't think he needed protection from me. It's not that he didn't believe I was powerful enough to pull it off. Rather, he'd been just as confident as I had that you can't look at someone the way I looked at him in bed last week and then blast them apart with dark magic.

The full reality only seems to hit him once my blaze does.

For the third time since my return to Mannith, I wake up from an unconscious state. Just like after the casino, Chrissie is working healing spells and Liam's channelling magic into me to compensate for the sheer quantity I burnt through.

"She's awake," Chrissie calls, the moment my eyelids start to flicker.

I don't know what expression I'm going to see on my family members' faces. Am I a heroine for killing Gabriel or a monster for failing to save Connor? The thought of Connor makes me want to cry. But the thought of Gabriel makes me feel like I've torn myself in two.

I glance at my watch. It's four AM. Only a few hours until I need to be in court.

Mum throws her arms around me as I drag myself into a seated position. "Well done, sweetheart. I knew you had it in you. I can't believe you've been suppressing your magic all these years when you're that powerful."

"Is Connor dead?" He must be, surely. He'd almost passed when I decided to strike at Gabriel instead of bringing him back from the brink. But a miracle could have happened...

"You had no choice but to let him go," Dad says, perching on the end of the bed.

It's hardly a surprise, but his confirmation still makes my throat constrict.

"He'll have a hero's funeral," Dad continues. "Compensation for his family. Burial on the sacred hill he died to protect."

"And Gabriel?"

Dad twists the duvet cover between his hands. "According to our spies, he's not dead, merely dying. We'll see whether his supporters can summon enough power to put him back together again, but even if they do, he'll not be in a mental or physical state to try anything like that for a while."

I close my eyes and let the unwanted praise flow over me. If I'd saved Connor, if I hadn't attacked Gabriel, then what? He could have taken down the Dome, killed us all.

Or you could have kept the shield intact. Attempted to reason with him. Or let him burn his magic out against your combined defensive force.

"How's The Windmill?" I ask, desperately trying to block out my mind's internal debate.

"The décor and the clientele took a few knocks, but nothing that can't be fixed. Two of ours down, three of his."

Five people dead. This isn't a game, it's a war. Everyone's proud I've struck the winning blow, but my whole body is wracked with horror.

TWENTY-TWO

Somehow, I make it through court the next day on three hours' sleep. My job is to examine character witnesses who are sufficiently loyal—and therefore sufficiently biased—that I can rely on them to focus exclusively on Bren's good qualities—which are entirely real, but only half the picture.

In the evening, I shrug off my family's comments about my physical and emotional health and the need to rest, and tell them I'm heading back to The Windmill. Instead, I head straight to the hospital in Leeds. Mannith doesn't have a hospital for much the same reason it doesn't have a court. Nothing bad usually ever happens unless we want it to. And most injuries can be dealt with by magic more effectively than by human medicine. But sometimes, a combination of the two yields the best results.

I'm styled in full Kate Elner costume today. Smart suit, natural make-up, hair scraped back. The disguise would not fool any of Gabriel's acolytes—or my own family's supporters, for that matter—but if things kick off, it'll be good to look like the one whose side the authorities should be on.

"I'm here to see Gabriel Thornber," I tell the receptionist. "Could you tell me where he is?" Even as I say the words, I can't quite believe I'm doing this.

"Are you family?" she asks, in a tone that confirms everything I'd suspected about his condition. She's clearly lightly mesmerised. Goodness knows what she believes caused Gabriel's presumably horrific and unusual injuries.

"I'm his fiancée." I lie with a certainty that would make a Jedi proud. It'll be near-impossible to snap back out of the mind-tricks and mesmerism habit once all this is over and I go back to London.

"I'm sorry," the receptionist whispers. "I've never seen burns quite like it before—but I guess that's an explosion at a chemical factory for you. Anyway, it's Nightingale Wing. Third floor. He's in a private room. Fifth door on the left if you turn right at the lifts. There are lots of other family members with him already."

Of course there are. Family members. Bodyguards. Heartbroken admirers. Incidentally, there must be hundreds of patients in the hospital. It's fascinating the way Gabriel has not only lingered in her memory, but brought a tragic expression to her face.

Once I make it to Nightingale Wing, it becomes clear she hadn't been exaggerating about the number of "family" members. A selection of the more aggressive and muscular ones stand outside the fifth door on the left.

"I can't believe you've come here," one of them snaps, the second he sees me. I recognise him from the night of the BBQ. *Jamie*, I think. "You want to go in there and finish him off, you'll need to go through all of us."

Jim Thornber is standing by his side and nods sternly. He'd been Niall's chief lieutenant. It's not clear quite what relationship he has with Gabriel, beyond being his uncle, but whether it's based on respect, familial love, or fear, there's something in his eyes and in his stance that makes it quite clear that if needs be, he'll lay down his life to keep his nephew safe.

"He ordered us not to kill you, you know?" Jim explains. "That's the only reason I'm attempting a polite conversation instead of knocking you out. While he's alive, that order holds. But if he dies, all bets are off."

"I can't believe you did this to him," Jamie adds. "I know all Sadlers are scum, but I thought maybe you were different. He thought the world of you."

I force air into my mouth. "I'm not here to kill anybody, but can we stop acting like Gabriel is some martyred saint? He was fighting my family and friends, destroying our businesses, and trying to collapse the Dome that protects everyone in Mannith. And I blasted him because he murdered Connor."

"Who you apparently didn't care about enough to save," Jamie snaps.

I flinch. It's a fair point as far as my failings go, and it's a decision that's going to haunt me for a long time. As is my decision to attack Gabriel. But all that doesn't take away from the fact that Gabriel shot Connor without a second thought.

"What are you here for, Sadie?" Jim sounds like this has been the longest night of his life.

The million-dollar question. What the hell *am* I here for? To assess the damage? To complete it? To reverse it?

"I need to... to see him."

Jamie shakes his head. "Bullshit. No way in hell would your family let a Thornber in if one of you was lying unconscious at our hands."

I hold out my arms, and the two massive men flinch. *Wow. I seem to have acquired a reputation.*

"I don't want to do him any more harm," I say. "And I'm happy for you to do whatever it takes to ensure that. Whack those blocking bracelets on me and let me in there."

Jim frowns. "I'm not sick enough to put those things on

anyone. If someone's an enemy, you put blocking handcuffs on them, nice and simple. If they're a friend, an ally, or above all, someone you love, you don't block their magic with pretty trinkets and pretend that's okay."

"*He* put them on me."

"I'd never normally say a word against Gabriel, but he was wrong to do that, just like my brother was wrong to use them on his wife. I told him so when I heard. I've got some standard blocking handcuffs if you really want to go in there."

I'm not sure I entirely understand the distinction—blocking someone's magic is blocking their magic, isn't it?—but I guess the whole Thornber family is squeamish about the bracelets after what Niall did with them. Something uglier and sturdier would have led to the same outcome as far as Gabriel's poor mother was concerned, but they'd have left less room for the hypocrisy of pretending that blocking her magic was an act of love.

Right now, though, I need to get in that room, and I'll accept whatever conditions Gabriel's family impose.

I nod frantically. "I do."

Horribly dangerous to face them all with my defences down, but I believe them when they say Gabriel gave an order for me not to be killed. The thought torments me on more than one level.

Jim snaps the cuffs on me. Once again, all the colour and drama fades from the world.

Jamie opens the door. "There are plenty more of us in there, and we'll be watching. Don't try anything."

The room is surprisingly full. Thornber acolytes more endowed with magic than with brute strength crowd around, working healing spells. They're mostly pretty young women, but there are some pretty young men, too, as well as some motherly types deep into middle age.

Some of them are sobbing, others are lost in concentration. It takes both camps a moment to notice me, but once they do, everyone freezes. It's not clear whether they intend to attack me, defend Gabriel at all costs, or flee.

I ignore them, grip the door handle for support, and stare at the bed at the epicentre of their ministrations. Gabriel's utterly unconscious, mercifully. He's hooked up to who-knows-what combination of drips and monitors, and is swaddled in bandages. Modern medicine is working in tandem with the healing magic his supporters are channelling into him, but none of it seems to be doing much good. The force I unleashed should have killed him. It surely would have killed anyone else. There's little that can be done to undo that. Where his skin is visible through the dressings, he's a burnt, gory mess. *I did that.* It's a weird juxtaposition with his usual all-encompassing beauty.

It's usually a relief to get proof that you're not as shallow as you think, but I hate the fact that his burns don't make me desire him any less. Wanting someone as gorgeous as he was is human nature, despite his faults. My surging feelings for this wreck of a man suggest something much deeper.

"You! How could you do this? Are you here to gloat?" one of the glamorous female practitioners screams at me in between the tears that have clearly been flowing for hours.

"I don't know how anyone could hurt him. Not like this," another attractive practitioner—this time of the male variety—adds, shaking as he speaks.

Presumably these mysterious orders not to kill me extend to these people, too, not just the enforcers. But they all seem capable of breaking rank at any moment.

I step towards the bed, and they close the circle and throw up their shields. If only I could inspire this much raw loyalty and affection.

"Your magic's doing nothing," I whisper. "I doubt anyone could heal this. But I can reverse the spell."

One of the women frowns. "You'd turn it back on yourself? That would be suicide."

"No. But if you were willing, I could draw it back from him and turn a little on each of you. Divided that many ways, it'd be like a bad case of sunburn each."

It'd be the most complex bit of magic I'd ever attempted. It'd involve them putting a high degree of trust in someone who just attempted to kill their beloved boss. And it's utterly insane for me to risk myself trying to save him, when I let Connor die so I could kill him. But I did it to protect the Dome, and however well he heals, he won't be in a fit state to attack it again for months—by which point, if all goes to plan, I'll have got Bren out and he'll be able to protect it.

Or enlarge it, with all that entails, a disloyal part of my mind whispers. I push the unwelcome thought back down and focus on the situation at hand.

Both those without the blood and Born Practitioners of the less impressive sort sometimes act like it's necessary to learn every new piece of magic from scratch. They're like your grandad using a computer. Needing to be talked through each individual programme and each update step by step. Whereas those who've grown up with technology understand the underlying principles. Right clicking in one app is much the same as doing it in another. It's the same with magic. Since I was a child, I've learnt the basic ideas of opening programmes, saving files, and copying and pasting—so to speak. So, though I've never reversed a spell, and certainly never divided it between tens of people as I turn it back, the idea of how to do so is entirely intuitive to me.

"You're going to need to take off my handcuffs," I say.

The gathered fans converse amongst themselves, then someone makes a phone call.

Nikki stumbles in. Outwardly, she's a little calmer than most of the others—no wailing or hysterical tears for her. But she's walking in a daze as though she's hit her head, and her eyes are so red-rimmed from private tears she almost looks like a Born Practitioner.

Those eyes settle on me and widen. She walks over on trembling legs, grabs my arm, and with a pointed look at the others, drags me aside.

"How could you do it, Sadie? I know you felt the same way he did about you, deep down."

I close my eyes. "You're the one who told me to be careful."

"I told you not to marry him. I didn't tell you to murder him!" She manages the world's most unconvincing laugh.

"He was going to kill me. Either directly or by bringing the Dome down."

She tightens her grip. The rest of the room are watching and trying to hide that fact. "He would never have hurt you. He'd have found a way to get you out of harm's way before striking the final blow."

"He was happy enough to kill his own father. Whatever feelings he might have had for me, he clearly has no compunction about hurting those he claims to love."

"His mother made him swear to kill his father, in order to avenge her. She made him swear to a lot of things. He'd been psyching himself up to do it for years, but for all his usual ruthlessness, he could never quite put his qualms to one side."

"And what, he finally found his nerve when he realised he could use it as a way of getting at my brother?"

"That helped. As did the fact Niall wanted to send me away from Mannith—he didn't like a Taught Practitioner being that close to his pedigree heir. But what tipped Gabriel over the edge was when Niall decided to send assassins after you."

"After me? What on earth? I was in London. No trouble to anyone."

Nikki stares at the far wall and keeps her voice calm through sheer force of will. She sounds like she's reading out an email.

"Niall was plotting a grand dynastic marriage for Gabriel with one of the daughters of the Cornish Enclave. Consolidate the family power, keep the grand breeding programme going, take over the town—and probably put the new daughter-in-law in Maeve's old blocking bracelets if she started getting ideas above her station."

"And I presume Gabriel wasn't a fan of this idea?"

This time, Nikki can't quite keep up the act. There's fury in her voice. "There was no way he was going to agree to marry anyone but you. So Niall decided to remove that obstacle. And Gabriel killed him before he could do so. Because he may always have at least two reasons for everything, but the one thing he's always put over every other rational consideration is Ms Sadie Sadler.

"So, for all his grand claims, he wouldn't have brought the Dome down if it meant killing you. But you were perfectly happy to try to kill him."

I close my eyes. Just when I thought my conflicted emotions had surely taken everything the world could possibly throw at them, here comes yet more revelations to make me feel worse about what I've done.

I believe Nikki about the circumstances surrounding Niall's death. It makes it harder to hate, blame or fear Gabriel for what he did, if it was partially in defence of me. But it's yet more proof of just how deep his obsession goes. And that's arguably even scarier.

I place a hand on Nikki's arm. "I'm going to heal him." Words are my currency, but right now, I can't manage any response more complex than that.

Nikki scowls and jerks away from me. "I'm not letting you touch him."

"It's the only way."

She closes her eyes and for a full five minutes, no one moves or says a word. It's like she's attempting to commune with a god or will the universe to show her what to do.

"Give me your hand," she says eventually. "I'll take the cuffs off. At the slightest hint you're about to do anything to hurt him, to hell with his orders and with the fact you're stronger than me; I'll blow you apart."

I nod and hold out my arms. It seems unlikely she could do anything magical to hurt me, but while I'm vulnerable, there's a chance she could stab me or put her impressive boxing skills to lethal use.

As she opens the cuffs, everyone else keeps their arms raised. It's difficult to believe they think I'd actually hurt Gabriel again, while he's already laying scarred and unconscious at my hands.

After ten seconds have passed, and I've not obviously attempted to obliterate Gabriel, the mood in the room relaxes, infinitesimally. No one drops their defences, but they look less likely to attack me.

"Form a circle around the bed," I order. "I'll stand in the centre, one hand on him. Two of you will put a hand on each of my shoulders, then everyone else needs to take the arm of the person in front of them."

Everyone does my bidding, though their movements are slow and hesitant. Take a step. Glance at me to check I'm not attempting anything deadly. Take another step.

Nikki attempts to take hold of my left shoulder. I grab her hand, give it a little squeeze of appreciation, then pull away. "You'll need to step outside the circle," I whisper. "This sort of practical, applied magic will tear apart someone who's got the learning but not the blood."

"Screw you. I'm joining the circle. I'm holding on to you. If I burn, I burn."

I sigh. She really cares about him. Who am I to deny her? "Fine. On your head be it."

When I step forward towards the bed, the entire room tenses again, but everyone forms themselves into a circle, and, in the case of Nikki and a man I've never met, put their free hand on my shoulder.

I focus all my attention on the broken figure of Gabriel. I take a deep breath, cross my hands, and place them on his chest.

It would be the work of seconds to exert my will on his unconscious form and finish him off. Protect myself. Protect my family. The Thornbers think they have me surrounded, but if there's one thing the last few weeks have taught me, it's that I'm more powerful than I or anyone else has ever realised. I'd have a fighting chance of getting out.

I have to run it through my mind. It would be odd not even to consider it. But already, the idea seems laughable. God help me, I want to save him.

"Those of you who are able to reliably do core meditation should do so now," I say. "It'll help you with the pain and help me to find a way in."

Before I attempt anything more complex, I throw a light spell around us all to prevent anyone from dropping their hands and breaking the circle. Then I forget about everyone else in the room.

I think about the moment I'd unleashed the spell in the first place. The entire span from Gabriel's bullets hitting Connor to my fire striking Gabriel had only lasted a few seconds in total, and I'd been barely conscious of what I was doing. But now, in my memories, I break each of those seconds down to their constituent parts.

I'd connected with some part of the earth hundreds of miles down, where everything is just heat and pressure. I'd let those qualities flow through me. I'd clenched my fists together and curled into myself as I built the forces up to breaking point, then thrown my arms out, palms up, and forced them out of me in a concentrated blast. Or something like that, anyway.

Now, I have to do all of that in reverse. I lift up my top hand and move it over Gabriel's prone body. There are remnants of my magical force spiralling around him. Most of it would have exploded outwards as the blaze took hold, but what's left is enough. A spell reversal is a strange mixture of the literal and the symbolic.

I draw the free-floating traces of the earth's heat together, letting them build and become more tangible. This bit is ultra-sensitive. Too little pressure and focus and I won't achieve a thing. Too much, and I'll burn him alive from the inside out. I'm paying no attention to the rest of the room but they're no doubt terrified I'll do precisely that, whether deliberately or through a lack of control.

The memory of the spell rebuilds until Gabriel's glowing all over with a ghostly fire. It covers the hand I've placed on him, too. For now, it doesn't burn, just feels like something's lightly touching me. But that won't last.

I sweep my hand all over his body, trying not to be distracted by thoughts of the last time I'd done that, back in the hotel room. I gather the fire together until instead of an amorphous mass encircling him, it's a fiercely concentrated ball at his chest. It burns like holding your palm above a candle. Not particularly painful if just for a few seconds, but the intensity quickly grows.

This is it.

I lean over and touch my forehead to his. Then I tighten my mental and physical grip on the phantom fireball, wrench it away from Gabriel's chest, and clasp it into mine. The fireball enters me, dragging all its effects—the pain, the damage —with it.

I scream like a woman possessed. I'd known it was going to hurt—in what possible world would being burnt alive *not* hurt? But I'd not anticipated quite this level of agony, quite the extent to which my entire world narrows to that feeling of heat and destruction, breaking down any capacity for rational thought into a primordial urge to survive, to make the pain go away.

The key now is to get the magic out of me and dispensed amongst the others. But that takes focus and control, and right now, they are in short supply. All I have is screaming.

At least I've worked the circle-binding spell. Without the magic keeping us all locked in place, the Thornber acolytes may well just have chosen to drop their hands and let me burn. And failing that, I'd probably pull away in shock.

Nikki's hands at my shoulder tighten. "Breathe. You've got this. And we've got you."

I know it's him that she and the others care about, not me, but it's still enough to make me rally. I force oxygen in through my burning lips and send a few gentle blasts of the fire magic out in both directions around the circle.

I long to throw it all out of me in a frenzy, but that'd just kill the two people next to me and probably other parts of the circle. I have to let it out slowly, bit by bit, and let them spread it between themselves, watering it down with each person. But that means keeping most of it inside me, torturing me, for several more seconds, which might as well be years.

I'm still screaming, but I can barely hear myself. Like the time Gabriel unleashed the Greenfire on me, I'm fighting my own magic and will as much as the original spell and the pain. Like the Greenfire, it won't do me any real harm until I lose concentration.

A cry towards the back of the room cuts through my disembodied state. It shows the first lots of magic have made it right round the circle. I release another few blasts. My pain starts to lessen, but it's still more than I can reasonably stand.

Cries are coming from all directions. I shunt two more blasts around the circle, then release my control, letting the remnants of the magic either soak into me or disperse into the air. The pain lessens, which is ironic, because before, it was only really tearing at my psyche, and now it's burning my skin. But it's at a level I can manage.

I take one more deep breath, then break everything, including the circle spell. I drop my hands, lift my forehead off Gabriel's, then collapse onto the bed.

Behind me, the rest of the circle breaks apart. There are a few moans and whimpers, but these are good, solid northerners and they seem to be remaining stoic. Still, if I'd lost control, they'd be passed out or screaming no matter how high their pain threshold.

"Is everyone okay?" I whisper, after what feels like hours, pushing myself to a standing position.

General murmurs of agreement run through the room. I manage to turn and look at them. Where their skin is exposed, it looks badly sunburnt. The sort of sunburn that blisters and needs steroid cream rather than the sort that turns into a glowing tan, but nothing worse than that. Everyone's eyes are bloodshot and their hair is wild. There's a general air of exhaustion.

"Nikki passed out," someone says. "She should have sat this one out. Cath's healing her. We'll all heal each other later."

I nod. My own body doesn't look great. Despite my best efforts to filter it, I still took more than my fair share of the fire. But whether because of adrenaline, triumph, or just because there's only so much your mind and body will let you endure, I'm beyond pain.

"You'll need to heal him first," I say, preaching to the converted. "Reversing the spell won't do it all. There's still tissue damage and general depletion. I'd do it myself, but I'm burnt out."

Everyone crowds round like they want to be the first to touch Gabriel, the one to work the healing magic.

It's clear something's changed. I can't see much of him under the bandages, but where it's possible to catch glimpses, his skin is reddened rather than charred. His breathing and heart rate have stabilised. The hospital monitors tell the same story as my heightened senses. He's still unconscious, but it's more like a deep sleep than a coma. At my best guess, he'll be up and about within twelve hours. What he'll do then—to me, to my family—is anyone's guess. I don't know whether to feel guiltier about attacking him or about healing him.

"In fifteen minutes, I'm going to leave this hospital and return to my family." I speak deliberately formally. "For that fifteen minutes, I want you to leave me alone with him. Hopefully I've shown I can be trusted. If I do anything to hurt him, I guess you can all kill me on the way out."

I suspect Nikki would have led the resistance to my arguments, but she's still out cold. I can't help but admire both her bravery and her learnt grasp of magic. After a few pointed looks and what I can only assume is some telepathy on a frequency I can't access, the others seem to reach an accord.

Jamie, who's seemingly entered while the spell was under way, speaks for the group. "Fifteen minutes then. We'll be outside. Don't make us regret this."

I don't know what they think I'm going to do, but once they leave, I simply collapse back over the bed, resting my head on Gabriel's chest and feeling the increasingly steady rise and fall of his breath and beat of his heart.

I'm sobbing within seconds. If only he were awake. If only we could speak. If only I could apologise for hurting him. If only he could apologise for hurting me and those I loved. If only he could thank me for healing him and promise me there'll be no repercussions. If only we could kiss like we had before.

I think I liked it better when I felt nothing for anyone.

I kiss his cheek and let the tears flow. God help me. He's the worst person I've ever met, and I love him with more force than I could ever have imagined.

TWENTY-THREE

The next day, I'm due back in court yet again. I could quite happily sleep all day, and probably should. But this is it. It's time for my closing arguments—my last chance to strike a blow for Bren.

I'm praying both that he'll get out and that what he's sworn about enlarging the Dome isn't a lie.

I down three cups of the awful instant coffee that the courthouse has to offer. I'd normally never touch the stuff, but right now, the priority is staying awake, not appreciating the aroma and the taste.

Once I get into the courtroom, Bren can't stop grinning at me from the dock. He clearly heard what happened. The bit where I blasted Gabriel, anyway. Maybe not the fact I subsequently revived him. If he's feeling any sadness about Connor's death, his thoughts on his fallen friend are clearly outweighed by joy at his fallen foe.

On the subject of whom, there's no sign of Gabriel. It's always easier to focus when he's not attracting my attention, but his absence is worrying. What condition is he in now?

I thrive on the thrill of examination and cross-examination, but when it comes down to it, the closing statement is probably my favourite part of a trial and my greatest strength. At this stage, I'm entirely in control, and I can take all the loose threads of evidence and weave them into my own story.

The second I start to speak, all the exhaustion falls away. I stand up straight, smile at the judge and jury, and underline my key points with expansive hand gestures. There's no magic to contend with today. No witnesses who might be lying or bewitched, and no one I'm forcing to speak. There's just me and my words.

There's nothing new to say. It's an exercise in ensuring the jury understand how everything they've heard comes together to lead them to the unavoidable conclusion that Bren's not guilty.

I remind them of the basics of Bren's story, and why it makes sense. I bring in Leah's testimony—the parts that give Bren an alibi and corroborate his account, and the parts that explain that it was a set-up. I take apart the prosecution case bit by bit, painting Gabriel as an entirely biased and unreliable witness and the others as some combination of lying on his orders and confused. Without being able to explain the magical disguise angle, it's not the most compelling explanation, but hopefully it's enough to cast the necessary seeds of doubt in the jury's mind. They don't need to believe he's innocent, just that they can't be sure beyond reasonable doubt that he's guilty.

I exhale as I draw my speech to a close. I've done the best I could. No one could have done it better.

I'm about to sit down and hope for the best when I see the look on Bren's face. He's staring into the distance like he's watching the rest of his life play out in front of his eyes. A life of imprisonment. A life of his magic slowly draining away, until the lack of it either kills him or makes him wish he were dead. A life in which the Thornbers take over his beloved town or take down his precious Dome.

Even in this moment, he's far too conscious of his reputation to plead or break down, but to my absolute horror, a few tears trickle down his face. Even as a child, I never saw him cry. He always took his role as the heir, the oldest brother, and the family's protector and hope far too seriously for that.

I'm not much of an empath or a clairvoyant, but his pain and worry seeps into my blood. A horrible sense of foreboding hits me. I've done a good job, from a legal standpoint, but it's not been enough.

Bren stares at me and swallows hard. He's begging me with his eyes to do what needs to be done.

The way I've had to risk everything to get him out of trouble —again—would have been a lot to take if he'd been grateful and accommodating. But at best, he's taken me for granted and been demanding and unforthcoming. At worst, however much I've tried to convince myself otherwise, there's a chance he's been lying to me and planning something awful.

I've pushed my professional ethics to the brink. I've broken my vow to avoid magic a hundred times over. I've spent more time injured and unconscious this summer than I have in the rest of my life. And that's before I even factor in the way I've faced the only person I've ever truly feared and wrenched my heart open in the process.

I stare at the jury and though their faces are blank, there's something there that confirms Bren's fears and my gut instinct. They're going to find him guilty.

When all's said and done, Bren might not be an uncomplicatedly good man, but on balance, he was always a great big brother. And if our roles were somehow reversed, then despite everything that's happened since those long-ago childhood days, I have no doubt he'd do whatever it took to help me. I've done my best to play fair and respect the rule of law. Somewhat against the odds, my family have stuck to their agreement not to help the case along with intimidation or magic. But there's no reason I have to obey my own rules. I've already broken them in order to get Leah to testify. I've done all I can with my legal prowess. To hell with it. It's time to put my other skills to use.

I lift up my arms and draw an arc over the jury, then another over the judge. I imagine the judge's summing up being entirely in Bren's favour. I visualise the jury delivering a not guilty verdict. It'd have been a lost cause if Gabriel were in court, but thanks to what I did, he's not around to stop me and no one else is capable of it. By the time I sit down, the spell's fallen into place.

There's a moment, just after the jury do my bidding and find Brendan not guilty, where it all seems worthwhile.

His cuffs are removed, and the magic in the air swarms towards him like a pack of dogs whose beloved master has returned. He smiles once at the room in general, then once directly at me.

It takes about thirty seconds for my doubt and guilt to start creeping in.

I've betrayed all my principles as far as the rule of law goes, but I'll just have to live with that—I know for a fact that Bren was at least not guilty of the crime he'd been charged with. Now I just have to hope with every fibre of my being that I was right to trust him on everything else.

By ten PM, I'm drunk as hell. Usually, I tend to pace myself. But tonight, at what's simultaneously Bren's welcome home party and a celebration of Connor's tragically short life, no one's taking it steady.

The garden and conservatory of my parents' house are bedecked with flowers, lights, and incense. Music plays from unseen speakers, and the champagne never seems to run low. It's unclear what's been accomplished with money and influence and what's been achieved with magic.

In the aftermath of the Ritual, I'd told my mum I couldn't condone the family's actions, and I'd need to keep my distance. But some of that resolve fell away the night we all defended the Dome together. And there's no way I could stay away from tonight's festivities.

I'm leaning against a rowan tree, swaying in time to the music and drinking yet another glass of fizz, while chatting to some woman I barely know, when Bren strides into view.

He's looking more sober than anyone else there, crackling with magic, and glancing around him like he wants to soak up every sight and scent of freedom. He takes my glass, nods to my companion, who immediately blushes, then sweeps me away.

"I've barely spoken to you all night," he says.

"You've probably seen enough of me in the last few weeks. I'm glad you're getting to talk to other people."

He leads me to the furthest reaches of the garden, to the bench hidden under the branches of a weeping willow where I'd prepared for the Ritual—it had been one of our favourite childhood spaces, somewhere to get away from the adults and from the world.

I smile as I sink into its familiar ridges. "I'm so glad you're out. I just can't find the words."

"And I'm so grateful for everything you did for me. The legal stuff, the magical stuff, the investigation and intimidation and everything in between."

I don't tell him how guilty and conflicted most of that makes me feel. I've sacrificed my principles to save my brother. And whatever the rights and wrongs, I *am* glad he's free. For tonight at least, I want to enjoy that fact, and not taint our victory.

We sit in silence for a moment, appreciating the warm night air.

"Can I do that long-delayed portrait of you now?"

"Shouldn't we wait until morning?"

"I don't need light to draw, you know that."

I settle back on the seat, getting myself into a position I can hold.

He plucks a sketchpad and pencils out of thin air and starts to sketch. He stares at me for a moment, glances at the paper, then looks back up and seems to let his subconscious take over the artistic process.

"When are you going back to London?" He asks the question as his hand races over the paper.

I shrug, then quickly correct my posture. "In a few days, I guess. It'll be fantastic to relax with you all without the case hanging over us, but then I need to get back to my job, my life."

The words make my chest heavy. Does it have to be this way? I could move my practice to one of the northern chambers. Embrace my magic and my family.

"And will you be back to forsaking your powers?" He's still drawing, but all his attention seems to be on the conversation.

I laugh. "That's a pretty dramatic way of putting it. I don't need to be so all or nothing in future. I can't see myself doing rituals or joining a coven, and I certainly don't want to use magic in court ever again, but it'd be nice to be able to traverse myself places or wave my hand and be dressed and ready to go."

"I need to be strong for the family." Bren looks at the sky instead of at me or the sketchpad, and speaks almost like he's thinking aloud. "I don't know if anyone's dared to tell you yet, but Gabriel-fucking-Thornber survived your attack after all. According to my spies, he's already back on his feet and no doubt rapidly regaining his powers."

I try to turn my unconscious sigh of relief into a horrified gasp. Goodness knows quite what I sound like or what weird expression is on my face. I long to go and see Gabriel before I leave town. But it'd be hard to justify and it's anyone's guess what reaction I'd get—possibly a lethal one.

"The Thornbers will try something again," Bren continues. "I need to be able to stop them and protect Mannith properly. To do that, I have to consolidate our power."

I merely nod. It's not the sort of statement that needs an answer.

"I'm powerful, but not powerful enough," he continues. "I'm stronger than almost anyone else, but much as it pains me to admit it, Thornber has the edge." His pencil falls still.

I put a hand on his arm and remain silent.

"But with our powers combined, we'd be a force to be reckoned with."

"Are you asking me to stay?"

"You never would. And if you did, you wouldn't want to do the things that need to be done. So, no. I'm asking you to give me your magic."

I flinch back, as though he's about to start dragging my power out of me, though of course, he'd never do such a thing. Besides, what does he mean by 'the things that need to be done'?

Please, please, please let me have done the right thing in trusting him and getting him out.

"I'd never take the magic of someone who relished it. But for you, it's little more than an inconvenience." He makes a few final, furious scribbles on the paper.

"I'll think about it tomorrow." I stand up and stroll back towards the sounds of the party. By which I mean I'll think about how to break it to him gently that there's no way in hell I'd do what he's asking.

"Don't forget this." He hands me the sketch. It's perfect,

despite his apparent lack of concentration. Flattering, but still an accurate likeness. Showing my face and body, but also capturing something of my inner self. But it's not enough to put my mind at ease. Would one night of calm really have been too much to ask?

TWENTY-FOUR

The Witches' Church is spooky enough in daylight. In the darkness, with only the light of the moon to guide my path, it's terrifying. Logically, any lingering spirits will be broadly on my side, and anything more corporeal should be more scared of me than I am of it. But the logical part of my brain isn't really in control.

I feel my way through the graveyard, putting one foot in front of the other with careful precision. Sheer muscle memory carries me to my nan's grave, then I kneel before her statue, drop into a core meditation, and search for any trace of her. There's no sign.

I stay in my kneeling position long after it becomes clear no spirits are trying to commune with me, attempting to listen to my own mind.

Afterwards, I glance over at the statue of Gabriel's tragic, powerful mother. It's easy to pick out because of the way it glows in the moonlight. He must have charmed it recently. She's the only spirit I've ever managed to reach, and I'm half-tempted to speak to her again now. But the sorts of things she'd tell me probably aren't the ones I want to hear.

There's still no statue of Gabriel's father. Maybe he's intending never to erect one. It's still shocking to think he killed him. Did he hate his father? Or did he love him deep down but still manage to do the deed? I'm not sure which version is worse.

Connor's family have already erected a statue of him, though the funeral's not yet taken place. Looking at it brings tears to my eyes. I quickly lay some flowers on top of those placed there by others, and I whisper a blessing and an apology, but I'm too much of a coward to attempt to commune with his spirit.

There's a slight chill in the air, and a few leaves are starting to fall. Summer is almost over, but it's not the only season Mannith does properly. Within days, the temperature will have fallen to the point where you need to wear a jumper every day, and everything inside the Dome will be in shades of orange and brown, with the scent of bonfires in the air. I'll be sorry to miss it.

I step around the perimeter of the building until I reach the entrance door, then lean against it, waiting for Bren.

We've agreed to meet out at the Witches' Church for privacy from the rest of family. Though I've not yet given him an answer to his request, Bren presumably thinks this is so we can carry out the magic exchange undisturbed. But there's no way I can give him my magic.

Voluntarily choosing not to use it is one thing, but the thought of it not actually being there is like a physical pain—and now the lien isn't an issue, I'd like to keep using it a bit more anyway. Besides, however much I want to believe that he has no intention of further expanding the Dome, Chrissie had reassured me that even if he did want to, he didn't have quite enough power to do anything large-scale. And I guess he'd sort of hinted at something similar. I can't risk my magic tipping the balance.

I've chosen this private, sacred place so I can let him down gently, without our family listening in. And so I can try once more to get a straight answer about what he's done in the past and what he intends to do in the future.

"Hey," Bren says, suddenly traversing into place. He's clearly forgotten Nan's old advice about the walk here being half the point.

"Shall we go in?" I take his hand and lift it up. We open the door together and step through the ruined arch and into the perfectly preserved church inside. However many times I activate this particular piece of magic, it never ceases to thrill me.

"You're doing the right thing," Bren says, the second we're inside. "With your power added to mine, the family will be unstoppable."

I study the stained-glass windows, trying to memorise every pane. "Bren, listen to me—"

"At best, you sit on all that power, fighting the urge to use it. Which must be exhausting." He paces up and down the aisle, barely looking at me. "At worst, it bursts out of you. Power and no control."

I sit down on the pew nearest the door. "Bren, I haven't said I'll do it. You're out and you've not got to worry about the risk of me dropping the case. I'm back to being your sister rather than your lawyer. And we're somewhere it's hard to lie. So I'm going to ask you one more time for the truth about you and the Dome."

Brendan sits down on the back pew next to me. It's cosy, safe, like something from childhood. No need for drama, though it's unclear whether he's about to tell me everything or try once more to persuade me to give him my magic.

"Sadie, please don't do this."

Gabriel appears out of nowhere in the pew in front, facing towards us. He's back in the white linen suit and there are no traces of his injuries.

Brendan's hands are up in a fraction of a second. "Don't push me, Thornber. This is Sadler family business."

I lift my own hands in turn and mentally raise my protective shields. I don't think I'll need them, even after what I did to Gabriel, but it'd be madness not to do so.

"I sensed this was happening," Gabriel says, speaking to me and entirely ignoring Bren. "On some subconscious level, you were calling out for help. I couldn't just stand by and let it happen."

"Why are you so desperate to stop this?" I ask. "Because you don't want me powerless, or because you don't want my brother more powerful than you?"

He smiles. "You know me. At least two reasons, always."

Bren stands, murder in his eyes. "Just this month, you've had me falsely imprisoned, killed one of my best friends, slept with my fiancée, and done God-knows-what to my baby sister. So, let's settle this the old-fashioned way. One-on-one duel to the death, magic only."

I grab his arm and try to force him to sit back down. "Bren, no. This is crazy."

He shrugs off my grip. "Because you don't think I can take him, or because you don't want me to?"

"You know I trust your powers. You know I'm loyal to this family. There's just no need for these extremes. I've got you out of prison. Renegotiate a peace."

"I'm sorry, Sadie. You've been away too long. You don't understand how these things work." He takes a few steps away from me and fronts up to Gabriel.

Against all the odds, I look to Gabriel to be the voice of reason, but he's nodding. "Fine, let's do it. I'm not going to be as cocky as I would be with anyone else and say I'll win for sure. I respect your power too much for that, and I'm still recovering. But I've got a fighting chance."

I get to my feet. "What? Seriously, don't do this."

"Sadie, get the hell out of here," Brendan orders. "This isn't about you. This fight's long overdue. But I don't want you getting involved or getting caught in the crossfire."

"I agree," Gabriel says.

It's probably the first time they've ever agreed on anything.

"No way am I going anywhere," I snap, moving my hands and letting my defensive shield morph into something more controlling. "You both need to stop this right now."

"Bubble of protection around the two of us, keep her out of range?" Gabriel muses.

Brendan nods. "Sure."

They shake hands, and a bubble closes around them and drags them away towards the altar, leaving me languishing in the pew, locked out. What the hell am I supposed to do? Whatever happens, someone I love is going to get hurt, perhaps even killed. Neither of them is exactly innocent, but I don't give a damn about that right now.

The fight starts before I can gather my breath. Power is absolutely radiating out of the two of them, mingling in the air above until I can't tell which spells belong to whom. I've seen both of them fight other people before, and it's always been over in seconds. No one can stand against either of them. But they can stand against each other in perfect balance.

There's a physical pressure in the room, as though a storm's about to break. In my mind's eye, Bren's power is red, Gabriel's green, and the two meet in mid-air, mingling in the middle. Their exertions cast an eerie light that illuminates the stained glass and reflects off the polished wood and brass of the pews and candleholders.

I run over to the limits of the bubble they've cast around their makeshift arena. "Stop it!"

I claw at the incorporeal barrier, visualising it collapsing. But it's no good. However much power I can muster, there's no way I'm capable of breaking through a protection bubble created by the combined powers of Gabriel and Brendan.

Each of their spells are repelling the other like magnets and forcing the two men backwards as though shoved by a huge invisible hand. I can't take my eyes away from the scene.

I alternate between screaming at them until my voice is hoarse and launching magic at the barrier until my hands are trembling, but none of it makes the slightest bit of difference.

I'm not quite sure what suddenly gives Gabriel the upper hand. Maybe he finds some strength even he didn't know he had, or maybe Brendan lets something slip. Everything's moving too fast for my brain to keep up. Either way, Brendan drops to the floor, and his magic falls away. Gabriel towers over him, hands raised, presumably intending a killing blow.

I run over to the edge of the bubble. "Please, Gabriel. Please don't do this. For all your faults, I'd forgive you practically anything else. But kill my brother, whatever he's done wrong, and there can be no future for us."

It's unclear if he still cares about all that after I tried to kill him, even if I did bring him back, but it's got to be worth a shot.

Brendan nods. "We can figure this out."

Gabriel's hands are trembling. It's not like he hasn't killed people before. He didn't hesitate before blowing a hole in Connor's chest, for a start. Not to mention what he did to his father.

"You're the one who wanted a duel," Gabriel says. "You're the one who laid accusations at my feet. Give me one good reason not to strike."

"Unlike you, I don't have two reasons," Bren replies. "I don't even have one. But I've got a bet to place."

Gabriel's still hesitating, which is more than I could ever have hoped for. I lift my hands experimentally. They're both weakened. Could I summon enough force to blast a hole in the bubble then knock both of them out and give things time to deescalate?

"My little sister told me an interesting story," Brendan continues.

I frown, hands frozen. What on earth is he talking about?

"She told me about the moment you killed Connor Colson. How she had enough power to bring him back to life or to kill you, but not both. And how she chose hate over love. Well, I say love... I guess it was only really lust that existed between her and Connor.

"But it got me thinking. No one has enough power to resurrect with one hand and kill with the other, not even the two of us. And someone who's *actually* in love would choose to save their beloved every time. I despise you, but before you made her betray me, I'd always have saved Leah instead of killing you."

"What's your point?" Gabriel hasn't lowered his defences. He's scrutinising Bren for any hint of a trick or distraction, the green-tinged magic still flickering at his fingers.

"You hate me as a concept, you hate me as a person, and you hate the things I do. There's almost nothing that would give you more pleasure than killing me. But here's my bet and here's my escape route: I'm gambling everything that you'll choose love over hate."

I glance around, uncertain of his meaning.

Brendan lifts his hand and gathers every last strand of his magic into his palm.

Gabriel tightens his shield, but still doesn't strike the final blow. Brendan's managed to get under his skin.

Brendan draws a quick jagged shape in the air. He really must be exhausted if he's resorting to hand signals, but it works. The bubble comes down from the inside out.

"Sadie, get your shield up!" Gabriel screams. He fires at Brendan, but my brother manages to roll aside and launch all the power he's built up straight in my direction.

Despite everything, I've grown to trust Gabriel. Grown more and more sure that he'd never really hurt me. But I always keep my literal and metaphorical defences up when he's around. If he'd turned towards me with fire in his eyes, I'd have had shields all around me in a second.

But despite all the hints in his words, the thought that my big brother might attack me has never even crossed my mind. So, in contradiction of all common sense, my shields stay down and my eyes stay wide until it's too late.

I stand there, too stunned even to scream let alone to fight back, as Brendan's killing blow cascades into me, and sends me crashing to the ground.

TWENTY-FIVE

I wake up in an unfamiliar bed, surrounded by a group of armed Thornber acolytes, who might be bodyguards or might be jailors.

I must have come close to death and been healed. Perhaps even started to pass through to the other side, only to be dragged back. I ought to be in agony, or at the very least exhausted, tender, and drained. Instead, I sit up in bed without the slightest issue. Were it not for the guards, I could walk out of the room unaided. My mind, on the other hand, is a mess. There's something about being murdered by your beloved older brother to score a cheap point that'll do that to a person.

"Am I free to go?" I call out the words, startling the guards.

"God, you're awake." Nikki pushes through the men surrounding me. "No visible damage, eyes bright, sitting up by yourself. I thought you were dead for sure when you arrived."

"Our boy really can work miracles," one of the guards says.

The last time I'd seen Nikki, immediately after the spell reversal, she'd looked like she'd been in a fire, but there's no hint of damage to her hair or skin anymore, either.

"I want to go home," I say. I'm not sure which home I mean.

London? The Windmill? My parents' house? None of the options seem entirely appealing.

"This is your home now." Gabriel appears from nowhere, right by the bed. His hair's all over the place and there are shadows under his slightly swollen eyes. Even so, he only has to give his guards the slightest glance for them to file out of the room. Nikki hesitates for a moment, but he looks directly at her, nods, and she follows the others.

"This isn't my home, Gabriel. Still, I guess you chose to save me rather than destroy my damn brother. I should thank you for that."

He sits down on the bed. "Bloody hell, Sadie. You make it sound like I had a choice."

He grips my hand, and it's like a dam breaking. Suddenly, he's clutching me against his chest, all traces of his icy composure and supercilious charm disappeared.

"I thought you were gone. I thought he'd hit you with too much power, pushed you straight over the edge. I couldn't believe he would do that to you—I killed my father in large part to keep you safe, but for all Brendan's other faults, I never thought I'd have to protect you from *him*. I couldn't even begin to imagine you dying."

He's actually shaking. Mostly from panic and emotional turmoil, judging by his words, but probably from overuse of magic, too. I didn't think there were enough spells in the world to push Gabriel into magical burnout, but apparently, a fight to the death with the one person who can match you followed by a near-resurrection will do the trick.

"I did almost kill you," I whisper into his chest. "I'm a little surprised you're able to forgive that this readily."

"You blasted me in the heat of the moment, to protect your family as part of a war. What matters is that you made the conscious choice to bring me back."

"Lie down," I say. "You need the rest more than I do. I feel totally healed." Physically, anyway, but I don't draw that distinction. It's not like the emotional pain is his fault.

He does as I ask, fully clothed, and I snuggle into his shoulder. "Take a little of my magic, if you need it," I whisper. "I still owe you some back from that night six years ago."

"Never. Or not unless I was actually about to collapse like you did at the casino. I love the way the magic flows through you. I'd never take any of it away. I'd never try to dampen your power."

There's a note of hysteria in his voice. Perhaps he's thinking of Brendan, angling to take all my power for himself. Or perhaps of his poor mother, wasting away in her golden bracelets. Just like his father had wanted him to do to his hand-selected bride.

I stroke his hair. "I know. Just like I know you're not a monster, whatever anyone says." There are a hundred and one reasons not to be with him, but he'd respect my power, that much is clear.

"What happened to Brendan?" I ask after a moment.

"Once I'd got you stable, I got off a quick attack before bringing you back here for fuller healing. To the best of my knowledge, he's recovering at your parents'. We'll have to negotiate a truce or else accept all-out war. Hence the guards."

His arm tightens around me. "Sadie, I know your head must be all over the place right now. And I'm not exactly feeling at my most relaxed and stable either. I ought to lie here in silence and let us both rest. But there are so many words that have been building up inside me. I've got to let them out or I might burst."

"Gabriel, I've kind of gathered you're a little intense and over-dramatic at the best of times. Say whatever you need to say."

He takes a few audible deep breaths and manages to get his trembling under control. "Firstly, when I thought you were going to die, I felt like Brendan had killed me, too. If I hadn't been able to drag you back from the brink, I honestly believe I'd have wasted away from the lack of you the way my mother wasted away from a lack of magic.

"Secondly, I despise your brother, and I like to win. I had him in my grasp. If I'd been forced to make the choice between killing him or saving anyone else, I'd have struck the fatal blow. With you, I didn't hesitate even for a second."

I close my eyes. I can barely breathe. "What are you trying to say?"

"I'm trying to say I love you. Really and truly and honestly, on some fundamental level. I know I've said it before, and you think it's a chat-up line at worst and obsession at best, but it felt real to me, and now I know for sure."

I run a hand down his chest. His heart rate is utterly out of control. I let his words soak into my brain, without trying to think about them or formulate a reply. He was right. I'm in no mental or emotional state for this conversation.

"When you came over to trade in the lien, I got my hopes up that you felt the same way. More so that time we spent the night together. But sex is sex and a date's a date. It was the evening you almost killed me that really convinced me."

Despite everything, I laugh. "It wasn't my most romantic gesture ever."

"Well, the bit where you put me back together again. It's no small thing to heal someone that deeply. And now we've both done it to each other. There was a bond before, but since that exchange, there's something unbreakably strong."

I still don't feel up to replying, but I can't avoid a tiny nod. Laid against him like this, I feel it. Something almost physical where our two magics meet.

"I want to give you this. It can be a symbol of as much or as little as you like. Of the connection neither of us can stop or deny, or of something more voluntary and official."

He slips a hand into his jeans pocket and pulls out the rose-gold ring, speckled with tiny flecks of emerald in a swirling pattern, which he normally wears on a chain around his neck.

"It's my mother's engagement ring," he explains, holding it out to me. "Though don't worry. It's not like the bracelets. Dad was a better person at that stage."

I clasp my hand to my mouth as I stare at the ring. "I can't accept that." My voice is shaking. "I've only known you for about a month. And the majority of that time's not exactly been romantic."

"Like I said, it can represent as much or as little as you want. One day, I truly hope you'll marry me. I hope you'll make this your home and be a Thornber instead of a Sadler. But I know that's too much to ask right now."

"I always thought I'd probably keep my own name on marriage," I say, with a little forced laugh. "Or maybe double-barrel it. Sadler-Thornber. Everyone would love that."

I take refuge in jokes because this is all too much to take in. *What is he thinking? Maybe we could make something work against all the odds, but not this much this fast.*

"I like tradition, I don't deny it. But I don't care about any of that a tenth as much as I care about you."

I shuffle away from him and sit up. It's too hard to think with his skin against my skin. "Gabriel, this is crazy. Who knows what could happen in the future, but right now, I can't get engaged to you. And I can't take your mother's ring as a symbol of anything less than that."

He sits up, too, despite his evident exhaustion, and looks me straight in the eye. "She wanted you to have it. Just like she wanted me to kill my father."

I frown. "I never met your mother." *Other than that brief conversation in the graveyard at least.*

"But she met you. In a way. She was a true clairvoyant and prophet. It was the only power left to her after Dad did what he did. I've got hints of the gift, though not enough to do anything constructive with, and it sort of works on a different channel."

"Wow." Even amongst the strongest practitioners, the ability to see into the future with any clarity and accuracy is vanishingly rare. As I've always argued, most magic is just manipulating the same forces in different ways. But clairvoyance involves something slightly different. It's not a gift I'm blessed with, so I can't quite put it into words.

"She saw you. She told me I was the right person for you and you were the right person for me. Just like she asked me to avenge her, she made me promise to make our relationship happen and to give you this ring. It was one of the last conversations we ever had."

I smile and my breathing stabilises as a little fluttery feeling builds up in my stomach. It all sounds so romantic. A bit like what happened with Chrissie and Ray. Perhaps we really are fated to be together? I reach out, take the ring, and lay it on my palm for a closer inspection.

For a second, all I can think about is how pretty it is. It's sweet that Gabriel's so insistent about giving it to me, even if it's a bit over the top. Then, as I stroke my fingers over it and examine it more carefully, I recognise the swirling, twisted pattern and freeze. I feel like I'm going to be sick.

"You planned all of this, didn't you? You didn't quite trust fate, so you decided to give it a helping hand."

The emeralds and engravings on the ring combine to make the same pattern that he marked me with all those years before. Everything falls into place, and I can barely breathe.

"You found a way to manipulate me into offering myself up to you. You gave me the lien. You couldn't give me the ring at that point—that'd seem insane even by your standards—so you did the next best thing and branded me with its design."

My voice is trembling. I liked it better when his actions were one unpredictable thing after another. Gabriel just looks at me, his eyes wide and his arms outstretched. He's got no comeback, for once.

"And then later, you put my family in a position where they needed the exact combination of skills that only I possessed, so I'd come back and have to face you." I'm twisting the duvet cover hard enough to tear it in two.

Gabriel tries to put his arm around me, but I flinch away. "You make it sound so cynical," he says, his voice catching. "I wanted to get you close and keep you close. Not to force anything, but to let you get to know me, fall in love, and see how good we could be together. Is that so wrong?"

"Of course it's wrong!" I throw off the cover and get to my feet. "This is all completely twisted. And it sounds an awful lot like a self-fulfilling prophecy. Like your mum told you you'd love me, so you built me up in your mind into someone you could love."

Which doesn't explain why I'm increasingly sure I love him, too, but that isn't the point.

I thrust the ring back into his hand. I'm oddly sad to see it go. It's so beautiful. I throw myself at the door before I can crack and kiss him.

"Take my car to get home. Bring it back tomorrow. We can discuss all this when we're both feeling calmer and stronger." His eyes are heavy again.

I walk out without replying, though I do take his precious Jag.

"So, what are you going to do about this?" I'm standing in my parents' kitchen, clinging to a mug of freshly brewed coffee like my life depends on it.

My mum sighs. "According to the Old Ways, it's you Bren's betrayed. His life is in your hands, and the traditional thing would be for you to declare it forfeit. But he's still your brother. I hope we can make a compromise work."

"What compromise?" I have no wish to kill Brendan, but I do want to make him pay. And now I know what he's capable of, the idea he might be plotting to expand the Dome seems far more likely—and I want to ensure that's impossible. Not to mention prevent him from taking revenge on Gabriel. Even if Gabriel is a manipulative bastard.

Liam strides in. He's glowing with power. "We're draining his magic. A third to each sibling. A fitting punishment and a way to stop him doing anything stupid in future, but no death and no real pain."

I laugh bitterly. "So, we're back to square one. We could have let Gabriel drain his magic six years ago and avoided all this."

"I'm not sure that's what you'd have wanted," Chrissie says, slinking into the room. From the sparkle in her eyes and the buzz in her aura, it's clear she's taken her share. I dread to think what her enhanced empath powers are showing her regarding me and Gabriel.

Neither Chrissie nor Liam have ever been particularly magically gifted, at least by my family's standards—their talents have traditionally lain elsewhere. But presumably, that's going to change.

"Thornber's formally asked for an alliance, you know," Dad says. "Unite the families. Combine our powers. Stop the fighting and make Mannith better than ever."

"What did you say?"

I imagine the answer is going to involve obscenities, but Dad merely shrugs. "I'm thinking it over. I've heard worse ideas. We could use the extra magical firepower."

I find Bren upstairs in his old bed, bound by the rest of the family's collective magic. It's far too reminiscent of that night six years ago. Sometimes, it's like the whole town is caught in a time loop. I trudge slowly over to him, gazing into the distance.

"Hey, Sades. Come to take the last third? Ironic, isn't it? If you'd given me your power a few hours ago, I'd have been the strongest practitioner in town. Now I'm going to be left with nothing." His voice is flat and his posture slumped.

I sit down on the edge of the bed. There are dark circles under his eyes and scars on his arm. The symptoms of burning through too much magic and of Gabriel's attacks, respectively.

"You did try to kill me, Bren. I don't think you can push too hard for the sympathy vote."

He shrugs—a tiny movement between his injuries and his bindings. "I had a winning hand. I knew—absolutely knew, with the surety of a clairvoyant—that he'd save you. I wouldn't have risked it if I'd been anything less than certain."

I touch his arm. "You happened to be right. But there's no way you could have been sure enough to risk it. He's utterly unpredictable. Always scheming."

"Not when it comes to you. Besides, on the million-to-one chance he hadn't taken the bait, I'd have healed you myself."

"If he hadn't 'taken the bait' as you so charmingly put it, he'd have killed you in an instant. You'd have been in no position to save me."

"I'm not pleading for mercy. I just want you to know I was sure."

I stand and pace the room. I can't bear to look at him. "I don't need any more magic. And Chrissie and Liam have taken enough to stop you attempting anything insane. Taking the rest would be a needless cruelty."

I expect Brendan to be grateful. Instead, he frowns. "I was the only one who could stand against Thornber. Now that power's split three ways and the family's basically ready to agree to an alliance, he can do whatever he wants. And you're naïve if you believe he won't do something awful."

I don't answer. I don't want to think about that now.

"Take my power," he demands. "Add it to yours. Then, when and if the time comes, you can stop him."

"No. I've got enough magical power to take him if I really tried. Though... I don't think I could hurt him again."

"Are you going to form your own alliance then? Give yourself to him and have little Thornber babies?" His tone is half scorn, half longing. Perhaps he's thinking about Leah and their abandoned family plans.

"I don't think I could do that either. Keep the rest of your magic, Bren. Get over all this."

I lean over him, place a hand on his sternum, and take the tiniest hint of magic as a token gesture. He puts up no resistance, and it flows into my blood, bringing with it a warmth and a sense of nostalgia and home and safety. Ironically.

After a few seconds, I tap lightly to close the connection, then step away. "For the last time, what really happened with the Dome? There's no point lying now—I'm leaving town, your magic's weak, and you've got nothing to lose. Besides, after what you did to me, if I don't get a convincing answer, I'll feel entirely justified in resorting to mind reading again."

He closes his eyes. "You had it right. I tried and failed that night six years ago. I extended the boundaries a little back in May—the after-effects were the other reason I was so weak the night of Niall's murder. I was planning to attempt a larger expansion in the autumn—though I genuinely was far from confident that my powers were up to the task. The rest of the family didn't know about any of the recent stuff, in case you're wondering.

"And yes, everything I'd already managed required a pretty hefty sacrifice. The things I wanted to do would have required a larger one. I know it's not exactly conventional morality, but I still believe the trade-offs would have been worth it if I had managed to pull it off. But that's all academic now I'm in this state."

I stare at him in silence with my heart racing. He sounds more upset about the depletion of his magic than about all those people he killed. Not to mention all the others he'd been planning to kill in the future. Even after Bren had shown his true colours by trying to kill me, I'd been clinging on to the hope that Gabriel had either been exaggerating or mistaken about my brother's Dome plans and degree of comfort with murder, but I was wrong. Now, at least, the family have left him too weak to pull it off. There's a strictly limited amount of trouble he could ever cause with the relatively small amount of power I've left him.

I walk out of the room without another word.

Afterwards, Mum cooks a roast. We sit and eat as a family, minus Bren, who gets a tray taken up to him.

Despite everything, it's somehow not awkward, even though we all know it's a farewell meal.

TWENTY-SIX

I drive the Jag back out to Thornber Manor first thing the next morning. My suitcase is packed and in the back. I've said my goodbyes to the family.

There's a part of me that's longing to stay, for all sorts of reasons. I love Mannith. I love my family. But I can't stay here, knowing what I know. I can't be a committed member of the family, knowing what they do. I don't need to compartmentalise quite as fully as I used to. I'm going to stay in touch, continue to rebuild our relationships. Eventually, I hope I'll even be able to visit... but for now, I need to stay away and keep my distance. It's that or be entirely sucked back into a life I can't justify.

And that's just the family side of things. As I'm going to have to tell him, all that goes double for Gabriel.

Gabriel's waiting outside when I pull up, pacing back and forth across the gravel driveway. It's not clear whether he sensed my arrival or whether he's been there all night. I park his beloved car carefully.

"Come and sit next to me," I insist. "I've always found cars to be the best place for a difficult conversation."

"Is this going to be a particularly difficult conversation?" He slides in beside me.

"I think so."

I put on some music then stare fixedly at the dashboard while my hands tap out a discordant rhythm on the steering wheel. "Let me get one thing straight. I love you, and I believe you love me. It's sudden and it's irrational, but that doesn't make it any less true. I don't know whether it's matching souls and auras or a reaction to each other's chemical compounds. Maybe there's no real difference between the two concepts. Either way, when I look at you, I want to tear off your clothes, and be held by you, and tell you all my secrets and worries, and build a life together, us against the world."

He puts a hand on my knee. "Oh God, Sadie. I can't believe I'm hearing these words from you. You've said exactly what I was thinking." He puts his other hand on my shoulder and draws me in for a kiss.

Everything I've just said is true. As a result, it takes every ounce of resolve I have to push him back.

"Let me finish. Whatever love is, I feel it for you. And I lust after you, too, because you're gorgeous and weirdly charismatic. But there's nothing in between. I don't like you. I barely know you. And I'm not convinced you could give me any objective explanations for why you like me either."

Gabriel's grip on my knee tightens. "How can you say that?"

I close my eyes. If I look at him, I'm not going to be able to finish this little speech. "Perhaps when it comes to the dispute between my family and yours, you're secretly on the side of the angels. But you've still done some awful things to me. Liens and Greenfire and Leah and who-knows-what else. And all the stuff you told me about how you've plotted to get me physically and emotionally closer to you isn't romantic, it's unhinged."

Every word is absolutely fair, but saying them aloud is breaking my heart.

"Your love is wonderful," I conclude. "But it's not enough."

Gabriel rests his head on the dashboard. "Sadie, I might have gone about all of this the wrong way, but you're wrong if you think my feelings for you are just some idea Mum put into my head. You're gorgeous. You're clever. Confident. Funny. You stand by your family and your values, but you're not afraid to be ruthless when you really need to be. We never run out of things to say to each other. And our chemistry is off the chart.

"Just tell me you'll be mine, and then I'll be yours, and there'll be no more need for any of this scheming or any of my more over-the-top gestures. And my family and yours are going to be allied now. So there'll be no plotting in that direction either."

I could imagine it all too well. Living with him here at Thornber Manor. Sex. Long conversations. Honing our magic and growing together. Visiting my family and working together with them. Operating as a lawyer out of Leeds, because even in the wilder reaches of my imagination, there's no way I'm giving that up. In due course, babies with beautiful faces, glowing eyes, and extraordinary amounts of power. Loving and being loved.

I sit up straight, turn to face him, and place a hand on his chest like I'm about to do a magic transfer. "It's not like flicking a switch, Gabriel. I don't believe you can act like you have for years and then suddenly start being perfectly reasonable. I'm scared that when things don't go according to your grand plan, you'll try to force them in that direction, through magic or manipulation."

"Just give me a chance."

I nod. "I'm going back to London this afternoon. I'm making zero commitment to you about what happens after that. I will not say I'm yours until I understand more about who you are.

Stay in touch. Be my friend instead of my enemy. Be flirtatious instead of obsessive."

"I don't know whether I can manage that. It's not quite the way I am with anyone. And when I'm with you, my brain short-circuits. When I'm apart from you, I feel like something's missing."

"I know. I feel the same way. But you're going to have to try. It's that or draw a line under this whole thing and never speak again."

He reaches into his shirt and pulls the ring out again. "I'll try. But I want you to take this. Not as an engagement ring. Just as a token."

I swallow hard. "A token of what? You're really failing at the first hurdle here."

Offering me the ring again is completely against everything I'm trying to say. Taking it would be an utter capitulation, but it's drawing my attention, calling to me.

"Just a token. I know you understand."

I take it from him and hold it tentatively above my middle finger, where no one could mistake it for an engagement ring.

"Are you sure you want to give your mum's ring to someone who's basically walking away?"

He nods. "She wanted you to have it. I've kept the rest of my promises to her: Stay in Mannith. Increase the family's power. Avenge her. Besides, I believe you'll come back."

This is crazy. Perhaps I should give into my heart and fall into his arms. Perhaps I should listen to my head and cut off all contact. Instead, I'm attempting something that feels like the worst of all possible worlds. And yet, I slip the ring onto my finger.

"Thank you," I say. "Now, in ten minutes time, I need to head to the station. But, in the meantime..."

I lean over and kiss him. I half expect him to push me away

after everything I've said, but he presses me towards him and kisses me back like his life depends on it.

"Can you cope with missing this train and getting the next one?" he asks.

"Yes," I breathe, breaking the kiss just long enough to speak, then clamping my mouth back on his. I don't want to leave. I don't want to do the right thing, the sensible thing. I'm going to, I've sworn it to myself. But I really don't want to.

He lays his seat down, as flat as it will go and lounges back. I scoot over to him, open his belt and unzip his fly. You'd think my earlier words might have deflated him, but clearly, some combination of the kiss and the ring have turned him on past the point of all endurance. I feel exactly the same. I kick off my shoes and straddle him. At first, we just continue to kiss, while I grind against him and he holds me against him.

Then his fingers touch between my legs and my hand closes around him. The emotional intensity of the moment is basically all the foreplay I need. I feel ready to come within seconds.

"Nope. Not like that. When you're back here, when we're together, we can do this in all sorts of different ways. But for now, we'll only have this memory to sustain us. I need you to come with me inside you."

I nod shakily. There's a mad part of me that's tempted to break my golden rule and forego protection for once. Let fate take the decision on whether to stay out of my hands. But that's not the person I am, so I do the semi-sensible thing and grab a condom from my bag.

Normally, whenever I go on top, I bounce around putting on a show. Now, I lean over to kiss him, and rock myself all too gently back and forth, drawing moans from both of us. We never break the kiss, and we never stop gripping onto each other with all our strength. Time seems to blur. It's just me and him and the movement of our bodies. No regrets about the past, no worries about the future, no thoughts of anyone else. Just us, together in this moment. When my orgasm hits, it's like snapping out of a trance. He comes a split second later, holding me firmly in place as he thrusts upwards, again and again.

We break apart, then I fall back into his arms.

"That was wonderful. I mean it, when I say I love you. But equally, I mean it when I say I need to go."

"That *was* wonderful. I love you, too. And I understand. I just hope that one day, I'll manage to do enough to change your mind. Now, let's get you to the station."

We drive in dazed silence. I look at him, at my ring, out at the view. I'm trying to commit every inch of his face and every corner of this town to my memory. Goodness knows when I'll see either of them again.

I kiss him again at the station, with just as much passion, even though there are several people around.

When the train pulls up, I long to throw myself back in his car. Instead, I do the adult thing and climb aboard. And then I do the childish thing and close my eyes as we pull away. I'm still aware of his presence, even through the walls of the train, even as the distance increases. And then we go through the invisible barrier of the Dome. The temperature drops slightly, the sky looks slightly greyer, and I can't sense him anymore. Against the odds, I manage not to cry.

EPILOGUE

Four hours later, after two trains and a taxi, I make it back to my flat. My next-door neighbour gives me a nod of greeting as I fumble with my keys while holding my suitcase upright. I don't know her name, and I doubt she's noticed I've been gone all summer. It's such a contrast to the way everyone knows everyone else's business in Mannith.

I get inside, close the door behind me, then collapse onto the sofa in a heap. The flat is so much smaller than I remembered. A fraction of the size of my parents' row of terraces or Bren's house, never mind Thornber Manor.

Even indoors, the air feels different. More pollution, less magic, and about ten degrees cooler.

My eyes settle on the wall of drawings. I focus my gaze on the one of Leah, and it burns away into nothing. I probably ought to remove Bren's, too, but I can't bring myself to do that. Will he carry on sending me his art? Will losing two-thirds of his magic have affected his artistic skill?

After being away for so long, you'd expect there to be post piled high, but all my bills and correspondence are done online. There are a few pieces of junk mail, and sitting on top, two heavy envelopes, neither of which bear a stamp. That could mean someone had pushed them through the letterbox themselves, but in my experience, it usually means they've been delivered by magic.

I will the letters to drift from the floor over to my sofa. There's no point going back to doing everything manually, just because I'm in London.

It takes me a moment to place the familiar handwriting on the first envelope, then I realise it's from Bren. Had it been there when I arrived, or had I willed it into being by wondering about the drawings?

I open it with shaking hands, unsure what to expect. An apology? An explanation? An accusation? We said everything that needed to be said last night, but my brother likes to have the last word.

There's no letter inside. Just one more drawing in Bren's distinctive style. It shows Gabriel lounging on the sofa at my parents' house. It's unclear whether it's taken from life or from his imagination and if it's intended as a peace offering or a taunt. I stare at it for minutes on end, drinking in Gabriel's features. Then I fold it up and carefully place it in a drawer. There's no way I can cope with it being on the wall.

I can't help but hope that the other letter is from Gabriel himself, though again, it feels like we've already said everything that could be said for the moment. When I finally brace myself enough to open it, I find a blank sheet of parchment. But as I watch, words appear, drawn letter by letter with an invisible quill.

Sadie Sadler,

We've been aware of your presence in our city for some time now, but you've kept yourself in the shadows, denying your power and fighting to live a normal life. After this summer, I suspect that's going to change.

We've heard the basics of the things that happened in Mannith. We always like to keep a close eye on our provincial cousins and old allies. And now, we find ourselves in need of someone with your unique combination of magical strength and legal prowess. There are all sorts of ways in which I could make good use of a practitioner lawyer, but above all, I need you to help me prove that vampires can't always get away with murder.

I'll admit that my motivation is revenge and that they're a dangerous group to cross, considering most of our powers don't work on them. But if it helps, bloodsuckers are all reactionary bastards. Perhaps you'd like an opportunity to teach some stuck-up rich guys who regard people as livestock a lesson in human rights?

Meet me on Hampstead Heath at midnight, and we can discuss the terms of your membership.

Yours,

Lavinia Morven, Matriarch of the London Coven

*

Want to find out next what happens to Sadie and Gabriel?
Their story continues in *The Binding Mark!*

A LETTER FROM THE AUTHOR

Dear reader,

Huge thanks for reading *The Twisted Mark*. I hope you enjoyed Sadie's adventures. If you want to join other readers in hearing all about my new releases and bonus content, you can sign up for my newsletter.

www.stormpublishing.co/sophie-williamson

If you enjoyed this book and could spare a few moments to leave a review I'd be incredibly grateful. Even a short review can make all the difference in encouraging a reader to discover my books for the first time. Thank you so much!

The Twisted Mark brought together so many elements from my own life and from the varied books I love. I practiced witchcraft in my teens and practiced law in my twenties. I don't do either anymore, but I loved combining them in this book.

I have also always been fascinated by families and their dynamics. And I wanted to create a big, sprawling, close-knit happy family who love each other but do some terrible things. Similarly, I thought it'd be entertaining to have the classic perfect small hometown for the big city lawyer to return to, but to make it very dark under the surface—I hope you love both Mannith and the Sadlers as much as I do.

Probably my number one obsession in literature is characters who tread a fine line between love interest and villain. I had so much fun writing Gabriel. I'm equally fascinated by morally ambiguous heroines, but in the end, that wasn't where I went with Sadie. It was a refreshing contrast to write someone who's so determined to be a good person, and who's so professionally and magically competent. I love her confidence, her sense of humour, and her sex positivity. Not to mention her low-key coffee addition. I'm so looking forward to spending more time with these characters.

Thanks again for being part of this amazing journey with me and I hope you'll stay in touch—I have so many more stories and ideas to entertain you with! Starting with the sequel in a few months' time, where the action moves to London.

Sophie Williamson

www.williamsonwords.net

 twitter.com/williamsonwords

ACKNOWLEDGMENTS

I'm the sort of person who always reads the acknowledgements section at the end of books. And I've dreamt of writing my own for a long time. So forgive me if I get a little carried away.

Starting with the writing side of things, thanks to my agent, Marlene Stringer, for your determination to find Witch Trials a home and for making all of this happen.

Thanks to Storm Publishing for giving me this opportunity and being generally fantastic. Thanks in particular to my amazing editor Kathryn Taussig for all her incisive suggestions —even if I can't believe she is Team Connor! And thanks to all the other Storm authors—I love all the mutual support.

Thanks to all my CPs past and present, whether you helped me with Witch Trials in particular or helped to hone my writing skills through comments on older manuscripts. In particular, though, thanks to Eve Pendle, for shoring up the romance; Marith Zoli, for shoring up the magic; and Rachel Chaney, for shoring up the villainy. And thanks to Adrianne Karasek, who is usually amongst the first to read anything I write, but somehow missed this one until it was already on sub. But who subsequently gave me such an enthusiastic positivity pass that I think she singlehandedly manifested me a deal!

Thanks, too, to everyone I've interacted with—or indeed, just silently admired—on Book Twitter and especially in various pitch competitions over the years. A million and one little tips here and there have made me an exponentially better writer and convinced me not to give up. Shout out in particular to everyone involved with RevPit 17, where I was a runner up with an old manuscript and found several of my long-term CPs and writing pals; and with AMM 21, where I was a mentor and found a whole new amazing community amongst both the mentors and mentees.

Moving on to the more personal side of things, thank you to my parents and brothers for some Sadler family inspiration, though despite some similarities here and there, I'd like to emphasise that no one is actually meant to be a one-to-one replica. Even so, please assume all the good stuff is taken from life and all the bad stuff is taken from my imagination. And for goodness' sake, please skip the sex scenes or I will die of embarrassment!

More seriously on the family front, thanks to my mum, who's encouraged my writing since I was tiny. And my Nannan Beatrice, who I think was the only person to make it through the terrible YA fantasy manuscript I wrote at 17. Thanks, too, to my wider family and my in-laws, who have all always been so enthusiastic about my writing.

Georgiana and Archie, unlike everyone else I've name-checked here, I'd be lying if I said you'd helped with the creation of this book. Caring for a three-year-old and a new baby while working on edits was not easy. But the sacrifices are so worth it.

Georgie, I love how you're already following in the footsteps of your Great-Nannan, Granny, and of course, Mum, with your love of books and storytelling—it's a magic that flows down the matrilineal line. The monster story you dictated has a better villain redemption arc than I could ever manage. And I smile every time you solemnly tell people about "Mummy's scary witch book."

Archie, you're still a bit too tiny for anything like that (what are words?), but you're utterly adorable and make me smile every day. I love you both so much.

Adorable as my children are, probably my biggest thanks of all go to Freddie, for all the weekends when you took them out of the house so I could blast my edits! But beyond that, thanks for always believing in and supporting my writing, year after year, as well as supporting me more generally and keeping me calm and happy amidst the chaos. For someone who consistently writes such psychotic love interests, I have a very lovely husband. To quote Sadie, *"I want to tear off your clothes, and be held by you, and tell you all my secrets and worries, and build a life together, us against the world."* Please ignore the rest of the scene that line is taken from!

Made in the USA
Middletown, DE
18 July 2023

35389237R00222